THE ELECTRICIAN AND THE SEAMSTRESS

THE ELECTRICIAN AND THE SEAMSTRESS

Monica Granlove

Published by Granlove Legacy Publications, Raleigh, North Carolina
MonicaGranlove.com

Edited and designed by Girl Friday Productions
www.girlfridayproductions.com

Cover design: Emily Weigel
Logo design: Lydia Granholm and Birgitte Sundstrøm
Project management: Kristin Duran
Editorial production: Reshma Kooner

ISBN (paperback): 979-8-9904347-0-7
ISBN (e-book): 979-8-9904347-1-4

Library of Congress Control Number: 2024911101

First edition

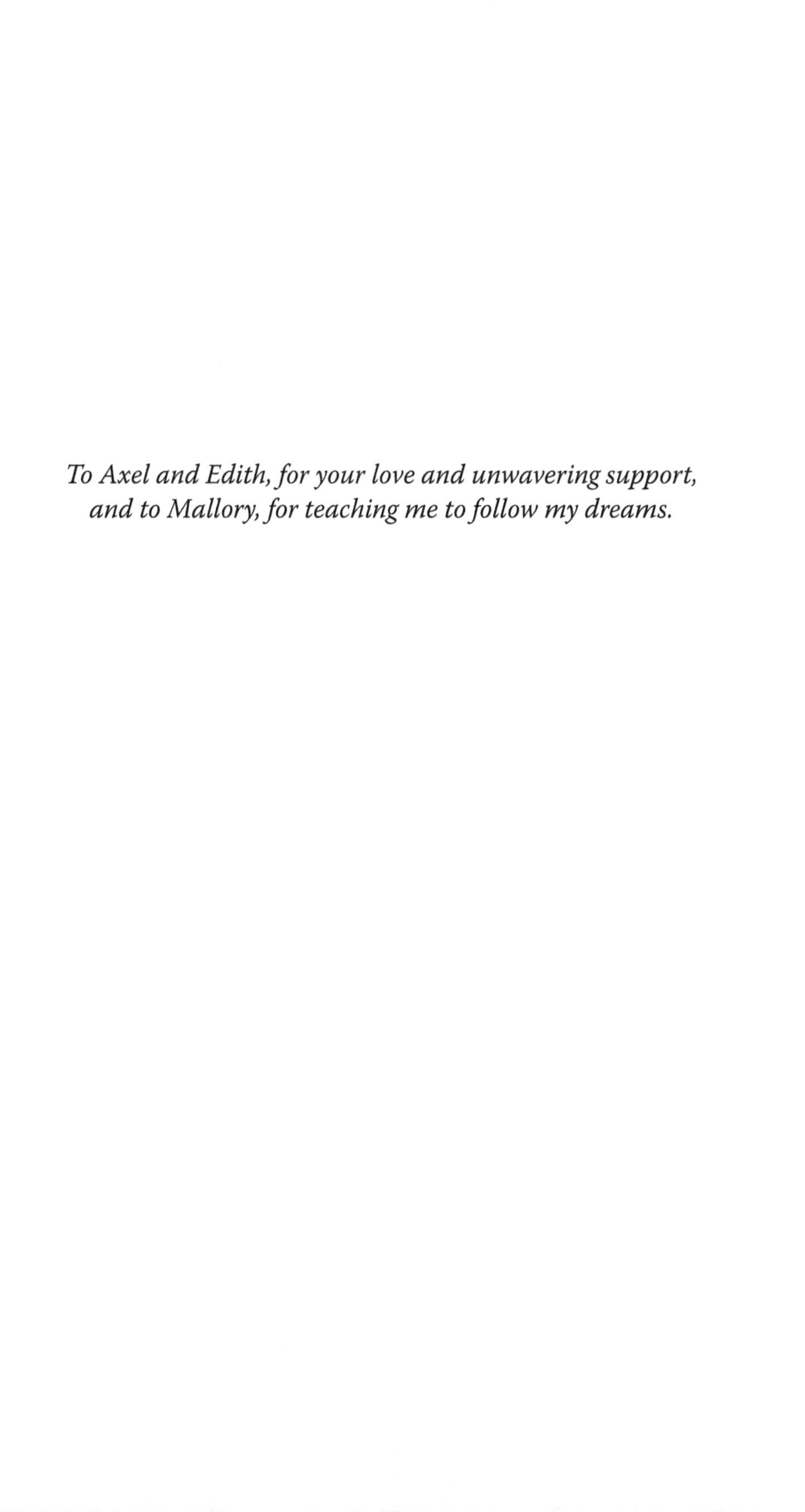

*To Axel and Edith, for your love and unwavering support,
and to Mallory, for teaching me to follow my dreams.*

ACKNOWLEDGMENTS

I express my deepest gratitude to my husband and business partner, Axel, for his steadfast and enduring support. He patiently listened to me on many nights, offering suggestions as I described scenes.

A special thanks to my mother, Edith, for generously sharing a treasure trove of family stories that served as inspirations for bringing Bruno and Karla's story to life. My sincere appreciation also goes to Lydia Granholm for her consulting, which added valuable perspectives to the narrative.

The collective contributions of all three have enriched this journey, and I am truly grateful.

INTRODUCTION

Many factors contributed to the complex nature of World War II, among them its vast geographical scope, which included numerous countries across Europe. The conflict played out on various fronts, from the Western Front, where Allied forces faced off against Nazi Germany, to the Eastern Front, where the Soviet Union clashed with German forces in brutal battles. Occupied territories experienced widespread devastation as their cities were bombed and their civilians subjected to oppression and persecution. The war's impact extended beyond military operations, profoundly affecting European societies through displacement, forced labor, and the Holocaust, resulting in immense human suffering and loss. The ideological struggle between Fascism and democracy further intensified the conflict, leading to complex alliances and political divisions.

Amid the complexities, the Nazis' stringent control over media and information dissemination added another layer of oppression. The Nazis owned all media outlets, so information was strictly controlled. They shaped narratives to fit their propaganda machine and further their agenda of totalitarian control and ideological dominance.

The Electrician and the Seamstress is a work of fiction based on the remarkable experiences of my grandparents against the backdrop of World War II. Through the enduring lessons of their kindness, tolerance, and celebration of diversity, their legacy has touched multiple generations. Their compelling stories, passed down by my mother and her siblings, serve as a poignant reminder that the human spirit can persist during tumultuous times.

This novel aspires to preserve their narrative so that future generations may learn from my grandparents' resilience and compassion.

Moreover, it encourages reflection about today's political climate and the importance of conscientious voting. Any resemblance of additional characters to real people is purely coincidental. Their storylines may not be completely factual to history. Historical figures such as Adolf Hitler and Otto-Heinrich Drechsler were added to enrich the story for the purpose of entertainment.

I hope you enjoy the stories. Please visit me at MonicaGranlove .com, where you will find information about my novels, short stories, articles, character analyses, recipes, and much more, and where you can join in conversations about learning from history.

PROLOGUE

October 1959

Frankfurt, Germany

Karla and Bruno walked up the steps of the administration building at Goethe University. They had agreed to give interviews about the journey of their lives after being asked by a history professor. As they walked through the front door, Karla laughed quietly, thinking about their stay in a hotel the night before. It was the first time in their lives that she and Bruno had spent the night at such a place, and they had been captivated by the television. Although television had been introduced in the 1930s, they'd never been able to afford the luxury of one. The stay in the hotel and the nine-hour train ride from their home in Kiel, Germany, to Frankfurt was an adventure that was tempered by their feelings of trepidation about dredging up old memories.

After they checked in at the administration office, Bruno and Karla were shown to a room with a dark-gray metal table surrounded by six matching chairs and walls painted a lighter shade of gray. The room felt drafty and cold. Karla wrapped her black coat tighter around her as she sat at the table quietly, lost in her thoughts.

Bruno stood at the window, looking at the clouds. The anticipation he felt was tinged with sorrow and dread as he gathered his thoughts and summoned the courage to recount his experiences in World War II.

He walked slowly to the table in the center of the room and looked at Karla with sad eyes that seemed to ask, *Can we really do this?*

Needing something to do with his hands, Bruno walked to another table located against the wall opposite the windows. He perused the food and drink on the table, trying to focus his mind on the present moment until the interview began. He poured two cups of coffee from a silver carafe and placed a delicate, flaky croissant filled with sweet apricot jam and dusted with powdered sugar on a plate, then brought the snack to Karla, balancing the coffees carefully as he walked.

Karla thanked him and took the treat. Her face did not betray whatever emotion she might be feeling.

"Aren't you nervous at all?" Bruno asked.

Before she could respond, the door opened and three people walked in, each carrying a notebook and pen. A man with glasses who looked like he was in his fifties carried a tape recorder stacked on his notebook, along with extra reels piled precariously on top of that. A young woman with hair pulled neatly into a bun and wearing glasses took a seat opposite Karla, then gave them a soft smile and began to write in her notebook. Another man, this one younger, acknowledged Bruno with a nod and sat next to the woman.

The older man spoke first. "Herr and Frau Arnold, I'm Doctor Schmidt, and these are my colleagues, Fräulein Neumann and Herr Peters." Dr. Schmidt placed the tape recorder in the middle of the table and then sat in the chair at the head of the table, arranging his notebook and pen in front of him before continuing.

He opened his notebook and perused his notes. "I know that you lived through two wars, and you are fifty and forty-nine years old?" He looked up for confirmation.

"I'm sure we look much older than that," Bruno said jokingly. He looked at Karla for her input, but she only shook her head softly and gave him an impish smile.

Their love was a force that had long sustained them. But fourteen years after the end of the war, Bruno and Karla were still coping with its effects, just as Germany was still in the process of rebuilding and recovering from the conflict. Since 1949, the country had existed as two separate new states: the Federal Republic of Germany, a democratic country to the west, and in the east, the German Democratic Republic, which was run by the Communist leaders of the Soviet

Union. Tensions between West and East Germany were palpable, and newspaper headlines regularly blared warnings about escalating conflicts. Meanwhile, citizens murmured anxiously on street corners, their nervous chatter reflecting widespread concern that another war could arise.

Dr. Schmidt and his associates were part of a research team that was interviewing survivors of the war. It was Karla who found the small advertisement on the third page of *Kieler News*. She'd told Bruno they should participate so the world could have a firsthand account of the terrifying experiences of war. Karla saw giving interviews as a way to confront the past and contribute to the healing process, both for her own sake and for future generations. Even after fourteen years, both Bruno and Karla suffered from nightmares and attacks of anxiety.

The U.S. army had interviewed Bruno extensively when he returned from a Soviet prison camp after the war ended. However, the current research provided the university an opportunity to go deeper and create a more accurate historical record. These interviews elicited valuable firsthand accounts of life during the war, including the hardships people endured, the atrocities they witnessed, and the resilience they demonstrated. Such interviews would later prove to be instrumental in preserving people's memories of World War II and would make it possible for future generations to learn from the lessons of history.

Dr. Schmidt pointed to the voice recorder. "May I record your story?" He pushed the Record button when he saw Karla nod. "Now then, where would you like to begin?"

Karla was the first to speak. "To give you a deeper understanding of the experiences of the war, it's essential that we first revisit the events that led up to its outbreak."

Bruno rubbed his hands on his thighs and agreed.

The interviewers indicated that the couple should proceed. They were aware of the pivotal role the First World War had played in setting the stage for the onset of the second, but they had come to listen to Bruno and Karla's experiences, and they were eager to hear what the two had to say.

As Bruno and Karla began, the room changed. A moment before, it had been a simple university meeting room. Now, it became a repository of history—a place where personal stories intersected with the broader narrative of a nation grappling with the consequences of totalitarian rule.

PART I

Bruno and Karla

CHAPTER 1

January 1928

Karla

My mother's illness and death were a turning point in my life. The day of her funeral was veiled in snow, with frigid wind gusts sweeping off the Baltic Sea.

I grew up amid Kiel's cold and dark winters, in Germany, but the weather on the day of her funeral was particularly unforgiving. The chill seeped into my bones as the men lowered my mother's casket into the frozen ground. I was eighteen years old when the plans my mother and I had made for my future unraveled. I had secured admission to the University of Music and Theatre in Leipzig, a remarkable feat for a woman in 1928. Acceptances for women applicants were scarce, but I had earned scholarships for my academic achievements, and I had aspired to delve into the realms of music and language. All my dreams had revolved around becoming a music teacher. Now my dreams were as cold as the icy winds sweeping across the frigid expanse of the Baltic Sea. Those winds seemed to freeze my dreams, and I knew that, in time, without my mother's warmth and nourishment, they would eventually die.

I barely heard the words of the pastor as he delivered the eulogy.

The funeral was held in the graveyard behind the Lutheran church where generations of my family were baptized. But my mind was only slightly present. My mind kept going back to the months before Mutti's death, when I had been forced to take on her caretaker role in our family.

My mother, whom I called Mutti, had grown increasingly frail over the past year. Then one morning, I got up and found her still in bed, unable to rise and attend to the simplest tasks. She was not physically unable to get out of bed, but from that point on, she spent most of her time there. There were days when I returned from school to a silent apartment, where I was greeted only by the sight of dirty dishes piled high in the sink and the realization that there had been no groceries purchased, no meals prepared.

My father, Friedrich Ferdinand Petersen, whom I referred to as Vati, struggled to comprehend the gravity of Mutti's condition, and he was unable to navigate the daily chores of our household. Given this, I knew I had no choice but to step into the role of caretaker, taking on the responsibilities that were formerly Mutti's. Two months before she died, she was completely bedridden from chronic kidney disease, and the weight of responsibility fell heavily on my shoulders.

In the early days of taking over care of our home, I found myself frustrated with my father for not even trying to help tend to the apartment or Mutti. He was by then a different man than he had been before the war that ended in 1918. He used to laugh easily and smile most of the time, and people loved his gregarious nature. But in the aftermath of the war, he became distant and adrift, with no sense of purpose.

At the graveyard, standing in the cold, I thought about the great upheaval in our country that I now understood had been the background of my young life. Despite the pervasive chaos, my parents had tried to shield my younger sister, Erna, and me from the harsh realities of war and politics. But they had been unable to do so entirely.

One morning as I was drying dishes, I finally asked a question I had been afraid to ask. "Mutti, why do you and Vati only listen to the radio after Erna and I are in bed?"

Mutti waved her hand as if to toss the question back to me. "It's all boring news about war and politics. You're fifteen. You shouldn't be concerned with such things," she said.

I nodded as if I agreed, but I was thinking about the small ways I stayed connected to the world beyond our doorstep. Whenever my sister was visiting friends, I was concealed in the shadows of my room, my ear to the door, catching snippets of news and updates from the front lines as my parents listened to the radio. And on the rare occasions when a discarded newspaper found its way into my hands, I devoured its contents eagerly, hungry for any scraps of information that offered a glimpse of the outside world.

Following the Great War, political upheaval swept across Europe, leaving a trail of shattered empires and burgeoning ideologies in its wake. The once-mighty Austro-Hungarian, Ottoman, and Russian Empires had crumbled under the weight of defeat and internal strife, creating power vacuums in Europe and Asia and clearing a path for the creation of a wave of newly independent nations. Amid these ruins, radical ideologies and movements such as Communism, Fascism, and nationalism found fertile ground as they promised to provide solutions to the social and economic turmoil that were plaguing war-torn societies.

This was the state of the world around me, though I was also focused on my smaller, personal world. At school, I excelled at English, Danish, and history. At home, I focused on my music. I loved everything about opera and classical music. I practiced the piano every day, especially my favorite music by Franz Liszt and Robert Schumann. If opera was playing on the radio, I sang as I did my chores, practicing in various octaves. And my interest in history extended into my own life. My passion for current events about the war was not crushed even after Vati once caught me reading the paper.

I clearly remember the event as well as the article I was reading at the time. It happened in the summer of 1925. My best friend, Martha, and I were fifteen at the time, and we were lying on our stomachs on the grass outside my apartment, enjoying the warm sun on our backs and reading a newspaper that Martha brought.

National Socialist German Workers' Party Offers Hope Amid Rising Tensions

Germany today finds itself embroiled in a whirlwind of political upheaval, with rival factions jostling for control within the delicate democratic framework of the Weimar Republic. Simmering tensions between left-wing and right-wing ideologies continue to add fuel to the fire of social unrest and political discord. The landscape is further complicated by the resurgence of political parties, including the burgeoning influence of the National Socialist German Workers' Party, referred to as the Nazi Party, which promises a bold new vision of Germany's future.

Despite the chaos, some view the rising momentum of the Nazi Party as a beacon of hope for a nation grappling with economic turmoil and social fragmentation. Amid the clamor for change . . .

"Karla! What are you doing there?" I looked up sharply to see Vati standing over us. We hadn't heard him approach. I scrambled to my feet as he bent down and picked up the newspaper. My heart was racing as I waited for him to say something.

He glanced at the headline. "This is none of your concern. Go inside, Karla." He turned to Martha. "Go home, Martha."

I looked up as the pastor finished talking. The weight of grief was heavy in my heart. I felt overwhelmed with the depth of my grief and with anger over Mutti's dying at such a young age. She should have lived long enough to help me pick out my wedding dress and hold her grandchildren. I took my handkerchief out of my coat pocket and dabbed at my tears as I watched my father step forward. His eyes were filled with sorrow. He took a deep breath of the cold sea air and began to speak, his voice steady and resolute. "My beloved," he said as he looked at the coffin. His voice carried across the somber gathering. "Today, as we lay you to rest, we mourn not only the loss of a devoted wife and mother but also the guiding light of our family. Your love, your kindness, and your unwavering strength have touched us all in ways words cannot express."

He paused, his gaze sweeping over the assembled mourners. Each one was bearing their own burden of sorrow. "In the face of life's trials and tribulations, you remained steadfast, a beacon of hope and resilience. Your unwavering faith and unyielding spirit inspired us all to persevere, even in the darkest of times."

A soft breeze stirred the air, carrying with it the scent of salt and sea, as if nature itself was lending its voice to the solemn occasion. My father's words, filled with love and longing, echoed against the backdrop of the crashing waves in the harbor: a poignant reminder of the fleeting nature of life.

"And though you may no longer walk among us, your memory will live on in our hearts forever," my father continued, his voice tinged with emotion. "We will never forget the sacrifices you made, caring for our two daughters in a time of war, ensuring they felt loved and protected even in the midst of chaos and uncertainty."

I knew that he was right: my mother had indeed faced immense challenges while raising children in a time of scarcity. Kiel was home to the formidable German High Seas Fleet, yet those ships had proved powerless against the might of the British Royal Navy's Grand Fleet during the earlier stages of the war. The consequence had been a devastating Allied naval blockade, one that severed the flow of essential supplies and support to our nation.

Food scarcity was a way of life during wartime. People were given monthly ration cards for food, and grocery shopping had to be done each day if we wanted fresh vegetables and eggs. On rare occasions, we were given meat from Kiel's surrounding farms.

Unfortunately, the war's end had not brought relief; instead, it exacerbated our plight. The Treaty of Versailles, signed in June 1919, imposed crippling penalties on Germany, including the loss of territories and the burden of hefty financial reparations to the Allied powers of France, the United Kingdom, Italy, and Belgium. The harsh measures plunged our country into further turmoil, deepening the hardships endured by families like ours who were struggling to secure even the most basic necessities of life.

Our neighbors were facing the same trials we were facing. A small number of them had come to the funeral, but through my tears, I could barely see them as they followed Vati and Erna out of the graveyard. I continued to stand in the cold, hardly registering the disturbed earth and small headstone.

ELISE JULIE BERTHA MARTENS PETERSEN
2 APRIL 1888–8 JANUARY 1928

I wondered, as I had done so many times in recent months, how my father would be able to cope without my mother. He had a good job as an engineer designing ships for the German navy, which allowed us to live comfortably in a one-bedroom apartment. But in every other aspect of life, Mutti had been my father's anchor.

I considered the changes I had seen in Vati in recent years. It was clear that the war had had a profound impact on him, as he had sometimes become quieter and more introspective. Before the war, Vati's work had been his passion; he'd poured his heart and soul into crafting vessels that would sail the seas with pride and strength. However, the outbreak of war changed everything.

As the conflict raged on, Vati had witnessed firsthand the devastating consequences of his creations. The ships he designed were not merely instruments of naval power; they became symbols of destruction and loss. Each vessel that went into battle carried the weight of countless lives, both friend and foe, that had been lost amid the chaos of war.

As a girl, I had lain awake some nights, listening as Vati told Mutti his feelings about the war. He grappled with the realization that his expertise had been used to perpetuate violence and suffering on a massive scale. The once-gleaming ships he had labored over now bore the scars of battle, their once-proud hulls battered and broken by enemy fire.

Since then, as Germany grappled with defeat and devastation in the aftermath of the war, Vati had struggled to find meaning in his work. For Vati, the scars ran deeper than the wounds inflicted on the ships he'd designed; the war had left an indelible mark on his soul, forever shaping his perspective about the world and his place within it.

My memories turned to the months preceding my mother's confinement to her bed. My father had sought solace in the companionship of other people, frequently welcoming associates and colleagues into our home. Their visits became so routine, Mutti set an extra place at the dinner table each night and prepared additional food in anticipation of their arrival. While occasionally an associate's wife would join in, more often than not the gatherings were predominantly male. The men would linger into the late hours, sipping on watered-down coffee and puffing on cigarettes, engaged in fervent discussions about politics and work.

These gatherings between my father and his associates were marked by intense political debates that cast a veil of intrigue over my teenage years. This included discussions regarding Germany's national parliament and went on from there. The men dissected the latest news from the Reichstag, analyzed the shifting dynamics of international relations, and debated the merits of various political ideologies. As a young observer, I was both fascinated and unsettled by the intensity of their discussions, which seemed to echo the tumultuous times in which we lived.

I can recall one particularly memorable encounter with Vice Admiral Conrad Helfrich of the Norwegian navy from these times. He and Vati met when Vice Admiral Helfrich traveled to Kiel to learn about new shipbuilding techniques. I was excited to meet him after I learned he spoke fluent English, as I anticipated this would give me a chance to practice.

Vice Admiral Helfrich and I spoke in English for a few minutes about the weather and school before Vati cleared his throat and looked at me pointedly. I received his message: *you are only to be present to serve dinner and to help translate if needed.* The vice admiral then spoke to my father in German, which he spoke well. I helped only when there was a word he couldn't think of.

At one point during dinner, my father paused and said, "Mutti, coffee." I watched as my mother slowly rose out of her chair, her face contorting in pain. Her body was visibly weak as she shuffled to the other end of the table. I made a move to help, but she waved me off.

She poured coffee for Vati using a coffeepot that had been standing on the table directly in front of my father. This—a wife pouring her husband's coffee from a pot that was on the table next to him—was a normal occurrence in my family. A surprised look came over Vice Admiral Helfrich's face. The vice admiral was quick to cover up his expression, but I caught it. That was the first time I started to understand the role my mother was in and how far her role of taking care of my father extended. It was at that moment that the notion first occurred to me that I would have to step in as caretaker to my parents.

At the graveside, another wave of sorrow washed over me. The reality of my mother's passing hit me like a crushing weight, leaving me struggling to comprehend a world without her presence. Finally, I took a deep breath and whispered, "Goodbye, Mutti. You'll be missed." After another minute, I started walking, resigned that my dream of becoming a music teacher was no longer within my grasp. The streets were quiet as I walked home, snowflakes drifting gently from the sky, softening the sharp edges of grief that weighed heavily on my heart. The occasional echo of church bells in the distance added to the solemn atmosphere, reminding me of how great was my loss.

❦

"You're quieter than usual tonight, Karla." Vati leaned forward, concern in his eyes. I glanced at the empty chair that was my mother's and then at my plate.

"I would still like to attend university in the fall," I said quietly.

"You can't leave. Who will take care of me?" Erna's words held a twinge of jealousy and anger. *Was that because she was thirteen years old, or was there another reason?* Since Mutti had gotten sick, Erna had been left on her own with little supervision. She lashed out about everything. Once, I had told her she shouldn't eat so much candy. She threw the chocolate bar at my head and told me to go to hell before slamming the bedroom door.

"I suppose I can see if someone can come take care of the apartment," Vati said with doubt in his voice. "Where will you live? Who will watch out after you?" he asked quickly. He looked away, which I took as evidence that he really didn't want to find answers to these questions.

That was my last effort to go to university. I knew from the tone of his voice my decision was made. Vati and Erna couldn't function without me, and I felt duty bound to remain in Kiel, in Vati's home. Perhaps I had just needed to make one last attempt to help me close the door on that future. After that, I didn't bring the subject up again. I chose to stay and to embrace the transition from daughter to the head of household.

CHAPTER 2

May 1933

Bruno

The massive naval ships in Kiel's harbor always made me feel so small, and it was no different on that day. My older brother, Karl, and I had been working a job there all morning, trying to repair a faulty generator. I had just left Karl to retrieve some tools from the truck when I heard a tiny meow. It took me a few minutes to find the kitten. It was sitting behind the front right wheel of our father's old farm truck. I lay on my stomach to reach for it, then wiggled forward as it shifted from my grasp. Finally, I managed to grab the little gray ball of fur. It lay nestled in my hands as I stood up and glanced around to see if there were any others.

"What do you have there?" a female voice asked.

I turned and found myself standing before an astonishingly beautiful woman, the hue of her eyes a captivating blend of blue and green. Her eyes seemed to contain the essence of the sea on a calm day, their depths reflecting both serenity and mystery. I held the kitten in both hands as it let out another nearly imperceptible meow.

The woman reached for the kitten, which I gladly handed over, feeling the softness of her hand as she gently scooped up the small creature. I watched her tenderly stroke its soft fur. The woman had a calming presence. "What will you do with him . . . or her?" She laughed.

"Well . . ." I thought about it. "If I can't find the mother, I'll take it to my niece. She's talked about having her own kitten for years, so this will be a nice surprise. My brother and his family live on a small potato farm." I paused, then asked, "What is your name?"

"Karla." She brought the kitten lovingly to her cheek and smiled as she listened to it purr.

"I'm Bruno."

Karla explained that she had brought her father lunch and was on her way back home. A flicker in her eyes told me there was more to the story, but I didn't want to intrude.

"Would you like to sit and have lunch with me? I can offer you a delectable half of a cheese sandwich." I gave her my most charming smile.

Her laugh sounded like music. "Perhaps I will sit with you for a moment, although I have already eaten."

We walked to the back of the truck to sit on the tailgate so I could eat. We sat in silence for a few moments, listening to the kitten purr under Karla's gentle strokes. The silence was comfortable as we both sat, enjoying the warmth of the sun.

"Do you work there?" Karla glanced around the naval yard.

I swallowed the small bite I'd taken before answering. "I'm helping my brother with a job. We're electricians." I pointed toward the building where we were working, and I wondered, *Is Karl missing me?*

"It must be nice to work with your brother."

"Most of the time. Though there are times when he takes advantage of his older-brother status. Like when he disagrees with me."

"Is he your only brother?"

I laughed, thinking about the chaotic home I grew up in. "No, there are eight of us! I had four brothers and three sisters. I'm the youngest." My heart sank a little. "One of my brothers died in the war."

Her eyes dimmed. "It's terribly sad about your brother." After a few moments, she said, "You must have had big, noisy dinners growing up?"

"Yes, they can get quite loud, especially when all the spouses and children come. But we all get together at the same time only once a year."

The more we talked, the more I was taken in by this woman. She was curious, intelligent, and I could tell well bred. Her clothes were clean and pressed. She had white gloves peeking out from the top of her purse. There were no holes or runs in her hosiery, and her hair, cut in a modern style, reached nearly to her shoulders.

"Karla!" I turned to see a man wearing a tailored jacket, matching waistcoat and trousers, and a fedora on his head. He was walking toward us from the administration building. His walk and his mannerisms as he touched his hat were precise. His eyes were shaded by his hat, so I couldn't tell if he was angry or concerned.

Karla eased off the tailgate of the truck. "My father," she whispered. I couldn't see the resemblance between him and his daughter and thought she must take after her mother.

This well-dressed, refined woman was intriguing me more and more.

She gave the kitten a kiss on its head and gently handed it back to me. As our hands brushed, I saw a small smile appear on her face. It quickly vanished as her father said, "Why are you still here? You need to go home, now!"

Karla looked at me with sad eyes and said, "It was nice to meet you." I watched her walk away toward the street.

CHAPTER 3

August 1933

Bruno

It had been three months since we had last worked at the naval base. The supply chain problems for most goods around Germany, plus the cost of the parts we needed, were proving a challenge. I finally decided to see if I could find an old motor in the scrapyard located about five kilometers south of the city. I was pleasantly surprised when, after half a day of looking through old engines, I found twenty-four bearings I thought might work.

The next day, as Karl parked the truck in the dirt parking lot close to the worksite, my thoughts naturally turned to Karla. In truth, I had thought of her often since meeting her in May. Her beautiful eyes and soft voice were forever seared into my brain. My heart fluttered as I thought about how wonderful it would be to run into her. No other woman had ever affected me like Karla had. She was special.

That day, Karl and I had to dig a hole about one meter deep and half a meter wide adjacent to the generator. The hole would allow us to get ourselves into a position from which we could pull the rotor out. The soil was wet and heavy as we dug, and it seeped into my shoes.

The first time I went into the newly dug hole, my feet began to sink, creating a suction effect that pulled my right shoe off. Each time I tried walking, the mud would suction off one shoe or the other. Karl eventually found some boards I could stand on. As I did that, I pulled my shoes out of the mud and tried unsuccessfully to wipe them clean.

Later, as we worked, Karl remarked, "You're quiet today, brother."

I had just put the rotor with the new bearings back into the generator. "I'm just focused on the work. Try the generator now."

He did. It came to life for thirty seconds and stopped.

"I'll get the other bearings from the truck," Karl said. "Let's just replace all of them." He started walking toward the truck.

I climbed out of the hole and reached for my canteen. I was still waiting for Karl's return when I heard the silky melody of her voice.

"Hello, Bruno."

I turned to see Karla smiling at me. Her jacket was open, revealing a simple yet refined dark-blue dress and matching hat. Her impeccably styled hair framed her lovely face. She exuded beauty and grace.

My pulse quickened as her gaze swept over me, scrutinizing every inch. With a gentle smile, she retrieved a pristine white handkerchief from her purse and extended it toward me. A sparkle in her eyes and the hint of amusement coloring her voice told me she was teasing when she said, "You've got a smudge on your cheek."

I looked down at my clothes. My shoes were caked with mud, and the dirt extended up to my chest. I laughed as I held my hand up and said, "Karla, I'm a mess. I didn't know I would see you, but I'm happy you're here."

"Hello, I'm Karl." I hadn't heard my brother walk up. He glanced at me with a knowing smile.

Karla looked over at him and said, "Hello, I'm Karla." She laughed. "It seems we have the same name; I hope no one gets confused." She looked back at me and said, "I see you're very busy, so I'll leave you to it." With a small wave, she turned to leave.

My pulse quickened at the thought that I might not have the chance to get to know her more. My network of people in and around Kiel was huge, but it was this one woman who had stirred something deep in me. I stepped forward and gave her my most endearing smile. "Karla! Would you like to take a walk sometime? I can come back later today after I clean up."

"I'm sorry, that won't be possible. My father . . ."

I felt a sinking sensation, but before I could accept her excuse or she could walk away, to my surprise, Karl stepped forward. "Karla, my family is having dinner at our farm on Saturday. Perhaps you would like to join us? Bruno can meet you at the train station and drive you in the truck." Karl shrugged, adding, "If you can get away."

Karla licked her lips, thinking for a moment. "I would like that very much."

Karl nodded and glanced at me before looking back at her. "Bruno will meet you at the main train station in Kiel at nine o'clock. The meal will be at noon, so you two should have time for that walk."

She looked at me. I nodded with a hopeful smile. "I promise I'll be more presentable."

She smiled back. "Okay, see you then."

Karl bumped my shoulder as I watched her walk away. Saturday was only three days away, but I already knew that it would feel like a lifetime.

∗∼∗

On the way to pick up Karla, I reflected on my current living situation, wondering what she would think about it. I was well connected throughout Kiel, and people were in the habit of calling on me all the time for any type of repair job, from a leaky roof to adding electricity to a house. Eli Meyer, the owner of a house in Kiel, had asked me to fix a leaky faucet. It didn't take long for us to become friends, and he had offered to rent me his attic room at a reduced rate.

I lived in a community called Kiel-Pries located just thirteen kilometers north of Kiel. However, much of my work was in the city of Kiel. My parents, along with Karl and his family, lived on a farm just outside the small town of Felm, thirteen kilometers west of both Kiel-Pries and Kiel. My arrangement with Eli allowed me to live affordably while staying close to my family. But my workdays varied in length, depending on weather conditions and on whether I had ridden a bus, cycled, or walked.

I enjoyed Eli's sense of humor, and we laughed often. His wife, Ilse, participated in our crazy humor as well. I remember one dinner when we sat down to matzo ball soup, with dumplings made from unleavened bread.

"I heard your matzo balls are so light, they float away before you can even taste them!" I said with a straight face.

Eli and Ilse stopped passing dishes and looked at me, then burst out laughing. With a twinkle in his eye, Eli retorted, "Well, I heard your sauerkraut is so sour, it puckers your lips for a week!"

The first time we shared a meal together, I brought a present for Eli's sons, four-year-old Jacob and two-year-old Daniel. The gift was a box that included various-sized pieces of scrap metal, bolts, screws, small wheels, and pieces of copper. I had also cut about thirty small pieces of wood in varying sizes and sanded them down before drilling holes for the screws and bolts. The set of items allowed them to build anything they could imagine, like the bridge I crossed over the canal on my way to the train station to pick up Karla.

As I arrived at the train station to meet her, I tried to distract myself from my nervousness about the coming day. I turned my mind to the Friday night Shabbos meal I had shared with Eli and Ilse the night before. They celebrated Shabbos every week, and I felt honored every time they invited me, a non-Jew, to participate.

The Shabbos celebration began at sundown on Friday and lasted until sundown on Saturday. Just before the Friday evening meal every week, Ilse lit candles and recited blessings to usher in the Sabbath. Then everyone sat down for a special meal. The meal began with Eli saying the blessing over the challah bread and sanctifying the Sabbath with wine. No work was done on the Sabbath, allowing for spiritual reflection and spending time with family and community. Time with family—like the time with my own family that I was about to share with Karla. And there I was, thinking of her again. Trying to distract myself did not work. All I could think about was spending the day with her. She had been so easy to be with on the day we first met.

As I pulled up to the curb outside the train station, I saw her before she saw me. She looked radiant in an emerald-green dress that buttoned down the front and had a wide white lapel. Her matching hat complemented it perfectly. She held her purse and white gloves in one hand and pink cornflowers, the German national flower, in the other.

She finally looked over and gave me a smile, then walked quickly to the truck as soon as I parked at the curb. She reached for the handle to open the truck door, but I quickly ran around to open it for her. After she was settled in the passenger seat, I couldn't help but smile as I nearly danced around the truck to the driver's side.

Karla was very quiet for the first ten minutes of the ride. I started to get nervous, thinking perhaps she regretted her decision to spend the day with me. Perhaps she was as nervous as I was. She seemed much more introspective today than she had the other times we met.

I glanced over. "Karla, are you okay?"

"Yes, I'm sorry."

I nodded, encouraging her to continue.

"Last night, my father shook his head when I told him I was going to Felm for the day, so this morning I told him I had decided to visit my cousin. I hated to put my cousin in the position of potentially lying for me, but she said she was so happy I had met someone." Karla's eyes looked sad. "Forgive me. I don't mean to be melancholy during our time together."

I touched her hand. "I'm sorry you're in this position. I can bring you home if you want."

"No! I very much want to spend the day together . . . if you still want to spend it with me?" Her eyes looked so hopeful.

The fact she didn't want to lie spoke volumes about her integrity. I covered her hand with mine. "Karla, I'm exactly where I want to be. I want you to have a wonderful day today. It sounds like your cousin is supportive. Perhaps someday you can repay the favor."

Her smile lit up the truck. "I didn't think about the opportunity to repay her. I will do that." She seemed to brush off her guilt over lying after a few minutes.

Not wanting to be too forward or make her uncomfortable, I reluctantly let go of her hand and asked, "Is it that your father wouldn't like you to go on a date with anyone or is the problem specifically me?" I did not refer to our obvious class differences, but I didn't have to. It was clear right away that she understood me.

She looked down at her clasped hands. "Probably both, but that's mostly because the war changed him. Before the war, he was trusting and happy. Honestly, I find his behavior a bit confusing sometimes. With the Nazis, he is open and trusting, but he's wary with other people until he knows whether they support the Nazis. It's as if . . . he knows a person is in the same club as him, then he can trust them, and if they are not, he acts like the person is going to commit a crime or something." She paused, seemingly considering her words. "He obsesses about things like my sister's and my safety and whether we can afford to buy food."

I nodded, trying to understand, but there was a lot to consider when it came to this man, including factors Karla had not stated out loud. Although the middle class was emerging, in the 1930s, there was still a class system in Germany. Karla came from an affluent family. My family was lower class, working paycheck to paycheck, and had no aspirations to curry favor with the Nazi Party. Food was always scarce, but my family was close and happy. My father had worked on the farm and had done electrical work on the side for as long as I could remember. He typically would bring me or Karl to his electrical jobs, which is where I started to learn the skills that enabled me to become an electrician.

Later, when Karl was of age, he grew the family electrical business from a side business into a full-time one. However, like most German businesses, his had been impacted by the depressed economy and high inflation. Every electrical job he managed to get was a blessing. Karl; his wife, Anna; and their daughter, Rosemarie had moved into the family farmhouse when Rosemarie was born so they could save money and care for our parents. Our parents helped take care of Rosemarie in return.

After our conversation, the remainder of our drive was much more relaxed. Karla told me funny stories about the children she taught piano to as a side job. I laughed as she told me about one student who'd decided to make his own "symphony" by tapping the piano keys with wooden spoons. It sounded like she had some precocious students. I told her stories from my life growing up with seven siblings. Having so many children in the family had meant that living in our home was a nonstop adventure. One evening, we had decided to have a "fancy dinner" and had dressed up in our parents' clothes. The sight of my brother struggling to walk in my mother's too-big high heels while attempting to serve potatoes that were rolling off the plate had us all in stitches for days.

I took my time driving to the farmhouse, telling Karla stories like these and showing her around Felm and the quiet countryside.

My heart started beating faster as I finally rounded the corner onto the familiar dirt driveway of my childhood home. There was a barn just forty meters to the left of the house, and across from the barn, two outhouses stood about twenty meters away. Our potato fields surrounded the compound. I wondered what Karla's impression was of it all. I was so nervous; I couldn't even bring myself to turn and try to read her face. *I really hope my family will like her as much as I do and vice versa.*

CHAPTER 4

August 1933
Karla

German people are generally more formal and shake hands in greeting, so I was surprised when Bruno's mother, Therese, gave me a hug. She was shorter than me and slender, wearing a well-worn but crisply laundered apron over her dress. Her dark-brown hair had gray streaks and was swept neatly into a bun. Her strong grip on my shoulders hinted at a lifetime of hard work.

I could tell she had been cooking, as the house smelled divine, the tantalizing aroma of hearty stews and freshly baked bread wafting through the air, wrapping around me like a comforting embrace. I sensed the pride Bruno's mother took in maintaining their home as I surveyed the modest yet meticulously tidy living room. The worn but neatly arranged furniture and the fresh scent of soap from the scrubbed floors spoke volumes about her dedication to keeping her home beautiful.

I walked around, looking at the fresh-cut daisies on the side table. I smiled at Therese as she placed the flowers I'd brought beside them on the same table. She hurried toward the back of the house, saying that she needed to check on dinner, leaving Bruno and me in the living room. I walked to the small piano in the corner and touched the keys.

"Do you play?" I turned to see a man who I presumed was Bruno's father. Otto Arnold was a doppelgänger of Bruno: older, but with the same height, same build, and same mannerisms.

"Vati, this is Karla," Bruno said.

I walked over and shook his hand. "Hello. And, yes, I do play piano, Herr Arnold."

He released my hand. "Please call me Otto. We are more informal in this house than most Germans are used to, but I prefer it." I smiled at him, unsure of how to respond but liking his energy and openness.

Just then, a young girl walked in with a creature I recognized. I reached over and scratched the little gray cat's head, feeling surprised at how much it had grown. "Hello, you must be Rosemarie. I'm Karla. What did you name your kitten?"

"Max," Rosemarie whispered with a small grin. She added, "He sleeps with me, but don't tell Vati. My friends call me Rosie. You can too." She seemed excited as she said all these things in a single breath.

I smiled and said, "Your secret is safe. And thank you. I shall call you Rosie, then."

"Would you like a piece of cake?" Rosie asked the question as if it were a serious offer, but she wore a mischievous look on her face. "Oma has been baking since early this morning, and I am forced to wait until after the meal. But if *you* wanted cake . . ." Rosie was smiling at me with hope in her eyes.

I smiled back and shook my head as Bruno stepped forward. His eyes were twinkling with humor, but his voice held authority. "Rosie, we will have cake after the meal, but right now I want to show Karla our farm. Would you like to come?"

Just then, Therese called from the kitchen. "Rosemarie, come help me with setting the table, please."

Rosie rolled her eyes and said to me, "She has ears like a bat. No one can get away with anything!"

During our time at the farm that day, I felt very comfortable with Bruno and his family. Being with him was easy and fun. As he showed me around the property, Bruno told me about life on the farm, and then we discussed personal things before talking about some of the things we were hearing in the news.

When I told him about my mother's illness and death, he was kind, patient, and a great listener, offering insightful comments and asking probing questions that showed he understood and was genuinely interested. He spoke words of encouragement and offered thoughtful reflections about what I had gone through. He was the first person I had met who really listened to me, other than my mother. I told him about my mother's beautiful singing voice and our shared love for the piano. I spoke about how she had taught me how to sew, instilling in me a sense of creativity and self-reliance.

I told Bruno about my sister and explained how, since my mother was sick for so long and my father didn't handle anything in the household, Erna had had no discipline. My father could not say no to her, and I was not a parent who could set limits with her. As a result, she had become a willful child who always got her way. She even knew how to get what she wanted when the answer was no—and it rarely was no. For example, Vati spent a lot of time with Nazi friends, and Erna was supposed to make herself scarce when these men were around. But she did not.

Both Erna and Vati were, like many people in Germany, drawn to the fervent energy of the Nazi Party's gatherings. They were seduced by promises of national pride and unity. And so, they eagerly attended rallies and events, swept up in the fervor of the movement.

As I was telling these stories, I wondered to myself, *Is Bruno in favor of the Nazi ideology that's becoming so popular?* I wondered if I should tell him I was turned off by all the hype and didn't agree with any of the antisemitic propaganda. *If I told him that, would he run away from me?* Whenever I looked out at the sea of swastikas and salutes displayed by the Nazis who paraded down the streets of Kiel, I felt a little appalled at the seemingly blind devotion people were giving them. The Nazis were very adept at fostering a sense of belonging, camaraderie, and purpose. They were promising things that our country, and people like Vati and Erna, desperately needed. But I didn't trust any of it.

Still, that day with Bruno, I didn't talk about my experience at the rally or my disdain for the Nazis and Hitler or about feeling a sense of dread for the fate of Jews and other ethnic minorities who were being unfairly scapegoated. Although I sensed that Bruno had deep integrity, my upbringing had instilled in me a deep-seated wariness about divulging too much too soon, particularly in the area of expressing dissenting opinions. I did attempt to decipher Bruno's stance on politics by reading his expression, but his demeanor remained inscrutable, his placid facade betraying no hint of his true beliefs.

As we navigated our conversation around weighty subjects, our discussions gravitated toward the grim realities of Germany's current state: things we'd heard about on the radio or read about from the newspaper. The Treaty of Versailles continued to loom over our country like a specter, and anger over the harsh reparations imposed after the war was widespread. Bruno and I talked about how Germany's economy was in a state of distress, plagued by soaring prices, meager wages, and scant opportunities for advancement. The infrastructure lay in ruin, having been neglected since the war's end. Dilapidated roads and buildings served as grim reminders of our nation's struggles.

There was more than just my hesitation to say too much that kept me talking about weightier things. I was also fully aware of the threat of severe repercussions—prison or death—faced by those who voiced views contrary to the Nazi doctrine, and I was sure Bruno was aware too. Yet I also sensed that a silent understanding hung between the two of us, a shared hope that perhaps one day we could delve deeper into our beliefs without fear of persecution.

As we walked back toward the house, I felt a little frustrated that I wasn't comfortable speaking about my beliefs, so I changed the subject back to my life at home and how I kept myself busy. My mother had left me her sewing machine, and I found great joy in creating new clothes, especially dresses. I loved the creativity involved in taking old curtains and making dresses or shirts. I twirled around and said, laughing, "I made this dress from a neighbor's old tablecloth. She burned a corner of it with her iron by mistake and gave me the rest!"

We were about thirty meters from the house when Bruno tentatively took my hand. "Is this okay?"

I felt my cheeks warm but smiled and nodded. As we walked together, I could feel that Bruno was becoming someone incredibly special to me.

Bruno held the back door open, and I walked into the kitchen where Therese was taking a lid off a pot to stir what smelled like a stew.

"Can I help you with anything?" I asked.

"No, everything is ready, and we can all sit," Therese said.

Bruno introduced me to Karl's wife, Anna, as we walked into the dining room. She was taller than me and slender, her dark hair falling neatly to her shoulders and framing her face in an understated elegance. I guessed that both she and Karl were in their thirties. Anna seemed much more formal than her husband, and I wondered if I should call her Frau Arnold. We shook hands hello and found seats at the table.

The dining table comfortably seated six, plus there was an extra chair tucked in the corner which I assumed was for Rosie. A pair of candles cast a soft glow, and white-and-brown napkins added a touch of elegance to the mismatched dishes. I watched the steam rise from the bowls in the center of the table containing hot stew, cured ham, potatoes, and green beans. The meal was simple but tasted wonderful. Unlike conversations at dinner with my family, which were quiet and always focused on politics, the conversation at the Arnold home flowed and covered everything *but* politics. I had never laughed as hard as I did at their stories of being part of a large family.

Karl laughed too as he told the story of Therese tying Bruno to a tree when he was four while the whole family harvested potatoes. "To be fair," said Therese, "it was for his own protection." She looked lovingly at Bruno. "Our youngest was always in the habit of running off to play in the woods."

Otto took a sip of water and launched into another story. "I remember when the kids decided to figure out how they could avoid walking in the pigpen. They thought their plan was foolproof." He pointed to Bruno. "And this one was at the center of the mischief: building a zipline from the hayloft to the fence around the pigpen." I saw Karl and Bruno looking at their plates, laughing.

"How old were they?" I asked.

"I think I was nine at the time," Bruno said.

"They launched their first trial run, and there was nothing except chaos." Otto looked at his sons with amusement. "Instead of soaring like birds, they found themselves tangled in a mess of hay and laughter."

After dinner, Anna, Therese, Rosie, and I started cleaning the kitchen. Anna left a few minutes later to sit with the men. The kitchen was small, so one less person was fine, but I didn't miss the look of irritation across Therese's face. There seemed to be an underlying story between Therese and Anna, but Therese said nothing and continued to clean.

"Therese, why don't you let Rosie and me finish this, and you go sit. You cooked all day, and it will give me a chance to get to know Rosie better," I said.

Therese worked efficiently through the kitchen, placing the dishes in the soapy water. "You are kind, but I will not have a guest cleaning for me. Cleaning won't take long, and then we can sit together with cake and coffee. I would like to get to know you better too." She washed the dishes one by one, then put them in the clean water, at which point I picked them up and dried them. Rosie just danced around the kitchen, laughing.

"I can already tell that my son has certainly picked someone good to be with," Therese continued. "I see how he looks at you, and you should know that he has never brought anyone home with him." I felt my face warm. I really liked Bruno and his family.

Now that we'd finished cleaning, Therese picked up a plate with a bee sting cake, made with honey and pudding, and a white carafe of coffee. I followed her into the living room, carrying a tray with cups, saucers, spoons, sugar, and cream. Bruno stood up and took the tray from me, then placed it on the coffee table. I didn't miss the look that Karl and Otto exchanged.

Otto moved to squat in front of the radio, its polished wooden cabinet gleaming in the warm glow of the afternoon and began to turn the dials in search of music. All that was playing was Nazi propaganda, so he switched the receiver off and turned to me. "Will you please play the piano for us, Karla?"

Feeling relieved that we didn't have to listen to the news in case someone asked my opinion, I smiled at him and said, "Of course."

CHAPTER 5

August 1933
Bruno

I was mesmerized as Karla played "I Lost My Heart in Heidelberg" by Fred Raymond and Fritz Löhner-Beda. I was astounded at her talent when she started singing while playing "To Music" by Franz Schubert. My entire family was captivated. My father sat on the sofa with his eyes closed, appearing to be totally immersed in the music. My mother's face was serene and focused as she watched Karla play. Rosie danced around in the corner. It was always hard to tell what Anna was thinking, but Karl smiled at Rosie's dance.

I moved a chair from the dining table to a spot against the wall by the piano so I could watch Karla play. A smile tugged at her lips as her hands moved effortlessly over the keys. She glanced at me, and the small smile grew so that it reached her eyes.

Finally, after an hour and a half of her playing, I said, "Karla, we should go so you can get back home before dark. The streets are becoming more dangerous, and I couldn't bear it if something happened to you."

She nodded and gathered her hat and purse, then turned to my parents and said, "Thank you for such a lovely day and wonderful dinner."

"We would love you to come back anytime." Mutti glanced at me with a twinkle in her eyes and added, "With or without Bruno." She turned back to me, smiling brightly. I couldn't help but laugh. Secretly, I love every minute of my family's mischief.

Finally, we found ourselves in the truck after a wonderful day together. I decided to tell her what I was thinking. "Karla, I would like to spend more time with you."

Karla gazed pensively out the window for a moment. Then, after a deep breath, she said, "I would like that too, but I'm not sure it's possible. My father prefers me to stay close to home." Her eyes lingered on the view outside. "Since my mother's passing, he has become more dependent on me, as well as increasingly obsessed with the Nazi Party. He seems to find solace in being part of a group. Politics never held much sway for him while we were growing up, but the war and my mother's death spurred him to seek . . . something." She shook her head. "It's hard to explain."

I began to try to think of ways we could spend time together. My mind flashed through long walks around the harbor, dinner with Eli and Ilse, and maybe even a shopping trip to Hamburg, one and a half hours south of Kiel.

It seemed that Karla was doing the same thing. "Bruno, your father said you could fix anything." She paused. I glanced at her and squeezed her hand, urging her to continue. "Will you fix my sewing machine on Saturday morning? Erna and my father will be at a Nazi rally."

"It would be my pleasure, Miss Petersen." I grinned. "Especially if we can have a picnic after."

CHAPTER 6

October 1933

Bruno

Ilse pushed the newspaper across the table toward me as I sat down with my cup of coffee. I unfolded it and read with a feeling of apprehension. It seemed that every day the Nazis were announcing something new.

Germany Asserts Sovereignty with Withdrawal from League of Nations

In a bold move aimed at asserting Germany's sovereignty and independence, Chancellor Adolf Hitler announced Germany's withdrawal from the League of Nations, effective 19 October 1933. This decision, made in the best interests of the German people, reflects Chancellor Hitler's commitment to breaking free from the constraints of unjust treaties and to restoring national pride.

> Chancellor Hitler emphasized that Germany's withdrawal from the League of Nations is a necessary step toward regaining control over its own destiny and forging new diplomatic and economic alliances. The decision has garnered widespread support from the German populace, which views it as a crucial move toward reclaiming Germany's rightful place among the community of nations. As Germany embarks on this new chapter, free from the constraints of international organizations, the world watches with anticipation to see how this bold assertion of sovereignty will shape the nation's future.

I put the paper down and thought back to when the League of Nations had first been established. I had applauded its goals of promoting peace, cooperation, and collective security between nations. "I'm not sure what to think."

Ilse took a sip of her coffee. This must have been difficult to do because her hands were shaking. "I think Europe's political climate is fragile," she said. "I'm afraid this decision will trigger conflict with other countries."

Her hands were shaking so hard that when she lowered her cup to the saucer, I was surprised the porcelain didn't break.

CHAPTER 7

December 1933

Karla

I couldn't believe how well Bruno understood me. His consistent empathy and perceptiveness made me feel truly seen and heard, as if he intuitively knew my innermost thoughts and feelings. Over the next several months, we met up in different areas of the city. After delivering lunch to my father, I brought lunch, usually some cheese and bread, to whatever job site Bruno was working at during the week. We spent those thirty minutes together while Vati was at work at the naval base. We also spent many Saturdays and Sundays at the farm while Vati and Erna attended Nazi rallies and parties.

During one of our many lunches together, Bruno told me all about Christmas at the Arnold house. His family spent the weeks before the holiday getting ready for their annual family celebration. Otto cured meat throughout the year in anticipation of the Christmas season. I wasn't surprised that preparations took so long with a family of twenty-three. I laughed when he explained that everyone couldn't fit in the house at the same time, so tables were set up in the barn. I couldn't imagine how cold that must be in December, but Bruno explained that they were all out of the wind, and with everyone dancing and singing, no one suffered.

Christmas with my family was mostly a small and quiet affair with just Vati and me. Erna joined us if it was convenient for her to do so. Occasionally, we would have a cousin or aunt over. The most fun part was going to our neighbors' apartments for coffee. Each day, between Christmas Day and New Year's Day, one family hosted the others, with each of us taking a turn: a tradition Mutti started when I was young.

Bruno and I decided to take a Saturday to visit a Christmas market in Hamburg. The famous markets were a long-standing tradition in our country. Amid the darker things that were happening socially, politically, and economically, the markets offered a festive atmosphere with food, crafts, and holiday decorations for sale. Bruno and I decided it would be easier to meet at the train station in Kiel since he was going to spend the night before at his parents' house in Felm.

My eyes scanned the terminal until I found him. When I did, I started walking toward him. He still had not seen me. I stopped a few meters behind Bruno to watch him entertain two other men, who both laughed at his antics. My Bruno could tell a story like no one else I knew. I looked at the two men facing him. One was younger and had a wooden toolbox in one hand and a cigarette in the other. The other man's old bike leaned against him as he used his hands to light his own cigarette.

I stepped forward and heard Bruno say, "She was this tall . . ." He brought his hand over his head. "And could get apples out of the trees." Bruno looked over at me and put his arm around my shoulders, smiling. "Suddenly, everyone was standing around this poor woman." All three men laughed at the story. I only heard the last part of the story, so I just smiled. Bruno said to the two men, "I'm off to Hamburg. Have a good day." He waived and guided me toward the train platform.

"Are those your friends?" I asked Bruno. He seemed to know everyone and, if we came across someone he didn't know, the person never left us as a stranger.

"Not really. I just met them," he answered.

As we waited for the train, I said, "You must be cold. Your coat isn't heavy enough, and you don't have a scarf or gloves!"

Bruno just smiled. "Karla, I'm a tough German who is used to cold. I'm fine." He bumped my shoulder with his and added, "Thank you for worrying about me, though."

I felt myself blush as a train pulled into the station with a lot of noise and wind, blowing my hair and skirt. I tried to think of what to say back to him, but it was too loud for me to respond. The moment was lost as the train came to a stop and people climbed down to the platform while others climbed on board.

Our train ride took about an hour and forty minutes with no stops. There were a few people in the same car as us, but it wasn't overly crowded. Bruno and I were in our own world, talking and laughing. We always had a great time together.

It was a short walk from Hamburg Central Railway Station to the market. The streets where the market was set up were closed to any car or bicycle traffic. The market was crowded. It seemed all of northern Germany was there, there were so many people. The atmosphere was lively where locals gathered to share in the holiday spirit and purchase gifts for loved ones. Traditional holiday music was being played by a band, decorations hung everywhere, and Christmas trees stood on every corner.

Wooden stalls decorated with garlands of evergreen stood along each side of the street. Their foliage made the market smell like a forest. Within the stalls, shelves were full of a variety of handmade crafts, ornaments, and sweets. I licked my lips when I saw gingerbread cookies, shortbread biscuits dusted with confectioners' sugar, and flaky pastries filled with spiced fruit compote. Hand-painted signs with seasonal motifs guided visitors through the bustling marketplace, where the air was filled with a sense of holiday anticipation.

Bruno and I walked hand in hand up one side of the street before crossing over to walk down the other. At one point, he brought our joined hands to his lips, kissed the back of my hand, and said, "Karla, I'm going to find a place where we can sit for a coffee."

"Oh, that sounds wonderful. I'll look for you in a few minutes. I just have to run a small errand."

I went into the store I had noticed from across the street. I'd seen that they had winter clothing, and I wanted to get Bruno a gift. I found a pair of gloves made of leather and lined with rabbit fur. The leather was smooth and supple. I pulled one of the gloves onto my hand and felt the soft fur against my skin. I held the gloves to my nose and breathed in the subtle earthy scent. I knew the gloves would be just the right gift for Bruno.

I noticed a moment later that the gloves were eight marks. I only had seven. Resigned, I put the gloves down. As I was walking toward the door, the lady behind the desk stepped out and said, "Those are beautiful gloves. Sure to keep your man's hands warm."

I smiled and nodded. "I don't have enough money to buy them."

"How much do you have?"

I pulled my wallet out of my purse and showed her.

I watched the shopkeeper walk over and pick up the gloves. "There haven't been many people buying things," she said. "I'll sell you the gloves for what you have."

I didn't want to take advantage of her, but I was only short one mark. And I did want to get Bruno the gloves.

She handed them to me as I replied, "Thank you?" I said it as a question because I still wasn't quite sure I understood her correctly. But she didn't take the gloves back. Finally, I handed her my money. "Merry Christmas," I said. I felt grateful for her kindness.

As I walked out of the store, I hid the gloves in my purse and went to find Bruno.

Bruno was sitting in a café a few doors down. I saw him through the window, surrounded by men and women. He was telling a story, raising his hands for more drama as the crowd laughed. I shook my head with a smile, thinking, *I can't leave him alone for a minute without him telling stories to anyone who will listen.*

As soon as I entered the café, Bruno jumped up and pulled me over to the table where there was a cup of coffee waiting for me. I nodded at the people surrounding him. A few people smiled at me and walked away. Some others stayed to talk some more. Bruno was in his element, and I loved seeing him happy. Everywhere we went, people were drawn to him.

As we were walking back to the train station, Bruno pulled me over to a small park with a decorated Christmas tree in its center.

"I'm having a wonderful time, Bruno." I opened my purse and pulled out the gloves I had bought. "Merry Christmas," I said, handing them to him.

He looked at me and said, "Karla, these are wonderful. They're beautiful."

"I hope they fit!" I had been so concerned about the money, I hadn't even considered whether the gloves would fit his hands.

He slipped on the gloves and moved his hands around to show me they were perfect. It was as if someone had custom-made them for him. He said, "I love them."

Bruno then pulled a small red pouch out of his pocket and handed it to me. Happiness bubbled over me as I pulled the necklace out. "Oh, Bruno, this is too much." I touched the necklace tenderly. Despite my protests, I couldn't help but think it was the perfect gift.

"No, Karla. I want you to wear it. I want you to know how much you mean to me." He took the delicate necklace from my hands and motioned for me to turn around. Then he gently put it around my neck and secured the clasp.

The chain was elegantly designed with small interlocking links that created the impression of fluidity and movement. The links were subtly textured, which I thought added a touch of sophistication. At the center of the necklace was a gold cornflower with a delicate loop attached at the top for the chain to pass through.

I touched the necklace where it fell just below my collarbone and imagined how lovely it must look. "It's so beautiful. Thank you. I will treasure it always." I felt my feelings for Bruno grow as I reflected on the thoughtfulness he'd obviously put into selecting the perfect gift.

CHAPTER 8

January–July 1934

Bruno

I sat at the kitchen table with Eli and Ilse, drinking coffee with them as we discussed the changes that had occurred in Germany. It had been a full year since Hitler was appointed chancellor. I had been having morning coffee with Eli at that very table when the announcement came on the radio twelve months before, in January 1933.

Eli reached over to turn the volume up on the small radio at the end of the table.

"Ladies and gentlemen, this is the Reich Broadcasting. We interrupt our regular programming to bring you an important announcement."

Eli's expression hadn't changed as he took a sip of coffee.

"In a historic development, President Paul von Hindenburg has appointed Adolf Hitler as chancellor of Germany. This decision follows the recent Reichstag elections, in which the Nazi Party emerged as the largest party."

We remained silent as Ilse walked in and sat beside Eli. Hitler's voice came through the radio speaker loud and clear.

"My fellow Germans, I humbly accept the responsibility entrusted to me by President von Hindenburg. Together, we will work tirelessly to rebuild our nation and restore its greatness. We shall embark on a journey of renewal, guided by the principles of unity, strength, and prosperity for all true Germans. With unity and determination, there is no limit to what we can achieve!"

Next came the sound of applause. Ilse shifted back in her chair and started chewing on her bottom lip. She looked nervous but remained silent as she listened to the rest of the broadcast.

The announcer concluded with, "So let's join hands and celebrate this historic moment! Stay tuned for more updates and exciting developments as we march forward toward a brighter tomorrow!"

Eli turned down the radio. "He speaks of unity but not for all Germans." He stared down into his cold coffee as if he was looking there for the right words. "They started with taking outspoken Jews to 'reeducation camps' last year. Now, they are taking more and more of us." He looked up at me solemnly. "I wonder when they're coming for my family." Ilse moved closer to Eli and took his hand.

I felt helpless as I tried to find words of comfort. There was nothing I could offer. Propaganda promoting the Nazi ideology was everywhere: in the newspaper, on the radio, on signs, on pamphlets, at cultural events, and in films. It all centered around the notions of racial supremacy and on creating a racially pure Germanic state. "All this propaganda about being racially pure is damn barbaric," I said. "People are unhappy, I know. But this is no answer."

"I wonder how much of the disillusionment people feel is actually caused by the way the press talks about all the issues we're facing," Eli said.

"All of it," Ilse replied. "The government runs the media, and people don't have a balanced view of the world."

Eli stood up and walked to the counter, then back to his chair but remained standing. "I think the appointment of Hitler as chancellor is one the president will come to regret—and the people too. Look how quickly the regime is moving to consolidate its power."

The Reichstag fire had followed a month after Hitler's appointment. I remembered it as vividly as if it had happened yesterday. The headlines told of chaos and destruction. There was a devastating fire at the Reichstag, the heart of our democracy where parliament held sessions. The Nazis blamed the Communists for the fire. In March, many of our civil liberties, like freedom of speech, freedom of the press, and the right to privacy were taken away. The Law to Remedy the Distress of the People and the Reich—an act that allowed Hitler and his cabinet to make and enact laws independently—was passed that same month. Soon, the people's liberties were replaced by fear and oppression. This was a turning point, the moment when our democracy was snuffed out and the path to totalitarian rule was paved. The Reichstag fire would forever be etched in my memory as the day our freedom was lost.

I had since believed that most Germans accepted the new laws because their fear of Communism was even greater than their fear of losing liberties. In our country, Communism was associated with political instability, economic hardship, and loss of individual freedoms and, of course, the Soviets—formerly the Russians, who had been our foes in the Great War. It felt almost as if that war had forced us to become a society that sought safety at the expense of all else.

I thought now about what Karla had said about her father: that he had been a happy man before the war. Today, he seemed the very model of a society that was desperately seeking safety amid chaos. *Maybe I understand that man a little better than I knew,* I thought.

Eli's words brought me out of my reverie. "I knew passing those laws last year was going to be a big mistake. Now that the Nazis have power and Hitler is in a position where he can do the most damage, I don't see a way back. No one in the government is strong enough to stop him." Eli shook his head and whispered, "And people voted for this."

"Now we must live with the choices the voters made when they backed the Nazis," Ilse added. "I think the boys are old enough now to understand that discussions in this house are private and the danger of us going to prison if they repeat anything."

"Or they could just shoot all of us," Eli added.

By early 1934, there were two main police forces in Germany. The SS, or Protection Squads, handled internal security throughout the country, including arrests of Nazi opponents. The Secret State Police, referred to as the Gestapo, had emerged in 1933 and had broad powers to arrest anyone seen as an enemy of the state, including political dissidents, Jews, and Communists. Neither group was shy about using violence and fear to control the population.

It was Ilse's practice to leave the daily newspaper on the steps going up
to my attic apartment so that I could read it after work. Each evening, I
unfolded the paper and slowly walked upstairs to my apartment while
reading. One night, one particular article caught my attention for its
example of the Gestapo's brutality and of the way the media manipu-
lated public opinion.

> In a demonstration of unyielding resolve to
> uphold law and order, the Gestapo, operating
> under the meticulous direction of Heinrich
> Himmler, swiftly apprehended a group of
> individuals suspected of plotting against
> the state. Acting on reliable intelligence, the
> Gestapo conducted targeted raids, resulting in
> the arrest of several alleged conspirators aim-
> ing to undermine the stability and unity of the
> Reich. "We will not tolerate any threat to the
> safety and security of our nation," asserted
> Hermann Göring, minister of the interior and
> founder of the Gestapo. This decisive action
> underscores the authorities' unwavering
> commitment to safeguard the interests of the
> German people and to preserve the sanctity of
> the National Socialist vision.

Over the past year, I had experienced a disturbing shift in our
neighborhood dynamics as neighbors, driven by a desperate urge to
curry favor with the Gestapo, began reporting even the slightest in-
fractions, like a person hiding a book the Nazis deemed undesirable.
Witnessing these betrayals had left me deeply unsettled, as I had always found it easy to trust the people in my community. The experience served as a harsh awakening, forcing me to confront my feelings
about the actions and choices people made in the name of survival in a
society governed by fear and betrayal.

Because I didn't support the Nazis, I had to remain on guard and take care every day about what I said in public, even to those that I considered friends. Aside from Eli and Ilse, no one knew my political opinions. I had not even expressed them yet to Karla, though I felt certain, given her kindness and intelligence, that she must have similar thoughts.

One day in May, as I passed by the library, I saw men in Nazi uniforms gathered there, their hands firmly gripping rifles while they scanned the surroundings, ever watchful for signs of dissent or other potential threats. There were stacks of books on carts, and a few men nearby were stacking wood. *Are they going to burn those books?* I stopped to watch and asked the people around me what was happening. "The 'un-German' books need to be burned," said one woman. A man on the other side of me nodded. "Anything written by a Communist or Jew must go." I moved closer and saw there were books by prominent authors such as Thomas Mann, Erich Maria Remarque, Heinrich Heine, Sigmund Freud, and many others. These books were the same ones I saw stacked on Karla's dining table, ready to be returned after she read them. She was going to be upset that the Nazis were burning books.

Nazi ideology, whether we agreed with it or not, was now permeating every part of our lives. I knew by then that dissenters were eliminated by being shot or sent to prison camps with their families. I didn't understand where the authorities could take so many people who were arrested.

Eli seemed to be under more stress than ever. It seemed that each night we listened to the radio, he stood up to pace the room. Most people I knew were living in fear of not being able to provide for their families and of saying something that could be interpreted as not supporting the Nazis. Eli feared all these things too, but he also feared people's growing hatred toward Jews, and he feared what that hatred might do.

The air was sticky as I watched my friend walk back and forth in the living room like a caged lion. "Do you think people understand that the Nazis are chipping away at their civil liberties piece by piece?" he asked. I couldn't tell if he wanted an answer, so I looked at Ilse, who was sitting quietly in the corner of the sofa with her feet tucked under her. She shook her head, which I took as advice to remain silent and let Eli blow off steam.

Eli threw his arms in the air as he walked back and forth. His voice got louder as he expressed his frustration. "I heard someone say, 'It's a small thing the Nazis took away, but since they gave us jobs, we're willing to sacrifice.'" He stopped pacing and stood at the window, looking out at the dark, rainy night. From where I sat, the patch of darkness looked like an abyss. I wondered if that's what he was seeing too.

"They think that one small thing isn't doing harm," he said, "but this one small thing is adding up to other small things and expanding to include big things. They seem willing to give up freedom of the press and for what? A lousy job they hate at less than ten Reichsmarks a day?" Eli sat on the sofa and looked at me. "I'm not even talking about the freedoms the Nazis took away from Jews. People who aren't Jews don't care about that. That doesn't surprise me. But they don't care about the freedoms that were taken from them either. The authorities took away freedom of the press and freedom of speech, so now Germans see only one opinion of the world: the one being presented to them by the Nazis. People can no longer make informed decisions."

Ilse had remained silent all this time, taking everything in. Now she took a deep breath and said quietly, "Hitler is spreading hate and using people's insecurities to feed Nazi power, and the Nazis are using Jews as a way to manipulate support by blaming us for our country's problems and presenting Jews as a common enemy to rally behind."

None of us said anything else after that. I knew what she said was true, and I knew that whatever came next would not be good for Germany or for any of its people. But I had no idea how much worse things would one day be.

CHAPTER 9

September 1934

Bruno

It was a beautiful night in September when I was invited to dinner with Eli and his family. I walked down the stairs from my apartment to the smell of cooked cabbage. I loved the taste of cabbage, but the smell was pungent to me. The windows were open, letting a soft breeze in, making the home feel comfortable and relaxing. Ilse had also made potatoes along with the flounder I brought home from fishing just a few hours ago. I smiled, remembering how impressed Ilse had been that I cleaned it before handing it to her.

Jacob and Daniel were sitting beside each other at the dining table when I walked in and pulled out my usual chair. "Am I supposed to say 'Heil Hitler' when I meet people?" Jacob asked just then. Eli and Ilse were already seated at the ends of the table.

I sat down but remained silent as Eli and Ilse looked at each other. I imagined they were wondering how best to answer the question.

Eli leaned forward and looked at his son. "Jacob, what do you understand about what is happening around our country? I assume maybe you have heard things in school?"

"I understand that Hitler doesn't like the Jews, so I guess he hates our family." The boy was looking down at his plate, but then he looked up at his father and said, "And the kids don't like me and my friends. They call us 'nasty Jews' and throw rocks."

Ilse passed the platter of fish to me. "That's horrible!" she exclaimed. I took a small piece of fish, placing it on top of my cabbage.

Eli shook his head and looked at Ilse. "Maybe it's time to take Jacob out of school and teach them at home."

Jacob scooped some food onto his fork, nodding. "I hate school. The teachers don't even like me, and I didn't do anything mean to anyone." He put the food in his mouth and chewed. There was sadness in his eyes.

"Okay, so it's decided." Eli tapped his hands on the table. "You will learn from home. Mutti will teach you." He shifted to the edge of his seat, his eyes moving from Jacob to Daniel as he said, "My sons, there are people who are, indeed, spreading hate. In our family, we will continue to be respectful. If someone approaches you with anything other than kindness, you run home."

Jacob furrowed his brow. "But why do they hate us?" I noticed Eli had barely taken a bite of his meal. I looked down at my nearly empty plate, then across the table at Ilse. "Delicious," I whispered.

Eli didn't seem to hear me as he addressed Jacob's question. "Some people need to blame others to make themselves feel better. But we know what is in our heart, and that is kindness, always."

Daniel was sitting next to me. He touched his elbow to mine to get my attention. "Uncle Bruno, you're not Jewish, but you're our friend?" I wasn't sure why he'd said that as a question.

I covered Daniel's hand with my own. "You are not just my friends. I am your friend forever." The boys smiled and wiggled in their seats upon hearing that.

Eli took a bite of his food, which by now, I was sure, was cold. "Uncle Bruno is our family," he said.

Thinking it would be a good time to break the tension in the room, I released Daniel's hand and stood up. "Ilse, as always, the meal was perfect. Thank you!" I looked at Jacob, then Daniel. "Boys, I have a surprise for you." I glanced at Eli, and he nodded, then mouthed the words "thank you."

The boys slid off their chairs and jumped up and down with big smiles on their faces in the way that excited children do.

I held up my hand. "First, you help your mother and clear your plates."

Ilse arranged Jacob's knife and fork on his plate to make it easier to carry. As he was walking toward the door to the kitchen, he asked, "But what is it?" A few seconds later, I heard the clank of dishes being dropped into the sink. Ilse laughed. Daniel struggled to coordinate getting out of his chair and carrying his plate, so Ilse put his plate on top of her own. Jacob ran back into the room, looking at me expectantly.

I pulled Daniel's and Ilse's plates to mine and stacked all of them, then stood and started walking toward the kitchen. "I found all the things we need to build a wagon. Would you like to help me build it?"

Both boys jumped up and cried, "Yes!"

In the backyard, I helped the boys lay out the supplies I brought home from the scrapyard. I stacked the wooden planks close enough to where I intended to work so the boys could watch me, but far enough away that they wouldn't get in my way. I gave them each a piece of sandpaper with which to sand the wooden planks. I laughed inwardly at how seriously Jacob took his sanding job. "With the grain of the wood." I demonstrated, smoothing my hand across the board.

Once I was satisfied that the boys were occupied, I started laying the rest of the parts out in a way that allowed me to better visualize the completed product. I placed the chassis from a damaged two-seater Goliath Pionier car flat on the ground. Next, I bolted a wooden flatbed from a wrecked horse-drawn carriage flat onto the chassis. I lifted each corner of the chassis to put the wheels on and stepped back to survey the masterpiece.

I glanced up at the boys, surprised they weren't peppering me with questions. They were still seriously occupied with their sanding job.

The flatbed's wood had shrapnel scars, so I reinforced the weakened places with metal sheets I had ripped from some household appliances that had been left to decay in the rubble: remnants of domestic lives shattered by the war.

Now it was time to add the planks. I picked one up and held it in the air. "Boys, this looks wonderful! You did a great job sanding!" Jacob gave me a sweet smile while Daniel ran into the house calling after his mother. I couldn't hear anything after the door slammed shut. I held up a board and started to sand. "I'm just going to add some finishing touches." Jacob had sanded the same place for so long that there was a dip at one end, and no sanding was done anywhere else.

I sanded four boards that had been sawed down to one meter and four that had been sawed to half a meter. The boards were extra pieces my father had had sitting on the ground behind the barn. Karl had cut them to size and brought them to Eli's house in the truck.

Now I fastened the side planks together using hinges I had pried from old doors from the waste disposal site. This design allowed the sides to be let down for easier loading. I used a bolt at the front of the chassis to hold a rope in place so the wagon could be pulled. Lastly, I added a pillow that Karla had sewn from scraps of fabric, giving the wagon a seat cushion that would make riding in it more comfortable.

The sun had nearly set when I heard the door slam and saw Eli walk toward us. He walked around the wagon and whistled slowly.

"That is some wagon, Jacob."

CHAPTER 10

October–November 1934

Bruno

The Sunday Karla and I decided to spend in Hamburg was a beautiful day. We had a wonderful picnic at Inner Alster Lake. Karla brought cheese sandwiches, sliced carrots, and two apples. It had rained overnight and the ground was wet, so we sat on a park bench, enjoying the sounds of children playing and the view of ducks gently swimming in the water.

After a long walk around the lake, we decided to walk to a café for coffee. On our way, I noticed a large crowd of people around the steps leading up to city hall. I wondered what event was about to take place. Large flags featuring the Nazi swastika hung on either side of the large entry doors. At the top of the steps was a podium. To my surprise, Hitler was standing behind the microphone. It looked like he was about to give a speech.

Both Karla and I had heard him speak many times on the radio, but neither of us had heard him speak in person. Out of curiosity, we both agreed to stay and listen. Karla and I had not yet talked about our political opinions. But she was the kindest person I knew, and I couldn't imagine she would have a pro-Nazi ideology. She had told me previously that her father was a Nazi, but she had not indicated she shared his beliefs. I couldn't blame her for her father's decisions. After all, several of my brothers had pledged their allegiance to the Nazi regime, including Karl. He had been forced to join the Party to keep the jobs he had with the German military. It was a hard spot to be in, but I understood his priority was to care for his family.

The Nazis told me several times to sign my allegiance to the regime, but signing went against my beliefs. I gave them my most charming smile and dropped the names of the Nazi families in whose homes I had done electrical work. I then thanked the person for bringing me the form and promised to sign it the first chance I got. I was not going to do it willingly. I told myself someone was going to have to hold a gun to my head before I signed.

Karla and I stood on the fringe of the crowd to listen. As she stood watching Hitler on the platform, I took her hand in mine. She looked over and gave me a small smile. At first, I wasn't sure how to interpret that smile. *Was she happy that she was going to get to hear Hitler's words? Was she simply telling me she cared about me? Or was she only pretending to be happy to hear Hitler to protect herself in the pro-Nazi crowd?* I looked into her eyes and saw sadness and nervousness. I gently squeezed her hand. We would have to talk soon.

I looked back at Hitler. Outwardly, I feigned interest as he began.

"When our venerable Field Marshal and Reich President von Hindenburg closed his eyes for the last time after a blessed life, there were no few people outside the Reich who wished to see in his death the beginning of heavy internal fighting within Germany."

I thought to myself, *This guy is justifying his move to merge the positions of chancellor and president instead of asking for a vote.* I looked around at the crowd and saw that everyone was enthralled. He was a good speaker; he was articulate and dynamic. I looked at Karla. At first, she scanned the crowd with a look of frustration on her face, and then she looked down. She shifted from foot to foot. *She seems frustrated,* I thought. *Maybe I was right, and she really doesn't trust Hitler or believe in the ideology and propaganda he's spreading.*

I squeezed Karla's hand again and whispered in her ear. "Do you want to get out of here?" She nodded without hesitation. We turned, but by that time, many more people had joined to listen to Hitler speak, and we were in the center of the crowd. I looked around. Everyone was watching and listening intently.

"And I am now responsible to the entire German Volk," Hitler was now saying of our country's people. "And no action will take place for which I will not vouch with my life, as this Volk be my witness."

I was afraid to move too swiftly through the crowd. A hurried exit could bring unwanted attention from the SS or Gestapo. The SS officers were easily identifiable by the black uniforms and swastika armbands they wore and the guns they carried. The Gestapo, however, were in plain clothes and could be anywhere. I could feel their eyes on us as they searched the crowd for any sign, however small, of political opposition. If the SS or Gestapo got the impression that Karla and I were uninterested in Der Führer, they could arrest us, calling us dissenters. The thought of that happening made my heart race and my palms sweaty. I was not going to take any chances with Karla's safety.

I leaned over to whisper again. "If we make our way too quickly, I'm afraid of what will happen. Let's move slowly that way." I nodded to Karla's left, seeing it was the shortest walk to get out. We took only a few steps at a time, gradually, so as not to draw attention.

"In this state, everyone is called upon to fight and work in some way or another."

We took a few more steps with our eyes on Hitler as he continued. I glanced over to the left and right of the crowd and saw SS officers standing around, listening as they scanned the crowd, looking for problems.

"I myself have no other aim in the future than the aim I have had for the fifteen years lying behind me. I wish to devote my whole life, unto my dying breath, to one task: making Germany free, healthy, and happy once more."

Karla looked over at me every few steps. I saw the worry in her eyes. I wasn't sure if it was because she thought someone might harass us for leaving early or because she was feeling claustrophobic in that tight crowd. Either way, I felt guilty for suggesting we stop and listen in the first place.

"It has always been Germans who have sacrificed themselves as allies of a foreign design."

I stopped moving and thought, *He's teaching people it's Germans against all others instead of trying to unite in peace. His whole speech is laced with propaganda as he tries to push through his agenda and ideology.*

"I aspire to be nothing but the representative of your life and the defender of your vital interests."

I stopped myself from shaking my head at the people who all appeared to believe him as he stated that he was one of us. *With the laws he has been passing, he is simply targeting everyone he deems "marginal" to gain more power.* I glanced at the officers, keeping a straight face, even though inside I was a nervous wreck and angry. I felt the SS officers looking right at us several times, but we were sure to keep our eyes on Hitler.

We continued to make gradual progress until we were almost outside the crowd.

"Did you enjoy the speech?" a male voice demanded.

I looked up to see an SS officer suddenly standing under half a meter away from me and Karla. He was my height but appeared younger. His hand was on the gun in the holster at his hip. I felt Karla stiffen, and her hand squeezed mine tighter than I have ever felt my hand squeezed. *Was she scared?* I looked at her and smiled, trying to signal that I was going into what she called my "charming Bruno mode." I felt her hand relax.

I smiled at the officer. "Yes, we did. We had never heard him in person, so this was a real treat for us." I looked at Karla, and she nodded her agreement. I went on. "I always knew he was a wonderful speaker, but it's hard to tell how charismatic he is until you see him in person." I paused for effect and asked, "Did you enjoy the speech?"

"You seemed to be in a hurry to leave," the officer stated flatly.

I waived my hand, dismissing his concern. "We were moving over to this side because I need to get my girlfriend home. I promised her father we wouldn't be out late. He worries." For better standing, I added, "Although I'm sure he'll understand that we couldn't miss the opportunity to hear Der Führer."

Another officer joined us, making my nerves rattle. He was shorter than the first and looked at us curiously. The first officer looked at the shorter one and said, "We're done here." He then turned to me, clicked his heels standing at attention, and put his arm straight out. "Heil Hitler!" My throat tightened as I lifted my arm halfway and said quietly, "Heil Hitler" with a large smile on my face. I learned that people don't notice I hate saying "heil Hitler" if I do so with a smile.

I pulled Karla's hand, and we walked swiftly away to, as I'd told the officers, get her home before her father worried.

One Sunday in November when I was visiting the farm, my father led Karl and me into the woods. We walked in silence until we were well under the cover of the large oak trees across from the barn. Once he was sure no one could overhear us, my father finally asked us, "Did you sign your allegiance to the regime?"

I shook my head.

Karl looked down. "I was required to in order to keep my job on the base."

Vati nodded. "Hitler is beyond dangerous, my sons." He rubbed his chin. His tone was firm, leaving no room for discussion. "Hitler just implemented the draft and is expanding the military at a rapid pace. You must never publicly state your opinions, or you will be sent to a concentration camp." Vati looked around as if someone could be listening.

He lowered his voice. "Our neighbor's son, Reinhart Müller, was part of a group of Catholics who spoke against Hitler's new policies, and Reinhart, his brother, and their parents were taken. They have been gone for months, supposedly to a reeducation camp, but I believe it was to a concentration camp." That was the second time he'd used that term. Vati rubbed his chin and shifted from one foot to another. "Our entire family will be at risk if anyone talks negatively about the regime or Hitler. You are smart boys. Stay diligent."

"Concentration camp?" I asked.

"Yes. There are camps that have been built around the country to house all the people being arrested for speaking out against the regime. Jews are also being sent there," Vati replied.

"How do you know this, Vati?" My heart started racing, and the hairs stood up on the back of my neck as I thought of Eli and his family.

Vati paused, seemingly considering whether to explain further, then said, "The less you know, the better."

Karl bent backward and to each side, stretching his back. "The Gestapo and SS have too much power," he said in a grim voice. "They're out for blood."

CHAPTER 11

May–August 1935
Karla

Bruno and I traveled north to Flensburg for the day to check in on my ninety-year-old aunt. A two-hour train ride took us out of Kiel, through the countryside, then back into the city landscape. We arrived at my aunt's apartment just in time for lunch.

"Tante Helene, we're here," I called as I took off my gray coat and hung it on the peg just inside the door. It was overcast and windy outside, so I hadn't worn a hat. Tante Helene shuffled into the foyer, her cane making a dull thud on the wooden floors.

She reached up and gave me a one-armed hug. I was taller than she was, so I had to bend to hug her in return.

"Is this your man?" she asked.

"This is Bruno," I put my hand lightly on Bruno's arm.

After Bruno and Tante Helene shook hands, she shuffled back into the living room as we followed. Tante Helene sat down slowly on the moss-green sofa, laying her cane at her feet. She looked at me with a small smile. "You know where the food is. Please make us lunch while I get to know this gentleman of yours."

We had a wonderful lunch with my feisty aunt, and Bruno spent some time fixing things in her apartment. She had a door that constantly stuck, and one dresser had a broken leg. I felt guilty because I hadn't brought Bruno to work, but he took it all in good stride and said he was happy to help.

Whenever a person is invited to lunch in Germany, it is customary to stay for the entire afternoon to enjoy coffee and dinner, but Bruno and I had to return to Kiel. There was not enough room for us to stay with Tante Helene, and we couldn't afford to stay at a guest house, which would have required two rooms because Bruno and I weren't married.

We decided to take a walk along the waterfront before going to the train station, so we bid goodbye to Tante Helene and started in the direction of the harbor. Both of us were preoccupied with our thoughts. It was a comfortable silence, and Bruno's hand felt warm around mine as we walked the one kilometer to the harbor.

As we neared the waterfront, we watched the seagulls gliding just above the water, hunting for their next meal. I imagined most people were staying indoors with the wind and dark clouds. This left us completely alone, except for people working on the docks and on the ships about a hundred meters away. It looked like timber was on one ship. There were also a couple of fishing boats, their sails tied down. We couldn't make out the features of the people or see what they were working on, but the wind carried the sounds of their trucks and the hammering of tools and an occasional yell from one worker to another.

When we came to a low stone wall, Bruno stopped. "Karla . . ." He sat down on the wall, then shifted to the side to look out over the water.

I waited patiently, securing behind my ear a strand of hair that had blown across my face. I followed his gaze and was quickly mesmerized by the patterns on the water that the wind was making. There was a raw beauty to the scene, an untamed energy that was captivating.

Bruno stood up so he could look me in the eyes, then he took both of my hands and said, "This could be a dangerous conversation for both of us. I have strong feelings for you, but we must discuss an important topic."

My heart started beating a little faster. Perhaps he wanted to talk about our future, or maybe his intention was for us to understand each other's political opinions, a subject we danced around constantly. He released my hand and pushed another stray lock of hair from my face, securing it behind my ear. I tried to reassure him. "You can discuss anything with me, Bruno." He seemed to be struggling to find words, which was very unlike him. I took a deep breath and asked, "How do you feel about the policies that Hitler and the Nazis are enforcing?"

Bruno licked his lips. "Our families could be put in concentration camps if we disagree with any of the Nazi's policies," he said carefully.

I glanced at the dockworkers, then back at Bruno. "Yes, I know."

"Do you trust me?" His brown eyes looked so serious.

"I love you, and I trust you with my life."

"I feel the same about you." He took a deep breath. "Karla, my best friend is Jewish. I am frustrated, saddened, and terrified of what is happening to our country. My father warns me all the time to keep quiet, but I want you and I to be honest with each other." He said the words very fast, as if driven by pent-up energies he had been waiting to release for months.

We started walking slowly again, trying to dispel a little energy that seemed to hang in the air following his confession. "My father is a member of the Party," I said quietly.

"I know. You told me. Several of my brothers are as well. They'll have to live with their own decisions," he said.

I stopped walking so I could look straight into his eyes. I wanted to make sure he understood. Bruno stopped too. "I never speak to my father about politics. Erna and I don't agree on anything, so I never voice my opinion near her." Bruno shifted closer and bent over to hear my words more clearly. "I know the Nazis are spreading hate," I continued. "And I don't agree with it. It is deplorable, and I don't understand how people voted for the Nazi Party." Someone yelled from the ports, and I looked over to make sure no one was coming toward us. "I think my father is becoming disenchanted with them. He brings fewer people from the Party home for dinner." I shook my head. "I can't stand them, Bruno."

His smile reached beyond his eyes. His entire body seemed to relax as he brought our joined hands to his lips. "I'm glad we had this talk. But we must be very diligent and not speak of this with anyone else or out in public."

I nodded and looked up at him. "Can I meet your friends?"

+‿+

Eli's house had a beautiful front porch. I walked in the front door, entering a foyer with closed doors to the right and left and a staircase that led upstairs. Further back was another staircase that went down. I walked up the stairs and knocked on the third-floor apartment door. I had been invited for coffee to meet his friends. I was both excited and nervous as I knocked a second time. *Had I gotten the wrong day?* Finally, I heard a door open from downstairs.

"Karla?" I heard Bruno's voice.

I walked over to the stairs and looked down to see my Bruno standing at the bottom of the stairs, looking up at me. "I'm sorry. I thought I would hear the front door," he said. I walked down the stairs, holding the banister with my right hand and a bundle of daisies in my left. Bruno waited at the bottom, watching me with a big smile. He was wearing brown pants, a crisp white shirt, and suspenders.

He took my elbow and guided me through the open door into the living room. The walls were covered with rose-patterned wallpaper, adding character to the room. There was a plush, light-mustard-yellow sofa with bright-blue pillows arranged at each end. A wooden coffee table stood between it and a comfortable-looking chair that matched the sofa. Across the room was a dining table with intricately carved legs. The table was set with cups, saucers, small plates, forks, spoons, and napkins.

In the corner, sitting on the floor, a young boy was building a tower with some wooden blocks.

"This is Daniel," Bruno said. "Daniel, come say hello to Miss Petersen." Daniel looked to be about three or four years old.

I bent over and shook his hand. "Nice to meet you, Daniel."

Through an open doorway, I saw a kitchen and heard a woman's voice. "Jacob, put this plate of cookies on the table, please." A second boy, who looked to be around seven, walked in and carefully set the plate of sweets on the dining table.

"And this is Jacob," Bruno informed me.

Just then, a woman walked in with a carafe of coffee and set it on the dining table before turning to us. I handed her the flowers I'd brought, and she introduced herself as Ilse.

"Karla, I'm Eli," a man's voice behind me said a moment later.

I liked Ilse and Eli instantly, and I felt right at home. They were welcoming, funny, and smart people. Their sons were energetic but respectful. I loved that the boys took part in our conversations, something that made the experience of getting to know the family even richer.

It made me very sad to learn that Jews were being excluded from various professions and faced increasing restrictions on their economic and social activities. Eli had recently been told to leave his job, and the family stayed home most days. The only money the family received now was from the rent Bruno paid. I knew from our conversation on the way back from Flensburg that Bruno tried to help the family out as much as he could, catching fish and giving them his rations and even doing the shopping for them.

The only grocery store that still served Jews was on the other side of the city, and many streetcar operators turned Jews away after seeing their last names on travel papers, so the family had to walk to get to the store. But with walking came the risk of people harassing them, both verbally and physically. As Eli described how much their lives had changed, I couldn't help but be terrified for their well-being.

After a wonderful afternoon, we made promises to see each other again before saying goodbye. Bruno and I were about to step off the front porch when we turned around at the sound of the front door opening again. Daniel squeezed through it, ran over to me, and handed me a piece of paper. It was a drawing with a sun and some flowers and two stick people holding hands.

"Is this for me?" I asked him. He nodded, and I stooped down to give him a hug. "Thank you. I will treasure it."

After Daniel ran back into the house, Bruno took my hand to walk me home.

"Do you want children?" he asked.

"Yes, of course!"

As the summer unfolded, it brought with it the warmth of the sun and the scent of blooming flowers. Yet I found it hard to enjoy, as I was increasingly troubled by the developments in our country. During the summer months, the Nazi regime continued to implement the discriminatory policies and propaganda that were aimed at consolidating power and reinforcing its ideology.

The persecution of Jews and other marginalized groups intensified as propaganda campaigns spread hateful rhetoric and fostered even more division in our society. Ongoing efforts were made to solidify control over various aspects of German life, including education, media, and the economy, as well as to further spread the broader agenda of Nazi totalitarianism. By August, the oppressive atmosphere weighed heavily on my conscience. I worried about Eli, Ilse, and the boys constantly, but I was powerless to help.

CHAPTER 12

September 1935

Bruno

I arrived home from work to find Ilse in the living room, sitting on the sofa, crying. I quickly knelt in front of her.

"What happened?" I asked. I was certain this had something to do with new laws that had been announced earlier in the day.

She took a deep breath, trying to compose herself, and handed me the newspaper.

Nuremberg Laws: Safeguarding German Heritage and Unity

In a bold move to fortify the national fabric, the German government has introduced the Nuremberg Laws, a vital initiative aimed at preserving the integrity of our nation and promoting social cohesion. These laws, including the Reich Citizenship Law and the Law for the Protection of German Blood and German Honor, reaffirm our commitment to safeguarding our unique cultural heritage and upholding traditional values.

Under these prudent regulations, individuals with strong ancestral ties to the Jewish community, with three or four Jewish grandparents, are recognized as part of a distinct group, ensuring the preservation of our German identity and the continuation of our cherished traditions. By prohibiting marriages and relationships between Jews and non-Jews, these laws serve to strengthen the bonds of our community, fostering unity and solidarity among our people.

Moreover, the Nuremberg Laws provide a legal framework to protect the sanctity of German bloodlines and honor, safeguarding our nation against the encroachment of foreign influences and preserving our distinct national character. Through these measures, the government demonstrates its unwavering commitment to the well-being and prosperity of the German people, laying the foundation for a brighter future rooted in unity and pride in our shared heritage.

As we look to the future, let us rally behind these important laws and embrace the spirit of unity and solidarity they embody. Together, we can build a stronger, more resilient Germany, ensuring a legacy of prosperity and stability for generations to come.

I stared at the paper in my hands. I did not fully grasp what the effect of these new laws would be.

Eli appeared in the doorway to the kitchen. "It is illegal for Ilse and me to be married now." He carried two cups of coffee across the room and handed Ilse one.

I shook my head, still not understanding.

"The Nuremberg Laws prohibit marriage between Jews and non-Jews," Ilse said.

I racked my brain trying to connect them with what I knew of the new laws.

Eli sat down beside Ilse and looked at me. "You already know I am Jewish. Ilse, however, is from a non-Jewish family."

I sat down as Ilse stood and looked helplessly around the room. "What's next?" she said bitterly. "There's nothing more of our lives for them to take."

I searched out Eli's eyes, and he stared back at me. *How could anyone know she wasn't Jewish?* I asked silently. Eli gave a shrug of his shoulder. "If anyone looks closely at her background, her family, they will know she is from a Lutheran family. People assume she is Jewish since we are married. It seemed easier just to let people assume Ilse was Jewish when we moved here. She had already been studying the Torah, and she knows more about the religion than many others in the congregation." Eli wiped his face with his hand. "Although she didn't formally convert, Ilse is Jewish in every way that counts."

The three of us talked long into the night about all the news and what might happen next. Would they pass a new law that said Jews could no longer live in Kiel? Were the Nazis going to publicly hang Jews? We agreed to continue to keep abreast of new information as it came out but to also remain in the bubble we had created, keeping our opinions to ourselves.

"Bruno, I know we talked about it before, but please. You must be careful and not trust anyone," Eli said insistently. He paused, and the room filled with a tense silence. Then he said quietly, "Maybe you should move out." I looked up at him sharply. *Was he serious?*

I shook my head. "You are my best friend. I will not be forced to stay away."

"Please promise me that you and Karla will be careful," he said. "It isn't safe to be friends with the Jews, much less live with a Jewish family."

I suddenly remembered our neighbor, Herr Martin. *Was he not Jewish? Would he have a problem living in the same house with a Jewish family?* I couldn't remember the last time I had seen him. "What about Herr Martin? Has he given you any trouble?" I asked.

"I haven't seen him for months, so I'm not sure what is happening. Perhaps he moved in with his daughter," Ilse said. I made a mental note to knock on Herr Martin's door and see what I could find out. If he was still living here, the last thing we wanted was for him to over-hear our discussions. Hopefully, he had moved out.

CHAPTER 13

November 1935

Karla

"I'm bringing someone home for dinner tonight," my father said one autumn morning. I was sitting at the dining table, making a list of things I needed from the grocery store. He was sitting across from me, sipping his coffee.

He placed his empty cup on the saucer and nodded at the carafe in front of him. With a sigh, I stood up and poured his coffee. This was the last time I would get up to serve him, I promised myself.

"His name is Heinrich Drechsler. He's the mayor of Lübeck." Lübeck was a town ninety kilometers east of Kiel.

"Why is he in Kiel?"

Vati feigned nonchalance. "Learning how to remodel ships."

My mind flashed to my recent visits to the naval base, when I'd brought Vati his lunch. I had seen guns and turrets on the deck of what I thought looked like a passenger ship. There had been extra security around the ship.

"Are passenger ships being converted to warships?" I asked. He had been upset when the ships he designed were turned into warships in the earlier war. *Was he now supporting converting civilian ships into warships? Are we going to war?*

"Drechsler was a doctor of dentistry before he joined the Party. He has an impressive resume." Vati folded the paper and placed it on the table as he stood up, and then he walked toward the front door. "He lost his leg in the war, but that hasn't slowed him down a bit." He put his hat on his head and draped his coat over his arm as he opened the door.

"Vati—"

The door closed before I could finish my question.

Later that evening Vati introduced me to Dr. Drechsler. Drechsler's eyes were stern, and he wore a fake smile as I shook his hand in greeting. I didn't mind a firm handshake, preferring that over a loose one. However, his handshake was so strong, it hurt my hand. It was as if he wanted to let me know he could overpower me anytime he wanted. Right away, I was nervous and didn't trust him. I served dinner and coffee, then stood up to excuse myself to the bedroom I shared with Erna. I wanted to spend as little time with the Nazi dentist mayor as possible. He gave me the chills.

But before I could make my escape, my father said, "Karla, I was hoping you would play the piano and sing for our guest." I watched my father take a drag of his cigarette and blow out the smoke. *Was he serious? Couldn't he see how uncomfortable I was around that man?*

"I'm sorry, Father. I had a long day. Maybe another time. Please excuse me, Mayor."

After the mayor left, my father knocked on the bedroom door and entered. I was sitting on my bed with my back against the wall, reading *On Liberty* by John Stuart Mill. The book was an essay that defended the principles of individual freedom and argued the importance of allowing diverse viewpoints in political discourse, which Mill said was essential if voters were to make informed decisions about candidates. *Will this book get burned if I return it to the library?*

I looked up at my father as he loomed over me.

"Karla, I brought Dr Drechsler over to meet you. I would have thought you could stay and get to know him."

"Vati, I have nothing in common with him."

My father shrugged. "You should be thinking about marriage."

"Then who would take care of you?"

"Karla, think about it. I would like you to meet him for coffee and get to know him. He knows how smart you are. I told him about how talented you are playing the piano and singing. He already knows you are an amazing cook." He paused, then said, "He's interested." Before I could say another word, he closed the door behind him.

I thought about Bruno and how he treated everyone with warmth and respect. I thought about how thoughtful and attentive he was. Bruno was the one I could picture spending my life with. I looked at the small calendar on the wall and started planning when would be a good time to invite Bruno to coffee to meet Vati.

Two weeks later, I thought about my plan as I pulled a small Linzer torte out of the oven. I decided that I would invite Bruno to coffee soon. I was poking at the crust, thinking how perfect it had turned out, when I heard a knock on the door. Wiping my hands on my apron, I opened the door to find Dr. Drechsler looking down at me. He had the same fake smile that didn't reach his eyes. It was a calculating smile.

"Karla, I was wondering if you would like to walk with me," he said.

I tried to think of what to do. I glanced outside and saw children and their mothers out enjoying the day, and this made me think about Bruno's Jewish friends. I did not want to go with Dr. Drechsler, but it would have been rude not to, and I didn't want to raise any suspicions that might lead to him following me. Finally, I said, "I only have a few minutes for a brief walk. Please let me get my coat."

The walk lasted for twenty-seven minutes. It was the longest walk of my life. I walked for hours with Bruno, and it was never enough.

This man, Heinrich Drechsler, a dentist, mayor of Lübeck, Germany, was passionate about one thing: the Nazi regime. He talked of climbing the ladder of the regime. He blamed the Jews for everything wrong in our country, from inflation to the state of our education system. My emotions were a mixture of anger and terror. I felt physically dirty just being in his presence, and I couldn't wait to get away.

"Karla, I am leaving for Berlin tomorrow and will be there for several weeks before returning to Lübeck. May I write to you?"

I searched my brain for an answer that wouldn't lead him on. He could write me a thousand letters and I wouldn't be interested in a single word he had to say. "I'm sorry. I have a lot of projects that I am working on at home right now."

He looked down at me with a frown and said, "I see." Then he raised his hand with a "Heil Hitler!" I think that was the first time I had heard those words directed at me. I thought, *Is this a test?* I smiled and said quietly, "Heil Hitler, Mayor."

I walked up to my apartment, hoping that was the last time I would ever see that man. As I hung my coat on the hook beside the door, something on the sidewalk caught my eye. It appeared that Erna was on her way home and had struck up a conversation with him. As I watched them, I noticed she became very animated. *Are they making plans?* I felt a bit guilty when I thought, *They deserve each other.*

A few hours later Vati, Erna, and I sat down to eat dinner. Dinner was always a quiet time in our home—boring, really. I thought of the dinners at Eli and Ilse's house and how lively the conversations were. The conversations at the Arnold farm were also very entertaining as the family teased each other with stories of the past.

"I understand Dr Drechsler came to see you today?" Vati took a sip of water, looking at me pointedly over the rim of his glass as he waited for me to answer.

Erna piped up. "I met him, and I think he is divine. We are going to write while he is in Berlin." For once she saved me from having to answer.

Several weeks passed. Then something happened as I was putting clothes away in the dresser. The long walnut dresser had three columns of two drawers. Erna and I each had two drawers. When I opened Erna's top drawer to put away clean stockings and underwear, I saw a letter postmarked Berlin. I picked it up and held it to the light streaming in from the window. Reading it would be a gross invasion of privacy. But this man felt dangerous.

My curiosity won out, and I pulled the letter out of the envelope. Drechsler wrote about how Hitler was a great man and about all the things Hitler was doing to improve life in Germany. His words sent chills up and down my spine and filled me with a strong sense of foreboding. *This man is up to no good,* I thought as I put the letter back in the envelope and returned it to the drawer.

♒

Vati continued to encourage a relationship between Heinrich and me, making comments about how wonderful he was and asking me if I wanted Heinrich to come for dinner. One day I had enough. "Vati, I will never ever be interested in that man, so please stop talking about it. Besides, Erna and Heinrich are the ones that have the relationship."

Vati looked at me but said nothing.

I thought about the ships he'd told me were being "remodeled" and asked the question that had been on my mind for weeks. "Are we going to war?"

"No, of course not. The regime simply wants us to be prepared just in case."

"In case of what?"

Vati was quiet for a moment, then he took a deep breath. "Karla, there's so much you don't understand right now. Please know that everything I do is to keep you and Erna safe. I lived through a war and don't want another, but sometimes I must do things I don't want to do to keep you and your sister safe."

He walked across the living room, put his hat on his head, and slid his arms into his coat. Then he silently left the apartment.

I still had so many questions. But his actions told me the conversation was over.

CHAPTER 14

March 1936

Bruno

I had just replaced rotten pieces of the wooden frame on the back door leading into the kitchen in Eli's house and was painting. Ilse was adding ingredients to a bowl. I heard the radio announcer say, "Special report."

"Will you turn the radio up please, Ilse?"

She wiped her hands on her white apron and walked to the table where a small radio stood.

"Attention, citizens of the Reich! Today, we bring you news of our triumphant reoccupation of the Rhineland! After the unjust Treaty of Versailles stripped us of this vital territory following the Great War, our führer, Adolf Hitler, has boldly reclaimed what is rightfully ours. The Rhineland, with its rich cultural heritage and strategic significance, has long been an integral part of the German nation. By returning to this historic land, we restore not only our territorial integrity but also our national pride. Under the visionary leadership of the National Socialist government, we assert our rightful place on the world stage and reaffirm our commitment to a strong and prosperous Germany.

Let us stand united in celebration of this historic moment and march forward with unwavering confidence in our future!"

I thought back to a conversation between my parents that I had once overheard. I was nine years old at the time. My father had been telling my mother that, in accordance with the Versailles Treaty that ended the war, Rhineland was required to be demilitarized—a move that was intended to create a military-free buffer between Germany and the countries west of the Rhine River.

Next, my mind flashed to a recent newspaper article that portrayed Germans as being resentful and frustrated by the demilitarization of the Rhineland. According to the article, Germans saw this as an unjust constraint on their national sovereignty and a humiliating reminder of the Treaty of Versailles' punitive measures. *How much*, I asked myself, *had the media contributed to the present chaos and to people's feelings of disenchantment with the democratic government?*

⚮

I met Karla at the bus stop to walk with her to my apartment for dinner with Eli and Ilse. We only had dinner with them on special occasions now, to reduce the risk of Nazis following us. It was a cold Sunday evening, with light snow drifting down to the ground. It was already dark out, and there was no wind coming off the Baltic. The streets were nearly empty, and this created a soothing atmosphere.

Karla walked off the bus and into my waiting arms. She hooked her arm through mine, and we walked the two blocks to my house in silence, enjoying the peacefulness of the night.

We walked in the front door and stomped our feet to get the snow off our boots. "I have to tell you about my day," Karla said. I hung her coat over the banister while she took off her boots. She took slippers out of her bag and put them on her feet before taking my hand and walking into the living room.

She called hello to Ilse and Eli, who were in the kitchen, and we sat on the sofa next to each other.

"Heinrich and Erna arrived unannounced at Vati's apartment. I guess that sounds silly since Erna technically lives there, but she's never around," Karla explained. Ilse walked in and handed Karla a cup of tea.

"Where does she go?" Ilse asked.

Karla blew on her tea and took a small sip. "I know she used to go to Nazi rallies and parties, but honestly, I have no idea these days. I stopped asking a long time ago." Karla put her cup in its saucer and placed it on the coffee table. "They got married. Erna was all smiles when they walked into our apartment, radiating bliss and showing me her ring." Ilse sat across from us, and Eli walked in with the boys behind him. Seeing Karla, Daniel ran over to her.

"Happy birthday, Daniel," Karla said as she hugged him. She turned back to me. "My downstairs neighbor, Frau Bauer, was visiting when Erna and Heinrich walked in. I watched as Heinrich scanned the room, as if he was sizing up potential allies and adversaries. It's disconcerting, as if he was assessing our worth." Karla picked up her teacup for another sip.

"How did your father take the news of their marriage?" I asked.

"He seemed a little surprised at first, but then he was all smiles and seemed happy."

I saw Eli and Ilse exchange a look. "What is it?"

Eli rubbed his dark beard, which was now flecked with specks of gray. "Do you think Heinrich would have you followed, Karla?"

Karla looked at me and back at Eli. "I suppose it's a possibility, but I don't see why he would." She looked worried when she asked, "Should I not come anymore?"

"I think we all need to stay diligent." Eli stood and clapped his hands. "Now, let's talk about other topics. Ilse cooked a wonderful meal!"

As the family talked and laughed, I thought of how seamlessly Karla had slid into my life with my Jewish family. After dinner, I watched her from the doorway to the kitchen as she blew soap bubbles from the sink at the boys.

Ilse walked up behind me with dirty dishes in her hands and said quietly, "She's a good one. You should ask her to marry you before she gets away."

Eli was behind Ilse, and he added, "I am happy to see you in love, Bruno."

I had dated women before, but I had never been in love. Watching Karla with my adopted family, I knew without a doubt that she was my partner and that she would be my partner forever.

CHAPTER 15

August 1936

Bruno

It was a beautiful summer day with a clear blue sky, warm sun, and a light breeze. It had taken me six months to save enough money to buy Karla an engagement ring. I stood at the counter with a diamond ring in one hand and an emerald in the other, debating with myself which one she would prefer. The shopkeeper seemed a little antsy, so I finally settled on the emerald to match Karla's eyes. The ring was a simple gold band with a small emerald embedded in the gold.

Karla and I met at Schrevenpark, our favorite park with its open lawns, walking paths, and pond that we loved. Although the SS police in their black uniforms and swastika armbands were always in full view, and I was sure the Gestapo secretively watched everyone who came there, many families enjoyed the park when the sun was out. That day, some children were playing Heaven and Hell, and there were mothers on the paths, pushing their prams while talking and laughing.

When I rounded the bend, I saw Karla sitting on a bench, looking in the opposite direction as she watched some boys play football. Her ankles were crossed, and she was wearing a light-blue dress. She clutched her black purse on her lap with both of her hands. I walked up quietly and sat beside her before gently taking her hand. She jumped, then turned her head and smiled as I kissed her cheek.

She pointed to the other side of the bench where she had a folded black wool blanket with a bag on top. "I packed some food for us so we can have a picnic."

I picked up the blanket and bag, then held out my arm. She laughed as she hooked her hand in my elbow, and we walked to an area under a willow tree. I was nervous about asking her to marry me, but I reminded myself of the many words of love we had exchanged over the past several years.

My hands shook as we worked together to lay the blanket out on the grass. Karla took the apples, rolls, and cheese out of the bag and set them on the blanket. I walked on my knees toward her, careful not to squish the food.

"Karla, I would like to marry you," I blurted out. I admonished myself, thinking, *That wasn't how I rehearsed the proposal in my head, but at least the words are out.*

"Are you asking me?"

I laughed as I saw the twinkle in her eyes. Karla was the smartest woman I knew, and I loved the mischievous side of her.

I took her hands in mine. "Karla, will you marry me?" I released one hand and dug in my breast pocket for the ring. My hand trembled as I held it out to her.

"Yes."

I slid the ring onto her finger, holding my breath and hoping that it fit properly. It was a little loose, but that was okay. We would fix that.

Her smile was radiant as she held her hand up so she could see her ring.

"Bruno, this cost so much money; how did you . . . ?"

I put my finger on her lips and said, "You should not worry about such things."

There were some people close to us, watching. I heard a man's voice say, "Way to go, Bruno!" I waved, not taking my eyes off my fiancée and not really caring who had seen us. "I'd like to talk to your father as soon as possible."

She licked her lips nervously and said, "Okay, Bruno, come to coffee next Sunday . . . maybe at fifteen hundred hours. He should be home then."

CHAPTER 16

September 1936

Karla

It was Sunday, and I was expecting Bruno to arrive soon. Vati was at the dining table, trying unsuccessfully to repair a lamp. The stained-glass shade was lying on the coffee table and the metal base was lying in front of Vati as he tried to fix the pull chain. Pliers and a screwdriver sat on the table, ready to be used. Vati moved the base around to get a better look.

I took the bee sting cake out of the oven and placed it on the stove to cool. "Vati, I need to tell you something."

"What is it?"

"I have someone I'd like you to meet. He is coming for coffee," I said as I placed some plates around the table.

"Who is it?" Vati asked as he continued working.

I placed the cups and saucers on the table around his lamp and tools. "His name is Bruno, and he is important to me."

Finally, he paused and looked up at me and then at the table. *Was he surprised to see the table was set?* "Is this why you declined Dr Drechsler?" he asked.

I was careful with my answer, not wanting to irritate him and risk him saying anything to Heinrich. "Partly. But mostly that was because we had nothing in common." He looked at me curiously but said nothing more.

A minute later, there was a knock at the door. Bruno took off his black fedora and his jacket as he entered our apartment. My stomach did a somersault when he gave me a small smile and a wink.

"I know you! You're the electrician." I couldn't read Vati's expression, but his voice held a tinge of surprise.

Bruno held out his hand. "Yes, I am. I'm Bruno Arnold, Herr Petersen."

Vati slowly shook Bruno's hand. It was clear from Vati's thoughtful expression that he was mentally navigating through the various reasons why the electrician Bruno Arnold might be in his living room for coffee.

Bruno's eyes lit up as he saw the broken lamp still on the table. "Can I help you with that?"

"I think it's trash, though we can maybe use the parts," Vati said with doubt in his voice. I wondered what he was thinking.

Bruno walked to the table and said, "May I?" Vati gestured with his hand, inviting him to try.

I walked into the kitchen to get coffee and cake. By the time I returned to the dining area, Bruno had the lamp fixed and was plugging it in to test it. Vati looked both happy and frustrated at the same time, but Bruno quickly said, "I'm a bit of a savant when it comes to fixing things. This often frustrates my father and brothers. I'm sure you would have figured it out."

Bruno had a way with people. I saw Vati relax as I handed him his tools and smoothed the tablecloth and adjusted the plates and cups.

Over the next fifteen minutes or so, we drank coffee and ate cake while the two of them talked about the generator at the shipyard and made small talk about some of their mutual acquaintances who worked with my father. I was so nervous, I could only take small bites of my cake, but Bruno ate all of his and even complimented my baking skills in front of Vati.

At a pause in the conversation, I poured my father a second cup. Bruno declined more coffee, and I saw him move to the edge of his chair. He looked thoughtful as he said, "Herr Petersen, I love Karla very much, and we wish to marry."

Vati took another sip and looked at me but addressed Bruno. "You are in no position to provide for her and keep her safe. It is out of the question." He put his cup on its saucer and took the last bite of cake from his plate.

I stood up. "Vati! Bruno is a trained electrician, and he can provide for me just fine. I can also work."

My father pursed his lips together and glanced at each of us in turn. He sat silent for a few minutes, observing as Bruno and I looked at each other. When I caught my father's eye, I gave him no room to discuss the matter. "We are coming to you as a formality," I said quietly. "Not to ask for permission."

✌

We drove out to the farm the following week to tell Otto and Therese. They were thrilled with the announcement. The kitchen table was immediately cleared of dishes, and the women took over the table to begin making lists of guests, food to be served, and other details. Even Anna participated. She always seemed standoffish around me, and I hoped the party would bring us closer.

Bruno, Karl, and Otto shook hands, and there was a lot of slapping on Bruno's back as they all walked out of the kitchen into the yard, lighting their cigarettes as they went.

After thirty minutes of the ladies planning, I laughed and shook my head. "It's too much. Perhaps we should have a smaller gathering?"

"Nonsense! We all need a reason to celebrate. I think this is perfect." Therese laughed as she added, "You're marrying into the wrong family if you are thinking of a small gathering."

I smiled and agreed that everyone could use a reason to celebrate.

Things happened fast, and three weeks later, we were on our way back to the farm for our engagement party. Our families had never met, and Bruno's family was huge. Everyone brought their spouses, and there were nine grandchildren. Even Bruno's aunt and uncle came from the next town over with their two children. My father arrived with Erna and Heinrich. It was a little overwhelming to have so many people engaged in so many conversations, but everyone seemed to have a good time.

There were people everywhere: on the front porch, outside, and inside the house. Bruno held my hand and introduced me to each person. Bruno's cousin Hans wore a uniform, and I nodded as he held up his right hand in a salute and said, "Heil Hitler." I glanced at Bruno with a raised eyebrow but was, thankfully, pulled away by the next family members I needed to meet.

It took some time to be introduced to everyone, as everyone wanted to get to know me. Everyone wanted to ask questions, and several women complimented the dress I was wearing.

"Karla made it. She is the best seamstress in all of Kiel. In all of Germany!" Bruno said proudly as he put his arm around my shoulder.

I touched his shoulder and laughed as I remembered how happy I had been to find the material. Rosie had come for a visit by bus for the day. While we were shopping, I found striped cotton fabric on sale. I also had a few extra pieces of white material from the wedding dress I was making, and this scrap worked nicely for making the new dress's collar and elbow-length sleeves. This meant I was already wearing a piece of my wedding dress at my engagement party.

It felt like hours passed before I finally was able to sit and have a drink. Just as I was doing so, I heard Karl enter and say, "We need music! Vati, the radio."

Otto squatted in front of the radio in the living room. It was in a beautiful carved wooden cabinet with dials that Otto adjusted, trying to find a station with music. But it was all news. Frustrated, he finally turned the dial to the off position and stood up. "Karla, will you entertain us?"

Everyone clapped and cheered for me to play the piano, so how could I say no?

I sat on the wooden bench in front of the upright piano and began to run through scales while Rosie came over to sit beside me. Bruno's brother Walter had a guitar in his hand as he put a chair against the wall next to the piano. "May I accompany you?"

Grateful to have company to help with the entertainment, I nodded my head eagerly.

"Do you know this one?" I played a few notes of "I Wish I Were a Chicken." I heard Bruno laugh as he walked over to stand next to the piano opposite Walter.

"Yes," said Walter, and he started playing. I had to speed up to catch up on the fast-paced song. I joined in the singing, and everyone in the room started clapping.

It was wonderful to play the piano and provide entertainment. Even Erna and Heinrich were clapping their hands and laughing. I was surprised that they were content to let Bruno and I have our day. When I voiced my concern about them attending and taking over with their need to be the center of attention, my father had said it would be disrespectful and hurtful not to include them.

After a couple of hours, Walter and I decided it was time for us to take a well-deserved break and enjoy our meal. With the house brimming with people, we had opted to dine in shifts, with everyone taking turns at the table in order to accommodate everybody.

Bruno and I found ourselves seated together. Therese sat beside me, and Otto sat on the other side of her. My father occupied the seat opposite Bruno. Across from us sat Rosie, Karl, and Anna.

Our meal consisted of sumptuous rouladen, which is tender beef rolled with mustard and onions, accompanied by red cabbage, freshly baked bread, and potatoes. It was truly a feast to behold. Beef was a rare treat, but the entire family had contributed to making our celebration unforgettable.

We were nearly done with our meal when Rosie looked at me and said, "Karla, before you leave, will you take my measurements for the dress I want to wear at your wedding?" I saw Anna tense up in her chair but wasn't sure why. Anna and I were cordial to each other but had not yet become friends. Rosie and I had become very close over the years, and I wondered whether Anna was jealous of our relationship.

Therese looked at her granddaughter with a stern look and said, "This is Karla's party. She doesn't want to work!"

I waved my hand, dismissing Therese's concern. "It's fine. I'd like to get the measuring done so I can tell you how much fabric to buy. It will be my pleasure to make your dress."

I don't remember who had a camera, but after we'd finished eating, someone told Bruno and me to turn around and look toward it.

Someone handed me a bouquet of chrysanthemums, and other family members gathered for a group picture. Bruno put one arm around my shoulders and touched my hands with his other hand. I wasn't surprised when Heinrich and Erna sat in the front, but at that point I didn't care. I looked into Bruno's eyes and thought, *How did I get so lucky?* I couldn't wait to get married. Looking into his eyes, I could feel his love for me.

After pictures, Bruno stood up with his glass held high and said, "A toast. To my bride. I promise to give her a good life and love her always!" He turned in several directions to make sure everyone could see his face and participate.

Everyone held their glasses up and said, "To Karla."

My cheeks warmed with the attention. I caught Bruno's eyes and mouthed, "I love you."

To take the focus from me, I stood up and said, "Music!" and carefully walked to the piano so I didn't step on Heinrich or Erna since they were still sitting on the floor.

The rest of the evening was full of laughter, dancing, and singing. Everyone joined in the fun.

CHAPTER 17

August–December 1937

Bruno

I stood in my apartment for what would perhaps be the last time, buttoning up my white dress shirt as I got ready for my wedding. I would miss that attic apartment. It had been my home for six years. But Friedrich had offered to let Karla and I live with him. At first, I had said no because I didn't want to live with a Nazi. But Karla felt that she couldn't leave him, and she asked me to set my opinions aside and understand that Friedrich was her father first, before he was a Nazi.

Germany had a housing shortage, so sharing an apartment or house was very common. Karla's apartment had only one bedroom, and Friedrich was used to sleeping on the sofa, having given up the bedroom to Erna and Karla after Karla's mother died.

It was Eli who'd had the final word, settling the matter when he told me I could no longer rent their third floor. "What will you do for money?" I asked Eli.

"We have money hidden in the house for emergencies. I promise, we will be fine, Bruno," Ilse said, answering for him. I wasn't sure about the hidden money, but I wasn't going to call my friends liars either.

Ilse's father was a surgeon in London before he died, so maybe they did have money.

Now, I finished tying my tie. I only had one suit, a black one with a white shirt, so my wedding attire had been an easy choice. Karla had made a handkerchief out of the same fabric as her dress, and I carefully folded it and put it in my breast pocket.

I looked around my small apartment. It was just one room with a small sink and a two-burner cooktop on which I could heat water for coffee. There was a small oak table that had been old and scratched when I moved in, but I had sanded it down and put a new coat of varnish on it. The two matching chairs were also scratched up, as if someone had left them out in a hailstorm. I hadn't had time to refinish those. In the corner, on the opposite side of the room from the bed, was a small dresser with six drawers. A mirror hung over the dresser. The single bed wasn't the most comfortable for my back, and my feet would hang off the end, so that, at least, I wouldn't miss. My quilt was folded with my pillow and a bag of clothes on top of it, ready to be moved to Karla's apartment.

I shared the only bathroom with Eli and his family. Located on the first floor, it had been converted from a closet, so it was very small, with a toilet and a small sink and a shower head on the wall above the toilet. I had to bend slightly to fit under the spray of water.

I walked to the door and scanned the apartment once more, then closed the door behind me, already missing my adopted family.

I had invited Eli and Ilse to the wedding, but they'd said they would have to think about it. It was dangerous for them to be out in public, so they limited their excursions as much as possible. The fact that Friedrich and Heinrich were Nazis that we knew were attending made the risk of facing persecution or violence, by the Nazi regime or its supporters, very high.

I had seen for myself the brutality of the SS when I was walking to work one morning. As I approached, I saw that two SS police were harassing an elderly Jewish man in the street, their shouts of intimidation echoing through the air. One officer was using his nightstick to beat the man, who was already in a submissive position on the ground. I had felt overwhelming guilt for not helping the man, but there was a very real chance that if I had, the officers would have shot me and put my entire family in prison. Three weeks later, I still felt angry and disappointed with myself, even though I was certain I'd made the only decision I could make for my family. *How could my countrymen be so brutal?*

I walked downstairs to find my family waiting for me in the living room. Mutti walked over to give me a hug, and Vati patted my shoulder. Eli was sitting at the dining room table with a glass of water in front of him. He took a small sip then looked at me. "We would like to celebrate with you and Karla when you return from your honeymoon. Ilse will make a special dinner."

I walked over and put my hand on Eli's shoulder. I could feel the unshed tears in my eyes. "I understand and look forward to our celebration."

My parents and I took a streetcar to the administration building that held the registrar's office. I smiled as I stepped off the streetcar into a crowd of friends and family cheering at me. I was touched when I saw a few customers among the crowd of about fifty, half of the people being my immediate family.

Anna passed me a bouquet of flowers. "For Karla," she said. I looked down at the flowers and thought how much Karla was going to love them. The bouquet of wildflowers tied with a blue ribbon was made up of delicate daisies, vibrant poppies, and lavender that evoked a vivid but calming smell. I looked at Anna and said, "Thank you." Then I walked up the stairs of the building and through the front door. The first door on the left was the registrar's office.

✢✜✢

Karla stood up from her seat against the wall when I entered. My mouth went dry, and I felt a lump in my throat as everyone else in the room faded away. I handed her the flowers as I tried to find words, any words. But for once, I was speechless.

Karla had remade her mother's wedding dress, adding new material to it to update the design. The new dress fit her perfectly. Frau Bauer, Karla's elderly neighbor who lived below her, had contributed a few marks toward the purchase of sheer white fabric with delicate light-green flowers running down the skirt in graceful stripes.

Though I was unfamiliar with different types of fabric, I had been able to sense Karla's joy as she worked with it. During my visits to her apartment for dinner over the past several months, I'd often found her serenading her sewing machine, her melodious voice filling the room as she dedicated herself to perfecting her dress.

After the registrar had married us and we'd signed papers, we walked out of the building hand in hand to the waiting crowd. I raised our joined hands above our heads and said, "We did it!" After a few minutes of hugs and congratulations, the entire group started walking toward a pub along the water that had been my grandfather's favorite. It was only two blocks away, but we took our time enjoying the happy mood. My father started singing loudly, and everyone else jumped in.

As you start this life together, hand in hand,
May your love forever bloom and expand.
Through every joy and every tear,
May your bond grow stronger each passing year.

Here's to love, pure and true,
For the newlyweds, that's you two.
May your journey be filled with endless delight,
As you navigate life's path, together, in flight.

We'd been in the pub celebrating for several hours when I pulled Karla to the back room to share a quiet moment. A young girl was folding napkins in the corner. I knew her from the times I had spent in the pub with my father and brothers, and I waved to her. "Hi, Sara!" She smiled and waved back but continued to silently fold the napkins.

Karla leaned against a table while I stood in front of her and gave her a kiss. We were surprised when Erna and Friedrich suddenly walked in. Erna glanced at Sara, and my heart beat a little faster. I hoped Erna would leave the poor girl alone.

"Isn't that Herr Rosenberg's daughter?" Erna sneered.

I felt Karla's shoulders tense under my hands. I glanced at Sara again. Her eyes were big, and she stood up so quickly she accidentally pushed against the table, causing stacks of napkins to fall on the floor.

"You stupid Jew, get yourself together," Erna yelled. "This is my sister's wedding, and you're ruining it."

Karla stood up, and my hands dropped to my sides. She hissed, "Erna!"

Before I could admonish Erna for being insensitive and abusive, Friedrich stepped in and said, "Erna, that's enough. She's doing the best she can." He looked at the young woman and said, "I'm sorry. Please forgive us and let me help you." Friedrich walked over then, bent down, and picked up the napkins. Sara's face went from fear to shock as she watched Friedrich kneeling on the floor in front of her as he collected the napkins.

Erna cried out, "Me? I'm not the one dropping napkins and ruining the wedding party."

I saw Heinrich walk in, although I wasn't sure how much he had heard. When I glanced at Sara, she was looking at Heinrich in his Nazi uniform, a look of pure terror on her face. She turned and ran out the back door.

"Erna, you and Heinrich should go, please," Karla said quietly. I was amazed at how calm she was when my entire being was telling me to scold Erna. For the first time in my life, I wanted to hit a woman.

"What? You're choosing a Jew over your own sister?" Erna shouted.

"Erna, Heinrich, let's find some drinks, shall we?" Friedrich guided Erna back into the party, and Heinrich followed. I couldn't read Heinrich's expression since his face was always stern, but I felt very concerned for the Rosenberg family.

"Karla," I whispered. "I'm going to find Herr Rosenberg and warn him."

I couldn't get over the fact that I'd just seen Friedrich, a member of the Nazi Party, apologizing to a Jew for his daughter's behavior. I had no idea what to think. I figured that since we would now be living together, I would have more opportunity to get to know this man. Maybe then I would better understand the many layers that made up who he was, and his apparent contradictions.

It didn't take long to find the Rosenberg family. They actually rented a room above the pub. I was relieved to hear that Herr Rosenberg had already made arrangements to travel to Sweden, and I urged him to leave as quickly as possible.

My sister Gertrude; her husband, Paul; and their two children lived in Hamburg, and they had invited us to stay with them for a honeymoon. Before we left the pub, Gertrude gave me a key and a note:

> Dear brother,
> We wanted to give you a wedding gift to remember, so we are staying with Kaethe for two days. Enjoy your time together.
> Love,
> Gertrude

The next morning, Karla and I took the train to Hamburg for the weekend. I had been saving money to give her a special time to remember. We opened the door to find an apartment that had been decorated just for us. There were candles on the table ready to be lit, and flowers were distributed in glass jars across the kitchen counter, dining table, coffee table, and side tables next to the sofa. There was a cake with white icing and blue flowers on the kitchen table along with a sign that said *Congratulations*. I picked up one of the forks sitting next to the cake and took a bite. It was a layered sponge cake, with raspberry and marzipan between the layers.

Karla walked up behind me and wrapped her arms around my waist while peering around to look at the sign. I turned around to hug and kiss her silly.

The weekend was going to be even more wonderful than what I'd hoped for.

The next day, we walked around the city, went to museums, and had a picnic in the park. Finally, we reached the destination to which I had led her. As we approached, Karla stopped and looked up at the building. We were standing in front of the most prominent opera house in Hamburg, home to the Hamburg State Opera, which had been in operation for centuries. I crossed my arms over my chest. The sight of the building's imposing columns, weathered cement and brick, and intricate carvings left me underwhelmed. I was struck by the lack of aesthetic charm. But we hadn't come to observe it from the outside.

"Karla," I told her, "I have a surprise. I have tickets to see *The Knight of the Rose* by Richard Strauss."

Karla looked down at her dark-blue dress with buttons down the front. She was carrying her black purse paired with black shoes. She looked back up at me. "Are we dressed okay for the opera?"

I held out my arm for her to take and said, "You are always beautiful." I pushed some hair behind her ear. "This is a present from Friedrich."

I don't think I have ever seen such a large smile on another person before. My heart soared.

✵

It seemed strange how naturally we fell into sync with one another after I moved in with Karla and Friedrich. I quickly learned Karla's daily routine. She was the first to wake up and start the stove, which was used for both cooking and heat. She made coffee and biscuits, or eggs if they were available. Later, while Friedrich and I were at work, Karla cleaned, did laundry, gave piano lessons to children from different parts of Kiel, and worked on sewing for the dress shop or for neighbors.

Evenings were stressful as we listened to the latest news on the radio. With Friedrich in the room, Karla and I chose our words carefully or kept silent until we went to bed and could discuss the news in whispers under the covers. I felt especially frustrated when we listened to an announcement in December.

"You're tuned in to the Voice of Germany, bringing you the latest news and updates from our great nation. Today, we have a groundbreaking announcement from SS Chief and Chief of German Police Heinrich Himmler, one that demonstrates unwavering commitment to maintaining law and order in our society."

Karla and I were sitting across from each other at the dining table, drinking our coffee. As we heard the words "special announcement," we looked at each other.

"Herr Himmler has enacted the Circular Decree on Preventive Crime Fighting by the Police, a bold initiative aimed at safeguarding our communities from those who threaten our way of life. Under this decree, individuals engaging in chronic asocial behavior, habitual criminals, and those making their living from criminal activity will be identified and dealt with swiftly and decisively."

I hated that I couldn't talk this through with Karla immediately. I could see in her eyes that she felt the same. She shook her head subtly at me, which I understood to mean that I should remain quiet.

"This proactive approach empowers our law enforcement agencies to take necessary measures to protect our citizens, ensuring that our streets remain safe and secure. By targeting potential threats before they escalate, we can prevent crime and maintain the peace and prosperity of our beloved fatherland.

"Together, we stand united in our commitment to building a strong and prosperous Germany. Trust in our leadership, trust in our police, and trust in the vision of a brighter future for all. Stay tuned to the Voice of Germany for more updates on this inspiring initiative."

Later that night, Karla and I talked about the differences between the Reichstag Fire Decree and the new development. The Fire Decree had allowed arrests of anyone who expressed dissent, whether that person had actually conveyed dissent or someone else had simply perceived that they had. The new decree expanded the powers to arrest to include everyone who committed an infraction—once again, perceived or real. The SS had already been making such arrests, but the new decree made it legal.

Karla and I were already on alert most of the time. This new development would only increase our stress.

At least once a month, on Saturday or Sunday, she and I traveled to the farm by bus for a meal with my family. We continued our long walks, even in the winter. It was the only time we could relax. It was the only time we could get away from the Nazis who constantly surrounded us.

CHAPTER 18

November 1938

Karla

One morning, after I started the fire and made coffee, I put on my coat and walked to the corner to buy a newspaper, a habit I had added to my routine. I was especially interested in the news after having heard the rumors that revenge might be taken against the Jewish community following the assassination of a German diplomat, Ernst vom Rath, by Herschel Grynszpan, a Jewish teenager of Polish origin.

I walked into the living room and opened the folded paper as I shrugged off my coat. I was just starting to read when Bruno walked into the room from the bedroom and stood behind me. My father was sitting at the dining table, waiting to be served his breakfast.

"You don't need to read it," Bruno said as he sat down at the dining table. "I can tell you: people smashed the windows and doors of Jewish businesses and synagogues across the country last night."

My father suddenly stood up, took his coat from the hook, and walked out of the apartment without a word.

Bruno helped himself to coffee from the carafe I had placed on the table earlier. "Friedrich knew it was going to happen. He told me so I could warn Ilse and Eli." Bruno took a sip of the hot liquid. "He probably just needs some time. I think he feels torn between being a member of the Nazi Party and doing the right thing."

My knees felt weak, so I pulled out the chair next to Bruno and sat. "My father knows about our Jewish friends?"

Bruno nodded and blew on his hot coffee.

"How? We were careful."

I watched as Bruno took a sip of the steaming liquid. "I told him."

"What? Why would you do that?" I could feel my heart rate increasing.

"Because after the incident at the pub with Sara, I thought maybe your father would be in a position to help." He put his cup on the saucer. "It was a gamble that paid off, Karla."

It was as I'd always told Bruno: my father was my father first and a Nazi second. But there was no denying that the country was becoming even more dangerous. "Maybe we should try to go to your cousin in America and build a new life," I suggested.

Bruno pulled my father's unused coffee cup over to me and thoughtfully filled the cup, then placed it in front of me. "I think it will be hard, and we have no money. But why don't you figure out the requirements, and then we shall see?"

I felt a wave of nausea from the smell of coffee. "Bruno, I need to tell you something." I pushed the cup away, then took the plunge. "I'm pregnant!"

Bruno was stunned. He just stared at me, so I told him again. "Bruno, you're going to be a father!"

That seemed to break the spell. He leaned into me and, even as we were still seated, pulled me into a hug. As we embraced, he stood up, pulling me with him so he could hold me even closer. "This is the best news! When? When will the baby come?"

"June or July, I think."

◦∽◦

Since there weren't many warm days in Kiel left as the calendar headed toward winter, I took the sunny day as a good sign that I would get information on how we could get to America. I was full of hope as I walked to city hall.

The administration office was located on the second floor. Large windows separated the hallway from the office. Through them, I could see a small lobby with three chairs and people working behind a counter. When it was my turn, a clerk told me that Bruno and I would first need to obtain a visa from the American embassy, which was in Berlin, a four-hour train ride from Kiel. A medical examination and background check were required to get a passport. We also had to prove that we had money and that there was a job offer in America. My heart began to sink as the clerk cautioned me that if we had any ties to Hitler's regime, we would most likely be denied. Relations between America and Nazi Germany were poor. There was also a limit to the number of people allowed into America and a very long waiting list.

The hope I'd felt earlier was dead. We had no money for medical exams and passports, much less for tickets for passageway on a ship. My father, Heinrich, and Bruno's brothers were part of the regime, and his nephews were in the Hitler Youth. We would have to climb a huge mountain of logistics if we wanted to try to leave Germany.

I thanked the administrator and walked out of the office. As I was passing the large windows, I saw that he was now on the phone. He stopped talking and stared back at me with a look of guilt. I knew immediately that I had made a huge mistake. Now, Bruno and I would have a target on our backs. Now there would be no more visits to see our Jewish friends. My heart raced as I left the building.

⚓

A few weeks went by, and I began to feel that someone was watching us. Every time I went to the store, I got goose bumps. I looked around at the people walking on the streets and sidewalks, but I couldn't distinguish who, if anyone, was following me.

Our dinner table was quiet. The only sounds through most of the meal were our forks and knives clattering against the plates. It was so different from the meals we ate at Ilse's or at the farm with the family. I wondered if the silence drove Bruno crazy. I made a mental note to ask him later. Finally, toward the end of dinner, I could bear it no more, and I asked, "Vati, is the SS or Gestapo following us?"

Vati looked straight at me, taking a moment to slowly finish chewing and swallowing before he answered. After a minute, he picked up a fork full of potatoes and said, "The SS patrols and the Gestapo ensure the safety of everyone. As good Germans, we shouldn't care."

I felt disappointed with his very Nazi-like answer.

CHAPTER 19

June 1939

Karla

On the eighteenth of June, I woke in the middle of the night with pain from contractions that had started six hours earlier. I stood up to get dressed, thinking I would give Bruno a few more minutes of sleep, but as I moved around the room gathering my dress and shoes, a dam of hot liquid burst between my legs. I found a towel to clean up the mess, but as I kneeled down, I had to pause, feeling a contraction rip through my body. "Bruno. Get . . ." I took a breath. "Up. The baby is coming."

I had never seen my husband move so fast. He was instantly standing over me. "What are you doing, woman?" he asked as he helped me stand.

"My water broke, so I was cleaning the floor."

Streetcars were not running at the early hour, so we had to walk to the hospital seven blocks away. It was the hardest walk of my life, with the rain pouring down and us having to pause twice, waiting for a contraction to end.

Bruno hovered next to me, trying to be helpful by distracting me with stories. But I finally told him to be quiet.

CHAPTER 20

June 1939

Bruno

I slept on and off in the most uncomfortable of chairs in the lobby of the hospital as I waited for word of my wife and baby. When I was finally allowed into the room, Karla was smiling with our baby bundled in her arms. She handed him to me when I approached and said, "Congratulations, Vati. You have a son." My feelings of joy and happiness overwhelmed me as I looked at this beautiful human Karla and I had made together. I pulled his little hand out from his swaddling blanket and let his fingers wrap around my pinkie finger. He was perfect.

"Bruno, the doctor gave me news before you walked in," Karla said softly.

I looked up sharply at my wife. "Is he okay?"

She put her hand on my arm to reassure me, "Well, yes. But . . ." She seemed to be trying to think of the words she wanted to say. "The doctor said he suspects the baby has some sort of disorder." She sat up straighter and pointed to the baby's features. "He has a flattened facial profile, small ears that are set back, and a flat nasal bridge. And do you see his tongue—how it protrudes? Those are all signs."

I got ready to tell Karla that I didn't care because I was already in love with this tiny human, and we would figure it all out. But just then the nurse walked in. "Here are his papers. This one"—she held the first piece of paper up—"is his birth certificate. Fill out his name, your names, your address, and your religion." She placed it on the bedside table. "This one," she said, pointing to a second piece of paper, "is for the registry."

"What registry?" I asked.

"All abnormal births must be registered. It's the law. It's so the government can be aware and protect your son in the future." She placed the registry form with the birth certificate and left the room.

✢✢✢

We named our beautiful son Klaus and brought him home from the hospital four days after his birth, embracing our newfound parenthood with unwavering love and acceptance. Regardless of the differences the doctor had pointed out, we were captivated by our son.

I had a demanding work schedule, so I felt immense relief when Frau Bauer in the apartment below ours graciously volunteered to lend a hand. The first morning Karla was home from the hospital, Frau Bauer surprised us by arriving unannounced and treating us to freshly baked biscuits and coffee, allowing Friedrich and me to head off to work without worry.

CHAPTER 21

September 1939

Karla

I was ironing one of my father's shirts and listening to the radio when the special announcement came on the morning of 3 September. Klaus was sleeping in the cradle Bruno had made from discarded wood. Reichssender Kiel Radio was playing Richard Wagner's "Ride of the Valkyries," and I felt the music filling me with energy right up until the radio announcer broke in. My mouth went dry as I recalled the most recent announcement from two days before, informing listeners that Germany had gone into Poland to protect German citizens living there. *What can we expect now?* I asked myself.

"This is a special broadcast. We bring you breaking news. In an act of aggression and provocation, the warmongering governments of Britain and France have declared war on the German Reich."

My heart dropped and my knees felt weak, so I put the iron down and sat in a chair at the dining table to listen.

"Their unwarranted and unjustified declaration of war against our peace-loving nation is a clear indication of their hostile intentions and disregard for the principles of diplomacy and sovereignty."

My hands shook as I thought about how hard the first war had been on the people of Europe.

"Germany, under the leadership of our beloved Chancellor Adolf Hitler, has always pursued peace and cooperation with our neighbors. However, in the face of this blatant aggression, we will not waver in our commitment to defend the fatherland and protect the interests of the German people."

The ironing forgotten, I stood up to get my purse and coat. I needed to walk. I gently picked Klaus up and held my breath, hoping he wouldn't wake as I walked to the door.

"We call upon all citizens to remain steadfast and united in support of our government and armed forces. Together, we will overcome any obstacles and emerge victorious against the forces of tyranny and oppression."

I heard the announcer say, "Heil Hitler!" as I closed the door.

CHAPTER 22

December 1939
Bruno

I was walking around the apartment with Klaus in my arms, trying
to soothe him. He cried a lot but seemed to calm somewhat whenever
someone held him and walked. I knew he would be much calmer if I
put him in his pram and walked outside, but it had just started snowing. I would not have heard the soft knock on the apartment door if I
hadn't happened to be walking by.

I opened the door and found Eli's family dressed in coats, hats,
scarves, and boots. Jacob and Daniel had red faces and dried tears on
their cheeks. They each had a suitcase, and they all looked defeated. I
looked around to make sure no neighbors were out and ushered them
inside.

Karla was instantly there to help the children take their coats off.
She turned to me and said, "Stoke the fire, please, Bruno." Then she
turned back to the family and asked, "What happened, Eli? Ilse?"

Eli glanced worriedly behind me at Friedrich sitting on the sofa
and whispered, "I'm sorry. This was a mistake. We should not have put
you at risk." I grabbed Eli's elbow before he had a chance to put his coat

back on and said, "No, Eli. It's fine. He knows." I looked pointedly at Friedrich, and my father-in-law subtly nodded.

Eli kept his eyes on Friedrich as he said quietly, "The Nazis came and gave us only ten minutes to pack and get out of our house. They said Jews were no longer allowed to own property. I'm sorry, Bruno. It's snowing, and we didn't have anywhere else to go. In all the chaos, we just started walking in the shadows, hoping they wouldn't notice and force us into a truck with the other families."

Friedrich was silent for a few minutes, then quietly said, "You can stay for one night, and then you must go."

Ilse took Klaus gently from me. I wasn't sure if Eli heard Friedrich, and so I prepared to repeat the information. But then finally Eli responded, saying, "Yes, I understand, and we are grateful."

✢

When I came home from work the next day, Karla was preparing the evening meal. I looked around to see where Friedrich was and, not seeing him, assumed he was still out.

"Where are our guests?" I asked quietly.

Karla stayed focused on the carrots she was cutting and replied softly, "I found an apartment for them."

Just then, Friedrich walked in. He hung his coat and hat on the hooks next to the door and looked around. Then he walked into the bedroom. After a moment, he came back out again and sat at the dining table. No one spoke a word as we sat down to eat.

After dinner, Karla packed up some leftovers and said, "I want to bring some food to Frau Bauer. Bruno, will you please help me?" She was holding Klaus and pointed to the basket of food on the table.

I looked at my wife. The look in her eyes gave no room for me to say anything other than, "Of course."

We walked silently down the stairs to the first-floor apartment. There were no lights on in the hallway since electricity was becoming more expensive, so we each kept one hand against the wall as we walked. Karla knocked softly on Frau Bauer's door.

I had met Frau Bauer just after Karla and I were engaged. She was already in her mideighties then. A small woman with a large personality. She made sure everyone in the building pitched in to keep the common areas clean. Every time I saw her, I got the feeling she would live until a hundred, she had so much feistiness in her. She'd lived in the apartment below us her entire life, having inherited it from her parents. Her husband had died in the war, and they'd never had children. Karla told me that Frau Bauer had a niece who visited occasionally. Other than that, she simply was the matriarch of the apartment building, and the neighbors were her family.

The door cracked open slightly, and Karla said, "Frau Bauer, it's Karla. Bruno and I brought you some dinner." We slipped into the apartment. The apartment had the same layout as ours. Even the furniture was arranged identically. To my amazement, sitting there in the living room on the sofa next to each other were Eli and Ilse. They appeared to be listening to a classical production on the radio. Jacob and Daniel looked up briefly from some kind of card game they were playing on the floor and waved to me. Eli jumped up and reached for the basket of food. "Let me help you with that." I looked at Karla, but she just smiled at me.

"How," I asked incredulously, "is this possible?"

Karla handed Klaus to me and walked toward the kitchen to help Eli with the food. "I introduced everyone, and Frau Bauer said it was okay for the family to stay here for as long as they want." She placed the plates and bowls of food on the dining table. "Frau Bauer will sleep on the sofa, and the family will sleep in the bedroom. I brought extra blanks and pillows earlier. It's all worked out."

I looked at Frau Bauer, who was sitting at the dining table, drinking tea and looking at the food Karla unpacked. "This could become dangerous for you, Frau Bauer."

She put her teacup down and waved her hand in dismissal. "What will they do to an eighty-five-year-old woman?" She laughed. "I have lived a good life, and these people are a gift!"

Ilse stood and walked to her. "You are our gift, Frau Bauer, and we will forever be grateful for you."

Karla came and stood beside me at the door. "It isn't much, but I will bring more food after Vati goes to work tomorrow."

Frau Bauer pulled money out of the pocket of her light-blue dress and handed Karla some Reichsmarks. Karla pushed the money back, shaking her head. "No, Frau Bauer. We want to contribute."

Frau Bauer pressed it on her again. "You listen to me, child. God didn't allow me to have a family of my own, as much as my Herr Bauer and I tried." She winked at Karla. "Today, you gave me children and grandchildren to spoil. You will allow me to pay. I can afford it; you and Bruno will save your money."

Reluctantly, Karla pocketed the money and said softly, "Thank you." Her body was so tense, I could tell she was conflicted about taking the money. But we really couldn't afford more mouths to feed, so I was grateful.

As we turned to leave, my mind started running through different scenarios. *Where would they go if Friedrich or another neighbor knocks on the door? What would happen if Heinrich walks by and sees people in the window?* "Karla, what about your father?"

"There's no other option. I don't think Vati will turn innocent people into the street and contribute to their imprisonment or death." She glanced at the boys with a worried look. "I think he will be okay with the arrangement as long as we don't push it in his face."

I turned to Eli. "Keep the curtains closed. I will see if I can create a safe room for you in the back corner of the basement just in case someone comes."

༺༻

There was only one bathroom on each of the three floors for all the families to share. Since Eli and his family could hardly go there, I fashioned a bucket toilet in the corner of the bedroom in Frau Bauer's apartment with an old discarded broken chair I found in the basement. It had a mesh seat that was torn, so I pulled the rest of the mesh out and removed the crossbar holding the legs so the bucket fit. Then I nailed the chair to the wall to keep it from wobbling. Karla sewed an old sheet onto a rope, and I hung it around the toilet for privacy. When I was done, I told the family I would be by late at night to dump the contents in the hall toilet.

CHAPTER 23

February–April 1940

Karla

Back in the winter of 1922, when I was twelve, it was so cold for so long that the Kiel fjord froze over. Now, eighteen years later, I felt just as cold as I had felt then. Perhaps that was because there was no getting away from the cold. The war was taking all our supplies. We only received a small allotment of coal to heat our apartment. Bruno, Vati, and I would make it stretch by only using a small amount in the mornings and hoping that a little sun would warm the apartment during the rest of the day.

My stress escalated as I witnessed, with mounting horror, the Gestapo or SS begin to arrive at neighboring apartments. Jewish families were forcibly loaded into trucks and vanished. I didn't understand where they were taking all the Jews and all the other people Nazis targeted as undesirable. A feeling of disgust churned within me as I listened to neighbors boastfully discussing their collaboration with the Gestapo, with whom they hoped to curry favor.

I think Vati was also negatively affected by the same scenes. He stopped entertaining altogether and became withdrawn. I didn't know if he'd stopped entertaining Nazis to keep them away from us or if maybe he had become completely disenchanted by the Nazis when the war started. I suspected both were a little bit true, but I didn't question him because I was happy not to have Nazis in my home.

Overwhelmed by it all, I found myself sitting in a chair at the dining table one day, silent tears tracing down my cheeks. Bruno found me there when he returned home from work that day. He rushed to my side and put his arms around me. He didn't have to say anything. I knew he understood because he was living the nightmare with me. One misstep, however minor, would bring the Gestapo to our door. There was nothing stopping them from searching any apartment they wished.

The room fell silent as Bruno continued to hold me. My heart quickened as I prepared to share my news. Amid the chaos of war and the constant vigilance in safeguarding Ilse, Eli, and the boys, I couldn't shake the fear of taking a wrong step. But I couldn't keep my news from him.

Finally, I mustered the courage to meet his gaze and softly whispered, "I'm pregnant."

Concern etched itself across Bruno's face as he absorbed the weight of the information. But a moment later, a radiant smile transformed his expression into one of happiness.

"A baby means life and hope, Karla," he told me. "And we will love it."

⌇

At the beginning of April, a letter arrived addressed to me. It was from the Nazi regime, and my hands shook as I opened it.

The letter said that I was to report to duty within one week at the uniform factory because I had a special talent as a seamstress. The German military, under the direction of the Nazi regime, had a vast network of factories and facilities dedicated to producing uniforms, weapons, and other military equipment. This included both government-run factories and private enterprises that were contracted to produce goods for the military. The Nazis were ordering me to turn my joy of sewing into support for war. My heart ached with the thought of assisting them.

I lay awake all night, thinking about the letter. I absolutely did not want to support the Nazis or the war in any way. *But how could I get out of it? What would happen to me if I refused? How would my refusal affect Klaus, Bruno, and Vati? Would my refusal bring the Gestapo here? To Eli and Ilse and their family?*

By the time the sun started peeking through the bedroom window, I knew that refusing wasn't an option. I couldn't risk the well-being of so many people who depended on me. I also knew that, with Klaus's needs and a baby on the way, it wasn't possible for me to work outside my home. Klaus was a happy ten-month-old, but he required a lot of attention. He couldn't feed himself, and I suspected he had a hearing problem. I packed Klaus in his pram and walked to the factory. I had an idea and was determined to make it work.

My heart racing, I explained to the manager in charge of the factory that I had no one to care for my children so could not work in the factory. He glanced briefly at Klaus and, seeing that he looked different, looked quickly back at me, glancing at my stomach. I casually put my hand on the front of my dress and smoothed it down so he could see my small bump.

"Of course, I want to contribute to the war effort." I forced myself to look straight at him, hoping my directness would make him think I was sincere. "I have a sewing machine at home so I can work there."

He rubbed his chin, thinking, and finally said, "Okay. I'll have someone drop off material and supplies each Monday morning. You will sew hats all week, and I will send someone to pick them up every Saturday morning."

I panicked as I thought about a Nazi coming to the house. Klaus began to cry, so I rocked the pram. "You all are much too busy. My husband will pick everything up at the same time he delivers the completed hats." I held my breath until he shrugged and said, "Suit yourself."

⌇

It took me forty-five minutes to complete each hat, and I had to complete forty hats a week at home. I also did my own family's work of cleaning, cooking, shopping, and taking care of Klaus. I was relieved

I had stopped taking in other sewing just after Klaus was born. After two weeks, my hands were so sore, I had to soak them in warm salt water.

One morning, I brought food to Frau Bauer's apartment very early. I walked in and handed the food basket to Ilse. Each basket only contained a small amount of food, just in case someone in the hallway got curious and looked inside. Ilse took one of my raw hands in hers and turned it over. "What is happening?" she asked.

I explained the situation to her, and she said, "Bring me supplies. I will sew too, and we'll use the bottom of your food basket to transfer material and finished hats back and forth." When I started to object, she put her hand over mine. "I need to do something, and I like the idea of helping *you*. Please!"

༶

It was just before lunchtime, and I was at the dining table, sewing. Klaus was sitting on the floor, content to bang a spoon on a pot. The small radio we kept on the dining table was turned low to classical music. When the announcer interrupted, I reached over and turned up the volume. I had grown to hate the words "important announcement."

"This is an important announcement! Today, we bring you news of a great triumph for the Reich. The valiant soldiers of the Wehrmacht have achieved a decisive victory in the noble campaign to secure the territories of Denmark."

I thought of my cousins in Denmark and tried to imagine whether they were afraid or grateful for the Nazis. I assumed the former, based on what I'd seen of the way the Nazis gathered support by instilling fear in people, squashing civil liberties, and delivering harsh punishments.

"In a swift and glorious operation, our brave forces moved with lightning speed to overcome Danish defenses and secure key strategic positions. The surrender of Denmark is a testament to the indomitable spirit of the German people and the unstoppable might of the Third Reich."

I paused my sewing and took a sip of water from the glass on the table.

"With Denmark firmly under German control, the Reich has

secured vital sea routes in the North Sea and the Baltic Sea, strengthening our position in the heart of Europe and ensuring the safety and
security of our borders. However, our victory in Denmark is only the
begi—"

Unable to stomach any more, I reached over and switched the
radio off.

CHAPTER 24

August–September 1940

Karla

It was late at night in August, and I was eight months pregnant, when I heard the wail of the first air raid sirens. I sat up in bed and knew right away what it was: the nightmare of my childhood when planes dropped bombs on Kiel in the first war. I listened for a minute, hearing the rising and falling volume of the siren, then I poked Bruno.

"Bruno, wake up!" I grabbed our robes from the hook on the back of the bedroom door and threw his over to him.

"Is it the baby?"

"Listen! The air raid sirens. Get Klaus. I'll wake Vati." I stopped at our closed bedroom door and looked back at him. "What about Ilse, Eli, and the kids?" I whispered.

Bruno put Klaus over his shoulder. With a serious look, he whispered, "They will have to stay in the apartment. Eli and I already spoke about this."

I opened the bedroom door. Vati was dressed and ready to walk out of our apartment.

On the way down to the basement, I knocked on Frau Bauer's door and yelled, "It's Karla, Frau Bauer. All the neighbors are out here to go down to the basement!" She opened the door, and I took her arm to walk down the stairs with her.

The basement was dark, cold, and smelled musty. Having lived in the same apartment building all my life, I knew all the neighbors. Many had been in the building since before I was born or had inherited the apartment from a relative. All the families from the building, except Ilse and her family, were in the basement when we got there. We were all silent as we listened to the bombs. They seemed far off, but it was hard to tell since the basement provided a natural sound barrier. Bruno held Klaus in one arm and put his other arm around me. I was shaking, I was so terrified, and I could only imagine what it was like for the Meyers.

✦

It was a crisp Saturday afternoon on 28 September when I felt the first contractions. I had just delivered the week's hats to the factory. Klaus was nestled in his pram. At fifteen months old, he was adept at crawling but had yet to find his voice—perhaps because he couldn't hear. He loved being outdoors, and he laughed as I talked to him while we walked in the direction of home. Bruno and I had planned to meet at the corner pharmacy, halfway between the factory and home, so we could walk the rest of the way together.

At the pharmacy, Bruno stroked Klaus's head. I saw him notice my white knuckles around the pram handle. I was taking deep breaths, working through the contraction that gripped me. Bruno looked at me with concerned eyes. "Are you okay?"

As the pain gradually ebbed, I nodded. "I'm having contractions."

Once we were home, I went straight upstairs to rest while Bruno stopped at Frau Bauer's apartment to let the family know I would be delivering our baby soon. An hour later, the air raid sirens went off, calling us to the new bomb shelter that had been built just two buildings away. I could hear bombs going off, but thankfully none were close to our building. I sat with our neighbors for an hour with my contractions growing closer together until the two quick beeps of *all clear* sirens signaled that it was safe to return home.

Bruno and I walked directly to the hospital, where they ushered me through the dark corridors. The blackout was still in effect, but there were candles that lit our way. Bruno and Klaus remained in the dark waiting room until the nurse called them back two hours later.

Bruno and I marveled at the two miracles we had made together. I held our new son, Rolf, in one arm and reached up to shake Klaus's little hand as Bruno held him.

"You're a big brother, Klaus," I said.

CHAPTER 25

October 1959

Frankfurt, Germany

The door to the meeting room opened, and a young woman with long blonde hair pulled a cart through. The top shelf of the cart contained a tray with small sandwiches. Each sandwich was made with a slice of rye bread and topped with mayonnaise, ham or turkey, a slice of cucumber, and fried onions. On the second shelf was a bowl of fruit and a plate of sliced carrots, celery, and cucumbers.

Dr. Schmidt nodded at the woman and flipped through his notes. "May I ask some clarifying questions?" He looked up, and both Bruno and Karla nodded.

"In reflecting on your experiences during that time, what do you think were the most significant factors or influences that contributed to your opposition to the Nazi regime?"

Bruno rubbed his chin and sat back while Karla answered. "At first the Nazis spread hate, blaming Jews, gypsies—everyone who wasn't Aryan." She looked at Bruno to see if he wanted to add anything. He simply nodded and gave her an encouraging smile.

Karla looked back at the interviewers. "After the war started, they were very public about rounding up the Jews. The Nazis treated the Jews terribly, yelling at them, pushing them, kicking them, and in some cases shooting them." Karla took a deep breath, apparently struggling with that memory. "They started treating other Germans poorly too."

"I saw them beat an old man," whispered Bruno. He wiped his face, and a tear started falling down his cheek as he remembered the scene.

Dr. Schmidt nodded and took some notes before asking his next question. "There's a widespread belief that many Germans were unaware of the full extent of the Nazi regime's actions, including the atrocities committed in concentration camps. Reflecting on your own experiences and observations during that time, what factors or circumstances do you believe contributed to this lack of awareness among the German population? And how do you reconcile this with the idea of individual responsibility and moral accountability?"

Bruno looked down at his hands as he gathered his thoughts. "The regime's control over media and public discourse shielded many Germans from the truth about the regime's crimes. A climate of intimidation and the gradual erosion of civil liberties also played a role. Still, I believe individuals bore a moral responsibility to question authority and seek out alternative sources of information. And yet the oppressive nature of the regime made it exceedingly difficult for many to fulfill this responsibility. I personally never had the courage to step in when I saw someone being terrorized in public, something I will regret for the rest of my life."

The woman who brought lunch finished putting the food on the side table and quietly left the room.

"One more question before lunch, please," Dr. Schmidt said. "Karla, regarding your father, Friedrich, it appears he transitioned from staunchly advocating for Nazi ideals to defection. What do you believe prompted this significant transformation in his beliefs?"

Karla clasped her hands together on the table and leaned forward. "It's difficult to pinpoint a single factor that led to my father's change in beliefs from being pro-Nazi. Many experiences, things he witnessed, and even his own personal reflections could have played a role in changing his perspective.

"I think the last straw came when Germany invaded Poland and started the war. The horrors of the first war affected him so deeply." She shook her head. "He didn't want there to be another."

CHAPTER 26

April 1941

Bruno

One Friday, Karl drove me out to Felm in the old farm truck. I watched the scenery go from city to country during the fifteen-minute ride to the farm. Vati had asked me to help Karl fix the root cellar under my great-grandparent's house. The house itself was broken down into a heap of wood on my parents' property. They needed help creating access to the cellar, which could be used as a safe place if war found its way to our family home.

I was reading the paper to Karl on the way. "Listen to this," I said. "The headline reads: 'German Forces Occupy Yugoslavia and Greece, Extending Reich's Influence.'" I rolled down my window to get a small amount of air before reading the whole article.

"In a momentous announcement today, Germany declares a significant military victory in southeastern Europe. Through a swift and decisive campaign, German forces have successfully occupied Yugoslavia and Greece, expanding the Reich's reach into new territories. Under the leadership of Führer Adolf Hitler, our courageous soldiers have demonstrated unparalleled strength, bringing these nations under the banner of National Socialism. This occupation not only bolsters

Germany's strategic position but also secures vital resources, fortifying defenses against potential adversaries. This triumph underscores the resilience of the German people and the vision of our esteemed leader, paving the way for a promising future under National Socialism."

Karl parked the truck out front and looked at me, his lips a thin line. He shook his head and got out of the truck, then headed to the house. It felt like the Nazis were making a land and power grab. *How many of these nations really wanted German occupation?*

Karl and I spent the weekend pulling the old wood to the side and stacking it for use later. We then brought lanterns down into the cellar so we could inspect both the stairs and the cellar itself. The cellar was a single room about six meters by six meters. The walls were reinforced with stone and wood, and the floors were made of wooden planks. There was a small single bed in the corner with no mattress or linens. A small round table stood in the middle. Three wooden shelves covered an entire wall. The place smelled of dirt and moisture.

"There's definitely some rotten wood we'll need to replace." I pointed to the areas I noticed, then walked up the steps to start cutting wood so Karl could install it. Karl stayed in the cellar to pull out the rotten pieces. We worked well together and just naturally fell into a groove in which neither of us needed the other to explain what he was doing.

After the cellar was fixed, I restacked the wood in case it was needed in the future. On Sunday, Mutti gave us linens, a bucket, and canned food to store in the cellar.

CHAPTER 27

December 1941

Bruno

It was snowing outside on 11 December 1941, adding to the coziness of our evening spent together as a family. We had just finished eating, and the kitchen had been cleaned. Karla was sewing at one end of the table, and I was fixing a small engine at the other. Friedrich was sitting on the sofa, watching the boys. Rolf kept pulling himself up and holding the sofa while taking some tentative steps, then falling onto his bum. He was very close to walking. Klaus lay on his stomach, pushing a wooden truck I had made him back and forth across the floor. The radio was playing Richard Wagner's *The Mastersingers of Nuremberg* until the announcer broke in.

"Ladies and gentlemen, this is an urgent announcement. In a momentous development, Germany has officially declared war on the United States of America in response to America's entry into the war following the Japanese attack on Pearl Harbor."

I looked at Karla. "Where's Pearl Harbor?"

Karla stopped sewing to listen and put her hand up to keep me quiet.

"Chancellor Adolf Hitler addressed the Reichstag today, declaring that America's decision to join the Allies leaves Germany with no option but to reciprocate. Hitler cited America's support for Britain and its aggressive expansionist policies as being a threat to the stability and security of the Axis powers."

I remembered when the Americans had entered the first war. The conflict had been going on for nearly three years at that point. After the Americans joined, the Allies made progress, and the war ended nineteen months later.

"This declaration of war is a crucial step to protect the interests of the German people and defend the sovereignty of the Axis alliance against American imperialism. By aligning themselves with the Allies, the United States has revealed its true intentions as a hostile and belligerent power seeking global dominance."

I wondered if Hitler had declared war on the Americans because he hoped to exact revenge on them for helping to end the first war. I looked at Friedrich, wondering what he thought about this latest development, but all I could see was an old man with worry lines etching his face. Then another thought entered my mind. *Hitler claimed the Americans were seeking global dominance. But wasn't that what Germany had done with the invasion of Denmark, Yugoslavia, and other countries?*

"While the American government claims to champion freedom and democracy, its actions belie a hidden agenda of domination and subjugation. The German people must remain vigilant in the face of American aggression and propaganda as we continue our struggle for a new order based on justice and strength."

Just then, the air raid sirens went off. We mindlessly moved into action. Friedrich put his coat on and waited next to the open door. Karla put Rolf's coat on Rolf, and I put Klaus's coat on Klaus, and then Karla and I grabbed our own coats, and we all left our apartment to go to the bomb shelter.

CHAPTER 28

July 1942

Bruno

In July, I asked Karla if she wanted to go to the farm for the weekend. We had both been working hard, and most nights the air raid sirens went off, prompting us to run to the bomb shelter. I felt we needed a break. "We can go Saturday morning."

I saw the excitement in Karla's eyes as she nodded and said, "I'll pack the boys."

On Friday evening, Karl arrived at our apartment in the old farm truck he drove to and from work. He pulled his bicycle out of the back and left for the farm while we finished getting the boys ready. Karla also went downstairs to bring extra food and to remind Frau Bauer and the Meyers that we would be gone for two days. I asked her if she was worried Friedrich would figure out how much food she'd taken downstairs, but she dismissed the question, saying her father didn't ask anything about the household.

We had to go through two checkpoints to leave Kiel. Both times, the officers reviewed our paperwork and told us to get out of the truck so they could search it. There were at least seven armed SS soldiers at each checkpoint, plus several jeeps.

The second checkpoint had a tank as well. I could tell Karla was nervous as she stood next to the truck and shifted from one foot to another, but she kept a straight face as she rocked a crying Rolf. I held Klaus as he watched the soldiers intently. I worried a little that he would make a fuss, but he seemed to sense how tense we were and remained quiet.

Finally, after twenty minutes, the soldiers let us pass. The mood in the truck felt strained at first, but as we got further away, that feeling of tension started to go down. Karla and I both looked out the window to enjoy the scenery—so different from the bombed-out buildings we were starting to see in Kiel. The land surrounding Kiel is beautiful: flat farmland with lush grass and an occasional patch of pine trees. When I noticed that we were passing a small field of yellow black-eyed Susans, I pulled the truck over.

"What's wrong? What are you doing?" There was alarm in Karla's voice.

"Everything is fine," I said calmly, "I just need a quick break. Stay here with the boys. I won't be long." I picked two bunches of flowers, one for Karla and one for my mother. My heart leaped with joy when Karla's face broke out into a smile as I handed her a bunch of flowers. The last of the tense atmosphere dissipated.

My mother was sitting on the porch when we drove up to the house. She walked over as Karla and I got out of the truck with the boys. I helped Klaus down, and he immediately took Mutti's hand. I heard the front door slam as Rosie came running out the front door. She ran to Karla's side and picked Rolf up, giving him a hug. Not knowing Rosie, he immediately put his hands out for Karla to take him.

Karla touched Rolf's hand. "You're okay with Rosie," she assured him.

Klaus started walking away to explore. Mutti put her hands on her hips and smiled at me. *Uh-oh.* I knew that look. *The ladies have been conspiring,* I thought. Mutti took Klaus's hand again and started toward the house as she said, "It's been decided. Bruno and Karla, you two will leave the boys with us and go on an overnight date. Rosie and I will take good care of them." Mutti walked through the front door with Rosie just behind her, carrying Rolf.

I wasn't expecting this surprise and called out, "Mutti, are you sure?" *An entire day and night with my wife? No kids? No father-in-law?* My heart started racing with excitement. I opened the door for Karla to walk through and glanced at her for permission to leave the boys. My heart sank a little when I saw she was uncertain.

Mutti sat on the sofa with Klaus next to her. She put her hands out for Rosie to hand Rolf over, then looked at me. "I raised eight children with no help. I think Anna, Rosie, and I can handle these two." She put Rolf on her lap so that he was facing out and clapped her hands. Rolf started crying, holding his hands out to Karla. Mutti looked at Karla and said, "It's only one night."

I put my arm around Karla's shoulder and said, "Let's do this. They will be very spoiled by the time we get back, and I need a night alone with you." I saw it in Karla's eyes the moment she relented.

While Karla was packing some food and blankets, I went to the barn with my father to find our fishing gear. We decided to go to Kaltenhofer Moor See, a lake about a twenty-minute walk from my parents' house. My grandparents had an old fishing cabin right next to the water that Vati, my brothers, and I had kept. To Karla's relief, we wouldn't be too far away from the boys.

Just inside the barn was a small utility closet filled with fishing gear. I opened the door and pulled out five poles that I propped against the barn wall. Next, I pulled out two tackle boxes, along with a net for catching minnows, and put them on the ground. As I rummaged through the poles to select two, Vati leaned against the jam of the big barn door.

"I heard the ladies plotting to keep your boys so that you and Karla could have some time alone." He smiled. "Mutti and Rosie are always up to mischief."

I squatted down and opened the tackle boxes, then began to transfer some lures back and forth between them. "I'm happy to take Karla on a date."

Vati crossed his arms across his chest. "I hear they are bombing Kiel a lot."

"Yes. The sirens go off almost nightly, although the bombs don't come all the time. Maybe three to four times a week." Satisfied that I had my favorite lures and other fishing items all in one box, I closed the lids and put the tackle box I didn't want back in the closet.

Vati ran his thumbnail along the wood of the door jam. "The British want to destroy the German navy base and the shipyards." He dropped his hand and looked at me. "Son, it's going to get worse. Why don't you move out to the farm?"

I stood up and stretched my cramped knees, which felt sore from squatting for so long. I stepped out of the barn and looked around to make sure no one was nearby and to take a moment to contemplate my next words. "I would, Vati, but I am looking after my friends."

Vati had been putting away the three poles I discarded. Now he looked up sharply into my eyes. "Let's go for a walk," he said, and he led me out into the yard, where we could see if anyone approached. He could always read my face, and he knew there was more to the story.

He crossed his arms over his chest and looked squarely at me, waiting for me to explain further.

"Do you remember my friends Eli and his wife and children?" Vati nodded, and I took a deep breath. But I didn't have to say anything more.

Vati dropped his arms and shifted his weight. "They're Jewish."

"Yes. Their home was taken by an SS officer, so they moved in with Frau Bauer, an elderly lady in our building. Karla drops food off to them each day, and I help as well."

Vati shook his head and wiped his hand down his face, as if washing off the news. "That is very dangerous for your family and for your friend's family. We need to get them out of there. Chances are good that a neighbor will notice and turn them in."

"I agree, but I don't know where to bring them."

"Does Friedrich know?" Vati asked.

"I told him." Seeing the shock on Vati's face, I put my hand out to calm him and quickly said, "He's been helping. Or at least he helped once. And he isn't interfering."

Vati rubbed a finger across his lower lip, then dropped his hand and took a step toward the barn. "You'll bring them to me."

I started walking with him. "Vati, the last thing I want to do is put you and Mutti at risk . . ."

Before I could say more, Vati stopped and laid a hand on my biceps. "I have helped other families escape. The hardest part will be getting them out of Kiel."

What the hell? I thought. I was completely shocked by this news from Vati. He ignored my surprised look. "You and Karla go enjoy yourselves." He started walking again and I followed, my mind spinning with endless questions. *How could I have not known about this? What families did he help? How did he help them?*

When we reached the barn, I picked up the poles and tackle box, and we turned back toward the house. "Vati . . . ," I began again.

He snapped at me. "Don't ask me questions I cannot answer. Just come back from your date by noon on Sunday so we have enough time to talk before you must return to Kiel." Vati paused, and I stopped as well. He pointed at me. "You tell no one. Not Karla. Not your mother."

I was still reeling from the news about my father. I knew his views on the war, the Nazis, and the treatment of Jews, but I'd had no idea he was helping Jews flee. I swallowed and tried to control my breathing. "Vati, I have no secrets from Karla."

We were now halfway between the barn and the house. Vati and I were the same height, and our eyes were on the same level as we stared at one another. Finally, he nodded his understanding, turned, and crossed the remaining twenty meters to the house.

I stood there, watching him walk, still in shock that my father had already risked so much and I'd had no idea.

CHAPTER 29

July 1942

Karla

Bruno carried the basket of food, and I carried two wool blankets. We walked for about five minutes in a comfortable silence. I could tell Bruno had something on his mind and was trying to figure out the best way to tell me. He is hardly ever quiet unless there is something big or complex to discuss. I waited patiently as we walked.

"Karla," he said at last, "Vati wants me to bring the Meyers here. He said he will get them out of Germany."

I stopped walking to look at my husband. He took two more steps before turning back to look at me.

I was shocked but not really surprised. Otto was a kind man. "Really? Your father has been helping Jews escape? That's incredibly dangerous."

"I didn't know anything about it until just a few minutes before we left the house," he said.

"Bruno," I said, considering the situation as I spoke, "it will be very dangerous for our family if you bring them here, but no more dangerous than what we are doing."

Bruno was silent for a moment and then answered, "Yes, I know."

He started walking again, and I followed. "Neighbors could very well turn them in, and I'm not crazy about you continuing to put yourself and our boys at risk by bringing food every day."

Suddenly, our conversation was broken up by the sound of a plane. My heart started racing, and I could feel myself starting to panic. My body tensed, ready to run back to the house. Bruno put his hand on my arm to keep me there. The silver plane was flying very low. I could see two men in it, one sitting in front of the other. There was a red cross painted near the tail.

Bruno watched as the plane landed and steered to a place near a cropping of trees across the field from us. "His engine was misfiring." Bruno put the food basket on the ground and started running toward the plane. All I could think was how crazy my husband was being. I was terrified we were going to get shot. "Bruno!" I yelled. I ran after him and grabbed his hand. "You don't know who they are!"

"The plane has a red cross. It's fine, Karla. We need to help." He pulled my hand, and we started running together toward the plane.

One man had the engine door open by the time we made it to ten meters from them. He was maybe two meters tall and was wearing a one-piece khaki flight suit with no insignias. The other man was jumping down from the plane. He wore a similar suit, but he was shorter than the first man.

Bruno stopped running to them, and we remained at a respectful distance. "Do you need help?" he yelled.

Both men looked up sharply, and the shorter one pulled out a gun. Bruno and I instantly put our hands up, and Bruno stepped in front of me. My heart was racing so fast, I thought it might jump out of my throat. I immediately thought of our boys and how they would cope with our deaths. At the same time, I felt a flush of anger at Bruno for getting us into the situation.

"We have no weapons," yelled Bruno.

The two men were silent for a moment until the taller man put his hand on the other man's, motioning for him to put his gun away.

Once I saw they wouldn't hurt us, my stress level went down just a little. I took a deep breath and stepped around Bruno. I asked them in English if we could help. The men looked at each other, both of them clearly surprised.

The taller man took two steps forward. "You speak English."

Bruno and I put our hands down and started walking, closing the distance between us and the two men. "Yes, can we help you?" I asked.

"America?" Bruno asked as he walked ahead of me and warmly shook both men's hands, welcoming them to Germany. Although Germany was at war with America, the country was still known for its democracy and the land of opportunities. Bruno felt a certain curiosity and excitement about America.

The short man looked angry but holstered his gun. The tall man smiled at Bruno and scratched the back of his neck.

Bruno walked to the plane to look at the engine. The short man walked over, shaking his head, trying to get Bruno to stop. The taller man strolled over, looking at Bruno in amusement. "Let him see what's wrong."

Bruno talked about the plane, and I translated, trying to put the men at ease. "Where did you fly from?" I asked.

Both men remained silent, clearly not willing to answer any questions.

After a few minutes, Bruno showed them inside the engine. "The ignition system wires are burned, causing the plane to misfire," I translated for him.

The tall man craned his neck to investigate the engine where Bruno was pointing and then nodded. "Can you fix it?" he asked in German.

Bruno wiped his hands on his pants and nodded. "I can figure it out."

I translated, even though the tall man seemed to understand. The short man's brows furrowed with suspicion, and his lips pressed into a thin line. He shifted his weight subtly, ready to react at the slightest hint of danger, his body and demeanor tense and alert.

Wanting to leverage the friendliness of the tall man, I stepped forward and offered my hand. "I'm Karla, and this is Bruno. You're American?"

The tall man shook my hand without smiling. My heart stuttered. *Did I say something wrong?* He scanned the field as I clarified, "We're not Nazis."

The tall man considered for a moment, then said, "I'm Viggo, and that's Mike." Viggo shook my hand.

"It's going to take me a little time to find all the wiring. Perhaps you can go back to the house for coffee," Bruno said. I couldn't believe he was inviting these men to the house, but Viggo seemed harmless enough, and they were in a Red Cross plane.

I was surprised when the tall man—Viggo—said, "Mike, help Bruno. I'm going up to the house."

I left the food basket and blankets and walked with the men toward the Arnolds' property. We eventually split up when the barn came into view. I took Viggo to the house, and Bruno went with Mike toward the barn.

Still concerned that I'd said something wrong, and still very nervous, I asked, "Do you have children, Viggo?"

"Yes, I have three boys: eight, four, and six months." I could see the love in his eyes as he added, "My wife is pretty busy."

"Oh, that's wonderful. We have two boys." I stopped walking and looked into his eyes. "Before I bring you into my home, can you answer my question? Where are you from?"

Something I'd said seemed to have put him at ease, because this time he answered. "We're American with the International Red Cross."

⌁

We walked through the back door into the kitchen where Therese was pouring milk into two glasses. Otto was sitting at the table, drinking coffee. Their eyes widened in surprise as I walked in with a tall man behind me. I quickly explained the situation, and they invited Viggo to sit and have coffee. Therese took the glasses of milk into the living room, telling Rosie to keep the boys occupied.

When she came back, Therese poured coffee into cups. Otto asked a lot of questions about the plane and whether passengers could be flown out. Viggo seemed to understand most of what was said, but I translated whenever he raised a brow at me.

Viggo shifted in his seat, subtly sitting up a little taller. "What are you trying to do?"

"We have friends—a family—we have been helping who are in grave danger." I paused, nervous about trusting a stranger and going too far. "They're good people." Viggo remained silent. I felt hot tears behind my eyes and whispered, "Please."

Just then, Bruno opened the back door to the kitchen and told us he was ready.

"I can't promise, but I'll see what I can do," Viggo said quietly. He took a tiny notebook and pen out of his front breast pocket and wrote something down. "For emergencies," he said as he handed me the paper. I looked at the Swedish address and folded the paper, putting it safely in my pocket.

Bruno explained that he had pulled wiring out of an old tractor. He said he would replace the tractor's wiring another time but wanted to get the two men on their way.

It took only thirty minutes for him to get the wiring fixed. Viggo climbed into the back of the plane and started the engine. After running it for a minute, he nodded to Mike and climbed back out. Mike nodded a thank-you to us, then helped Viggo push the tail of the plane so it faced the field instead of the trees.

While Mike climbed into the plane, Viggo jogged over to me and Bruno and handed Bruno a gift. "For fixing the plane. Thank you."

Bruno put his arm around me as the plane went up to the end of the field, then turned around. The plane gained speed and finally took off. Viggo waved his hand in the air, and the plane got smaller and smaller.

"What did Viggo give you?" I asked.

Bruno opened his hand and showed me. "A patch with the American flag."

✦

We walked back through the front door to the apartment building on Sunday afternoon. I held the boys' hands in each of my own and started upstairs with them. Bruno knocked on Frau Bauer's apartment door. "Frau Bauer, it's Bruno." Her door cracked open, and he entered.

The boys and I were on the landing to go up the next flight when the door opened again. "Karla, can you please come down?" Bruno's tone was ominous, so I picked up Rolf and pulled Klaus with me down the stairs into the apartment.

Ilse was preparing a meal, and the children were drawing at the table. I looked at Eli and said, "What is it? What's happened?"

Bruno took Rolf from me. "I'm so sorry, but Frau Bauer died last night."

Eli was standing on the other side of the room. "Last night, I took her body to the far corner of the basement, where it's cooler," he said. "I covered her with a blanket."

I pulled a dining chair out and sat down, releasing Klaus's hand so he could go see what Jacob and Daniel were drawing. Eli came and stood in front of me with his hands clasped. "I'm so sorry. I know she was family to you."

I had a lump in my throat as I thought of her dead body in a dark corner of our basement. Frau Bauer had always been so good to us. Especially since taking in Ilse and Eli's family. I blinked back my tears, wanting to save them for later, for the privacy of my own apartment. Ilse walked over and bent over to hug me. I sensed Ilse's sorrow at losing someone who extended so much kindness to her family. I saw the sorrow in Eli's eyes as I looked over Ilse's shoulder at him. I felt as if my whole being might become unglued from grief. Then a new thought occurred to me. I looked up at Bruno. "Someone is going to find out she's dead." I looked at Eli. "We need to figure something out. And quick."

CHAPTER 30

July 1942

Karla

Bruno ran his thumb along his chin, thinking, as he looked back and forth between Eli and Ilse. "We need to figure out how to get you to my parents' farm. Otto said he will find a way to get you out of Germany." Rolf reached his hands out to me, and I took him from Bruno, settling him on my lap.

I looked at Ilse. Her expression showed a mixture of fear and determination as the realization dawned upon her. Her eyes widened, reflecting the weight of taking the risk to leave the country. I could see the tension in her jaw as she processed the gravity of the situation.

Suddenly an idea came to me. I hesitated at first, wondering, *Would it work? Will God punish us for it? Will we be able to live with ourselves?* I looked at Jacob and Daniel as they laughed at what Klaus was trying to draw, then took a deep breath. "I have a thought, but I don't think you will like it."

Eli nodded for me to go on.

I looked over at Bruno. "You should build a coffin for Frau Bauer. She's a small woman. The top of the coffin will hold her body, and there will be a secret compartment under her that we will put the children into. You can then use the truck to transport the coffin to the farm for burial. That will work for the children. But then we'll need to figure out how to get Eli and Ilse there too."

Eli shook his head. "Absolutely not! My children cannot ride with a corpse, and they cannot be separated from me and Ilse. And besides, it's disrespectful to the body."

Ilse took a step toward Eli and put her hand on his arm. "Eli, it's a way to keep our children safe, and Frau Bauer wanted to help. It's why she invited us to stay so long. She knew the risks."

She didn't say what I was thinking—what I suspected we all were thinking: that this wasn't just a way to keep the children safe. It was the only way.

"Eli, I wouldn't want to do this either," Bruno said grimly. "But I think it's the only option."

෴

Bruno started scavenging for wood and nails right away. He went to the shipyard, where he dragged boards out of the trash and pulled old nails from them and straightened them for reuse. The work was tedious and time-consuming, and he did as much as he could in the dark of night to limit any questions. If anyone had asked, and if he'd said he was building a coffin for his neighbor who had died, the authorities would have been right over to check his story.

We had to move fast before the decomposing body attracted the attention of curious neighbors, so I left Klaus and Rolf with Ilse for a few hours to help Bruno. Vati asked me what was happening, but I said only, "The less you know, the better." He looked into my eyes for a long moment and finally walked silently away.

Once the coffin was ready, we found ourselves with a few fortunate circumstances. First, the relentless downpour outside would hopefully dissuade anyone from venturing outdoors. Second, the risk of an air raid was notably diminished because inclement weather would ground the planes. There was also the fact that, though they were thirteen and eleven years old, the boys had very slender frames. Lastly, we still had access to the truck after our recent weekend at the farm.

At three o'clock in the morning, the apartment building was quiet except for the sound of the rain. My hands shook as I put some lotion mixed with fresh mint, which I'd brought from the farm, under each boy's nose to help with the smell of the decaying corpse. After they'd hugged their parents, Bruno helped the boys into the coffin. Bruno smiled at them and said it wouldn't be long and that they should close their eyes and must be very quiet throughout the journey.

Next, Bruno and Eli took the blankets off Frau Bauer. Her body was bloated, and I coughed at the harsh, rancid smell. My eyes were watering both from the smell and the sight. This would be her last heroic deed to help people. I knew this was what she would have wanted, but it was still difficult. I knew I would have to work hard to picture her alive and to remember all her shenanigans through the years I was growing up, rather than remembering her as a corpse. Eli and Ilse's family, I knew, would honor her memory when or—though I hated to even consider the possibility that they wouldn't—*if* they got settled someplace safe.

Eli ran to a corner of the basement opposite where Bruno and I stood and had dry heaves. I didn't know if it was the sight or smell of a corpse or the fact that we were using a dead body to transport his family out that made him sick. All I could do was offer him a weak smile of sympathy.

Bruno sealed the coffin with nails. Then he and Eli carried the coffin to the top of the stairs just in front of the main door to the building. This was the point where Eli and Ilse had to go back to the apartment. The coffin was heavy with three bodies, and I could barely lift the end where their feet were. Vati emerged from the shadows and helped me. My heart beat hard in my chest because I didn't hear him walk down the stairs from our apartment. *Was anyone else awake?* Somehow the three of us managed to get the coffin out to the waiting truck. Once it was loaded, Bruno and I faced each other and held hands for a moment. We knew the words we both were thinking and didn't need to say them. He nodded once and got in the truck. *Please come back to me,* I prayed. Vati put his arm around my shoulders, and we silently walked back into the building. *Does this mean he is no longer a Nazi?*

Bruno left at four in the morning. It was five o'clock when I heard him pull up again, but he didn't come straight upstairs, so I whispered down the staircase, "Bruno . . ."

Bruno was at Eli's door, knocking softly. Vati, Klaus, and Rolf were still asleep, and when Bruno saw me there, he waved for me to come. Once we were in the apartment, Bruno said, "Ilse, let's go. We have a very small window to get you out of here. The soldiers at the checkpoint were just changing shifts on my way back. I think I can get you out now, and then we will figure out how to get Eli out."

Eli started to protest, but Ilse put her finger on his lips and said, "I must go to our children. Please be safe, and we will see you soon."

Bruno looked at what I was wearing, then said, "Will you give your house coat to Ilse so she can get to the truck? Hopefully, if anyone is awake, they will think it's you." I was already handing my house coat to Ilse, not caring that I was left standing in my nightgown in front of Eli. "I'll park in an alley to get Ilse settled in under Frau Bauer before we leave the city."

I watched from the window as Ilse lay down on the truck bed next to the coffin. There was no time to give her the mint lotion, so I hoped she would be able to tolerate the pungent smells.

As a mother, I was certain she could walk through fire to get to her children.

CHAPTER 31

July 1942

Bruno

I took deep breaths as I approached the first checkpoint, willing my hands to stop shaking. I tried to keep my mind busy by picturing my and Karla's engagement party as the officers approached me. There were men sitting in a jeep that had a machine gun strapped to the top. I gave the officer my papers while another officer walked around my truck.

"Where are you going, Herr Arnold?"

I had answers ready. "My neighbor died and wished to be buried outside of Kiel, near her family."

The officer walking around the truck looked through the passenger window and said, "Get out." I tried to swallow past the lump in my throat, but my entire mouth had gone dry.

The first officer opened my door, and I stepped out.

I glanced at another officer who pointed his rifle at me. I thought, *Do they know I came through here earlier?* I'd tried to make sure I'd calculated correctly regarding the shift change, but perhaps there was someone still held over from the previous shift.

The first officer pointed to the back of the truck and ordered, "Open the coffin."

I leaned in to get my hammer and grabbed a cigarette, thinking a smoke might calm my nerves. I lit the cigarette as I walked to the back of the truck, feigning boredom.

I used the back of my hammer to pry off the lid. The smell was incomprehensible, and the officers all stepped back.

"Fine, you can go." The officer handed me back my papers, and I nailed the coffin shut, wondering how Ilse could bear the smell.

⌁

As soon as I parked in front of my great-grandparents' old house, where the boys were hiding in the cellar, I opened the coffin, pulled Frau Bauer's body out, and gently laid her on the ground near the dilapidated house. Then, I pulled the panel up and helped Ilse out of the truck. She immediately bent over and threw up. As she wiped her mouth with her shaking hands, I motioned for her to follow me.

We picked our way around the fallen house. The sun was just coming up, giving us enough light to find the cellar door. I bent over and pulled the handle. "It's Bruno," I yelled. We went down the stairs as my father leaned his shotgun against the wall. The boys ran to Ilse for an embrace.

"Vati, I need to get back. But Frau Bauer needs to be buried or cremated," I said.

Vati nodded and both of us started toward the stairs. Ilse put her hand on my arm, then pulled me down for a hug. "When the war's over . . . ," she started. But we were both so emotional that neither of us could say anything more. I just nodded and left the cellar with Vati.

I closed the cellar door and moved some wood pieces over it. "Vati, can you and Karl handle Frau Bauer?"

Vati followed me to where I had left Frau Bauer's body. "Yes, go. I'll have Karl help."

I started unbuttoning Frau Bauer's dress, tasting bile as I shifted her body to take her dress off. *Will I be able to forgive myself for this?* I prayed Vati wouldn't ask me to explain and was grateful he remained silent as he got into the truck.

"Give me a ride," he said after several minutes. "If you are doing what I think you are doing, I saw a dead fox earlier today that you can add to the coffin."

CHAPTER 32

July 1942

Karla

It was nearly six-thirty in the morning before Bruno came home. I heard him stop at Frau Bauer's apartment to talk to Eli before he climbed the stairs to our apartment. He looked exhausted as he hung his hat on the hook next to the door. He wrapped his arms around me and whispered, "The children and Ilse are safe."

Bruno tried to pull away, but I held on to him and whispered back, "How will we get Eli out?"

He put his finger over his lips for me to be quiet and pulled me into our bedroom. Once the door was closed, he wrapped his arms around me again and said quietly, "I have an idea. Did you wash the blanket Frau Bauer was wrapped in yet?"

"No, I left it in the basement," I replied.

"I brought Frau Bauer's clothes and the empty coffin back. I think we can modify the coffin and wrap Eli in the clothes and blanket. Vati gave me a dead fox to add to the smells." Finally, unable to take the smell of a dead body from Bruno's clothes, I stepped back. "You need to change your clothes. You stink."

Bruno took off his clothes, leaving them in a heap on the floor, and climbed into bed. I followed him. He whispered, "When the soldiers opened the coffin with Frau Bauer in it, they immediately closed it when the smell overwhelmed them. Eli will have a horrible ride, but I think it will work. I will drive through the checkpoints at the same time tomorrow and see if the same soldiers are there or if they rotate."

I had a lump in my throat as I said, "Bruno, this is so dangerous for you. I'm terrified."

Bruno sounded determined as he answered me. "I need to do this for Eli. He is my family."

CHAPTER 33

September–October 1942

Bruno

I looked at Vati as he sat on the sofa. Klaus was sitting at one end, bouncing back and forth against the sofa. Vati looked so sad, so lost. My normally sharp and witty father seemed to have died along with Mutti. He had told us she was dead, but that was all he'd said. We'd been unable to get anything more out of him.

Karla sat down next to him, offering him a cup of tea, but he shook his head. She placed the cup and saucer on the coffee table, then put her hand on Klaus and shook her head silently, telling him to stop. Unable to comprehend subtle cues, Klaus continued bouncing.

I walked out onto the front porch, where Karl and Walter were waiting to take Mutti's body to the family cemetery at the edge of the farm to bury her.

Walter was sitting on a lower step, and Karl was standing on the top one. Karl reached up and touched the roof of the porch. "The Gestapo was here yesterday." I saw my brother Hans; his wife, Antchen; and their daughter, Anne-Rose, walking up the driveway toward the house.

"Did it have anything to do with the planes landing here in July?" Walter asked.

"Planes? There was only one." *Should I have said that? Can I trust Walter?*

Walter looked at me with curiosity. "What do you know about this?"

Karl shook his head so subtly, I wasn't sure I actually saw it. "Hans is here. Let's take care of Mutti," I said. I walked off the porch with a nagging feeling I couldn't quite articulate to myself.

After we buried Mutti, I walked to the broken shack to find Eli and his family, but they were gone. The nagging feeling from earlier became stronger. As I walked back to the house, Karl met me halfway.

"Did the Gestapo murder Mutti?" I asked Karl.

"I don't know. Vati still isn't talking." Karl crossed his arms across his chest. "She could have died from a heart attack or stroke for all I know." I looked at the ground as Karl pushed a rock with his shoe. "Anna, Rosie, and I were in Kiel visiting Anna's mother when the Gestapo came."

"Walter said planes, not plane. There was only one when Karla and I were here. Did it happen again?"

I glanced over when I heard the back door slam. Rosie and Anne-Rose started running toward the barn.

"Two planes landed here and took off thirty minutes later." Karl looked at me pointedly. "I assume they picked your friends up."

I tried to talk to my father several times, but he wouldn't answer any questions either about how my mother had died or about Eli and his family.

In October, my father died one month to the day after my mother had died. I took the bus back to the farm to help Karl bury him next to my mother. Karla stayed in Kiel with the boys because Klaus had been sick with croup, and she wanted to let him rest.

Vati's death was a hard thing, made even harder because now we would never know what happened to Eli and his family. I had hoped that after the war, he would tell me what happened to my friends, but those hopes died with him.

A week after I returned from my father's funeral, Klaus's cough was worse, and he started to have a fever. Karla tried everything for him. We heated water on the stove to make steam and took turns walking with him as he cried. We kept a bucket with ice and water so we could soak rags and wipe his body, trying to reduce the fever. Karla made tea from the bark of a willow tree to break the fever, but he wouldn't drink it. We even kept the windows open at night to let in fresh air. Nothing worked, and he seemed to get worse.

Finally, a week later, Karla sent a neighbor boy to get me from work. When I arrived at home, the apartment was a mess, and Karla looked exhausted. Klaus was coughing so much, he was struggling to breathe.

I left Rolf with Frau Hoffman, an elderly neighbor who lived down the hall from us, while Karla wrapped Klaus up in a blanket. Then we took a streetcar to the hospital.

The looks on the faces of the nurses and doctors who examined Klaus made me uncomfortable. They all tried to keep a blank face, but it seemed they were all in on some secret from which Karla and I were excluded. The doctor said Klaus had bronchitis, and we would have to leave him there so he could get steam, medications, and full-time care. The nurses wouldn't look at us, which increased my concern. They said bronchitis was contagious, and they assured us they would call when he was ready to go home.

"No, I'll stay here and help care for him," Karla said determinedly.

The doctor shook his head and told us that would be impossible. We knew that if we argued with the doctor, he could call the SS police or Gestapo. Our only choice was to leave our son in the care of nurses and doctors or risk being imprisoned or shot. I told myself that the doctors and nurses had taken an oath, so maybe it was going to be okay.

The nurse took Klaus away after we both kissed him.

Life at home changed immediately. Of course, we remained devoted caregivers to Rolf, who, by this time, was running everywhere with his tremendous energy and unending curiosity. But the day we left Klaus at the hospital, Rolf could sense a problem. As his calls for "K," the name he called Klaus, went unanswered, Rolf would get quiet with a confused look in his eyes.

On Saturday, the day after we'd left Klaus with the doctors, we received a letter from a messenger. Friedrich was reading the newspaper at the dining table and slowly sipping his coffee. He stopped and watched as Karla opened the envelope with shaking hands. I looked over her shoulder. *Your son died in his sleep*, the message read. Karla stopped reading and dropped the letter. I watched it float to the floor, trying to understand what I'd just read.

A moment later I collapsed to my knees, my heart shattering into a million pieces. "My boy! My son!" I cried out with anguish, my voice echoing through the room. I sat the rest of the way onto the floor. Rolf, sensing my pain, looked up and slowly made his way over to me, settling onto my lap. I pulled him close, desperate for solace, but the emptiness engulfed me.

Beside me, Karla sank to the floor, tears streaming down her face. Then Friedrich appeared, squatting down beside us, enfolding us all in a tight embrace. Amid the chaos of grief, the rhythmic ticking of the clock on the wall seemed to mock our pain, a relentless reminder that time marched on mercilessly.

"We must go get him and give him a proper burial," Karla whispered.

Leaving Rolf with Frau Hoffman again, we left the apartment and took a streetcar back to the hospital. My voice was flat when I spoke to the receptionist. "We have come to collect our son for a proper burial." I handed her the letter, and she told us to wait. I watched her walk down the hall until she turned and disappeared into a room.

After thirty minutes, the same doctor who had been treating Klaus the day before walked out of the room. I watched him walk toward us with a face like stone. The closer he got to us, the tighter Karla squeezed my hand. The doctor stood in front of us and took an irritated breath, as if our problems weren't worth his time.

"Due to the contagious nature of his sickness, the hospital cremated him. You can mourn him at home." Anger like I had never felt before surged through me, and I felt the urge to wrap my hands around his throat. Karla wrapped her other hand around my upper arm and whispered, "No, Bruno. We have to think about Rolf."

I'll never forget that doctor. He wore an SS patch, so he was obviously part of Hitler's party. I knew in that moment that they had taken my boy's life because he was born different.

I knew then what that registry was all about.

CHAPTER 34

October 1959

Frankfurt, Germany

Bruno stared at the floor as he tried to express the depth of his emotion. "That was the worst day of our lives." Tears streamed down his face as he looked at Karla. The sadness in the room was palpable. "The Nazis murdered my happy, innocent son because he didn't fit into their definition of a pure race."

He squeezed Karla's hand. "Karla and I walked home from the hospital that night overwhelmed with grief. We had no words as we grieved for my parents and mourned our son. Although we didn't agree with the ideology of Hitler and the Nazi regime, we had tried to be good Germans. We loved each other and our children and were never unkind to anyone. With the deaths of my parents and Klaus, it felt like we were being punished."

Karla spoke up then, adding, "I had never known sorrow so profound. Bruno and I expressed our grief only in our apartment. The political and social climate forced people to either suppress their emotions or channel them into the war effort. The second wasn't an option for us since we didn't support the war. The Gestapo would have shown up at our doorstep if they thought something was wrong."

As the interview continued, the three interviewers stopped asking questions and let Karla and Bruno's heartbreaking account flow.

CHAPTER 35

June 1943

Karla

The bombing raids intensified, and we found ourselves running to the bomb shelter with increasing frequency as the relentless barrage of explosions rattled our nerves. Each night brought the haunting echo of sirens, signaling the impending danger looming overhead. In the light of day, we walked around in a city that was being leveled. Buildings were destroyed either partially or fully. Smoke and fire became common sights.

Vati became more and more withdrawn after Klaus died. It seemed the only time he spoke now was when he sat at the dining table, listening to the news and crying out, "I'm sorry! I didn't know."

It was alarming to see him weep, since I had never witnessed him crying in my lifetime. "Didn't know what?" I asked him once.

He looked at me with tears in his eyes. "I supported those bastards," he whispered. He then stood up and walked out of the apartment. He did or said something like this at least once a week.

Even after Klaus died, I kept my same routine of waking up first to start the stove and make breakfast for Vati and Bruno before starting my daily chores. I worked from sunup to sundown sewing for the

Nazis, cleaning the apartment, going to the grocery store, cooking, and caring for Rolf. I welcomed the long hours as a way to keep myself from falling apart while thinking about my precious Klaus. *Had he felt pain,* I wondered, *when they killed him?*

One morning, however, I was tired and sick with nausea, so I stayed in bed longer than usual. After changing Rolf and getting dressed, Bruno sat on the edge of the bed. The movement sent a new wave of nausea through me.

"Karla, you look like you don't feel well," Bruno said.

"I'm just tired. Maybe I ate something last night that didn't agree with me. You can leave Rolf here, and I'll get up in a minute and get some water."

A few days later, I was still feeling poor. Bruno helped me clean the kitchen after dinner. As he was drying a plate, he said, "Karla, go to the hospital and get checked out."

I shook my head even before he finished speaking. "No, Bruno, I'm fine. We don't have the money, and anyway I will never set foot in that hospital again. Not with the doctors who murdered my son there."

The following morning, I was getting dressed and noticed that my breasts were too large to fit in my bra. *Had I gained weight?* Then a thought hit me like a freight train. I reached into my nightstand drawer and pulled out a small calendar. After counting the weeks, my heart sank. I was still mourning Klaus and didn't know if I could handle a new baby. I started crying when Bruno walked in. He took one look at me and ran over, then squatted in front of me.

I sniffled and handed him the calendar. He took it, placing it on the nightstand and looked at me with confusion in his eyes. "I'm pregnant," I said.

Bruno stood up, pulling me with him, and wrapped his arms around me. "I'm so very happy."

Over the months of my pregnancy, Bruno took on some additional side jobs fixing whatever people called him for. He fixed everything from a boat motor to a toaster. Any money he earned went to buying food from the black market since the ration cards we had hardly fed us. Bruno was well connected, and these connections allowed him into the black market. But it was very dangerous.

The morning sickness eventually went away. My feelings were a mix of joy for the new baby and guilt for feeling joy since Klaus was gone. I didn't have time to play the piano, but I sang every day to the baby and Rolf.

I asked around the apartment building to see if anyone knew of a midwife. The new neighbor in Frau Bauer's old apartment told me about her aunt who lived two blocks away. She said her aunt had delivered hundreds of babies, so one day, with Rolf in tow, I walked over to introduce myself.

The lady who answered looked like she was in her fifties. She was shorter than me and had a small frame and dark hair wrapped in a neat bun. She wore a blue light cotton dress with small pink roses across the scooped neckline.

"Frau Krüger? I'm Karla Arnold. Nina lives in my building and says you have experience as a midwife?"

Frau Krüger looked down at my growing belly, then scanned her eyes back up to mine before glancing down at Rolf. She then poked her head further out, looking straight down the hall and then to the right, down the stairs from her apartment. Appearing satisfied, she opened the door wider and ushered me inside. "Come in, come in."

I looked around her apartment. The living room was small but neat and clean. A two-seater gray sofa stood against the wall with a small walnut coffee table in front of it. Three books were stacked neatly on the corner of the coffee table. To the right of the sofa was a closed door. To the left of the coffee table was a beige oak chair in front of three windows.

"Would you like some coffee?" she asked.

Coffee could mean half a day of visiting. I didn't want to be rude, but I had a great deal of work to do, so I got to the point. "Thank you, no. I can't stay long, but I am in need of a midwife."

Frau Krüger smiled at Rolf and pointed to the sofa. "Let's sit down for a moment."

I sat Rolf on my lap, but he quickly wriggled down to the floor. I pulled from my purse one of the wooden trucks Bruno had made to distract him from getting into trouble.

Frau Krüger sat on the edge of the chair with her hands clasped over her knees. "Before I confirm anything, I need to know why you are looking for a midwife instead of going to the hospital to give birth."

My throat suddenly went dry with the thought of having to tell this stranger about my baby boy. My palms started to sweat, and I could feel the tendrils of anxiety begin to pull at me. I reached out and softly stroked the back of Rolf's head, needing to ground myself. I watched Rolf push the truck back and forth on the sofa for a moment, then I turned to Frau Krüger.

"I can't go to the hospital." I looked into her eyes and saw sympathy there. She patiently waited for me to go at my own pace. "My son, my first born . . ." I swallowed. "He died there."

"The Nazis prefer that women give birth in the hospital so the children can be properly registered," she said quietly.

I took a handkerchief out of my purse and wiped my nose, then looked at her pointedly. "I know," I whispered.

After a few moments, Frau Krüger reached over and touched my knee. "Let's talk about prenatal care first, shall we?"

I listened to her talk about drinking enough water and getting vegetables and meat in my diet. She asked me many questions about my day and gave me advice about taking breaks. I quickly found out that what she lacked in height, she made up for in personality as she spoke animatedly about other patients she'd treated in the past.

At some point during our discussion, Rolf climbed on the sofa and laid his head on my lap. I gently rubbed his hair, and he fell asleep. Twenty minutes later, I looked at my watch and exclaimed, "Oh my goodness, I've taken up so much of your time." I sat Rolf up to wake him and glanced at Frau Krüger. "Will you deliver my baby at home?"

As I stood and helped Rolf up, she said, "Yes, but you cannot tell anyone. I don't want the Nazis knocking on my door. Send your husband to get me when your water breaks."

CHAPTER 36

December 1943

Karla

The baby had dropped lower, and I knew I could go into labor any day.

My lower back started hurting the afternoon of 30 December. I thought at first it was from the extra weight I was carrying, but then the pain started coming at intervals. That evening, while lying in bed next to Bruno as he read the paper, I noticed the pains were starting to come more often. I got up and put my robe on to go to the toilet, which we shared with all the other tenants on our floor.

When I stood up from the toilet, I felt the gush of hot liquid between my legs. Gripped by another contraction, I sat back down on the toilet to breathe through it. *At least it wasn't all over the floor like it was with Klaus.* Klaus . . . I could feel the tears starting but pushed them away. This baby needed nothing but joy. After washing my hands, I went back to our room and said, "Bruno, it's time."

Not understanding me, he kept his eyes on the paper. "Okay, I'll turn off the light soon. I just want to finish this article."

I slipped into bed. "Bruno, my water broke!"

The newspaper went flying. I had never seen anyone get up so fast. "All right. Let's get to the hospital."

I felt another contraction starting. "No! I'm not going there. Frau Krüger is just two streets over at number forty-five A. She's a midwife, and I've already spoken to her." The contraction was consuming my body. "Go . . . get . . . her."

Bruno opened our bedroom door and yelled, "Friedrich, get up. Karla's in labor. Stay with her while I go get the midwife."

Rolf woke up and started crying in his crib in the corner, so I stood to get him. But another contraction forced me to sit down on the edge of the bed. Vati was at the doorway. "I'll take care of Rolf. You get into bed." I vaguely wondered how my father was going to care for a toddler but let the thought go while the contraction consumed me.

As the contraction slowly left my body, I heard Vati talking to Rolf, so I propped my pillow against the headboard. Just as I was laying back, another contraction gripped me. Bruno ran into the bedroom, followed by an out-of-breath Frau Krüger. Bruno must have run the entire way, dragging her with him.

Frau Krüger took charge, her voice commanding. "Bruno, get clean towels and sheets." I watched as she pulled a knife out of her bag and handed it to him. "Put this in the fire on the stove and clean it thoroughly with boiling water. Don't touch the blade." I was shocked at seeing the knife, but then another contraction took over, preventing any further thoughts.

Frau Krüger closed the door, leaving the men outside, and helped me pull my undergarments off. Then she positioned my knees up and checked me. "You're getting close, Karla. You're doing great," she said while she covered me up.

I watched her take the wooden chair from the corner and place it beside the bed. Then she took knitting out of her bag and sat down. *She's knitting?* I thought. *She needs to help me!* Things continued in that way, with my contractions growing stronger and Frau Krüger offering periodic encouragement in between making rows of stitches.

Twenty minutes later, Bruno walked in and placed all the supplies on the bed. Frau Krüger stood up to look through the towels as Bruno kissed me. Then she pushed Bruno out of the room as another contraction took over.

By one o'clock in the morning on 31 December, contractions were coming every two minutes, so Frau Krüger checked again. "You're ready to push," she said.

Bruno opened the door to bring me a glass of water. I reached for him, but Frau Krüger sent him out the door. "It's time for her to start pushing. Wait out there."

In the middle of a contraction, I yelled, "No! Bruno, I need you." Bruno made his way past the midwife.

Frau Krüger looked surprised but recovered quickly. She said, "Go sit behind your wife. When she pushes, prop her up a bit."

Bruno climbed on the bed and situated me between his legs with my back to his chest as Frau Krüger moved the chair to the end of the bed and lifted the sheet above my knees. "Are you ready?"

I nodded as another contraction came searing through my body.

"Push, Karla, push!" said Frau Krüger. At the same time, Bruno sat up straighter, and I pushed as hard as I could. The intensity of the pain was beyond comprehension.

As the contraction slowly faded, Bruno relaxed, but then another one took hold of me, so he provided more support, and I pushed again.

On the third push, I felt something give, and our baby slid out of my body into Frau Krüger's waiting hands. "You have a girl!" she announced.

I looked down as Frau Krüger placed the screaming baby on my belly. Bruno reached over and touched our little girl, even though she was covered in blood and a yellow waxy substance.

Bruno had not experienced Klaus's or Rolf's birth. Both those times, he had stayed in a dark waiting room at the hospital. Now, he seemed stunned by what he'd just witnessed.

"I'm overwhelmed, Karla. You did a tremendous job and this baby . . . our baby . . ." I felt Bruno swallow. "I had no idea. I . . ." But he could say nothing more. I laughed because it wasn't often my husband was rendered speechless.

"Bruno, get a clothespin out of my bag and put it on the umbilical cord as close to the baby as possible." Frau Krüger looked at me. "Karla, push once more to get the afterbirth out."

Bruno did as he was instructed, and I pushed. Frau Krüger nodded in approval at Bruno's placement of the clothespin and said, "Now take the knife and cut the cord, then wrap the baby in one of the towels. I'll wash her when I'm done here." Frau Krüger looked at me. "What's her name?"

"Edith," I answered as I watched Bruno. He was totally focused on cutting the cord. When he was done, he gently picked the baby up and wrapped her in a towel before turning to me with a huge smile.

"Edith is going to be a feisty one," Frau Krüger declared.

CHAPTER 37

January–April 1944
Bruno

Two days after Edith was born, Karla went back to her normal routine, seamlessly adding caring for our newborn to her many tasks.

Two days after that, on January 4, after nursing Edith in our bed, Karla carried the baby into the kitchen to make coffee and eggs. I got dressed, then walked into the living room, where I was surprised to see Friedrich still asleep, facing the back of the sofa. He was usually sitting at the dining table, waiting for breakfast when I emerged from the bedroom.

Karla placed a carafe of coffee on the table and looked toward him. "Vati, are you ill?" she asked. Friedrich did not move.

I walked over to the sofa and shook my father-in-law's shoulder. He felt stiff and cold. I took a deep breath and put my fingers on his neck to check for a pulse. Then I walked toward the dining area and caught Karla before she took another step. "He's gone, Karla," I said softly. "I'm so sorry."

She looked at me sharply. "What do you mean, 'gone'?"

She stepped around me toward the sofa, and I replied, "It looks like he died in his sleep."

The ground was frozen, but I was able to get a few friends to bring their pickaxes and shovels to help me dig a grave next to Karla's mother. I left a note from Karla with Erna's housekeeper informing her of Friedrich's death and saying when the funeral was. Erna didn't show up at the funeral, and she never replied. I knew Karla had mixed feelings. It had been an emotional week. We felt joy for our beautiful new daughter and sorrow over Karla's dead father and frustration at her sister. Karla hid all these feelings, focusing instead on her tasks in order to get through the days.

Karla received a letter in March ordering her to report to the uniform factory. She had been allowed to do her sewing work from home, and she sometimes worked late into the night to ensure she met her quota of uniforms for the week. Now suddenly they wanted her in the factory. She had no choice in the matter. If she did not report for duty, the Gestapo would find her and accuse her of dissenting from the regime.

I found Karl at one of his jobs and asked him to send Rosie to take care of Rolf and Edith while Karla and I worked outside the home. A day later, Rosie showed up with her suitcase and moved in with us.

At the end of Karla's first day in the factory, I found her sitting on the steps just inside our apartment building door, her head hanging low. I sat down next to her and took her hand. "What's wrong? What happened today?"

She looked at me with a troubled face. I could tell she had been crying but was trying to get herself together before facing the children.

After a few moments, she took a deep breath. "The regime is running low on everything." She looked at some imaginary spot behind me, then into my eyes. "The military is bringing uniforms from dead soldiers by the truckload." She shook her head. "They needed me in the factory to help clean them. I spent the day taking the uniforms to large baths for washing." She stood up and I stood with her, listening. "Bruno, blood was everywhere: in the truck, on the floor, in the water tubs with the clothes." She held up her hands. I could see they were stained. "I can still smell the blood!" She pointed at spots on her dress that an apron hadn't covered. "It feels like it's clinging to me."

I stood there with Karla, but I didn't have anything I could say to comfort her. This was yet another atrocity of the war that we had to endure; a war that we had never wanted.

✦

Just after breakfast on 1 April, a messenger knocked on our door and handed me a telegram. Karla was outside, hanging up laundry, and Rosie had taken the children for a walk. My throat felt dry when I opened the envelope. I was to report for duty on 10 April.

My heart sank, and my stomach rolled over. I dropped the telegram and covered my face with my hands. While there had always been the possibility that I would be drafted, I was nearly past the draft age limit and had hoped that I would be spared.

Anger coursed through me. The Nazis had murdered my son, and now they wanted me to be a murderer. I ran to the bucket we use for dirty water and threw up. Afterward, I poured some water from the clean water bucket into a bowl and washed my face. Just then, Karla walked in. She was carrying clean laundry from the line and singing. I stood up from the bucket and turned to look at her.

She immediately stopped. "What is it?" She glanced at the telegram on the floor.

"I have to report for duty." My voice was hoarse with emotion.

In her shock, Karla dropped the clean laundry. "This can't be happening. You're too old. How can they do this? We must fight this." With every word, my normally soft-spoken wife got louder and louder until she finally began to weep. I wrapped my arms around her. There was nothing I could say to comfort her, so we just stood there in the middle of the apartment and cried together.

That was a sleepless night for Karla and me. We cried and held each other all night. We hadn't been separated for longer than a workday since before we got married. The next morning, I sat on the edge of the bed and thought, *I won't be able to kill another human being.* I told Karla, "I don't know which will be hardest: leaving you or going to war."

I reread the telegram, looking for a way out.

> ATTN: BRUNO ARNOLD
> YOU ARE TO REPORT FOR INFANTRY SCHOOL DUTY ON 10 APRIL 1944 AT DÖBERITZ FOR TRAINING. YOUR DUTY STATION WILL BE ASSIGNED UPON THE COMPLETION OF TRAINING.

The telegram was from General Erich Becker. My only hope was that my superiors would see that I could fix anything and put me into a support role so I wouldn't have to carry a gun. I could not kill another human being. As I thought about all this, I wondered one more thing.

Were they forcing me into infantry because I hadn't signed my allegiance to the Reich?

CHAPTER 38

April 1944
Karla

The day after Bruno received the telegram, I came up with a plan to help him get out of the draft or maybe get a desk job. I left the children with Bruno and took the streetcar to Erna's house. I had never been to the house she shared with Heinrich, but I'd found her address in Vati's things after he passed. I had to go through a checkpoint to get there, but they waived me on after I explained I was visiting my sister and they had made a quick inspection of my papers.

I was surprised to see a guard at Erna's front door. I hadn't realized that Heinrich had climbed so high in the regime that a guard was necessary. The guard let me into the foyer and went to find Erna. Curious, I looked around the house. The foyer had a small table with a porcelain bowl. The floor was checkered with black-and-white squares. There was a set of stairs in front of me that led to a second-floor balcony. I saw three closed doors at the top of the stairs and assumed those were bedrooms and perhaps a bathroom. To the left of the foyer was a dining room with a table big enough for eight chairs. To the right was a closed door.

I heard a door close from somewhere in the back of the house, and then Erna walked up. She got right to the point. "What are you doing here, Karla?" Her voice was harsh, her eyes cold. *Who was this person in front of me? Why did she hate me so much?*

The guard walked in behind her and went to stand in the corner. I took a deep breath. "I need your help." I glanced at the guard. "Is there somewhere private we can talk?"

Erna stared at me and made no move.

"It's important. Please, Erna."

She told the guard to go outside. Once the door had closed behind him, she said impatiently, "Well, what is it?"

"Bruno was called to fight, Erna." I took a step toward her. "He isn't built to fight. Can you please help get him out of service?"

She shook her head before I even finished. "He should feel proud to serve the Nazi regime." She took a step back. "I can't help."

I had known it was a long shot, but I had to try. "Please. I'm begging you. Can you help to get him reassigned, at least? Maybe a desk job. He can fix anything and is a trained electrician. He can support the regime in so many ways other than at the front lines."

Erna looked at me angrily. "No, I cannot help. Heinrich cannot help. Bruno needs to go fight for Germany and stop spending time with Jew friends." She began walking toward the stairs, saying over her shoulder, "Please see yourself out."

Tears were too much to give my selfish sister. I was so angry and hurt. I marched out of her house and, needing to dispel the anger that coursed through my veins, walked home instead of taking the streetcar.

+~+

Karl had been included in the same wave of draft notices that went out, and he and Anna arrived at our apartment the night before he and Bruno were to leave. The two of them planned to travel together as far as they could. Karl was to report to a different camp, north of Berlin, to learn how to drive tanks. How the Army decided who went where for what jobs, I had no idea. I wondered if this was some kind of punishment. *Were the authorities doing this because someone had found out that we helped the Meyers?*

The week leading up to their departure, Rosie and I knitted socks and hats for the winter. I also bought new boots for Bruno. He tried to make me return them to the store, saying our money was for the children. I put my hands on my hips and gave him a stern look. "We will be okay," I said. "I found some money that my father had hidden in the back of the drawer he used." When he didn't make a move to pick the boots up, I insisted. "Bruno, not another word about it. You can't wear those threadbare shoes." He finally picked them up and softly said, "Thank you."

My heart ached, and my mind was spinning. *Will Rolf and Edith grow up without their father?* The future was so uncertain. So much death. So much destruction. Frau Bauer was dead. Therese, Otto, and Vati were dead. Klaus was dead. Erna may as well have been dead. Eli, Ilse, and their children were gone—to somewhere safe, I hoped. Our city was getting crushed by bombs.

⌁

The morning of 9 April, we all went to the train station to see Bruno and Karl off. Saying goodbye to a son without having a body to bury had been heart-wrenching. Now my Bruno was going off to war. I had no words. *Would we survive? Would I be okay raising two young children in the war all on my own?*

I had been to the main train station in Kiel many times while growing up, so it was very familiar to me. I wasn't expecting how different the experience would be the day we all walked from our apartment to the train station together.

My heart sank when we crossed the street and I saw what had become of the beautiful brick building. It had been bombed, so the front door was no longer accessible. Someone had built a temporary walkway to the back of the building. Karl and I carried Edith in her pram above the uneven walkway while Rolf rode on Bruno's shoulders. Anna and Rosie followed behind. Once we were inside, I looked around, and my heart sank further.

The smell hit me first: the stink of urine and body odor from so many unwashed people. I saw families camped out in corners, seemingly with nowhere to go. Probably their homes had been destroyed.

Some people were begging for food, and others were going through the trash cans, probably looking for whatever scraps they could find. Occasionally, trains would release water and replenish it to cool the hot engines, and I now saw people washing themselves with the water from the train that was parked on the tracks. It was a challenge finding water sources for bathing and laundry, so I couldn't blame people taking showers in public like that.

I saw young men in soldier uniforms hobbling on crutches, their legs missing or their faces burned. I looked into the eyes of some soldiers and saw emptiness. Others wore a look of horror, and some had sadness in their eyes. I just couldn't imagine what they had seen and endured. *What was going to happen to Bruno?* There were SS soldiers everywhere, constantly scanning the crowd for any infraction. I also felt the eyes of the Gestapo on me, but they were harder to spot as they worked undercover and in the shadows.

The train that had been first in the station when we arrived pulled out. Fifteen minutes later, another one pulled in. Fifteen minutes after that, another train arrived with a sign that said "Berlin" at the top of the engine car. White signs with printed red letters that said "Military Transport" were in the windows of the engine car and the third car. The coal car, second in line, didn't have windows.

Bruno dropped his duffel bag on the ground and squatted to give Rolf a hug. After a minute, he stood up and put his hand against Edith's cheek. Karl, Anna, and Rosie were about one meter from us in their own tearful embrace.

Bruno and I stood in front of each other, and I felt the chaos of the train station around us fading. "Bruno," I said, "please come back to me." I glanced at Rolf to make sure he wasn't getting into trouble. My right hand rested on Edith's pram, and I reached up to stroke Bruno's cheek with my left. "I know you said you cannot kill another human being. But, Bruno, if it comes down to it, I need you to do it and come home to us. I won't survive without you. You promised we would grow old together, and I'm holding you to it."

The unshed tears in Bruno's eyes almost brought me to my knees. He opened his mouth to speak but appeared to be struggling to find words. He wrapped his arms around me and held me tighter than he ever had. "I'll be back. I love you, Karla Arnold."

The train conductor yelled, "All aboard!"

Bruno released me, picked up his bag, and boarded the train behind Karl. I wasn't surprised when he didn't look back. It was just too hard.

Rosie walked over and picked up Rolf while Anna walked up next to me and took my hand. Together, we watched as the train pulled out, carrying our husbands away. There had been an underlying tenseness between Anna and me from the first day we met that I never understood. Now, however, we were joined by our mutual sadness of seeing our husbands going off to war.

I wasn't religious. But I prayed that day for our husbands to return safely.

PART II

Bruno

CHAPTER 39

April 1944

Karl and I sat next to each other, riding in silence. Many men around us wore the same look of tiredness, sadness, and resignation that Karl and I did. There were several in our car who looked ten years older than me and several that looked twenty years younger. I overheard one saying he was forty-five, the same age as Karl. I saw kids as young as fifteen and thought of my nephews. *Would they soon be drafted too, at twelve and fourteen years old?*

After five hours, the train stopped about three hundred meters from the central train station in Berlin. The train tracks and station had been heavily bombed two days prior. As we stepped down from the train, we saw hundreds of soldiers with guns. I saw and smelled smoke still smoldering from the rubble around the station.

Karl had to take another train two hours north, and I had to find a bus to take me to the camp just outside of Berlin. I felt a lump in my throat as we walked through a side door into the part of the building still standing. *Would I ever see Karl again?*

After we had found Karl's train, I dropped my bag on the ground and gave my brother a hug. He wrapped his arms around me.

"Stay safe, little brother," Karl said into my ear.

After getting ushered off the bus, I looked around the training camp. I saw a number of men marching in formation. Another group was also running, and I saw several groups doing calisthenics. I heard guns and other munitions going off in the distance. We were ushered into a two-story brick building to begin our registration.

Tables stood along the walls, and small groups of men waited in front of them. Some were dressed in uniforms, and others were in civilian clothes.

At the first table, I provided my personal information and completed some paperwork. The SS officer taking my information read through my paperwork, then wrote something on the top right. "This is your training group, barracks, and cot number." He stamped the bottom of the paper and handed it back to me, nodding to my right. "Go that way to get your uniform."

Uniforms were laid out on tables according to size. We each were given two uniforms. I looked at mine and asked about the stranger's name still on the breast pocket. The SS officer behind the table simply took out his knife and pulled the name tag off, leaving small holes where the stitching had been. I started to feel sick, thinking about Karla washing all the bloody uniforms of dead soldiers. And now I had to wear one.

Someone pushed me on the shoulder and motioned for me to go to the next table, where I picked up a knife and canteen for water. At the last table, I was given a rifle and a box of ammunition. My first reaction was to leave the rifle on the table, but the SS officer's stern look told me to take it and keep moving.

I looked around at the men and wondered if I would grow close to any. Karla sometimes called me "the mayor" because I liked to talk to people. I smiled inwardly at the memory but quickly pushed it aside because I didn't want to get consumed with missing her.

I followed the men I was in line with out to the barracks. There were seven long buildings, each with a small white sign painted with a black letter, A through G. I found my assigned C building and walked in. There were about fifty double-stacked cots made of metal on each side of the building. There were two trunks at the end of each grouping of cots for our personal items. Each cot had a small metal sign hanging on the bed-frame with a number on it. I found the one assigned to me, number 89, put my things away in the trunk and changed from my civilian clothes into my uniform. I tasted bile rising in my throat at the subtle scent of copper from the uniform: the unmistakable smell of blood.

Next, we headed to the clinic for medical exams. I moved around in only my underwear, holding folded clothes in one hand and a piece of paper in the other as I walked from station to station.

At the first station, a clerk typed up my family medical history. When he'd finished, he pulled the paper out of the typewriter and told me where to go next. At the next station, a doctor gave me a thorough physical examination to assess my overall health and fitness.

At the station after that, my vital signs were checked: heart rate, blood pressure, and temperature. They tested my vision and hearing and checked my feet and my teeth.

At the last station, I was given immunization vaccines for tetanus, typhoid fever, diphtheria, and smallpox. It both surprised and con-cerned me to get so many vaccines at one time, but I knew I couldn't question the authorities without getting a reprimand.

This entire process was the beginning of my mental transforma-tion from working-class man, husband, and father into a soldier. My instincts told me it was no longer time for me to be a gregarious man, urging me to become someone who was quiet, who didn't draw any attention. I decided to listen to my instincts.

The next morning came quick and loud as the training officers en-tered our building, yelling and banging a metal pipe on the end of our cots for everyone to get up. For breakfast, we were given coffee made from chicory and some biscuits. The morning was full of running, cal-isthenics, and weight training.

In the afternoon, we received basic instructions on handling and maintaining weapons. This included rifle drills, marksmanship train-ing, and other essential skills. We participated in live-fire exercises to familiarize ourselves with the use of certain weapons, including hand grenades and setting bombs. Housing, food, and household supplies were in short supply in Germany, but the country had plenty of weapons and munitions.

Having grown up on a farm, I was a great marksman. Before I met Karla, I had joined in competitions around my hometown of Felm and was always the first- or second-place winner. Now, I made a conscious decision to miss the targets on the shooting range. The training officers were disgusted, and my peers laughed and joked about how awful I was.

Pretending to be a horrible marksman was an act of survival for several reasons. I was hoping the army would put me in a support role instead of sending me into battle. I truly didn't think I would survive taking the life of another human being, especially in the name of Hitler and the Nazi regime. I would never be able to forgive myself. Also, if anyone tried to force me to kill another human being, especially an unarmed Jewish person, I planned to miss on purpose. I hoped that if they believed I was a horrible marksman, they might not punish me.

No matter what training we got, it was always laced with propaganda and Nazi ideology. Loyalty to the Nazi regime and to the concept of "total war" against the Allies were stressed. Military discipline was strictly enforced. We were expected to obey orders without question. The training was both physically and mentally intense.

I was relieved to see that being quiet and staying to myself seemed to be paying off. Most everyone left me alone. Even the officers didn't reprimand me for not constantly saying "Heil Hitler" like they did with other soldiers. At the end of each week, in private, I looked at my picture of Karla, Rolf, and Edith and at the patch Viggo had given me, and I pictured a better life after the war. I knew it was dangerous to have an American flag patch, but I took the risk because I figured the items I brought would ground me and keep me human in the inhumane circumstances I found myself in.

"Arnold!"

I looked up sharply, putting the picture on top of the patch and sliding both inside my boot. I looked to see if the training commander had seen the American flag patch, but he seemed to be more intent on the piece of paper he was holding in front of me.

"Why haven't you signed this?" he barked.

I glanced at the paper and knew immediately what it was without reading it. It had been given to me several times to sign over the years, and each time, I had told the person I would sign it and mail it in.

I stood up and took the paper. "Apologies, sir. I'll take care of it right away."

He looked at me for a moment. *Was he going to force me to sign it in front of him?* He turned and started walking, barking over his shoulder, "See that you do, and get it to administration."

Karla and I had agreed early on that we wouldn't sign, but things had changed. *Would they put pressure on Karla if I didn't sign?* I wondered. *Would they take the kids?* I thought about Klaus and how the Nazis had murdered him, then folded the paper and put it in my pocket. I figured once I was in the war, no one would care about this damn piece of paper.

After eight weeks of training, it was time for my group to receive their orders. The officer in charge for the day brought his clipboard and list of assignments to the barracks.

"Adler!" he called out. The man I knew as Johann stepped forward. "You're assigned to the 138th logistical team. Report to the front gate at five o'clock to board the bus." The officer clicked his shoes, put his hand out, and said "Heil Hitler." The recruit did the same, turned around, and started organizing his stuff to be ready to leave in the morning.

The officer then yelled, "Arnold!"

I stepped forward with my heart racing and my stomach in knots. I was filled with terror. I didn't want to die and leave my young family. I hoped perhaps the army would assign me to a desk since I couldn't shoot.

"You'll report to the Ninth Army, 352nd Infantry Division in Minsk."

I was stunned. I could feel some snickering and shifting around of the other recruits behind me. My throat immediately went dry, and I couldn't speak. I knew from the news that Minsk was a highly strategic city, and the prospect of being assigned there filled me with dread. I would be fighting against the Russians, who were known for their ruthlessness in war.

The officer finished the list and walked out. So many questions went through my mind about why I had been assigned to the Eastern Front, where some of the most intense fighting occurred. *Had someone found out I hadn't pledged my allegiance to the regime? Had someone discovered that I'd helped Eli and his family? Surely this must be some kind of punishment. But why recruit me to the army instead of just shooting me or imprisoning me as an example to the others?*

Needing to feel closer to Karla, I decided to write her a letter. I wasn't sure if I would get to send any more letters after that.

Dear Karla,

My training just finished, and I will be shipping out tomorrow. Training was hard, but I learned a lot. Know that I am thinking of you and our children. I know how much you are working to keep them and yourself safe. I will think of you every time I look at the stars. I love you.

Love,

Bruno

I folded the letter and brought it to the camp post office. The postmaster put it in an envelope, and I added our address. There were no guarantees she would receive it since mail was unpredictable. As I left the post office, I thought about walking out of the camp but quickly decided against it. The Gestapo would have imprisoned my family or shot them all for my desertion.

While going through my bag to organize my stuff, I found a folded piece of paper. I unfolded it to find a drawing of a train in the middle with "Berlin" written on the front. The sun was shining at the top right corner. A gun was lying on the grass under the train, and two men were shaking hands. "Praying for peace" was written across the bottom, and in the bottom right corner was the name Viggo. I couldn't believe it.

Somehow the pilot had seen me, but either he hadn't wanted to or had been unable to say anything to me. *How had this gotten into my bag?* The only thing I could think of was that he'd slipped it into my bag at the train station when I was hugging Karl goodbye. I never asked why he was flying over Germany but contemplated it a few times. *Was he an American spy, or was he really in the Red Cross?* Since he didn't say anything to me in Berlin, I had to assume the former.

I carefully folded the piece of paper and tucked it away with my American flag patch and the picture of my family. These were my treasures, and I would use them to give me strength.

CHAPTER 40

June 1944

The next morning, I took the bus back to the train station to board a train to Belarus with thirty-five other recruits from my training class. I overheard other men on the bus saying the Eastern Front was one of the largest and bloodiest theaters, confirming what I already knew. I rested my head against the side of the bus and closed my eyes, praying for the first time in my life: *Please bring me back to my family in one piece. Let me die if living would mean I need someone to take care of me.* I would rather have died than be a burden for Karla.

At the Berlin train station, we boarded a train, and I settled in for the thirteen-hour journey to Minsk. It was clear that the train had previously been used for the upper class as it had cloth seats and a toilet. I could tell that it used to be polished and well maintained, but its condition had declined as a result of being used to transport military personnel and equipment around Europe.

I had four grenades, a rifle, ammunition, a sidearm, and a hunting knife, along with a backpack filled with a few clothes, socks, gloves, and the hat that Karla had made me, plus a few pieces of dried fish and four biscuits. My canteen was attached to the strap of my backpack with a small piece of leather cord. I was grateful for the boots Karla had bought me. I think my training would have been much more difficult in the worn-out shoes I had.

Our train stopped just outside Warsaw, Poland. I don't know if that was because the tracks were destroyed or for some other reason. We were told to exit the train and get into the back of military trucks that were parked next to the train tracks. By then, it was early afternoon. Everyone was tired and hot from the train ride. There was barely room to sit in the trucks with so many men. We had to take turns standing around the sides, a move that created room for some men to rest and also made it possible for others to guard the vehicles. We rode for another five hours in the back of the truck to just outside of Minsk, Belarus, stopping once to fill the gas tank from the extra gas in the container attached to the back of the truck.

Minsk looked much like Kiel, with bombed-out buildings and rubble in the streets. A few more men stood up around the truck bed, guns pointed out. I heard small-arms fire around the city as we were driving through.

As we entered the military camp for the Ninth Army in western Minsk, a heavy sense of apprehension settled over me. The sight of the bustling activity only served to underscore the grim reality of war. Tents and makeshift shelters sprawled across the landscape: housing for the thousands of men assigned to the battalion. The air was thick with tension and resounded with a cacophony of voices and the clatter of equipment. The face on every man we passed seemed to echo the weight of the recent losses, a somber testament to the sacrifices made in this relentless conflict.

After registering at the administration office, I walked to my assigned tent: twenty-three on row X. Inside, I met my squad. Reinhard introduced himself as our section leader, stood, and shook my hand. He was younger than I would have thought a leader would be but seemed nice enough. He introduced me to the others. They all looked tired, and I could see in their eyes a weariness that went far beyond physical exhaustion. Helmut, who had red hair and freckles, sat on his cot and merely nodded at me. Franz stood over the stove, mesmerized by something in the pot with steam coming out of it. He glanced at me, then back at his pot. Horst appeared to be sleeping, although I wasn't sure if that was the case. Lastly, Gerhard was sitting on his cot, cleaning his rifle with a cigarette hanging out of his mouth.

Reinhard pointed to an empty green cot with stains on it. "Bruno, get settled. Get something to eat and a good night's sleep. We're assigned to set defensive traps tomorrow." He paused and looked at me. "We heard the Soviets may be positioning around the city to reclaim Minsk, and there is a lot to do. In a few days, we will replace another squad on patrol."

I nodded and dropped my things on my cot. I started to leave to go find the mess hall, and I heard a deep voice say, "Bring your weapons at all times."

It was Gerhard. His stern eyes gave no room for a debate. His eyes looked like the eyes of the toughest man I'd ever met, and there were weathered lines etched deep into his face: evidence of countless battles fought and hardships endured through years of military service.

When I returned from the mess hall, I noticed a battery backpack for a metal detector in the corner of the tent. Its wand sat at the end of Horst's cot. I picked up the battery pack and looked at Horst. "Do you need help fixing this?" He pushed the wand with his foot and said, "Have at it. Everyone else has tried."

I sat on my cot with the two parts. "Does someone have a screwdriver?" I don't know who threw it, but one landed in the dirt next to my cot. I took the cover off the machine and worked with the wires for a few minutes to figure out how to fix it.

Next, I took two new bullets and pulled them apart. Once I'd shaken out the black powder, I took the lead casings to the stove and dumped them in the now-empty pot. I watched the lead melt, then took the pot back to my cot.

Using the end of the screwdriver, I put the hot liquid around the wires I had joined and blew on them until the lead hardened. After putting the case back on, I waved the wand over my backpack. The detector emitted various tones as it picked up on metal: likely some coins or my canteen.

I could feel Gerhard's eyes on me as he lay on his cot, smoking his cigarette. "Is it fixed?" he asked.

I put the unit back in the corner and rinsed out the pot. "Sounds like it." Since I didn't know who'd thrown the screwdriver, I left it next to the stove.

Horst picked up the metal detector and turned it on. "You're fucking kidding me!" He walked around the tent, waving the wand and listening. The other guys laughed, and I shrugged. "Don't feel bad. I'm kind of a savant about fixing things."

"What do you do for a living back home?" Reinhard asked.

"I'm an electrician."

CHAPTER 41

June–July 1944

The following week, my section within the Ninth Army went out on patrol in the southwestern part of the city while the Fourth Army division patrolled the eastern part of it. We walked the city all day. Our orders were to shoot anyone wearing a Russian uniform or holding a weapon. The streets were eerily empty, as if people understood something was about to happen.

It happened quickly one day. One moment, we were walking. Then, as suddenly as if someone had flipped a light switch, the entire world was in chaos. Shots rang out in front of us, cannons went off behind us, and I heard the motors of large trucks and tanks driving through the city. Gerhard, walking on my right, called out, "Stay close."

We heard a rocket, and Gerhard screamed, "Incoming!" He dove down into an alleyway, dragging me with him. "Stay on my back," he yelled to me. I followed closely, and others did the same. We walked to the end of the alley, then turned left into a building that had been turned practically into rubble by a previous bombing.

My heart was beating fast, and I was breathing hard, trying to get control of my emotions. I had never been more terrified in my life. The men split up in the bombed-out building, with Reinhard, Franz, and

Horst hiding behind a large pile of debris, a partial wall behind them. I followed Gerhard and Helmut to hide behind a short partial wall about twenty meters away that looked like it was ready to crumble.

My hands started shaking uncontrollably at the sound of Russian voices. I knew enough Russian to understand someone shouting, "No prisoners. Just shoot the Germans." Gerhard turned to me and Helmut.

"We're going to have to sneak out of here when it gets dark. Fighting against them will be a suicide mission." Gerhard looked around. "Cover me." Helmut knelt so he could see above the wall and pointed his rifle out as Gerhard ran over to Reinhard. They spoke for a few seconds, then Gerhard ran back.

After a few hours of waiting and listening for Russians, it finally grew dark. Gerhard took the lead as we picked our way through the rubble, staying behind the cover of anything we could find. We walked along the walls of alleyways, crawled under bushes, and walked between trees to get back to camp. My nerves were frayed, but there was no chance for rest. The entire city was surrounded by the Russians.

When we finally arrived, the camp looked like complete chaos to me. As I followed Gerhard, I heard orders being shouted—in some cases, contradictory ones. Someone said this was a well-planned surprise attack by the Russians to take back the city. Another person confirmed we were surrounded and said we needed to figure out how we would manage supplies. I saw another group of leaders trying to figure out how to organize a counterattack. I also overheard officers talking about pockets of entire platoons that were under heavy fire and cut off from all communications.

Reinhard led us to our tent and took off his helmet. He looked at each one of us, then finally said, "We're going back out to save as many of our comrades as we can."

Gerhard nodded in agreement. "Load up, gentlemen. It's time for us to show what we're made of."

As we ran through the city, looking for fallen comrades over the next eight days, I saw a few Russian soldiers who were wounded. Although I couldn't take them back to camp to get medical attention, I tried to do small things to help. Once, as if by accident, I dropped a tourniquet and field dressing near a Russian soldier who was screaming with a leg wound. No one noticed in all the chaos. It was a dangerous

move, but it was a way for me to try to stay human in such a dehuman-
izing situation.

We brought back about ten wounded Germans each night. Our
task involved stealth, not direct conflict, and I was relieved that not a
single person in my section had to fire a weapon. On these missions,
Gerhard was especially skilled at directing us and keeping us safe.

On one of our trips out, I asked Gerhard why he wasn't squad
leader. He said he didn't want the role and was confident that his skills
were better used evading capture. During these nights, he also talked
to me about survival, explaining what to do if we were captured by the
Russians: techniques like resisting interrogations, looking for ways to
escape, and not trusting anyone. He taught me to pull a dead Russian
on top of me in order to hide. I learned more from him than from any
other person I'd met since I was drafted. Gerhard never talked about
life before the war or his family, but he was an amazing teacher.

By the end of June, we heard that most of the Fourth Army in
the east had been captured or were dead, so our division surrendered
Minsk to the Russians. There was a short truce that allowed us thirty
days to pack up and get out of the country. Thirty days was a very short
time to get a unit of our size moved out. Although there were still
pockets of fighting, everyone was tasked with helping to take down
tents and pack up. The rain and mud didn't help, but I think everyone
was grateful it wasn't winter.

Perhaps someone granted me a birthday present on 24 July by making sure I was on one of the first trucks out with my squad. Although
I didn't know these men well, war forced a bond with these five men
that I knew I would have for the rest of my life.

CHAPTER 42

August 1944

There were about one thousand men on the train heading north to our next assignment in Estonia. Our equipment, tanks, trucks, and supplies went with us in various cars. This train was not as nice as the train into Minsk. It was older and smelled of human waste, urine, and death. Despite the smell, I found a seat and leaned back to rest.

About twelve hours into our twenty-hour journey, I decided to stretch my legs and take a walk. When I returned to the car where my squad was, I saw that Reinhard had just sat down next to Gerhard. Reinhard's face was both stoic and sad.

"The rest of the unit was overrun by Russians after the deadline for leaving passed," I heard him say quietly to Gerhard.

Gerhard quickly sat up. "What happened to them?" I stopped in the aisle to listen.

Reinhard looked at Gerhard and then scanned the faces of the other men in the car. Everyone was listening now. "They were either killed or taken prisoner."

Gerhard hit the side of the train with his fist and let out a great cry. Reinhard stood up to give him some space but remained in the aisle next to him. Never in my life had I seen someone so angry. I felt angry,

I felt sad, and I felt guilty for also feeling grateful that we had been able to leave. I heard some talk of going back to save anyone who was still alive, but this was impossible. We had our orders. The remainder of the trip was quiet.

Our train traveled through Lithuania, Latvia, and Estonia. As I looked out the window at the countryside speeding by, I saw what seemed like thousands of people heading away on roads going west. They were in trucks, cars, or horse-drawn carriages or walking.

"What's that about?" I asked Helmut, who was sitting next to me, also looking out. Reinhard was sitting across from us with his eyes closed. When Helmut didn't answer, Reinhard glanced out the window and said, "They're running from the Russians."

It was a terrifying thought: not knowing which parts of the countries we traveled to were under German rule and which were under Soviet.

As we neared our destination, Reinhard briefed us about the situation. "Although the Russians overran the area a few weeks ago, there's still heavy fighting along the Narva river and in the town itself. We are going to be fighting alongside the Twentieth Waffen Grenadier Division of the SS." I looked across the aisle at Gerhard, wondering what he was thinking as he stared out the window while holding his sidearm on his lap. Reinhard continued, saying, "The Twentieth Waffen was made up of about fifteen thousand volunteers from Estonia before most were killed or taken prisoner." I wondered whether they were really volunteers or had been forced to fight like I was. From what Reinhard had told us, I assumed the latter.

I was surprised when Gerhard looked over and added, "There's no formal military base or outpost in Narva. The Waffen already dug trenches along fifteen kilometers of the river from the point going into the Gulf of Finland and out to the Baltic Sea, to an area just south of city hall."

So he hadn't been in a trance like I thought.

CHAPTER 43

August–November 1944

The day our train arrived in Narva, we immediately began unloading our equipment and marched to the front line along the river. My squad was assigned to protect about a kilometer stretch along the river. We were supposed to rotate every eight hours with another squad so men could get some rest and food. But troops were stretched thin because so many men had died and because fighting was fierce, so breaks were a luxury, and when we had them, they didn't last long.

Everyone had to pitch in to get additional ammunition or bring wounded soldiers to the safety zone located two kilometers away from the front lines. The safety zone provided food, water, medical attention, and access to supplies, if any were available. Fighting was so fierce, the inbound trains with supplies and more men couldn't come fast enough.

There was so much activity and noise along the river that I couldn't think of anything else except survival. I told Reinhard several times that I wasn't good at shooting. I let him know I'd failed at target practice, so he finally assigned me to be a runner. This was an extremely challenging and dangerous position because I had to simultaneously pay attention to the fighting, where I was going, and the task at hand.

I was assigned to run food, water, and supplies into battle along the trenches and to drag wounded soldiers out, all while staying low to the ground so that I wasn't shot in the head.

One day, I had an hour of downtime in which to walk through areas where buildings had been previously bombed. I was able to locate wood, nails, and pieces of metal. It took some time, but I finally found four wheels. Three matched in size, and one was slightly smaller. I built a wagon to carry more of what was needed back and forth.

Late September brought colder weather with a lot of rain and shorter days. From then on, my wagon was no longer effective because of the mud. This affected the speed with which I could do my job, but I continued as a runner, supporting my squad and others along the route.

In October, amid the chaos of battle, I made my way back to the trench where my squad had been fighting all day. As I approached, I noticed the others gathered around a figure lying motionless on the ground. Pushing through the group, I realized with a sinking heart that it was Reinhard. His lifeless form was lying in the mud. There was a bullet wound in his head, and his helmet lay at his feet. *Had he taken his helmet off? Why?* Despite the shock and sorrow that gripped us all, there was no time to mourn. Gerhard immediately took charge, barking out orders as the team resumed their positions.

With a heavy heart, I gently lifted Reinhard's body and carried him over my shoulder out of the trench to the nearby field hospital. The scene there was grim, with rows of wounded and fallen soldiers awaiting their fate. I watched as the orderlies prepared to move Reinhard's body to a temporary resting place among the fallen. I felt a sense of despair at the thought that his final resting place would be one of the mass graves I had seen when we first arrived.

I walked over behind the toilets and threw up what little food I had in my stomach. Reinhard was one of those men I knew I would always remember. He was smart, funny, and kind to his men.

Throughout the rest of October, the situation became even more horrific with so many dead bodies stacked up around the hospital. My uniform was caked in a mixture of mud from the trenches and blood from the wounded and dead I carried. Some days I was so exhausted from running back and forth, I could barely stand up.

One day I was squatting against the trench wall, trying to catch my breath, when someone screamed, "Incoming!" Men ran, but not fast enough to avoid a Russian soldier who threw himself, with a grenade in each hand, into our trench. I watched in horror as several men exploded, their limbs flying everywhere. I suffered some burns, but in time, the psychological damage would prove to be far worse.

I looked over and saw that Horst and Helmut were both among the dead. Franz was missing the lower half of his left leg, and he was screaming. I pulled his tourniquet and field dressings from his bag.

"I'll take him," Gerhard said as he put the dressing and tourniquet on Franz. I carried Horst's body first to the hospital, then ran back to help Gerhard with Franz, knowing I would return for Helmut's body as soon as possible.

Later that day, Gerhard and I joined another team that was engaged in the fight. The leader of the new unit stood in front of me and yelled for me to "shoot the fucking Russians," but I just kept running supplies and bodies back and forth. It had been snowing, so I was slipping and sliding as I tried to stay out of the leader's line of sight. His yelling was finally silenced the morning he was shot dead.

The Russians managed to cross the Narva river and break through our defensive lines. I was terrified but oddly relieved when we were ordered to fall back. Gerhard and I ran for the safety of the woods on the other side of the field hospital.

Our green uniforms stood out against the snow, making it nearly impossible to hide. There were no leaves on the trees or bushes to protect us, and the tracks our boots left in the snow were easy to follow. We kept running west for what seemed like hours. I heard shooting in the distance, but it was hard to tell which direction it came from. Finally, we found a small cropping of juniper trees. Pushing our way through the branches, we kneeled to rest.

"You better damn well be ready to shoot someone, Arnold," Gerhard whispered. He scanned the trees, looking for any movement. "It's shoot them, or they shoot us, and I'm not ready to die." He looked at me. "You got it?"

Just then, a murder of crows took off all together from a tree not too far from us. Gerhard put a finger on his lips and used his first and second fingers to point to his eyes and then out to the woods, signaling for me to scan the woods opposite of him. I heard their boots crunching as they grew closer. My breath became shallow as I scanned the woods, trying to see them. Gerhard and I were kneeling back-to-back. I put the butt of my rifle on my shoulder and took aim, preparing myself to shoot another human being.

Their steps were getting closer. I could hear the snow crunching all around us. *Maybe they were Germans?* That hope was immediately crushed when I heard someone yell in Russian, "You're surrounded. Give up or you're dead." I felt Gerhard shift and put his rifle down. I lowered mine as I saw about twenty men in Russian coats coming out of the woods toward us.

I put my rifle down and held my hands up as I turned to glance at Gerhard. He mouthed, "I'm sorry." The Russians pulled us out of the trees and pushed me face down onto the snow with a gun to my back. They took my knife, handgun, and pack. "Get up," someone said in Russian. A young soldier, maybe about twenty, yanked my wrists together and tied a rope around them so tight, I thought they would start to bleed. Someone from behind me took the hat that Karla had knitted and put a noose around my neck. I watched as someone dug through my bag, eating my food and pulling the gloves Karla had bought me onto his hands.

"Let's just shoot them and move on," one of the Russians said.

I glanced over, my body trembling. "You know Russian?" Gerhard whispered.

"A little," I responded. Vati, Walter, and I had spent nine months in Warsaw on a large electrical job when I was seventeen. We'd been surrounded by Russian speakers, so I'd made a point of trying to learn the language. I could still understand much of what I learned, but I didn't speak much. Someone kicked Gerhard for speaking to me, so I didn't elaborate.

I pushed all other thoughts out of my mind and scanned the woods and the Russians, looking for any opening to escape as the Russian soldiers pushed me and Gerhard forward.

CHAPTER 44

November–December 1944

We marched out of the woods and through the city scarred by war. More Russians appeared with more German soldiers and tied all of us prisoners together. Escape wasn't an option as we made our way to the train tracks. I started to panic as they loaded us into a cattle car. *Where were they taking us?* I knew the further east I went, the harder it would be to escape and get back to Karla. I started to shake as I stood in line waiting my turn to jump up into the car. The noose around my neck was pulled roughly off, and I was pushed forward.

I climbed up into the car full of men and turned to help Gerhard up, offering him my bound hands. He looked at them and then up into my eyes. *He's going to make a run for it.*

"No, Gerhard, don't," I whispered.

Gerhard took a small step back, then looked to his left and to his right. When he tried to make a run for it, three Russian soldiers pointed their guns at him. The scene unfolded before me like a film that had been slowed down.

"No!" I shouted as the shot rang out. The same soldiers turned and pointed their guns at me. I stepped back into the crowded car, my heart racing.

A few minutes later, Gerhard's body was unceremoniously thrown into the car with us, and the doors were closed. There was some light coming between the wooden slats of the car, but it was otherwise dark. I stepped over to Gerhard and felt a faint pulse in his neck. I ripped his shirt open and saw two bullet holes that I put my hands on to try to stem the blood flow. I looked around at the other men. All of them appeared resigned to their fate. When I turned back to Gerhard, his eyes were open, and I could see that he was gone. The train started slowly down the tracks. *Was I in hell now, or was I still going toward it?*

The car smelled of a mixture of urine, feces, and animals. I gently moved Gerhard to the corner and sat down next to his dead body. It was so crowded, men were sitting pressed against me on all sides. No one spoke; no one looked at each other. *How many men had been transported in this car before this? How many animals? Were we going toward the same fate as the animals?* I wondered. *Toward death?*

✢

I don't know how long we were on the train. It seemed like days, but time was like a deep, dark hole with no definition. The car started smelling of Gerhard's corpse, reminding me of Frau Bauer. The train stopped once, and we were allowed out of the car to drink water from a bucket, using a ladle that was provided. I had never been so thirsty before, and my thirst made standing in line very difficult. Some men were kicked for looking at the guards. I glanced quickly at our surroundings and saw that we were in the middle of a field with no cover, and there were guards with guns everywhere. I quickly looked toward the ground so I wouldn't accidentally make eye contact with any of them.

Exhaustion took over between that stop and the next. I fell asleep and stayed that way until the train made a jerking motion and forced me instantly awake with a sense of panic. It was nighttime, and I heard a screeching noise that went on until the train finally came to a stop. I heard the Russians running back and forth and saw their flashlights jumping around against the darkness of the night between the slats that made up the sides of the train car. The Russian guards were yelling too fast for me to understand.

Some time passed, and I heard the lock on the door, then felt the cool breeze as the door swung open. It appeared that we were to be allowed out for a few sips of water using the ladle from the bucket one of the guards carried.

As I waited in line for water, I cautiously looked around to try to figure out what was happening. Two soldiers were directing their flashlights at the coal car. Another stood pointing and saying something I couldn't understand. I saw a man with a black-and-red hat who I assumed was the conductor. The Russian men appeared to be arguing about some kind of problem with the coal car.

Would they give me more water and some food if I helped them? Without looking at any of the guards directly, I pointed and said in Russian, "I might be able to fix the problem." I could feel one of them staring at me for a moment, then he pushed me forward toward the coal car with one hand, his other hand holding a handgun to my back.

He yelled to one of the soldiers with a flashlight, "This guy says he can fix it." He pushed me again and said to me, "If you can't fix it, I will shoot you in the head." I nodded to show I understood. I wondered if the risk was worth it. Though, if I was going to die, I'd prefer it be a quick death. At this thought, I shook my head and told myself, *I can't die. Karla needs me.*

One of the guards reluctantly cut my bonds and gave me his flashlight so I could look under the coal car. I inspected the components but didn't see anything that was obviously wrong. I crawled out from under the car carefully, making sure the guards could see my hands.

"Can you see if there is coal in the engine?" I asked the conductor. He stared at me for a moment. *Had I gotten the words wrong?* He finally walked toward the engine and climbed the ladder. A few minutes later, he poked his head out of the engine room and yelled at me. "No coal!"

"Is there a coal shovel?" I asked.

The conductor stepped back into the engine room and came out holding a shovel that had a wide mouth and small handle. One of the guards ran over and brought the shovel back to me.

I climbed up the ladder on the coal car and saw the car was about a quarter of the way full of coal, enough that the train should still work. I climbed down into the car, holding the flashlight in my mouth and the shovel in my hand. Using the shovel, I moved coal out from the bottom of the long side of the car until I found the conveyor belt. I worked until I had uncovered the entire length of the belt. The movement of the coal created a lot of dust and forced me into coughing fits as I shoveled.

I glanced up and saw two guards with their guns pointed at me. They looked like they were losing patience with the number of times I had to stop and clear my lungs. *Focus on the task,* I told myself.

The conveyor belt was a long, continuous strip of rubber about seven centimeters wide with a textured surface on the outside of the belt that helped carry the coal to the engine. I didn't feel any tears in the belt, so I focused on the tensioner and soon found that it was missing a bolt. This was causing the belt to be loose, so no coal could get to the engine. After a thorough search, I found the missing bolt stuck in the machinery, but the outside of it was smooth, making it impossible for it to be held in place.

Putting the flashlight back in my mouth and holding up my hands, I walked over to the ladder and started to climb. Once I reached the top, I took the flashlight from between my teeth, held the bolt out to one of the guards, and said, "Stripped." I climbed down and walked over to the conductor. After handing him the bolt so he could see the problem, I started walking slowly around the train to find a replacement bolt, all the while keeping my hands in the air.

"Over here," the conductor called to me. He had gotten a toolbox out and handed me a wrench. I walked back to one of the cattle cars and pulled off a bolt from one of the planks of wood.

It didn't take me long to tighten the new bolt into place, adjust the tension, and reload the conveyor belt with coal. By the time I was done, I could feel the soot from the coal all over my hands, arms, and face. I was sure my clothes were black.

I handed the shovel and flashlight to one of the guards, then nodded at the conductor, signaling that it was fixed. I handed him the wrench. I then walked back to my car and stood next to it, awaiting further instructions. One of the guards brought me the bucket of water and allowed me to drink three ladles full. He also gave me a small biscuit, then bound my hands again.

The guards removed Gerhard from the car and left him next to the tracks for the animals to eat. I didn't want to look at him, preferring to remember him as the tough man I had known him to be. As the train started, I held my breath for a few moments, praying that the repair held. As the train continued to lurch forward, I slowly released my breath and closed my eyes.

The further we traveled over the following days, the colder it seemed to get. I assumed we were being moved to a prison camp deep in the Soviet Union, maybe even Siberia. Time had no meaning, with days and nights blending together. I tried to keep my mind off the cold by imagining what Karla and the children were doing. I pictured Karla at her sewing machine, singing as she made hats. I pictured Rolf laughing as he rolled down a hill. I thought of Edith crawling and putting whatever she could find into her mouth as drool dripped off her chin.

The train finally slowed and eventually stopped. When we were taken off the train, we stepped out into snow that was about forty or fifty centimeters high. I felt the cold wet slide into the top of my boots and run down my legs as we walked through the woods. Growing up in Kiel, on the Baltic Sea, I had thought I was used to cold winters. But this place was no comparison. The wind shot through my bones.

The guards pushed and kicked us forward in line. The skin around my wrists was starting to bleed as the rope rubbed back and forth with every step. Several men fell and couldn't get up on their own, so they were beaten and then shot. One was next to me when he was shot, and blood sprayed on my coat. I swallowed the bile that rushed to my throat. Once, I fell, and two guards approached me as I scrambled to stand up. I wondered, *Did they allow me to live because I fixed the train?*

Finally, I saw the guard towers as we approached: first one, then a second. As we got closer to the camp, I saw it was surrounded by a metal fence about two to three meters high and topped with barbed wire. At each corner of the fence stood a five- or six-meter-high tower with a guardhouse on top. Each guardhouse had two machine guns strapped to the railing, and two or three guards walked back and forth, their stern eyes scanning the camp both within and outside the fence.

Two oversized gates swung open to let the prisoners through. Approximately thirty-five were with us at the start of the journey and about twenty were still alive. I kept my face pointed forward but allowed my eyes to scan the camp. It was about fifteen hundred to two thousand square meters. On the far side, opposite the front gate and down a small knoll, staggered with one another, were three long white one-story buildings with no windows. The entrance doors may have been at the opposite end of the buildings; I only knew that they were not visible from where I was standing. Across from them was a small white house, and next to it stood a metal building that looked like a storage room. I could see a gate similar to the entrance gate behind the white house. I glanced to the right of the front gate and saw two additional long white buildings with windows along the sides. Guards were sitting or standing around, smoking cigarettes, so I assumed that was the guards' barracks.

We were shoved forward toward the white buildings in the back. As we walked, I could see that the three buildings were about twenty meters long and ten meters wide. I also saw a smaller building, about ten meters squared, tucked in the back corner with a door at the end and two stalls alongside it.

Much of the ground was muddy, but I saw some remnants of snow against the fence. The guards who walked us in from the train left us just outside the barracks but were quickly replaced by other guards. Inside the building were cots stacked up two high, with about fifty on one side of the building and fifty on the other. It was arranged just like the training camp had been. The guards pushed us roughly through the door, then started pointing: first to a prisoner, then to a cot. Each prisoner sat on his assigned cot and stared straight ahead.

My cot was a bottom cot about midway down. I shifted the thin cotton blanket with brown stains over to the end of the cot and sat. The guards pulled a couple of prisoners out of the barracks and then I heard the showers running. I assumed they were going to force all of us to strip and get under the showers, so I slowly pulled the patch, the drawing from Viggo, and my picture of Karla and the children out of the side of my boot and put them under the blanket. I could feel that they were wet, but I couldn't look at them for fear the guard standing at the door would take them.

I couldn't gauge how long it had been from the first time I heard the showers to when a guard pointed to me then the door. He pushed me roughly through the door. Two guards stood at each stall of the smaller building. The ropes from around my wrists were cut with a large knife. Two prisoners had to undress and walk into each stall. The water that rained down over me was ice. Within two minutes, it felt like needles on every nerve. After five minutes, we were told to get our clothes and get out. There were no towels. When I went to pick my folded clothes up off the small bench next to the shower stall, my boots were gone. I panicked and looked under the bench and all around for them. Someone threw some threadbare soft shoes at me, and I heard laughter among the guards.

My clothes were still sticking to my wet body when a guard walked in with a box. He stopped at each cot and handed a biscuit and a carrot or potato to each prisoner, barely enough to keep anyone alive. I felt under the blanket for the patch and my pictures and was relieved to feel they were where I had left them.

About an hour later, the barracks started filling up with other prisoners. Many of them wore threadbare pants and shirts that hardly covered their bodies. Most were German, but I saw a couple that were Asian. They all were so covered in dirt, the new prisoners could barely tell one man from the next.

CHAPTER 45

January 1945

The sun was barely up when the guards walked through the barracks, yelling. Two guards, each one taking a row of cots, walked by with a bucket of water and a ladle. When it was my turn, I filled the ladle up as much as I could and sucked down every drop of water. We were then ushered out of the barracks and marched out of the camp. In my soft shoes, my feet hurt terribly from the cold snow, and I was convinced I would have frostbite by the end of the day.

On this day, and the ones that followed, we walked around to the back of the camp and then about thirty meters farther to begin a grueling day of labor. The guards split us up into groups. I was in a group assigned to dig holes for mass graves and latrines. Another group cut trees for firewood. There was a third group, but I wasn't sure what they were assigned to as they were marched deeper into the woods.

At the end of each day, we were given three potatoes and some cabbage or beans. I wondered, *Were they limiting our calories so much because they wanted to keep us weak?*

In the camp, there were two generators to provide power: one for the guards' barracks and the other for the commander's house. Unfortunately, the prisoners' barracks lacked heating, which left us constantly shivering in the cold. Many of us, myself included, suffered from frequent coughing fits. I suspected I had pneumonia, but the fear of being shot if I didn't get up for work kept me from seeking help. The Russian guards shot anyone who they felt was slacking off for any reason.

One night, a guard came to me and yanked me out of bed. Since I had no other clothes, I was already dressed. I kept my inadequate shoes on my feet at all times for fear that they would be stolen too. My pictures and patch were securely under the laces.

I was too tired and weak to be scared, so I just followed the guard across the camp. He led me to the back side of the guards' barracks and pointed to the generator. "Fix it. Now." It occurred to me that someone must have remembered that I'd fixed the train. When I hesitated, he pulled his handgun out of the holster attached to his belt and pointed it at me.

I immediately stepped up to the generator to start figuring out what was wrong. Someone had left a wrench and screwdriver on the ground. The guard shined a flashlight at the generator so I could see and told me it wouldn't turn on. I took the top off the gas tank to make sure there was gas, then squatted in front of it and tried to turn it on. The guard kicked me in the ribs, and I fell to the ground. I got back up and tried to start it again. It started for two seconds and then stopped.

After spending a few more minutes troubleshooting, I pulled the ignition switch off and cleaned all the contacts, then put it back on and tightened everything I could get to with the screwdriver and wrench. By the time I turned the generator on, my hands were hurting from the cold as badly as my feet. Not wanting to be kicked or shot, I prayed the generator would remain on. After several minutes, I nodded to the guard and handed him the tools.

On the way back to the prisoner barracks, another guard walked out of the guard barracks and handed me two small raw potatoes and a piece of smoked fish. I nodded my thanks and made sure to eat it all before I entered the prisoner barracks, fearing someone would take my food.

That night proved to be a turning point for my life as a prisoner. In the days after I fixed the guards' generator, I found myself tasked with care of the camp itself. This was much easier labor than the work I'd been doing, and from then on, I was fed a biscuit or egg for breakfast in addition to the food I was given in the evening. I fixed everything from a door to a section of fencing to the roof on the commander's house. The guards seemed to trust me more each week, which allowed me to live and work on the fringes of both the guard and the prisoner populations.

As time went on, I started thinking about what I would do if I could escape, or if the war ended. *How would I survive? How would I get home?* The beginnings of plans started to take root in my mind. Anytime I was called to do a job, I looked for opportunities to steal small, inconsequential things. Once, I found a small knife that someone had dropped, and I tied it against my skin with a piece of twine I found to hide it. I was given tools to work with every day, but they were counted each time I received them and each time I gave them back, so I was always very careful to return anything I was given.

CHAPTER 46

May 1945

Spring was a welcome respite from the coldness of winter. One afternoon, I heard a commotion as I was standing in front of the generator located at the back of the camp commander's house, troubleshooting why it wouldn't turn on. The noise seemed to be coming from the front of the house, so I stepped quietly around the side to see what was going on.

Guards were taking boxes out of the commander's house and loading them into the back of a truck. I strained to hear what they were saying. "War ended," said one. "Ceasefire," said another. After a few minutes, the guards jumped into jeeps and trucks and drove off, following the commander's truck, leaving the front gates open.

I quickly ran through the back door into the commander's house and locked the front and back doors. I brought to mind the list in my head that I had been reciting for several months and started searching for things I would need to survive.

There was a single bed in the corner, covered neatly with a sheet and blanket. I untucked these and started looking for and putting provisions on them, all the while glancing out the windows to make sure no one was coming. I chuckled a little, thinking I would look like St.

Nicholas with my long beard and long hair and carrying a white sack over my shoulder as I made my escape.

I found a head of cabbage, two carrots, four potatoes, a half-eaten loaf of bread, one dried perch, an egg, a piece of cheese, and a half-eaten bowl of borscht. I put everything on the bed except for the borscht. That I quickly ate as I walked around, looking for other things. Next, I located a small pan, a knife, and a fork and spoon that I added to my pack.

I glanced out the window and saw a group of prisoners running out the front gate. I didn't blame them for wanting to get away from this hellhole as fast as possible. *But how did they plan to survive without provisions?*

I saw another group of prisoners running into the guards' barracks, presumably looking for food or water. I knew it was only a matter of minutes before they came to the commander's house. The house was located at the far end of the compound, but I needed to hurry. I searched through the house, opening cabinets, moving a dresser, and looking under the bed. My boots! I quickly traded the old shoes for my boots and carefully put my pictures and patch safely against my leg. I also found a Russian soldier's uniform. Knowing it would provide me, a German in Russia, a way to blend in, I took that too.

I gathered the ends of the sheets to make a sack and walked quietly out the back door. I was surprised to see the old truck I'd fixed the month before still sitting there. *Had the guards forgotten that I fixed it?* I could start it without keys with no problem, but I wasn't sure how much gas it had.

I walked behind the house to the truck and placed my collection in the back. It was then that I noticed the flat tire. Presumably, that was why no one had taken it.

I quietly opened the driver's side door and squatted down to reach the electronics that would start the truck. I pulled out the four wires I needed from under the steering wheel and connected the two ignition wires. At that moment, I heard one of the prisoners yell something from the front of the house. My heart jumped, so I waited, listening. I heard another prisoner yell from across the camp and focused on my breathing. My entire body was tense as I waited for someone to find me.

After ten minutes, no other noise came from around the house, so I scrambled into the truck, closed the door quietly, and lay down on the front seat. I decided to wait a few hours until dark. If anyone found me, I could tell them I was getting the truck ready for all of us. I knew not everyone would fit in the truck, but it was the best I could think of to buy time. I prayed no one would walk to the back of the house.

Once things started quieting down, I crawled out of the truck and over to the corner of the house to see what was happening. I counted about twenty prisoners sitting around a fire in various chairs they'd no doubt pulled from the guards' barracks. Another dozen or so men were sitting on the ground or in chairs just outside the guards' barracks front door.

I crawled back into the house to get a bucket I had seen just inside the back door. Then I went quietly back to the generator, disconnected the fuel hose from the carburetor, and watched the fuel run into the bucket. I then put the fuel from the bucket into the truck's gas tank. Satisfied with my progress, I replaced the flat tire with the spare. By then, the sky was completely dark, and the prisoners were quieter.

I opened the driver's side door and took a deep breath. *Was I strong enough to push the truck closer to the gate?* I wanted to turn on the engine at the last possible moment. If the other prisoners caught up with me, they would take both my provisions and the truck. *Can I really leave these men here to die?* I thought of Karla and pushed the truck forward.

I pushed the truck about ten meters from the back gate and bent down to touch the two starter solenoid wires together. The engine turned over and I jumped in, putting the truck in drive and pressing the gas as far as it would go.

The sound woke all the prisoners, and I heard them shouting as they ran toward me. I drove the truck right through the back gates. The truck surged forward, and time stood still as I navigated through the woods, down the hill to a small dirt road. I looked behind me and saw that a couple of prisoners had nearly caught up to the truck. One even tried to grab onto the back to pull himself in, but he couldn't hold on, and eventually, he too fell away.

I drove for two hours until my adrenaline started to dissipate, and then I pulled over. There by the side of the road, I cried like I had never cried before, hitting the steering wheel with both palms. All through the war, I had gone out of my way not to kill another human being. But in the end, I had left thirty or more men to potentially die in the middle of Siberia. I cried for Reinhard, Gerhard, Horst, Franz, and Helmut. I cried for all the men I'd seen die, regardless of their nationality.

When I was finally spent, I took a deep breath and changed into the Russian uniform I had found in the commander's house. As an afterthought, I used my small knife to cut the calf of my leg, then tore a piece of the sheet to make a bandage, which I wrapped around my neck after putting blood on it. If someone found me, I would pretend to be a Russian commander who was wounded.

I drove another couple of hours before pulling over to get some rest, dragging my sack into the cab, and waiting for the sun to rise so I knew which direction to go.

I woke up to the sun blinding me, so I knew I was facing east. I touched the two wires together to start the truck and turned it around so I was going west. I dug into my sack and pulled out a carrot to eat as I started my westward journey.

CHAPTER 47

May 1945

It was afternoon when the truck finally ran out of gas. I pulled out my sack and started walking into the woods, thinking I would have an easier time finding places to hide from prisoners or Russians there. I divided my food into rations: two pieces of cabbage and a carrot or potato each day. This would give me seven or ten days of food and hopefully time enough for me to find more.

After three days of hiking through the woods, I came upon a small field. It felt strange to walk out into an open space after having been cocooned in the safety of trees and shrubs for so long, so I paused at the edge of the woods to get my bearings. The field was about one hundred meters wide and one thousand meters long, with tall grass and a few rhododendrons. Directly across from where I was standing was a small cabin. There was a window to the right of the front door and a small porch with an overhang. Through it, I saw a wooden rocking chair next to a rusted basin. I stood watching the cabin for any movement. After about twenty minutes, it started to rain.

Soon, it was pouring, so I decided to take the risk and ran across the field, the tall grass rubbing against my pants, leaving wet marks. My eyes constantly scanned the cabin and the surrounding woods for any movement as I got closer. My hair was dripping, and my clothes were soaked by the time I stepped onto the small porch.

With my heart racing, I quietly lifted the small handle and pushed the door slightly open. I peered in and saw a dark, dusty cabin that smelled moldy with rotting wood. Satisfied that the cabin was vacant, I pushed the door wider. The cabin was only one room: about three meters by three meters. There was a small sink in the corner across from the door with a metal bucket under it and a wooden bucket beside it. A small oak table with three mismatched wooden chairs stood in front of the sink area. In the opposite corner was a pile of wood. A fireplace with a cast-iron pot sat in the center of the wall adjacent to the window. There was an old brown sofa in front of the fireplace. A single bed was behind the sofa.

My mouth watered as I thought about the two small perch I had caught earlier with a stick I carved into a spear. I decided to wait until dark to cook them to avoid the risk of someone seeing the smoke from the fireplace. For now, I laid the fish in the sink, then took my clothes off and hung them on two of the chairs around the table to dry.

I smiled, thinking that if anyone walked in, they would have a huge surprise seeing a skinny, naked bearded man walking around. I wedged the third chair against the door handle to give me time to get up if someone tried to enter. Finally, I lay down on the bed to rest.

I must have been even more tired than I thought because it was completely dark when I woke. I felt around until I found the lantern and matches I had seen on the kitchen table. After lighting the lantern, I kept the flame low just in case someone walked by the cabin. Then I got to work building a small fire in the fireplace and cooking my dinner.

After falling asleep again, I woke just before dawn and left the cabin. I would have liked to stay, but I didn't want to risk someone showing up, like the owner or other prisoners. Plus, I had to get home to Karla.

Over the next two weeks, the terrain started becoming hillier and harder to walk. One warm sunny day, I heard the sound of water in the distance, so I adjusted my direction somewhat, eventually finding a beautiful river with large enough rocks that I would be able to walk across it and continue my westward journey. I walked through a sandy beach area about ten meters wide and twenty meters long and started hopping from rock to rock across the river.

When I reached the middle, I stopped on a boulder to admire the beauty around me. I was surrounded by a mix of mature pine, spruce, and fir trees, along with a variety of bushes on each side of the riverbank. I pulled my bowl out of my pack so I could have a drink, and when I was done, I resumed hopping from rock to rock to get to the other side.

After a few moments, I paused once more to enjoy the peaceful sound of the water moving over the rocks and the small breeze that blew the ends of my long hair. Suddenly, I heard human voices and quickly crouched down behind the closest boulder to figure out where they were coming from. I scanned the woods and saw movement, squinting slightly to be sure they were on the east side of the river before starting again toward the west side.

Keeping my eyes on that movement meant taking my eyes off where I was putting my feet, and this was the cause of my downfall. In one swift motion, I stepped on an unstable rock, and my foot went into the water. Instantly, a sharp pain radiated from my ankle. I was three meters from shore, trying to pull my boot out, but it became stuck between two large rocks when one of them shifted.

I knelt as low as I could and untied my boot. This allowed me to slip my foot out, which in turn created room to shift the rock and pull out my boot. I caught a glimpse of three men, each carrying a rifle. I ran as low as possible to shore, feeling a sharp pain in my ankle that worsened as I stepped up on the riverbank. I knelt down and crawled the rest of the way into bushes of pine and honeysuckle, pulling my provisions behind me. I lowered myself to my stomach and used my elbows to crawl into the thicket, positioning myself so I could watch the men.

Hopefully, they will keep moving, I said to myself. My heart sank when I heard bits of their conversation above the flowing water: "getting dark," "camping," and "morning." I watched them as they set up a campsite on the small beach directly across the river from me.

As the sun went down, the men sat around their fire, cooking fish and sausage, the scent making my mouth water and exacerbating my hunger pains. They shared a bottle of what I assumed was vodka or schnapps, passing it back and forth. The more they drank, the louder their laughing and singing became throughout the evening.

Hours later, the campfire still blazed against the pitch-black night as the men continued their impromptu party. I desperately had to urinate, so I very slowly moved my body around and turned to my side to relieve myself. I hoped that no animals would want to explore the smell.

༄

I awakened to the noise of the men packing up their campsite. *Please don't cross the river,* I thought. My entire body seemed to relax as I watched them continue on a northerly trek.

CHAPTER 48

June 1945

My ankle was so swollen and bruised, I couldn't get my boot on. I added the boot to my provisions pack, then crawled around to find a branch suitable to be made into a walking stick. After testing the stick out, I determined that walking with my pack in one hand and the stick in another wasn't possible, especially in the mountainous terrain. I calculated that I had been walking just over three weeks. A day of rest, hiding in the bushes with a water source close by, was in order.

The swelling had gone down enough for me to put my boot on the next day. When I tested my ankle, the pain wasn't as sharp, so I continued my westward trek, although more slowly than before. I ate the last of my food and finding more quickly became a priority.

After a few hours of hobbling, I found a lingonberry bush and started gorging myself, enjoying the tart fruit immensely. I finally discarded my walking stick, filled up my bowl with lingonberries, and continued walking.

It was late afternoon when I heard the rhythmic sound of horse hooves striking the ground, along with the rattle of wagon wheels rolling over the uneven surface of the dirt road. I ignored the pain in my ankle and started running toward the sound. As soon as I saw the horse-drawn wagon, I squatted down to watch.

An old man sat on a bench, holding the horses' reigns. Sacks were stacked neatly in the back of his wagon, and a box stood just behind his seat. He was following the westbound road. *Could I make up the time I just lost and get a ride?* I looked down at my ankle and decided to give it a try, so I quickly pulled on the Russian uniform jacket along with the bloody bandage, securing it around my neck.

Despite the pain in my ankle, I ran through the woods to a point just ahead of the horses, then slowly walked out and put my hand in the air for the old man to stop. I reminded myself not to speak for fear he would hear my German accent.

The old man halted the horse, and I pointed to the seat next to him. "Do you need a ride?" he asked.

I indicated the bandage around my neck and nodded.

He pointed with his thumb to the back of the wagon. "Put your sack in the back and climb up here." He shifted over, pointing now to the seat next to him. Once I was settled, he clicked his tongue and slapped the horses with the reins.

I was grateful he wasn't the talking type. We sat in silence as the horses meandered down the road. After an hour, the old man pulled up to an intersection and started to turn north. I tapped him on the shoulder and pointed west.

He pulled on the reins to stop the horses. "Sorry, my home is another twenty minutes north of here," he said. "You're welcome to come. My house is full of family, but we'll make room."

The thought of a clean place to stay and a homecooked meal was enticing, but I couldn't take the chance, so I shook my head and climbed down. As I reached up to get my sack, I met the old man's eyes and nodded my thanks.

His stare made me panic a bit as a thought occurred to me. *Was he suspicious because of my long hair and beard? Wouldn't a Russian soldier have short hair and be clean shaven?* My entire body tensed, ready to run back into the woods, when I saw him reach behind his seat. *Was he pulling out his gun?*

He must have seen something in my eyes because he held up his left hand to reassure me and handed me a can of meat with his right.

I felt lucky that there were lakes and rivers for food and water as I walked. But the hills soon became steeper and the air cooler, making me concerned about what food I could find in the mountainous region. I made the decision to spend one day fishing.

I caught four small perches and one roach fish, cleaned them, then cooked them over a small fire. Afterward, I broke them up and put them in my bowl, then covered the bowl with a piece of sheet I cut off to carry food.

CHAPTER 49

August–October 1945

I was in the mountains and running low on food again when I heard water cascading. That meant fresh water and a source of food, so I followed the sound. As I came out of some evergreen shrubs, I looked up to find a beautiful twenty-meter-high waterfall. The crest of the falls was about ten meters wide, and the water fell into a clear pond that appeared maybe five or six meters deep.

I carefully walked across the wet rocks and boulders that formed a natural barrier around the pond. I could see some minnows darting around. *Does that mean there are bigger fish somewhere?* As I approached the bottom of the waterfall, I saw a shallow cave and rocks being warmed by the sun. The waterfall was so powerful, it was blowing my long hair and beard, and I could feel a cool mist on my face and hands. I couldn't resist the pull to take advantage of the spot further.

After dropping my pack in the cave, I found some wood nearby and built a small fire, thinking the mountains surrounding me would block any smoke. Still dressed in my clothes, I ventured into the clear cold water. I swam to the waterfall and used it as a shower, rubbing my hair and my clothes in an attempt to get some dirt off. I thought it was the best shower I had ever had, probably because I was so dirty.

When I returned to the cave, I undressed and wrung as much excess water out of my clothes as I could, then laid them on the rocks to dry in the sun. *What a sight. A naked German in the middle of the Soviet Union,* I laughed to myself.

༺༻

Days seemed to blend into each other as I walked, sunrise and sunset being the only things that marked the passage of one to the next. I could only guess at how many days it had been since I was captured. My time boiled down to walking, foraging for food and water, and indulging in my memories.

I borrowed a friend's bicycle, and with Rolf in the front basket, we rode the twenty minutes to the farm. I took Rolf camping just behind my parents' house in case he got scared, but to a three-year-old, it was a big adventure.

The leaves were starting to change color. *Would I make it past the mountains before winter set in?* As I climbed higher through the mountains, it got colder, and soon more of the leaves were on the ground than in the trees. I had no map and no way of knowing exactly where I was. I woke each day at dawn and followed the sun.

CHAPTER 50

November 1945

I made it past the mountains into the foothills on the other side, but the air was becoming too cold to sleep outside. Although I desperately wanted to get home to my family, I needed to find a place to stay until spring. The last thing I wanted was to get turned around and freeze to death in one of those severe Soviet winters I had heard about.

I had just climbed a huge rocky hill and was taking some time to tend to my feet since they had been bleeding on and off. I used pine resin and yarrow to make a paste to soothe them, something Vati had taught me to do when we were working in Warsaw. I wrapped each foot with strips of cloth I cut from the old sheet. *I need a new sheet,* I thought.

When I looked out over the valley, I saw a faint line of smoke trail up like a wispy ribbon in the breeze. *Was there a barn there I could stay in?* I packed my meager belongings and started down the hill, climbing over or around boulders as I made my way toward the smoke.

When I finally reached the source of the smoke, I stayed hidden behind some evergreen bushes and scanned the small farm. There was a small house, like the cabin I had stayed in, but larger. Across the yard was a two-story barn with a paddock surrounding the back side.

A horse was drinking from a bucket attached to the side of the fence. There was a chicken coop on stilts running along the side of the barn and a tractor to the left of the coop. The farm was surrounded by hills on three sides.

I stayed in the trees and bushes as I moved so I could approach the barn from the back. Leaving my pack on the outskirts of the farm, I slowly walked to the chicken coop. As soon as I put my hand on one of the eggs, I heard a bullet being loaded into a gun chamber behind me. I turned slowly around. Grateful to have remembered my fake bandage and Russian uniform, I pointed to my neck and shook my head.

"Get out!" she said in Russian. I put my hands in the air and took a step back. Just as I was about to take a few more steps, a pair of children came around the corner of the barn. They glanced at me and at the woman before running to hide behind her. The girl looked to be about six and the boy maybe eight. My heart was beating out of my throat as I kept one hand up and reached into my pocket with the other hand. The woman lifted her gun higher, ready to shoot. I slowly pulled out the picture of Karla, Rolf, and Edith and held it up so she could see my family. Then I let my jacket drop to the ground and turned around, lifting my shirt so she could see I had no weapons. I wanted to speak to plead my case, but I feared that hearing someone with a German accent would make her more likely to shoot me.

I saw a nearly depleted wood stack behind her, and an ax stuck in a larger piece in a nearby pile of wood. I walked over, pointed to myself and then to the ax and made a chopping motion with my hand. She didn't move, so I pulled the ax out and started chopping. The woman kept the gun on me and said nothing as I chopped wood and stacked the pieces against the barn wall. She started lowering her gun after about twenty minutes, so I kept chopping. After an hour, I stopped and handed the ax to her, handle first.

I smiled my most friendly smile. The woman turned to her children and said, "Go in the house." To my relief, she held the gun so the barrel was pointed toward the ground. I watched as the children took off running, and she started to follow. Then she paused and looked at me. "Wait here," she said.

A few minutes later, she came out with a glass of water and a bowl of cooked cabbage, which I gladly accepted.

She opened the barn door and pointed. "You can stay for one night." Then she turned around and walked back to the house.

It was late afternoon when I sat on a fallen log and ate my cooked cabbage. I didn't go to the barn yet. I wanted to understand my circumstances before getting my pack and settling in.

It was dusk by the time I finished eating. I walked to the front porch and placed the bowl and glass down next to the wooden rocking chair, then quietly looked in the windows, feeling like I was doing something illegal or immoral. The cabin was one large room with a large bed on one wall and a fireplace on the other. The woman sat on the sofa between her two children, reading a book. Feeling satisfied that I was in no present danger, I retrieved my pack and went to the barn.

The next morning, I woke at dawn and started working on the farm before anyone else got up. *Maybe my work will pay for the night she let me stay; maybe she will let me stay longer.* I milked the cow, cleaned out the horse's stall, fed and watered the horse, then started chopping and stacking more wood.

The woman watched me suspiciously from her porch before starting her own chores. No words were exchanged about me leaving, so I decided to stay as long as she let me. Every day that I worked, she brought me food and water around sunset and allowed me to stay in the barn. After a while, I started leaving wood outside her front door to make it easier for her to keep the wood stove burning for heat. There was also a small wood stove in the barn that I lit first thing in the morning and evenings for an hour. Having grown up on a farm, I knew what needed to be done. The work was hard, but nowhere near the work I had to do at the prison camp.

CHAPTER 51

December 1945–January 1946

I started working on the tractor that had a plow attached to it. It had been snowing since early morning, and I wanted to get it fixed so I wouldn't have to shovel out the paddock and barn area for the animals. The woman walked up to me with a white towel hanging on her arm and a bar of soap in her hand.

"You stink," she said. She handed me the towel and soap. "If you're going to stay here, you need a bath." She started to walk away, then looked back. "Follow me."

I had been married for eight years to an independent woman, so I knew better than to argue. Also, I knew I stunk because I could barely stand myself. I followed her to the back of the house where there was a smaller building I hadn't seen before. On a small table was a pile of neatly folded clothes. *Were those her husband's clothes?* She pointed to them. "Put these on, and I'll wash your clothes tomorrow." Then she turned and walked through the back door of the house.

Inside the bathhouse was a white metal tub next to a toilet with a wooden seat. I sat down and pulled my boots off as I watched the steam rising from the water.

I quickly closed the bathhouse door and got undressed, then slowly slid into the most amazing bath I had ever taken. I reached for the soap I left on the floor next to the tub and started cleaning layers of dirt off my skin.

The bath water was so dirty when I stood up, it was embarrassing. I got dressed and put my fake bandage back on my neck, then emptied the tub and wiped it out with the towel. Once I was satisfied the bathhouse was clean, I walked around to the front of the house and hung the towel on the porch to dry.

The woman was standing on the top step. "Come sit so I can cut your hair short. You may have lice."

I stepped onto the porch and sat.

"I'm Elena," she said as she started cutting off large chunks of my hair.

"Boris," I whispered softly.

When she was done, I rubbed my hand along my shaved jaw. It was the most human I felt since leaving home in April 1944. On the way back to the barn, I heard Elena giggle when I jumped up and twirled around, showing off my newly clean face and head.

Months had passed since I first arrived at the farm, and we had fallen into a comfortable routine of chores and playing with the children. But I still had not spoken above a soft whisper, fearing she would find out she was providing room and board to a German and either kick me out or shoot me.

⚭

It had been snowing for days, and snow drifts were forming against the barn. I was sipping my afternoon watered-down coffee and standing against the barn door jamb, watching the snow. *I'll plow tomorrow,* I thought to myself. Suddenly, I heard a gut-wrenching howl from the back side of the barn. I knew right away it was the boy, Nikolai. Dropping my coffee cup on the ground, I ran in the direction of the cry.

The scene was horrifying. Nikolai was lying in the snow, his leg stuck under one of the tractor wheels. He was screaming. Elena ran up behind me and screamed as she ran to him. I tried pushing the tractor off him, but it wouldn't budge in the snow. I knelt and tried pulling snow from around the wheels.

"Boris! We have to get it off him!" Elena shouted with tears running down her cheeks.

I was afraid to put extra weight on the tractor, but I had no choice. "As soon as the tractor moves, pull him out," I said in Russian.

I started the tractor and moved it. "He's out!" Elena yelled a moment later.

I jumped down from the tractor. "Pack snow around his leg but don't move him yet." I ran into the barn and got a thin piece of wood about thirty centimeters long from the pile of scrap wood I had stacked in the corner. I grabbed my old sheet and tore the remaining cloth into strips as I ran back to the boy.

Sofia was sitting next to her brother crying when I arrived.

"We are going to put this under his leg to stabilize it," I said as I handed Elena one of the boards.

I knelt down and gently ran my hands along his leg, feeling for any protruding bones or blood. I pulled his leg up slightly, and Elena pushed the board under it. We worked together to tie the strips of cloth that would keep the board in place.

I picked Nikolai up then and, cradling him against my chest, walked across the yard toward the house with Elena and Sofia following. Elena ran ahead and opened the door. I put the boy gently on the sofa and wiped the tears from his cheeks.

"Can you call a doctor?" I moved out of the way as Elena sat on the edge of the sofa next to Nikolai.

"No, they're all at war or dead." She brushed Nikolai's hair and pulled a blanket off the back of the sofa, tucking him in. "The closest doctor is at least two hours from here."

⌇

A few hours later, I heard a knock on the barn door. I pulled the door open, and Elena stood there with a plate covered with a light-blue towel. She pulled the towel off and handed me a plate of warm bread. We stood there for a few moments, looking at each other. I knew what

I had done. I had spoken Russian to her, and not in a whisper. *Had I given myself away?*

"You're not Russian, and you're not wounded," she said. She didn't sound angry. I looked down at the ground, then back at her.

"You speak Russian with an accent," she said lightly. My heart skipped a couple of beats. *Was she going to throw me out into the cold?* She stayed a few moments longer, but when I said nothing, she turned to leave. "I don't care. You seem decent enough, and I like hearing your voice."

CHAPTER 52

February 1946

In the days following the tractor accident, I was invited to the house for meals. Elena was impressed that I cleared my plate and helped clean the dishes. She said my wife had taught me well. I played cards with the children. And after they went to sleep, Elena and I talked for hours on the sofa in front of the fire. Between my time in the prison camp and my time with the family, my Russian had begun to improve.

I learned that Elena's husband had been called to serve in the Russian military. He had been gone for two years. During that time, her father and uncle both died, and life on the farm became very hard. I asked her why she hadn't moved closer to town. She looked at me in surprise and said, "The town is thirty minutes away by horse." Thoughts started running through my head. *What if someone comes to check on her and they find a German? What will happen to Elena and her children? What will happen to me?*

"You're tense. What are you thinking?" she asked.

"I don't want to create problems for you and your children if anyone were to come here," I replied.

Elena stood up from the sofa and folded the blanket she had wrapped around her legs. I took that as my cue to leave and stood up.

"I have no more family left, and most people are just trying to survive the winter," she said. "No one will come."

✢

One afternoon, Elena and I went hunting in the woods near the farm. I carried the rifle so she could focus on trudging through the high snow. I scanned the area, looking for animals or animal tracks in the snow.

"I was drafted into the war," I said quietly as we walked. I considered how much to tell her. "I pretended to be a horrible marksman so that I wouldn't have to shoot anyone."

I pointed to some rabbit tracks, and we started following them.

"Shooting one person was enough in my lifetime . . ." My words trailed off.

After a few minutes of walking, Elena said softly, "Do you want to tell me about it?"

"I practiced marksmanship with my brothers as a teenager for years. Eventually my ability was even greater than theirs." I put my hand on Elena's arm to stop her from walking. "I won a contest when I was sixteen." I put the butt of the rifle on my shoulder and fired at a white rabbit.

Elena walked ahead and picked up the dead animal, looking pleased. She said, "We'll eat rabbit stew like kings tonight." The sun had begun to go down, so we started back in the direction of the farm.

"There was this man from our village who had come back from the first war in 1918," I said. Elena walked a step ahead of me, and I watched a thin trail of blood drip from the rabbit. "Before the war, he was the mayor of our village. Everyone loved him. He always had interesting, funny stories and treated everyone with respect."

We climbed over a fallen tree. "When he returned from fighting in the war, however, he wasn't the same man. He was often angry and thought people were out to get him. For years, he barely left his house. If he occasionally ventured out, people tended to avoid him. His wife finally left him, taking the children to live near her brother in Hamburg, two hours away."

We stepped out of the wooded area. I could see the farm now. I paused and looked around as we walked, always vigilant, watching for anything different. Guarding against the possibility of anyone coming to harm us. "I don't know what brought Herr Koch to our farm that day."

We started walking toward the farm again. "I was sixteen at the time. I was in the barn when my sister Kaethe came running in, screaming for me to come. Kaethe pushed a rifle into my hands, and I followed her toward the house."

When we got to the paddock, I leaned with my back against the fence and looked back up the hill into the woods. "My mother was standing in the garden with her hands up. Herr Koch was pointing a gun at her. I yelled at him to drop his gun. When he didn't, I raised my gun as I walked toward them." I handed Elena her rifle. "I could see in his eyes that he was seeing something in his mind that we couldn't understand. His eyes were wild and glassed over. I heard a click as he pulled the hammer back to take his shot."

I looked into Elena's eyes and saw compassion. "I didn't have a choice. I pulled the trigger and watched him fall. My bullet went right through the center of his head. My mother screamed and had his blood on her cheek."

"I had known Herr Koch my entire life. He was one of my brother Heinz's best friends. The rabbit you're holding is the first time I have shot a gun and killed anything since that day."

There were unshed tears in Elena's eyes. "Was your brother angry?"

"No, Heinz died in 1917 in the first war. My father and my other brothers understood." There was nothing left to say, and I was drowning in sorrow, so I turned and walked to the barn, and I quietly shut the door.

CHAPTER 53

April 1946

By the beginning of April, we could see large portions of the muddy ground where the snow had been. Elena drew me a map of the Soviet Union and pointed out the location of her home, just west of the Ural Mountains. My heart raced as I thought about how much farther I had to travel. *Was it possible for me to walk all the way to Kiel, Germany?*

Seeing the look on my face, Elena touched my arm. "Maybe you should see if you can get on a train."

The following day, I had just finished pulling six eggs out of the chicken coop and was walking around the barn to bring them to Elena when I saw a man crossing the yard. I stopped short, feeling the blood drain from my head. I quickly stepped back into the shadow of the barn to watch and prepare myself mentally for killing this man if he bothered Elena and her children.

Then I heard the front door slam, and Elena ran outside into the man's waiting arms. Her husband had returned home. The children watched shyly from the front porch. I wasn't sure what they remembered of their father. *Will my own children remember me?* I was happy for her but knew I couldn't take the risk of him shooting me or turning me over to the authorities.

I quickly collected my provisions while keeping an eye on Elena and her husband through the door I left cracked open. Elena had sewn an old tablecloth into a sling pack so I could keep my hands free. I put my Russian jacket, an extra shirt, my knife, a cup, some dried fish, and my bowl with the six eggs into my new pack and quickly walked out the back and up the hill into the woods. It would have been nice to say goodbye, but I knew Elena would understand, and eventually the children would forget about me.

CHAPTER 54

June 1946

To keep from going crazy from the loneliness of walking, I talked to the animals. Squirrels were everywhere, collecting food and scurrying up trees whenever they saw me. I saw a bear and her cubs on the opposite side of a river I was walking alongside and picked my way carefully away to keep from disturbing them. The last thing I needed was an angry mama bear.

My favorite creature was the fox that one day started following me. He was curious enough to trail along after me as I threw a few small morsels of food at him but scared enough to stay a safe distance. I talked to him as if he was a human traveling companion, telling him stories about growing up on a farm. I enjoyed the company even though he didn't engage in conversation. He must have tired of me eventually, though, because I woke one morning to find him gone. I kept hoping he would come back, but I never saw him again.

An old man gave me a ride in the back of his truck one day. After an hour, I felt the truck slowing down, so turned to see what was going on. He stopped in front of a dead body. My hands started shaking when I saw the old tattered pants of a Nazi uniform. I watched the old man get out of his truck and poke the body with his boot. "Good riddance. Another German dead," he mumbled as he got back into the driver's seat and started driving again.

Finding water each day was always a big challenge. I needed to find something I could carry water in, and although I likely could have stolen a bucket somewhere, I thought carrying one would be a detriment to my progress. My bowl worked well, but it didn't hold enough water to last for days if I couldn't find a water source.

One day I came upon a dead elk. I worked quickly to cut a large section of meat with plenty of skin. I had been a boy the last time I dried animal skin, but I was sure I could use it to create a vessel for water.

Normally, I didn't want to get my feet wet, but I couldn't take the chance of animals following me for the meat I was carrying. So I walked for hours in the middle of a stream until I found a shallow dugout along the bank where the water had once flooded and eroded the area. It gave me a little protection and a good view up and downstream to see any unwanted visitors.

I built a small fire and separated the meat from the skin, then put the meat in my pan over the fire to cook so I could take it with me for meals. Then I wrapped the skin around a rock and added it near the fire to dry out in the shape of a vessel. The drying process took an entire night and part of the next day. I used my twine to close the skin, making a sack for water.

One day, two older women allowed me to ride in the back of their truck. It was raining, but I appreciated the opportunity to rest my feet. I felt immensely grateful as they drove across the bridge of a wide river with a swiftly running current. There would have been no way for me to walk across that torrential river. I saw a town ahead of us, so I knocked on the window for them to stop. Then I stepped back into the serene embrace of the forest, leaving the ladies to their own adventures.

After a while, I found myself in the woods of another mountainous region. Foraging for food was difficult there, but by then, I had learned to like lichen to survive. I found it growing on the rocks and was able to scrape some off to eat as I walked. It is a horrible-tasting fungus, but the particular lichen I found was full of nutrients and helped feed me as I walked. I also found a small bit of water coming off the boulders and was able to fill my water vessel.

Later, I came across a herd of elk lounging in a field in the sun. I saw one male elk surrounded by his harem, some teenage elk, and a few baby elks. They looked smaller than the ones I had seen in Germany but were majestic nonetheless. Living on the farm had taught me respect for wild animals, and elks were no exception.

I stayed in the trees, ensuring there was a lot of space between me and the elk. A few were eating the grass and turned to look my way, sensing I was there. But they made no move to run.

CHAPTER 55

July–August 1946

It had been weeks since I saw another human. I was walking through plains with some low hills for a couple of days when I saw city lights ahead of me. As I got closer, I could hear a train's whistle. *Do I have enough courage to walk into the city and get on a train?*

I adjusted the fake bandage around my neck so the dried blood was at my throat but decided not to wear my Russian solider jacket, not knowing exactly where I was or how the local people felt about soldiers.

Staying in the shadows of buildings as much as possible, I walked around, looking for the train station. As I walked, I heard music, so I made a quick detour and followed the sounds to a pub. Leaning up against the back of the building, I closed my eyes for a moment to listen. Karla would have been able to name the composers and their backgrounds. One memory was so clear, I could feel tears in the back of my eyes. Karla and I had danced in a pub similar to this one on our wedding day. She had smiled and looked at me with so much love and devotion.

A door slammed and I smelled a cigarette, so I shook off the memories and continued walking until I found the train station.

Once I was inside, I saw a sign that said I was in the city of Stryi. My heart started pounding as I thought, *This could be an area that was occupied by Nazis during the war. What would these people think about being in the presence of a German?* I adjusted my fake bandage and studied the Soviet Union map on the wall. I felt relieved to see how far I had come from Elena's house. The station wasn't full, but there were a few people milling around, waiting for the next train. I had no idea whether Budapest would be safe, but I couldn't ask. It was in the right direction, so I decided to take the chance and try to get a ticket.

My hands shook as I approached the ticket counter. I pointed on the map where I wanted to go and looked at the old man behind the counter. I had no money and prayed he would take pity on me. After a few moments of him looking into my eyes, I started to back away. To my surprise, he pushed a ticket under the window.

"My son went to war," he said. "And I am hopeful that someone will give him a ticket to come home."

∾

A few people glanced curiously at me as I boarded train number four, but they quickly looked away, dismissing me when I smiled. It was nice to take a break from walking. My palms were sweaty, and my heart raced each time the train stopped at a station to let passengers on or off. My stress level increased when I had to change trains. I had no passport and no travel papers, so the risk of getting arrested was high if someone were to check.

After fifteen hours of travel, I saw them. Two men in uniforms checking papers. I thought, *The train must be close to Budapest.* I casually threw my pack over my shoulder and walked to the back of the train. I kept my eyes on the men and prayed the train would stop before they reached me. Finally, it did, and I walked off, glancing back to make sure I wasn't followed. The city sign hanging from the ceiling in front of where the train had stopped confirmed I was in Budapest. The people around me weren't speaking Russian, or at least weren't using a dialect of the language that I understood.

Five minutes later, the train I had been on pulled out of the station. I found a corner where I could sit and watch the trains and the people.

Several Russian soldiers were walking around, and people seemed to treat them with respect, so I quickly pulled my jacket out of my pack and put it on.

After an hour of watching the trains leave, I had a good feel for when they started gaining speed. That was the point where I knew I could jump on. I located a train going to Szentgotthárd, a town further west. I ran around to the other side of the tracks, about twenty meters up from the depot, and stayed low to the ground, ready to run. As soon as I saw the boxcar of the next train to pull out of the station, I started running. I grabbed the handrail and struggled to pull myself up. Just as I found a foothold, a hand reached out to steady me and helped pull me in.

We took a moment to size each other up. He was young, maybe in his late teens or early twenties, and skinny. His clothes, inadequate and dirty, hung loosely from his body. It was hard to tell what he actually looked like behind all the dirt covering his face and the long hair. He looked at me from head to toe and suddenly came after me, screaming as he pushed me violently into the side of the car. The noise that came out of him was like that of an animal.

It took me a moment, but I was able to overpower him. I had him turned around with his back to the side of the car within seconds. With my left hand at his throat, I pulled my right hand back in a fist. I was ready to hit him when he cringed away. *What am I doing,* I wondered, *hitting a kid?*

I took a deep breath to control my adrenaline, then dropped my arms and backed away. I reached into my provisions, pulled out a piece of dried fish, and offered it to him. He hesitated, then grabbed it and sank to the ground against the wall of the train car wearing a resigned look.

I couldn't blame him for attacking. He probably was surprised that he had helped a Russian soldier get on the train with him. Whether his fear was of being put in jail for riding illegally in a boxcar or he hated Russians, I had no idea. He said something to me that I didn't understand. *Was that French?* Then something clicked in my mind. I remembered reading a newspaper article about French volunteers fighting alongside Germans against the Soviets.

I wondered: *Should I try to say something to him? Would German set him off? Would Russian?* I pulled another piece of dried fish from my pack and popped it in my mouth, chewing as I poured some water from my elk skin vessel into my bowl and handed it to the Frenchman.

Now, I've seen countless people on the brink of starvation. I have felt the desperation that being on the brink of starvation brings, and I understood firsthand the effects of dehydration. That is likely why, as I watched the Frenchman—a mere boy, really—consume the food and water, all I could feel was empathy. His trauma, resilience, and inner struggles related to all he'd done to survive mirrored my own.

As the train continued west, the Frenchman and I silently moved to the opposite ends of the car from one another. The car smelled of manure, urine, and fuel. *Did they transport military equipment and men in this car?* I leaned my back against the wall and slid all the way down to sit. The urine smell was stronger there, and I couldn't see what I was sitting in, in the darkness of the car. But despite the smell, I found solace in the rhythmic sway and steady hum of the train as it glided along the tracks, soothing my mind with its gentle motion. Each kilometer it traveled west brought me a kilometer closer to Karla and my children. *Had they survived the war?* Once again, I wondered, *Will my children remember me?*

Every ten or twenty minutes, the train slowed down as it approached a train depot. In some cases, it also stopped, presumably so passengers could board or disembark. Each time, someone would come by with a flashlight and scan our boxcar. The Frenchman and I hid in the dark corners, holding our breath, bonded by the same survival instinct.

We rode until I felt the train making a soft turn to the left. I stood up and peered through the space between the wooden panels that made up the car's walls. The train was going across a field, the sun shining brightly overhead and casting its golden glow upon the swaying wheat that danced gracefully in the breeze. I followed the path of the train and felt panic when I saw a checkpoint ahead.

I grabbed my pack and walked quickly across the car to the Frenchman, who was sleeping in the corner. I shook him awake and pointed to the checkpoint, then slid the boxcar door open. I hoped the train would slow down more when we got nearer to the crossing, but we couldn't get too close, or someone would see us run from the train.

After a few minutes, I knew I couldn't wait any longer. I put my pack across my chest, then took a deep breath and crossed my arms over my pack as I jumped. I relaxed my knees when I hit the ground and rolled onto my back. Every centimeter of my body hurt, and I had to take a moment to catch my breath before I moved. I heard the Frenchman hit the ground with a loud "umph."

I crawled through the wheat and positioned myself to watch the soldiers at the checkpoint. My skin started itching from landing in the wheat, but I stayed hidden, watching and listening for any danger. The Frenchman crawled up beside me.

I watched as the soldiers checked every part of the train, even jumping on board the boxcar we had been in. Eventually, the train was waved through the crossing. Although my skin was itching, I decided to wait until dark and walk south to see if there was another way to cross what I assumed was a border between countries.

CHAPTER 56

September–November 1946

At dusk, I started making my way south, not surprised that the Frenchman followed me. The sun was high when I turned and began to go west. The expanse of wheat fields turned into forestland as we walked.

While we walked, I taught the Frenchman how to live off the land. I pointed out lichen, mushrooms, and berries that were good to eat by rubbing my stomach, smiling, and saying "Mmm." For those that were poisonous, I put my hand around my throat and bent over with a retching noise. I taught him how to fish, and I taught him how to clean a fish and cook it. When I saw him limping from what I knew were bloody feet, I taught him how to make salve out of pine resin and yarrow.

Eventually, we came upon a small farm similar to Elena's. The Frenchman wanted to walk right in, but I held his elbow and shook my head. That night, as the Frenchman slept, I snuck to the farm to steal eggs. There was laundry on the clothesline, so I took a shirt and pants for the Frenchman. A quick look in the barn revealed a ham shank, obviously at the end of its curing cycle, hanging from the barn rafters.

The meat was like a Christmas present. I used my knife to cut off four large pieces and added them to my pack.

In the morning, we walked all the way around the farm, hidden from any prying eyes. The Frenchman kept pointing to the farm, but I shook my head vigorously and kept walking. Finally, I took out a piece of meat and handed it to him but continued walking and motioned for him to follow me.

We encountered farms every few days and stole what food we could find. I taught the Frenchman not to barrel into a potentially dangerous situation. I taught him to watch and learn about the people on the farm and to wait for nightfall. *How,* I wondered, *did he survive before me?*

Then one day, I saw an old truck parked beside a barn. Grass had grown up around the wheels, as if it hadn't been driven in many months. *Could I get it started? Did it have any gas? Was it worth the risk of getting caught?* I thought back on the number of seasons I had been walking and calculated I had been traveling for maybe fifteen or eighteen months. Cooler weather was starting to settle in, and it would soon be winter again.

The decision was made. I waited until late at night, then woke the Frenchman. I covered his mouth and put my finger up to my lips, then waived my hand for him to follow. I thought about how much easier it would be to leave him but quickly pushed the thought out of my mind. I had already left over thirty men to die at the prison camp. The young man was innocent, and although we had only communicated through sign language, I felt certain he was a good kid.

As we approached the house, I finally had to stop and motion for the Frenchman to take off his boots. *Does he even understand what quiet means?* As with any approach to a farm, I was hypervigilant, relying on all my senses to tell me if anyone was awake.

I signaled for the Frenchman to crawl in the back of the truck, not trusting him to be silent. I opened the gas cap and smelled gas, but it was impossible to know how much fuel was in the tank. I quietly opened the driver's side door and lay down to pull out the wires needed to start it. I put the transmission in neutral, and with the driver's door open and my right hand steering, I used the weight of my body to push the truck down the dirt driveway, which was about one hundred me-ters long, until I reached a narrow road. We were surrounded by trees, so it was too dark to see the ignition wires, but through trial and error, I was finally able to start the truck.

Relief coursed through me as I drove down the road. The truck worked! I drove a few hours to get well away from the farm before daylight, then stopped and took off the Russian uniform jacket. The Frenchman climbed into the cab with me, and I threw the uniform out the window. I had no idea whether we were still in the Soviet Union, but my gut told me to get rid of the uniform since we were well south of the checkpoint.

After the quick break, I drove another two hours until the truck shuddered to a stop. I assumed we were out of gas, so I got out and pushed the truck to the side of the road. It was still dark, and we were surrounded by woods. *Should I walk into the woods to sleep?* I looked at the sleeping Frenchman and decided not to wake him. I made my-self comfortable in the driver's seat.

CHAPTER 57

November 1946

The bright sun warmed my face as my head leaned against the driver's side window. *Was that the sound of a knock?* I heard the noise again and opened my eyes. My pulse immediately jumped, and I hit the Frenchman on the arm to wake him up. *How could I have been so stupid to have just fallen asleep on the side of the road?*

The soldier outside the truck opened the door and said something. *Was that English?* My hands started shaking as I got out of the vehicle. Another soldier was at the passenger door, waiting for the Frenchman to get out. A second soldier behind him had a rifle strapped around his neck, and both his hands were on the gun. I then saw a jeep with two soldiers: one in the driver's seat and another standing in the back, his hands on a machine gun strapped to the top. Another jeep was parked in front of our truck.

Something caught my eye, and a sliver of hope started to take hold. The soldiers were wearing American patches on their uniforms like the one Viggo had given me. Viggo's patch was a symbol of hope that had carried me through war and months of captivity and over a year's journey across the Soviet Union.

"America?" I held out my hand to the soldier that opened my door.

He smiled and shook my hand, nodding as he said, "Yes."

I held up my finger motioning him to wait and bent down to pull out my pack. "I have something in my pack to show you," I said in German. Just then, I heard multiple guns click and saw the end of several barrels of guns pointing at me. I immediately stood up and put my arms in the air.

The soldier that had opened my door said something to another soldier, who immediately pushed me aside and pulled my pack out. He placed it on the hood of the truck, then pulled at the knot that held it together. The contents fell out: scraps of meat, my water vessel sitting safely inside my bowl, a shirt I stole from one of the many farms we passed. There were two carrots and an apple, along with my knife. In the middle of my supplies were two flat stones about seven by ten centimeters held together with a rubber band.

Slowly, keeping my eyes on the soldier that had opened my door, I reached out and picked up the stones, then offered them to him. He looked at me curiously and took them. I nodded, looking at the stones.

He pulled the rubber band off and dropped the top rock when he saw that there were items sandwiched between them. He handed the bottom rock and objects back to me. The items were stuck together from sweat and dirt. I peeled the patch off and held it up. "America." I then held up the picture from Viggo and pointed to his name. Lastly, I used my fingernail to loosen the picture of my family from the stone and passed it to the soldier.

CHAPTER 58

November 1946

I couldn't help but enjoy the scenery from the back seat of the jeep I was in. The Frenchman was in the other jeep. We drove with rolling hills of forest land on one side and farms on another. I had no idea where they were taking me, but at least they hadn't shoved or kicked me, and they hadn't bound my wrists.

I held my precious pictures in my hand, feeling a surge of hope. Once-thriving villages dotted the landscape, a haunting reminder of the devastation conflict had wrought. Yet amid the ruins, signs of life emerged—a lone farmer tending to his fields, children playing in the rubble, and makeshift shelters dotting the horizon like beacons of hope in a sea of despair.

As we approached a camp, a knot formed in my stomach. The sight of barbed wire fencing and guard towers sent a shiver down my spine, stirring memories of my days as a prisoner. My heart raced as we passed through the gates, the camp's bleak surroundings a stark contrast to the hope I had felt just ten minutes prior. The air was thick with a sense of unease as we drove past rows of makeshift shelters, their flimsy walls offering little protection against the biting cold.

I tensed as the jeep parked in front of what looked like a hospital. I had to remind myself that I wasn't in the presence of Nazis as I entered a hospital for the first time since Klaus was murdered.

I was taken to a small room just to the right of the side door we'd entered through. Inside it was a gray metal table and four chairs. A soldier holding a shotgun across his chest stood in the corner. The two windows had bars on them. *Am I under arrest? Where was the Frenchman? Was he okay? Would he be able to survive prison?*

About ten minutes later, a woman in a light-blue uniform with a white apron and matching nurse's hat walked in carrying a small tray. She smiled at me and said something in English that I didn't understand, then pushed the tray in front of me. It was a glass of water and a plate with two sweet biscuits and a small piece of pork. There was also a small bowl of rice. A knife and fork lay neatly on a folded napkin next to the plate. It was more food than I had seen at one time in months. As soon as the nurse left, I ate every crumb of my banquet.

The nurse returned an hour later followed by a soldier carrying a stack of items. He placed them on the table and then stood with his hands lightly on the back of a chair across from me. "You're German?" he asked in a German dialect I was unfamiliar with. The nurse started organizing the items across the table.

I nodded as I glanced at another soldier who'd slipped into the corner and stood as a sentry across from the first guard.

"Can I have your name please?" the soldier asked in German.

My heart rate shot up. *Was he a Nazi?* I looked at his uniform and felt relief when I saw the American flag. "Bruno Arnold."

I looked at the things the nurse had spread out. A white towel with a bar of soap sat next to a stack of folded clothes: a pair of khaki pants, a long-sleeved button-down shirt, and a pair of socks. Next to the clothes was a pair of brown leather shoes. Beside these were a small white towel with a razor and scissors. *Were those all for me? Who were these people?*

I looked back at the German-speaking soldier as he started to speak. "I'm Lieutenant Werner. We'll get you cleaned up, and then the doctor will see you," he said.

I thought of the Nazi doctor who had told me Klaus was dead. "Are you American?"

"Yes." He paused for a moment, looking at me. "Does that make a difference?"

I shifted in my chair and considered my words carefully. "Who won the war?"

The lieutenant looked at me, surprised. "Where have you been that you don't know?"

I searched for the words, overwhelmed and unsure of how to answer. I looked at the nurse, but she just stood by the table silently, listening to the conversation.

"The soldier that brought you here, Lieutenant Reynolds, said you seemed happy to see Americans. But Germany fought against the Americans . . ." Lieutenant Werner's words trailed off.

"I have nothing against Americans. I have a cousin in America. My wife and I wanted to leave Germany for America . . . a country of peace and opportunity." I shrugged. "But it wasn't to be."

Lieutenant Werner indicated the nurse with a nod. "This is Miss Collins. She's going to shave your hair and beard, and then she'll show you where you can take a bath. I'm sure that will make you feel more comfortable before we continue our conversation."

Two hours later, I was back in the same small room, but this time I was clean shaven, bald, adequately fed, and wore clean clothes. I had also visited the doctor, who'd said I was malnourished and that my feet were infected. The nurse had put ointment on my feet and wrapped them in bandages before bringing me back to the same small room. I looked out the window and was watching people walking around in the late-afternoon shadows when Lieutenant Werner walked back in, followed by another soldier.

Lieutenant Werner handed me another glass of water and then sat across from me. The other soldier sat to my left.

"Herr Arnold, this is Captain Wilson," the lieutenant said.

I sipped my water and watched as Captain Wilson took out a notebook and pen. Then I turned back to Lieutenant Werner. "Are you German?"

He was lighting a cigarette. "My parents took me to America from Austria in 1930 when I was ten." He sat back and pushed the pack of cigarettes and a lighter toward me. "I work for the American army as an interpreter."

Captain Wilson started asking me questions, and Lieutenant Werner interpreted back and forth.

"Are you a Nazi?"

I took a drag of my cigarette and looked sternly at the captain. "No."

"Did you fight in the war?"

Lieutenant Werner pushed the ashtray toward me. I lightly tapped the ashes from my cigarette onto the ashtray. "I was forced to serve, but I never shot anyone."

The two men looked at each other. *Did they think I was lying?*

"Where are you from?"

"Kiel. I need to call my wife."

"We can arrange that, but first we need to continue our conversation," said the captain.

Edith's third birthday would be coming up soon. "Please," I begged.

"We have many questions before we can release you," he said.

CHAPTER 59

December 1946–February 1947

Each day they wouldn't release me, my frustration mounted. It was the middle of December, only two weeks before Edith's birthday. My frustration increased as I thought back to the day before, when one of the camp workers had said we were only ten kilometers from the German border. "Why are you holding me here, Lieutenant?" I asked.

"Even though the Nuremberg Trials are complete, there are still a lot of interviews to get through." The lieutenant leaned back in his chair. "You were in the German army, and you were a Russian prisoner of war." He leaned forward, putting his elbows on the table. "You told us that your father-in-law was a Nazi." He flipped a page in his notebook. "Your brother-in-law is Heinrich Drechsler . . . shall I go on?"

I stood up and put my hands on the table, looking directly at the lieutenant. "I was not and will never be a Nazi!" After a few moments, I sat back down and quietly asked, "Do you have children, Lieutenant?"

"Yes. Two boys and a girl," he answered.

"Then you know the love between a father and his children," I said flatly. I heard someone enter the room behind me but didn't bother turning around. "Even before the Nazis murdered my son, I was against them."

Someone put a tray with sugar cookies along with a glass pitcher of water and two glasses on the table and left.

"Your brother-in-law committed suicide and took many secrets with him that would have helped our investigations."

I felt my hope of being home for Edith's birthday floating away. "My wife and her sister were never on good terms. I barely had any contact with him."

✢

I had been at the camp for a month and was getting worried that my family was dead. I sent seven letters but did not receive a single response.

Every day, I sat in the room and answered the lieutenant's questions. Captain Wilson joined the interrogation two or three times a week, but mostly it was the lieutenant. Sometimes they asked the same question several times or several different ways, but I had nothing to hide and only had a few regrets. The guilt of not helping the old man that the SS was beating up was still with me. I also had left over thirty men to die in a remote prison camp.

It was January and had been snowing for several days. I leaned against the window frame, looking out across the camp from inside the same small room from the first day I had arrived. *Were people warm in their tents?* I remembered the prison camp, how my hands and feet had been so cold there it was painful. I glanced across the room as the captain walked in and sat across from the lieutenant. My eyes drifted back to the falling snow.

"Tell me about the Nuremberg Trials," I said. "What were they?" The room was quiet, so I turned and took a seat at the table as I waited for a response.

The lieutenant sat back in his chair, crossing his legs. "There were military tribunals held to bring some justice to the people the Nazis murdered or tortured."

I looked at him across the table, waiting to hear more.

The lieutenant shifted his chair back and put his elbows on his knees. "What do you know about the concentration camps?"

I lit a cigarette and blew out smoke. "I think they were prison camps."

The captain pulled some pictures from his notebook and slid them over to me. Emaciated people stared at me. Children. "They were torture camps. Mostly against Jews."

I touched one of the pictures. "I didn't know," I whispered.

"How could you not know?" the captain asked accusingly.

"The Nazis controlled every aspect of our lives," I said sharply. "They controlled all media, the radio, and newspapers." I heard someone yell something outside and looked over at the window and then back at the two men. "There were whispers, but nothing concrete." The tears came. "Those poor children."

The two men exchanged a look, and the lieutenant said, "Millions of Jews were murdered, starved, gassed . . ."

The nausea and dry throat appeared instantly, and for the first time in my life, I was ashamed to be a German. The two men watched me as I put my cigarette out in the ashtray. My mind flashed through scenes of my life: old men beaten, the Gestapo threatening people, neighbors reporting on neighbors, Eli's family standing at my door. I covered my face with my hands. "Oh God. No, no, no." My voice was a wail. My country had started a war! My country had focused on creating an Aryan nation! *Even if I had known, could I have done anything?*

I dropped my hands and let the tears fall. "People thought the Nazis would bring salvation from the impact of the first war . . . and then it was too late. I think they liked Hitler because he was a good speaker but didn't look at facts. Their votes for the Nazi Party released a lion from its cage."

The camp had been built next to a school so the children living in the camp could resume their studies and use the playground. The school gym was used as a common room for those living at the camp, where we could get coffee, tea, or water throughout the day. People strolled in and out of the gym, some getting a drink and leaving and others staying to catch up on the latest news.

Standing in line with the lieutenant to get coffee, I said to him, "My wife hasn't answered my letters, and I have no phone number for her. Please, I need to know if my family is still alive."

"I'll see what I can do, but you have to understand that Kiel was heavily bombed. Many residents were told to leave." We each picked up a coffee cup, then took turns filling it from the carafe. "She could be anywhere."

We walked back to the interrogation room where I'd spent the better part of the morning answering questions. *How could they possibly still have questions?*

"When I first arrived, you mentioned my brother-in-law as one reason I'm being held here. Aside from being a high-ranking Nazi, what did he do? Did he participate directly in killing Jews?" It was a question I had been thinking about ever since they first brought up his name, but I wasn't sure if I could live with the answer.

The lieutenant flipped through his notebook and, after a minute, found the page he was looking for. He read, "Otto-Heinrich Drechsler, known as Heinrich, was a dentist prior to 1933 when he joined the Nazi Party. He worked his way up the ranks and was finally assigned as leader of the Latvian concentration camps. He was married to Erna Petersen. No children." He turned his notebook to read some notes in the margins. "He left Latvia when the Russians liberated it, but he was captured by the British in Lübeck. On 5 May 1945, he committed suicide."

The lieutenant looked up at me. My hands were balled into fists at the thought of Friedrich trying to get Karla to marry that man. "If he oversaw concentration camps," I said, "that means he is responsible for murdering people."

The lieutenant nodded. "Mass murders," he whispered.

⌁

It was the middle of February, and I was done answering questions. They were going to have to arrest me if they wanted me to stay. I took the stairs two at a time from the second floor of the hospital where I had been living since mid-November and marched to the interrogation room.

I slammed the door open and walked to the table. The lieutenant was already seated, blowing on his hot coffee. He put his cup down and looked up at me.

"I'm leaving," I said. "I have answered more than enough questions. Now, I'm going to find my family." Since the lieutenant didn't immediately say anything, I turned to leave.

"You'll need travel papers," he said. I stopped just inside the door to the hallway. "Otherwise, you'll be stopped and interrogated again."

My heart sank. "How long will that take?" I asked.

"Give me five more days, and I will have your papers and a train ticket."

I turned to him and shook my head. "I evaded capture for eighteen months through hostile territory. I'm leaving in two days, with or without papers."

CHAPTER 60

February 1947

On 18 February, I boarded the train in Salzburg. At that point, I had been away from my family for nearly three years. When I left, Edith was not yet four months old, and Rolf was nearly four. I wondered, *Will Rolf remember me?*

Within ten minutes of leaving Salzburg, the train crossed over to Germany. I felt relieved to have so many kilometers behind me. Crossing the border was the final step home after having been in limbo for nearly four months at the camp. *Please be alive,* I prayed.

The Munich train station was a bustling and somewhat chaotic experience for me amid the postwar reconstruction efforts. The station was heavily damaged during the war and still undergoing repairs, and only limited services were available; however, I was happy to find coffee and potato salad while I waited for my next train.

The train slowed, waking me up. I scrubbed my face with my hand and looked out the window into the dark night. I saw a sign that said "Kassel" as the train stopped at the station. I picked up my sack and got off the train, then walked into the main terminal, where I was greeted by an image of both resilience and adversity. Amid the imposing architecture that still bore scars of war, the bustling atmosphere hinted at a city rebuilding itself. As I navigated through the crowds, I noticed makeshift stalls and vendors offering fruit, bread, cheese, and beer.

After consulting the train schedule, I bought an apple, then walked toward the hallway that would bring me to platform 3B, but I was stopped by border patrol. I was traveling from the American zone to the British zone, and everyone's papers had to be checked. Waiting for the travel papers had cost me an extra day, but the lieutenant had come through with the necessary papers and money for my journey.

I stood in line with other weary travelers. It seemed strange to now have a border in the middle of Germany. The customs area included two booths where papers would be checked. Three families stood in line in front of me.

Immediately ahead of me was a young boy, about three or four years old, holding on to the hand of a woman I assumed was his mother. My heart ached for my family as I looked at the boy. He was picking his nose as he looked up at me. I crossed my eyes at him, but he didn't have time to react, as his mother pulled him up to the customs booth for their turn.

I held my breath when the border patrol officer reviewed my papers. He glanced at me several times, which caused my stress level to rise. I feared he would arrest me or send me for more interrogation. But finally, he stamped my papers and handed them back. I was free to board my train.

The next leg of my journey, to Hamburg, took four hours. I wanted to go look for my sister, Gertrude, in Hamburg, but that would have to wait. The pull toward home that I felt was strong. I had to run through the terminal to board the final train to Kiel. *Two more hours, Karla.* Excitement and hope were coursing through my veins, tempered by the knowledge that my family may not have survived.

⌇

The train started slowing as it approached Kiel. Sitting by the window, I was confronted with the complete demolition of my city. A tear went down my cheek and then another as I shook my head. I closed my eyes, praying that what I was seeing was a nightmare from which I would wake. It had been a long journey, and I was home, but my home was gone. I could barely breathe. The hope I had felt was replaced by despair.

The train stopped at the edge of the city. It could go no further because everything was destroyed. People disembarked and stood looking around them, confused as to where to go. Nothing appeared the same. I started walking toward what looked like hell on earth.

Although I had lived in or near Kiel my entire life, I had to stop people and ask for directions because the streets were unrecognizable. Everything from small rubble to large walls from fallen buildings was covering the streets and sidewalks. I had to navigate around craters in many of the roads and sidewalks. I walked along the harbor, then tracked west to try to find my apartment building. Every building I passed was either partially damaged or a complete pile of debris. *How had anyone survived?*

I turned the corner to my street, and my heart sank even further. I felt a lump in my throat as I saw our building, or what remained of it. Ours was the third building on the left, number 16. I passed a few people who were making their way through the debris but didn't recognize anyone. I saw a man pick something up, then throw it back down on the heap.

The building we lived in was three stories high with five apartments and a shared bathroom on each floor. But what I was looking at was not a building anyone could live in. Where our apartment had been there was only one side wall and the back wall. The stairs were partially in place, and the apartments to the right of our front door had suffered damage but were mostly intact. I climbed through the rubble moving what I could out of the way. *Please don't let me find their bodies.*

I worked for three hours moving pieces of concrete, wood, and bricks. I climbed onto blocks of concrete with pieces of rebar shooting out like swords, scanning for any clues. As I made my way to the back side, I found Karla's piano crushed under the weight of bricks. It was getting dark, so I hunkered down in the outside corner of what had been Frau Bauer's kitchen and built a small fire to keep warm.

I was leaning up against a piece of the back wall, dozing, when I saw the shadow of a man on the other side of the fire. *A looter?* My pulse jumped, and I stood up and moved a few feet past the fire.

"Are you ready for a fight, little brother?" Karl's voice asked.

My entire body relaxed at the sound of his familiar voice. We moved toward each other and embraced tightly. I stepped back with my hands on his shoulders. We were nearly the same height. "You look old," I said with a laugh.

"Yeah? Well, you stink," he tossed back.

"Do you know where my family is?"

He shook his head and looked at me sadly. "I can't find either Anna or Rosie."

We made our way back to the wall I had been leaning against and spent the rest of the night catching up.

The next morning, I was famished so I decided to let Karl sleep and find some food. I went to the store on the corner that Karla and I had shopped at when she was in labor with Edith. The store shelves were mostly empty, aside from three old potatoes.

"Bruno?" It was the storekeeper whom I remembered had always had something nice to say to any customer walking in. He was in his seventies and had always worn a smile. I looked closer at Herr Lange and saw that his smile no longer reached his eyes. There was a shadow there now that looked like grief.

"Herr Lange! Hi." I rubbed my chin, looking at the potatoes.

He walked with a slight limp to the box with the potatoes. "Bruno, just take them. You can pay me another time."

I reached for them, feeling moved by his kindness. "Thank you." It struck me that he was perhaps one of the most likely people to know what had happened to my family. "Herr Lange, have you seen Karla?" I held my breath.

He shook his head and looked at me with sympathy. "It's been maybe a year or two since she came in."

My heart fell. *A year? Oh my God, Karla has been gone for a year!* My throat felt tight. "How is your family?" I whispered.

Tears appeared in his eyes, and he whispered, "Igor . . ."

I put my hand on his for a small amount of comfort. I understood fully what it meant to lose a son.

I was about to cross the street to my apartment building when I saw a movement, a flicker really, on the second floor of an apartment that had been down the hall from ours before the bomb hit. Frau

Hoffman's apartment. It was located in the middle of the building, where the second and first floors remained mostly intact, compared to the rest of the building. The windows had been blown out. There was a hole inside the first-floor apartment below it, at street level. *Are there people living there? Did I really see something?* I saw the curtains move again. Oh my God, someone was actually living in there. *Could it really be Frau Hoffman?*

I took a few steps, still staring at what I'd discovered, then saw a ladder tucked into the corner of the downstairs apartment. I tamped down the hope I felt, not wanting to face another disappointment, and crossed the street to climb up. Karl must have been watching for me, because he appeared after I'd stepped into the open first-floor apartment.

"What's going on?" he asked.

I started climbing the ladder. "I saw movement up here."

Once I got to the top, Karl started climbing up behind me. I saw that the apartment that had been located on the back side of the building was gone, but there was a small ledge of hallway that I could use to get to the front apartment. I shifted my weight onto each foot, testing its sturdiness, before putting my full weight down and taking a step. Three steps later, I was knocking on the door to Frau Hoffman's apartment. Karl was lightly walking across the ledge I had just crossed.

Someone opened the door a crack and peered out. I looked down into the eyes of the elderly lady who had lived down the hall from us. "Frau Hoffman?"

She looked at me, confused.

"Frau Hoffman, it's Bruno. Karla's husband."

The door opened, and she pulled me into her apartment. "Bruno! I didn't recognize you. Come in, come in." Karl followed and closed the door softly behind us.

I was surprised to see that her apartment was largely intact, a small oasis in the middle of the chaos and destruction outside. I made a mental note to find some boards to cover her windows after I found my family.

"Frau Hoffman, do you know where my family is?" I asked.

She walked to the small desk that sat in the corner. "They left about two years ago. Maybe two and a half." She opened the desk drawer and pulled out an envelope. "Everyone was evacuated, but I couldn't leave my home." She held out the envelope for me to take. "She left this for you."

My hands shook as I opened the envelope.

3 September 1944

My stomach rolled over as I read the date at the top. They'd left in 1944? That was nearly three years ago! Only five months after I left.

"I have these as well." Frau Hoffman handed me a stack of unopened letters. "I guess someone left them at my door since it was the only one in the building left."

They were the letters I'd sent to Karla from the camp in Austria.

I turned my attention back to Karla's letter.

My Dear Bruno,

We are being evacuated to a camp outside of Prasdorf. Anna and Rosie are with us. The children are well, and we miss you.

Love,
Karla

CHAPTER 61

October 1959

Frankfurt, Germany

The rain streaked down the windows of the interview room. The young woman who had brought lunch returned with her cart full of cups, saucers, and a carafe. On the lower shelf of the cart was a plate covered with cinnamon and spritz star cookies. She put everything on the food table, removed the dirty dishes, then arranged the fresh food.

"Karla, is Bruno different now than before the war?" asked Dr. Schmidt.

"In what way?" Karla inquired.

"Personality, behavior . . ."

Karla looked at Bruno, as if considering how to answer. He stood and walked to the table that held the coffee and food.

"Before he left for war, he was very outgoing and would strike up a conversation with anyone on the street. Everywhere we went, he created this convivial environment." She adjusted her position in her seat, uncrossing her ankles, then recrossing them. "He came back mostly the same around the family, but in public he was much quieter, more introspective."

After a few minutes of taking notes, Dr. Schmidt nodded. "Karla, we have heard a lot about Bruno's experience. Will you please tell us your story?"

Bruno had poured two cups of coffee, and he returned now and placed one in front of Karla. She blew on the hot liquid and took a tentative sip. She appeared to be gathering her thoughts before she continued.

Karla

CHAPTER 62

April 1944

I was heartbroken after Bruno boarded the train, but I knew there was no time for self-pity. Getting our basic needs met, including food, took endless work, and the nearly constant bombing was a regular distraction. There was no time in that moment to lose myself in my grief.

Rosie held Rolf's hand, and I pushed Edith in her pram out of the train station as we headed back toward the apartment. Anna lifted one end of the pram and I lifted the other over the broken concrete to the street.

I turned to Anna and Rosie. Rosie had already been staying with Bruno and me, helping with the children. I hated to think of Anna staying out at the farm alone. "Do you want to stay in the city with us, Anna?"

We walked in silence toward my apartment for a few minutes, then the air raid sirens went off. *Will Bruno be okay?* We watched to see where people were running and joined the crowd to the nearest bomb shelter.

Anna stood next to me in the shelter with her hand on Edith's pram. "Why don't you and the children come to the farm with us?"

"I can't. I may have to be at the factory. Perhaps we can stay at the farm during weekends and in the city during the week?"

⌘

Our first weekend at the farmhouse, Anna was kind enough to give me the larger bedroom with a full-sized bed. Rolf could sleep with me, and there was just enough room for Edith's pram, which would serve as a bed for her. Rosie slept in her room, and Anna slept in the room Bruno had shared with Walter and Karl when they were young.

The next day, while Rosie took care of the children, Anna and I worked in the garden, pulling weeds and bringing buckets of water from the well. I harvested some potatoes and carrots, a few turnips, one cabbage, and a basket of green beans. Anna took about eight eggs from the three chickens.

Just after lunch, Anna and I looked at each other when we heard the unmistakable crunch of a vehicle on the dirt driveway making its way toward the house. We both walked to the front of the house and saw a sleek black Mercedes parked next to the old farm truck.

Anna put her hand above her eyes to shade the sun. "Can I help you?" My pulse jumped at the sight of the man in a Nazi uniform standing on the front porch.

He stepped down and handed Anna a piece of paper, then gruffly said, "This is a notice for you to be out of the house by the end of day tomorrow. The farm is now the property of the Nazi regime."

"No, this house has been in my husband's family for generations. It's our home!" Anna said boldly.

"You may take your clothes and any family pictures." The soldier stood up straight and put his right hand out. "Heil Hitler!" He completely ignored Anna's protests, got in his car, and drove back down the driveway, leaving a cloud of dirt and dust in his wake.

"What does the letter say, Anna?" I asked.

She handed me the letter and walked into the house. The letter was stamped at the top with an eagle on top of a swastika.

Dear Herr Arnold,

This official letter is to inform you of a necessary sacrifice for the greater good.

In service to our nation's war effort, it has become imperative that your property be repurposed. Consequently, your occupancy of the property must be relinquished promptly.

You are hereby directed to vacate the premises 15 April 1944, ensuring that only personal belongings are removed. Furniture and vehicles must remain in the house. We suggest seeking refuge with other family members during this transition.

Your cooperation in this endeavor is crucial and greatly appreciated, as it contributes significantly to our collective efforts on the front lines.

"'Greatly appreciated'!" I followed Anna a few minutes later, feeling anger at how much the Nazis had already taken from us. As soon as I looked across the living room at her and Rosie huddled together on the sofa, crying, I knew I needed to set my feelings aside. I sat beside Rosie so she was in the middle and wrapped them in a hug.

After a few minutes, I leaned back again. "Let's harvest as much as we can from the garden and the fields. We'll spend the evening preserving the food and packing the truck." I stood up and put my hands on my hips. "I don't know about you, but I'm not interested in leaving them even a crumb of food."

"I'll bring the truck back after we move everything so we don't get in trouble," Anna said.

+∽+

We settled back into my apartment in Kiel and fell into a routine. Anna helped me sew soldier uniforms each morning, giving me time in the afternoon to play in the garden with the children or to play my piano. The neighbors asked me to leave my apartment door open when

I played. It seemed like every concert on the radio was interrupted by news of the war, and people just wanted to listen to music.

I also took some sewing jobs from neighbors. People needed sewing help for everything from a torn seam to making clothes from curtains, tablecloths, or any other cloth they could find. Most jobs were paid based on barter, typically with food.

I started writing letters to Bruno, thinking it would make me feel closer to him. I vowed to myself that I would write once a week. I placed each letter in a small box because there was nowhere to mail them. I had no idea where Bruno was, and even if I'd had an address, it was unlikely that my letters would have reached him in a war zone.

CHAPTER 63

July–September 1944

Nearly three months after Bruno left, I was called back to the factory to help wash truckloads of uniforms from dead soldiers. Resigned to having raw hands that smelled of blood and soap, I walked slowly on the day I was scheduled to return, delaying until the last minute my arrival at the factory I detested so much.

The building had been a clothing factory before the war, so it was easily converted to a uniform factory. I thought about the days I had spent at the factory before the war. Though I did not like being forced to work for the Nazis, I loved going in once a month to sort through discarded pieces to see if there was anything I could use. I once found enough pieces of the same fabric to make Therese place mats for her dining table. They had been fun to make, and Therese had been thrilled to show them off to visiting neighbors.

Before the war, the factory had hummed with activity as rows of machines rhythmically stitched together fabrics of varying textures and colors, producing garments destined for wardrobes across the country. From the clatter of looms weaving patterns to the whir of sewing machines stitching seams, the factory floor was a symphony of industry.

But since the war began . . .

I stopped walking. My memories stopped, and my mind went blank as I tried to absorb what I was seeing. The factory had been bombed the night before. The windows were blown out, the roof was caved in, and a portion of the corner wall had collapsed. The building was still smoldering from the fire the bombs had started. The familiar hum of machinery had been replaced by an eerie silence that was broken only by the occasional creak of twisted metal in the wreckage and the distant echoes of rescue efforts.

Someone walked up beside me and gently took my hand. I looked over and saw my childhood friend Martha. She squeezed my hand.

"Do you want to get some coffee?"

✙✙

When I walked in the door of our apartment, Edith was sitting in her high chair with a goopy piece of bread in her hand. She was kicking her legs in anticipation of the next spoonful of the applesauce Anna was putting into her mouth. Rolf was sitting on the floor between the sofa and coffee table, drawing on paper with his crayons.

Anna looked up surprised to see me. "You're home early."

"Remember the huge explosion last night?" I hung my purse on the hook next to the door. "Well, I no longer have to sew for the Nazis."

✙✙

One month later, I stood at the dining table, on which I had spread pieces of material. I held a few straight pins between my lips and was working on the hem of a skirt, folding the fabric and pinning it in place. Anna was at the sewing machine, working on the skirt's waistband. The radio was playing "The Watch on the Rhine," originally a poem by Max Schneckenburger but converted to a song by Karl Wilhelm. Edith was asleep in her bed. Rosie had taken Rolf to the park.

Suddenly, the apartment door flew open, and Rosie ran in, practically dragging Rolf with her. "Look at this!" She waved a piece of paper at Anna.

I pulled the pins out of my mouth and walked over. Anna scanned the paper, and her face paled.

"Where did you get this, Rosie?" Anna asked.

Rolf pointed toward the ceiling and jumped up and down. "From the sky!"

Anna handed me the paper to read.

Urgent Notice from the British Authorities

There was a drawing of bombs falling over a city. Anna stood up and walked into the kitchen. I heard her take something from the cabinet, then the sound of her pouring a glass of water.

> Attention Residents of Kiel,
>
> Due to imminent military operations, it is imperative that all civilians evacuate the city immediately. The safety of you and your loved ones is at risk.
>
> Bombing will commence at 21:00 on 4 September, at which time Kiel will be subjected to heavy bombing raids. To ensure your survival, we urge you to go to the relocation camp outside of Prasdorf, a safer area outside the city limits.
>
> Please gather your personal belongings and make arrangements to leave as soon as possible.

I closed my eyes for a moment and put the paper on the coffee table. It was already 2 September "There's no time to waste. We need to get organized and get packed. Only bring what you can carry—the most critical items." I walked to the apartment door. "Rosie, will you please help me get the wagon Eli left from the basement?"

By the time Rosie and I came back upstairs, Anna had carefully folded the material we were working on. She had stacks of clothes on the kitchen table, ready to be packed. She'd also laid out four sets of eating utensils, a spatula, one large bowl, four plates, and two small bowls.

Rosie and I helped her stack the dishes between the clothes. Rolf put his toys in his backpack along with some paper and his crayons. I put our family photographs and birth certificates in my purse. Rosie helped me put my sewing machine in the wagon, and I packed some of Bruno's shirts and pants along with the wrapped dishes around it. Lastly, I used some twine to tie two buckets to the outside of the wagon. I looked at the radio sitting on the dining table with its beautiful, polished wood. It stood thirty-eight centimeters high. There just wasn't room to bring it.

I packed the remaining jars of food from the farm in Edith's pram behind a blanket. Food was hard to come by and easily stolen. At the last minute, I put the aebleskiver pan in the pram. It was a luxury we probably couldn't afford, but Edith loved her aebleskiver. I pictured her sitting in her high chair with each hand holding scrumptious pancake balls, and I smiled thinking of the sticky mess.

Every time I walked by the wagon in our living room, I thought of Eli and Ilse. They used to dance around their home after dinner, so happy, so in love. I prayed they were living a happy and safe life. I thought about writing a letter to the address Viggo had left me, but each time I sat down to write, I had a vision of the Nazis finding the letter and hunting them down or putting me in prison.

It was late by the time we finished packing. By then, the curfew had already gone into effect. We were ready to leave first thing in the morning. After dinner, I touched the piano keys lightly.

Anna touched my shoulder. "Play for us?"

The Nazis kept strict control over music, forcing out any Jewish or other composers they deemed "un-German." But tonight, I decided to play whatever came to mind. I played Prelude in C-sharp Minor, op. 3, no. 2 by Sergei Rachmaninoff. Rosie opened the door so neighbors could listen.

Next, I played "Love's Sorrow" by Fritz Kreisler, which was about love and longing. Slowly, neighbors came into our apartment and sat on the sofa and floor until no more people could fit. Some stood against the wall, others just outside the door. I played Viktor Ullmann's Sonata no. 1. I did not stop as I went on to play and sing "Wandering Is the Miller's Joy," by Franz Schubert. I played for two hours. When I finally finished, the room was quiet for a few minutes. There was nothing to say. Many neighbors patted my shoulder, wordlessly thanking me for the concert.

Silently, I closed the door to the keyboard.

Would I ever play my beloved piano again?

CHAPTER 64

September 1944

Just before we left the apartment, I stopped at Frau Hoffman's apartment across the hall. I had a note for Bruno that I wanted to mail but needed an envelope and thought she might have one. Suddenly, it occurred to me that such a thought was ridiculous. I had no address for him. I was tired and wasn't thinking. I put the note in my pocket just as Frau Hoffman cracked the door and peered out at me.

"Hello, Frau Hoffman. It's Karla from across the hall."

"Karla!" She opened the door, took my hand, and pulled me inside.

I looked around, concerned that everything seemed to be in its place. There were no bags, suitcases, or boxes. "Frau Hoffman, we're being evacuated. Do you need help packing?"

She waved her hand, dismissing the notion. "No, I can't leave. I'll be fine."

I couldn't believe my ears. *She was just going to stay in the city and get bombed?* "No, Frau Hoffman. Please, won't you come with us?"

"No! My place is here in my home. I've lived here my entire life. My children were born here, and my husband died here. My parents died here too."

"It's not safe, Frau Hoffman."

She looked at me and squeezed my hand. "I'm an old lady. War took both my sons and my husband. I'm not going to let it take my home too."

I thought she was being ridiculous; it was just a building and stuff. Things that could be replaced. But I had known her my entire life and knew that when she made up her mind, that was it. *What was I going to do, throw her over my shoulder and carry her kicking and screaming all the way to the bus stop?*

She pulled me to the door. "You go now. Take care of those beautiful babies of yours."

Suddenly a thought occurred to me. I pulled the letter out of my pocket and handed it to the old woman. "Will you give this to Bruno if he comes?"

✦

Slowly, we made our way toward the bus stop just three blocks away. I carried Edith and held Rolf's hand while Anna pushed the pram with our food and Rosie pulled the heavy wagon. Everywhere I looked were women, children, and old men carrying what they could in a suitcase or bag. Everyone had the same look of overwhelming sadness. *Should they stay and risk their lives or go and hope to find a safer place? Was any place safe?*

The bus driver shook his head and yelled at me. "No wagon!"

I gave him what Bruno refers to as my "scary mommy look." I didn't have to speak. I stepped onto the bus and pointed to the first seat for Rolf to climb in, then I put Edith next to him. Anna and Rosie were struggling with the pram, but finally, Anna was able to pull it in and pushed it down the aisle. I stood on the top step, bending over to pull in the wagon while Rosie lifted it up. The wagon was too wide to fit down the aisle, so I left it next to the driver while Rosie ran to the back door and boarded the bus. It served the driver right! I ignored the disapproving stares from the other passengers.

✦

After a nearly two-hour ride, the bus came to a stop in front of a camp. I couldn't believe I was a refugee in my own country. Rosie stepped off the bus and ran to the front door to help me with the wagon. Then I helped her with the pram while Anna took care of Edith and Rolf. The people around us all seemed focused on themselves.

It was cold and rainy as we stood in the line of people. I counted at least fifty in line in front of us. After a while, another bus dropped off another load of people who got in line behind us. The line seemed to be never ending as it wrapped around the back of the building and down the side of the camp. Edith started getting fussy from boredom, rain, or hunger. My maternal instinct to try to make her more comfortable in an impossible situation added to my stress.

Anna pointed behind me. "There's a small overhang on the building next door. Why don't you take Edith over and give her a piece of bread while I stand in line?"

I took a sheet from the wagon with me and walked to the overhang. Edith cried harder when I sat her on the cold ground, until I gave her a piece of bread. I unfolded the sheet partway so that I had a long piece of cloth. I put it around Edith's back, then lifted her over my head and shifted her so she was riding on my back. Then I arranged the fabric across my chest, bringing it to my back and crossing it under Edith's bum and back to my waist, where I tied it into a knot. Now my hands were free, and hopefully, she would fall asleep.

I walked back to the line and watched as Rosie played with Rolf to distract him. It was nice to see them playing and laughing together as we stood in the cold. Thirty minutes later, the rain finally stopped, but the clouds remained, their presence adding to the ominous feeling of the day.

After two hours, we finally made it into the registration area. There were two tables, each with a clerk that was registering people. Two chairs stood across from each clerk. The clerk told us to all register on a single form so we could stay together. I sat at the edge of the chair, careful not to smush my sleeping baby, and used a pen to fill in the information on the ten-by-fifteen-centimeter card.

First and last names	Ages	Occupation/special skills
Karla Arnold	34	Seamstress, cooking
Edith Arnold	8 months	
Rolf Arnold	4	
Anna Arnold	47	Sewing, cooking, gardening
Rosemarie Arnold	23	Sewing

I showed Anna the paper to make sure I got everything. She took the paper and added to my skills: English, singing, and piano. The bottom of the page contained a statement that Anna and I ignored.

By signing below, I hereby pledge my unwavering allegiance to the ideals and principles of the Nazi regime.

She handed the paper to the clerk, who scanned it and handed it back. "Sign it."

Anna and I looked at each other.

"Sign it or leave," the clerk said.

Finally, I took the form back and added a nondescript scribble.

The clerk barely glanced at the registration form before placing it in a box. He then handed me a piece of paper with our assignment: row D, tent 222.

All I could think about as we collected our stuff and walked into the main area of the camp was how we would survive the winter in a tent. I was angry at Hitler and the Nazis for their power-hungry egos. I was terrified I wouldn't be able to keep my young children warm and safe. Most of all, I desperately missed Bruno.

We walked down the rows of tents. Every face we saw wore an expression of shock and sadness. Many women were squatting in front of a fire, cooking in front of their tents. The smells as we walked by were a mix of cooked cabbage, urine, and body odor. Even though the ground was wet and muddy, a few children chased each other between the tents.

Each row had a small piece of wood with a letter assigned. We found row D easily enough, but the walk to number 222 was long. The wagon and buggy kept getting stuck in the mud, so I finally turned to Anna and said, "We should carry them."

"Karla!" I knew that voice. I turned and there stood my friend Martha. She walked over and threw her arms around me, then stood back to look me over. "I'm happy to see you," she said. She looked down at Rolf, who was holding Rosie's hand, and smiled. Then she squatted and picked up the front of the wagon in one hand and the pram in the other while I did the same from the rear.

"Where are you staying?" I asked Martha as we began to walk.

"Just one row over. I'm in a tent with two mothers who don't like each other. They have teenagers who also bicker constantly. It's exhausting listening to them all."

I stopped walking so I could rest and adjust my grip. Anna walked up and took the rear of the wagon while Rosie took the front of it from Martha. "That must be awkward," Rosie said, having overheard Martha's description.

Martha laughed as she picked up the front of the pram. "It isn't pleasant at all." I picked up the back of the pram, and Rolf walked next to me, looking around. I wonder what my four-year-old thought of all this. He seemed more curious than concerned.

Finally, we found tent 222. We stood in the doorway to look at our new home. I felt taken aback. *How would we ever feel clean again living with a dirt floor?* There was a small cooking stove at one end and four cots at the other. The space smelled of smoke and urine.

Martha helped us pull our things in. "You should make sure someone remains in the tent at all times. I heard that people's things are getting stolen."

"Do you want to move in here with us?" I asked. Then I looked at Anna, embarrassed I hadn't discussed it with her before offering.

"If it's okay with you and Rosie."

Anna nodded and pointed to our sleeping area. "Another trusted adult would be good, but we need another cot."

"If you're sure it's okay, I'll just bring the cot from the other tent," Martha said.

Just then, Edith woke up and began squirming. I untied the baby carry bag and let her slide gently down. When I turned around and looked down at her, I cringed to see her crawling in the dirt.

CHAPTER 65

September 1944

It was difficult to settle into camp life. Every day we had to stand in long lines to get our daily rations, which consisted mostly of potatoes and cabbage. We also had to stand in line to use the community toilet. Each toilet had a well in front of it where we could get fresh water to drink after standing in line again. I wasn't convinced the water was safe, so I boiled it and let it cool before letting anyone drink it.

Four teams of women rotated cleaning the toilets, which had to be done at least two times a day. But getting them clean was nearly impossible considering the number of people sharing. Two weeks after arriving at the camp, it was my turn to clean the toilets.

We had to pour some unidentified chemicals into the pit to break down the waste. *Are the chemicals safe to handle?* I wondered. There were only three toilets for every fifty tents, and some tents had up to six or seven people living in them. The chemicals didn't have time enough to break down the waste completely, so we had to shovel what was left into buckets and carry the buckets to the cesspool at the edge of the camp. It was a grueling and smelly job that made me gag every time I slid the shovel in.

CHAPTER 66

October–November 1944

On the 10 October, a boy around nine years old brought us a note. Afraid of what horrible news awaited us now, my hands shook as I unfolded the piece of paper.

> Dear Frau Arnold,
>
> We are pleased to inform you that your registration has been processed, and you are now assigned to live at the Hermann farm, situated 1 kilometer north of Prasdorf at the end of Sandkroogsredder Road.
>
> Kindly check out from the camp registration office no later than noon on 12 October.

I knew that the farmers were required by law to provide housing to people who were being relocated. But my feelings were mixed. I desperately wanted to get out of the camp, but what was waiting for us at this stranger's farm? I didn't ask about Martha going with us because there was no way I was leaving without her. I was sure the camp wouldn't notice, and if someone did, they would be happy with one less person to feed and house.

It took us thirty minutes to walk from the camp to the farm, which was located just north of the town. We found the farmer on his tractor plowing a field when we arrived. *Was he angry that we had interrupted his work,* I wondered, *or that he had to provide housing and food to a family in need?* His expression when he climbed down to meet us was grim.

He showed us to our new home, a garden shed located next to the barn. The shed had just one room, which was about four meters long and four meters wide. In the corner to the right of the door was a wood stove for cooking and heating. An old door had been cut in half and was lying on top of stacked crates. This was our dining table. The table was surrounded by four mismatched wooden chairs. Two sets of stacked bunk beds lined the wall opposite the dining table. It would be cramped in there with four adults and two children, but the floor was made of wood, and the privacy of the arrangement told me this was many steps up from the camp.

"Rolf can sleep with me," Rosie said.

The old farmer was standing behind us just outside the open door. Rolf stood behind my leg, peering out at him. The man pointed to an area behind the house. "The outhouse is just over there, and you can get water from the well." His tone was gruff. "The children need to stay out of the barn."

"Did I see you have a garden on the side of the house?" I asked. When he remained silent, I added, "I'll work in the garden in return for half the food I gather."

"If you cook for me too, then you have a deal. You can take care of the chickens and milk the cow for a share of eggs and milk." He then turned and walked off in the direction of the field.

❧

I decided to prepare our dinners in Herr Hermann's house, since it had a better stove and oven than the ones in the shack. One afternoon, while the potato soup simmered and with nothing else to do, I started cleaning the kitchen.

I was stacking papers in the middle of the kitchen table when the words "Death Notice" in the subject line of a letter caught my eye. I looked out the back door, which stood adjacent to the table, then backed up a step to look into the living room. No one was there, so I read the letter while wiping the kitchen table.

> Dear Herr Hermann,
>   We regret to inform you that your son, Gerhard Hermann, was killed in action. He fought honorably and was a good Nazi soldier.

Oh, poor Herr Hermann. I imagined the small watermarks on the paper were tears and could imagine his sad face when he read the letter. We had been there four weeks and had not seen a wife, so I assumed she too was dead. I admonished myself for having judged him so quickly since the day we arrived. Maybe he hadn't been angry with us. Maybe he had simply been processing the death of his child. That was something I understood and could empathize with.

❧

After that, I had a new view of Herr Hermann. I saw that he wasn't angry or difficult. He was simply a humble, soft-spoken man who found comfort in setting rules and creating order around the farm.

One afternoon, Herr Hermann came in for lunch when I was just finishing making his plate of potato salad, sliced carrots, and biscuits. Rosie was taking care of Rolf and Edith in the garden shack. I put the plate and a glass of water on the table.

After washing his hands, he turned to me. "Would you like to join me for lunch?"

Was he lonely? Rolf and Edith were probably hungry, but I thought they would be okay for a few more minutes. "Yes, thank you."

I watched as he pulled apart one of the biscuits and took a bite. "My wife used to make biscuits like this."

I took a sip of water. "Do you like them?"

He scooped up a forkful of potato salad. "Yes."

"What happened to your wife?" I asked as I stabbed a carrot with my fork and popped it in my mouth.

"She died in 1942. She was visiting her sister in Kiel when a bomb hit." I watched him as he swallowed. He looked up at me, and I saw unshed tears in his eyes. "She didn't come home when she said she would, so I went to her sister's apartment." He wiped his mouth with his sleeve. "I was lucky. I found her body and was able to give her a proper burial."

I had a lump in my throat thinking about this poor man having to bury his own wife. *With his son gone, was he completely alone?* "Do you have children?" I asked.

He nodded. "Three daughters." He shifted in his seat. "My only son was killed in action not long ago."

I felt guilty for reading his letter. I reached my hand across the table and touched the back of his hand. "I lost my son too, and I wish for peace every day."

Our impromptu lunch seemed to relax Herr Hermann. After that day, he began engaging with Rolf with smiles and once even played toss with him for a few minutes, using an old ball. Edith was learning to walk with the help of whoever would bend over to hold her two hands as she tried to balance herself. She and I were in the yard one day, practicing this, when Herr Hermann walked out of the house and gave her an old doll one of his daughters had left behind.

CHAPTER 67

January 1945

The garden shed was made of steel sheets and had no insulation, and we couldn't keep the stove on all day for fear of running out of wood, so it was always cold in there. I remade Bruno's clothes into larger clothes for the children so that I could dress them in more layers.

It was rare for the sun to shine in the middle of January, so on the first occasion that it did, I took advantage of it and walked to the post office. I had mixed feelings about going. If I saw Bruno's or Karl's names on the list of dead, it would break my heart, but knowing the truth would also mean that we were no longer in limbo. I bundled Edith in her pram and let Rolf put his feet on the bar across the back of the buggy so he could have a ride too.

I was halfway down the road when Rosie came running up behind me. "Can I join you?" she asked breathlessly.

I put my arm around her waist. "Of course!"

"I got a job!" Rosie announced.

I adjusted my scarf so it covered more of my neck. "Really? Where?"

"I'm going to help Herr Braun in the afternoons."

The shopkeeper looked to be about ninety years old. It occurred to me that he could definitely use the help. He'd barely been able to walk when I went to his store the prior week. "That's great, Rosie."

We made it to the post office just as the postmaster was posting a new list of names. Since it was in alphabetical order, it only took a few seconds to see his name.

ARNOLD, BRUNO. 9TH INFANTRY DIVISION.
MISSING IN ACTION 5 NOVEMBER 1944.

I was numb. I backed away from the bulletin board as if it were dangerous. Rosie took my hand and squeezed, then put her hands on the pram and walked the children home with me following them. I simply followed her lead since I was unable to think for myself.

Once we were home, Rosie guided me gently to a chair at the dining table. "I'll find Martha," she said.

A few minutes later, Martha walked in from outside and sat down, adjusting her seat so she could sit in front of me. She took my hand but didn't say anything. She knew me well enough to know that nothing she or anyone said in that moment could comfort me.

CHAPTER 68

March–April 1945

An official-looking letter arrived for me two months later. My hands shook as I looked at the envelope. I was scared to open it. *Is this the letter that tells me Bruno is dead?*

I handed the letter to Martha, and she read it out loud. It said I had to report to the camp office before noon the next day. I felt relieved that it hadn't been a notification that Bruno was dead, but then panic crept in. *Had they figured out I didn't sign my actual name on the registration form saying I supported the Reich? Were they going to take my children to punish me?*

My heart felt like it was beating out of my chest as I walked to the camp. When I arrived, I was ushered to an office with the name "Director Keller" printed in black letters on a gold piece of metal attached to the middle of the door. I noticed my hands were still shaking as I knocked on the door, so I quickly put them behind me.

"Enter!" I heard someone call from inside the room.

I opened the door but stood in the hall. "You sent for me. I'm Karla Arnold."

Director Keller sat behind his desk. Stacks of papers were at each corner. He took a sheet from the top of one pile. "Come in. Sit, please."

He motioned toward the two chairs opposite his desk. He was maybe in his midfifties or early sixties and balding.

I sat down and pushed my hands under my thighs to keep them from shaking.

"I see you speak English. Do you speak it fluently?" he asked.

I focused on the map of Germany behind him. There were different colored pins pushed into various cities. "Yes," I answered.

He peered over his glasses at me. "Where did you learn?"

English was not something that was taught in public schools. "I went to a private school that taught English."

"Your family is rich?"

I shifted to the edge of my seat and clasped my hands in my lap. "No, I received a scholarship because of my good marks." *Where was he going with this?*

He tossed the paper he was reading from onto his desk. "I have a need for an interpreter. It comes with a small amount of pay."

My first reaction was that I could not possibly support the regime. *But could I tell him no?* We needed every penny of income we could get to support my family. And I didn't know what he would do if I refused. In any case, he wasn't asking. He was simply telling me what I needed to do.

I felt sick to my stomach as I agreed. The good news was that he didn't bring up the scribble I'd made next to the allegiance statement.

⚬⚬⚬

The following few weeks were a blur. I left Herr Hermann's farm at seven-thirty and returned almost twelve hours later. There was much to learn that I hadn't been expecting.

I was paired up with Lieutenant Maier, who specialized in interpreting coded messages. He would write the codes down in a notebook and translate them into letters of the alphabet using a codebook. I would then translate the words they made from English into German. There were also a few instances when someone was speaking over the airwaves or an uncoded telegram was intercepted, and I just needed to transcribe the information to German into one of the notebooks that were passed back and forth between me and Keller.

Lieutenant Maier and I worked at two desks that faced each other in a large room that had eight desks arranged in two rows. Each light-gray metal desk had a matching chair. The people at the other desks were part of the intelligence team, but we all generally ignored each other. I was there for one reason: to make money for my family.

The process of translating was easy and allowed me to practice English; however, the mental toll of thinking about the people who were about to be killed was difficult. In April, I had to translate a message from the American forces to British forces.

2 April 1945
Subject: Strategic Intelligence Update
Hanover has been identified as a key target due to its strategic location and potential as a logistical hub for further operations in the region.
The U.S. Army is prepared to advance from the south and will go north.
British units should advance from the north.
Intelligence expects heavy casualties.

The words were ominous. I couldn't help but wonder, *Was Bruno in Hanover, and would he be in that battle?*

✿

I was cleaning the kitchen after baking bread for Herr Hermann and his daughters when I found a newspaper on the table. It was dated 8 April 1945. I sat down to take a break and read the front page.

Hanover Holds Firm Against Allied Assault: Triumph of German Resolve

In the face of overwhelming enemy forces,
the city of Hanover stands as a beacon of
resilience and defiance against the advancing
Allied onslaught. Reports from the front lines

paint a vivid picture of heroic German soldiers and civilians steadfastly defending their homeland against foreign aggression.

Despite relentless enemy bombardment and fierce ground assaults, the defenders of Hanover refused to yield. Street by street, house by house, they valiantly repelled the invaders, determined to protect their city and its inhabitants from the horrors of war.

In a stirring display of unity and patriotism, Hanoverians from all walks of life joined the fight for their beloved city. Women, children, and the elderly support the efforts of the brave soldiers who stand as the vanguard of the city's defense.

Amid the chaos of battle, stories emerge of acts of heroism and sacrifice that inspire all who hear them. From the youngest child to the seasoned veteran, each resident of Hanover contributes to the city's defense with unwavering courage and resolve.

Despite the challenges they face, the people of Hanover remain steadfast in their determination to resist the enemy until the very end. Their spirit unbroken, their resolve unyielding, they stand united in the face of adversity, ready to defend their city to the last breath.

As the battle for Hanover rages on, the world watches with bated breath, witnessing the triumph of the human spirit in the face of overwhelming odds. In the heart of Germany, amid the ruins of war, the people of Hanover write a new chapter in the annals of history— a testament to the indomitable will of the human spirit.

Long live Hanover! Long live Germany!

I found it hard to believe women and children would join the fight. I also wondered, *Was the German army really able to fight off two strong armies surrounding the city from the north and south?*

CHAPTER 69

May 1945

I walked into the office and saw that every seat was filled with people working. I didn't care that I was late; I needed an extra ten minutes of sleep.

I placed my cup of coffee from the shared kitchen onto my desk, along with a blank notebook I'd picked up from the front of the room. I sat down and had just started to put my earphones on when Director Keller walked in. He stood at the front of the room and looked at each one of us with tears in his eyes. "It was just announced on the radio," he said. "Our führer is dead."

I watched with indifference as the others in the room began to cry and ask questions. Everyone was so emotional, but I had been wanting him dead for years. *Did I admit that to myself? Yes, I did want him dead.*

"Everyone should take the time they need to mourn," Director Keller said.

It made me sick to watch them mourn him. It was like they were in some kind of cult. I couldn't take it anymore. I pulled my purse out from under the desk and walked out. Although I had just arrived, I needed a few minutes. *Would the other people interpret my sudden departure as being my way to mourn?* I didn't care if they did or didn't.

It was a beautiful spring afternoon. As I walked, I tried to clear my mind. The sun warmed my skin, and a gentle breeze played with my hair. It was a moment of bliss, a respite from the worries that often plagued me about war, feeding my children, and Bruno.

Suddenly, amid the tranquil melody of chirping birds and rustling leaves, a deafening roar shattered the peace. My heart plummeted as I looked up to see three ominous warplanes darkening the sky with their silhouettes. Panic gripped me with icy tendrils, squeezing the air from my lungs and sending tremors through my body. The memories of bombs dropping from the sky flooded back, overwhelming me until I could hardly breathe. I stumbled, my vision blurred with tears, as the once-serene day turned into a battlefield in my mind.

✌

When I got home, I walked straight to Herr Hermann's kitchen to see if I could find a newspaper. It wasn't on the table, so I searched the house. Finally, I found it on the arm of the sofa. I sat down to read the front page.

The Reich Mourns: Führer Adolf Hitler Passes Away

Date: 1 May 1945
By: Reich Correspondent Franz Müller
    Berlin, Germany: The heart of the German Reich is heavy today as the nation mourns the passing of its esteemed leader, Führer Adolf Hitler. The news, though shrouded in sorrow, comes with a solemn determination to carry forward the vision and legacy of the National Socialist movement.
    Reports from the Führerbunker in Berlin reveal that our beloved führer succumbed to his injuries sustained in the defense of our

capital against the relentless onslaught of the Allied forces. Despite the valiant efforts of our medical personnel, Führer Hitler breathed his last breath 30 April afternoon.

In the wake of this tragic loss, the mantle of leadership falls upon the capable shoulders of Admiral Karl Dönitz, who has assumed control of the Reich as designated by Führer Hitler himself. Known for his unwavering loyalty to the National Socialist cause and his remarkable military prowess, Admiral Dönitz stands ready to guide the Reich through these tumultuous times.

In a statement issued from his headquarters, Admiral Dönitz pledged to uphold the ideals of National Socialism and ensure the continuation of our sacred mission to safeguard the German people and secure our rightful place in history.

As the nation grieves for its fallen leader, we are reminded of the unyielding spirit that has defined us as a people. Let us honor the memory of Führer Adolf Hitler by redoubling our efforts in defense of the Reich and remaining steadfast in our commitment to the National Socialist cause.

In this hour of darkness, let us draw strength from the legacy of our führer and march forward with unwavering resolve. The Reich shall endure, and victory shall be ours!

Heil Hitler! Heil Dönitz!

I felt like tearing the paper to shreds. They're carrying forward a legacy of hate. Bastards!

Edith was awake all night, pulling at her ears. She ran a small fever, and I walked with her in my arms, trying to keep her quiet so she wouldn't wake the others. At four o'clock, Martha stood up and reached out to Edith, saying, "I'll walk her a bit." She settled Edith over her shoulder with one hand under Edith's bum and the other rubbing her back.

I put some chamomile flowers in boiling water, then strained the flowers and let the water cool. Edith was quieter by then, but she was still fussy. I hoped maybe some tea would help with her pain.

Rosie took over walking Edith at seven so I could go to work. I was exhausted and felt guilty for leaving my sick baby. I knew the ladies would take good care of Edith, but I felt pulled between two roles: being a mother on one hand and a breadwinner on the other.

It wasn't often that an uncoded telegram came through, but around eleven o'clock, someone handed me one with English writing. I read it and looked across the table at Lieutenant Maier. He had his earphones on and his head down while he wrote in his notebook. My hand shook as I started to write.

From: Dwight D. Eisenhower, Supreme Commander Allied Expeditionary Force
To: Karl Dönitz, President of Germany
Date: 5 May 1945
Message:
Thank you for your prompt response. While I appreciate your willingness to discuss the terms of surrender, it must be made clear that the Allied powers demand an unconditional surrender of all German forces. This is nonnegotiable. An unconditional surrender will ensure the complete and total cessation of hostilities, paving the way for a just and lasting peace in Europe. I urge you to accept this demand without delay and instruct your representatives accordingly.
Sincerely,
Dwight D. Eisenhower, General
United States Army

I looked at the message and wondered if there was any way to avoid passing it on. *What would Director Keller do with it when he read it?* I tapped my pen on my notebook. I felt certain that the transmission had reached its destination. It's not like we kept the Allies from getting the transmissions we intercepted; we only made copies. I walked to Director Keller's office and knocked.

"What is it?" he asked gruffly.

I stepped into his office and waved the piece of paper. "Surrender negotiations are happening."

"Close the door, please, Frau Arnold."

I stepped in and closed the door softly.

"Frau Arnold, I will tell you this in confidence." He walked around to the front of his desk, facing me as he leaned against it. He looked at me intently. "Several German generals have surrendered. It's my belief that the war will end any day."

My heart raced as I thought about Bruno coming home, but in an instant, my hope dimmed when I remembered: Bruno was listed as missing in action.

~

I walked to work as usual on Tuesday, 8 May. It wasn't raining, but the clouds were thick. I felt grateful because thick clouds seemed to bring fewer air raids. My panic whenever a plane flew overhead, whether it was dropping bombs or not, was getting worse. I walked into the office to find Director Keller at the front of the room where I usually worked. *What now?*

"The announcement came out last night," he told us. "The war is over. Everyone go home." His tone was flat, so I couldn't understand whether he was happy or sad the war was over. Everyone in the room threw their notebooks, pens, and earphones into the air and cheered. I watched as everyone hugged each other and found it curious these people who had barely spoken to each other in all the months I'd worked with them were now hugging and celebrating together.

I was still standing in the doorway when Director Keller walked toward me. "Go home, Frau Arnold. There's no more work."

I turned and left to walk back home, my feet feeling like they wanted to dance all the way. The war was over!

✢

As I walked past the main house on the way to the garden shed, I saw Herr Hermann's daughters and grandchildren huddled just outside the open kitchen door. I walked over, thinking perhaps they were listening to the radio broadcast.

"Despite the valor and determination of our forces, it has become clear that the conflict that engulfed our nation has reached its conclusion. The enemy advances have forced us to reassess our position. While we may not have achieved the ultimate victory we desired, let us not forget the bravery and sacrifice of our soldiers who fought with unwavering loyalty to the Reich. As we navigate these challenging times, let us honor the memory of our fallen comrades and preserve the ideals that have guided us. Though the battle may be lost, the spirit of our cause endures."

"Preserve the ideals"? What ideals? The ones of hate and war? I thought.

I walked to my garden-shack home and was happy to see my children.

CHAPTER 70

August 1945

Rosie was kicking a ball with Rolf and Edith in the yard one afternoon while Anna was nearby, hanging clean clothes on the line. I was standing in the kitchen, rinsing the dishes we used for breakfast in one of the buckets. Martha was standing next to me, drying them. I handed her a plate.

"I was thinking about going into Kiel today to see my apartment," I told her. "Do you want to come?"

"Are the buses running?" Martha put down the dry plate and took a cup from my hand.

"Only one way to find out."

Anna decided to come with us, and Rosie said she was happy to watch the children. I felt safer leaving them on the farm. I didn't know what we were going to find once we entered Kiel.

The bus driver took us to a stop on the outskirts of Kiel. "End of the line . . . everyone out," he said, opening the door to the bus. I looked at Martha and Anna, but they were as confused as I was.

"Why are you dropping us here instead of the main station in Kiel?" Martha asked.

"The roads into Kiel are blocked. You'll have to walk if you want to get into the city." He impatiently waved us off the bus.

We walked west along the road and then turned north. There was a huge gap in the overpass, so we had to pick our way across the top of large pieces of cement and rebar to continue. I looked down at the train tracks. They were also partially destroyed. After forty-five minutes, we finally saw the Kieler Hörn, the beginning of Kiel harbor.

"What do you think is happening up there?" I pointed ahead of us. There were military jeeps blocking the entrance to the city.

As we approached, I saw a British flag on the back of one of the jeeps. There were four military men and two jeeps. My goodness, they looked young, barely even of age to drive, yet they all had rifles and sidearms at their waists.

"Excuse me. We're trying to get into Kiel to see our apartment," Martha said.

The one with red hair looked at her like he didn't understand. I stepped in and translated to English.

"Do you have papers?" asked the one with red hair.

"No, I didn't know we needed any to go home." I could tell Martha was getting ready to tell these men off, so I pulled at her elbow.

"Check back in a few days," he said.

"What do you want to do now?" I whispered. *Can we just find another way in?*

"I'd like to see if we can get to the farm," Anna said. She didn't have to distinguish her farm from Herr Hermann's. I knew what she meant.

"We can probably cross those train tracks over to the bus stop." I pointed to the west. "What do you think?"

✢❧✢

Nearly three hours from the time we left the Hermann farm, we were walking on the dirt driveway to the old Arnold farmhouse. The house looked vacant and sad. The porch swing Bruno and I had spent so many dates on was hanging by one rope instead of four. Ivy was crawling up the side of the house. The old farm truck was parked next to the barn with grass growing up around the wheels. All three of us stopped at the same time as we got closer and saw that the large oak tree in the backyard had fallen over onto the house.

We stepped up onto the front porch and looked through the cracked windows, using our hands against our faces as shields against the reflection. We could see nothing but branches, so we walked around the back of the house and saw the old tree's root ball had come out of the ground. The main part of the trunk went right through the roof over the kitchen.

Moving back to the farm was not an option.

CHAPTER 71

December 1945

At the beginning of December, Martha and I took the bus into Kiel, leaving the children with Anna and Rosie. The bus dropped us off just outside the city, and no one stopped us. What should have been a forty-five-minute walk to get to my address, Mittelstraße 16, took us two hours. Several streets were deemed too dangerous and had been roped off, so we had to go around.

I held Martha's hand as we stood across the street from the building that housed my apartment. My home and the one above us had fallen into what used to be Frau Bauer's home.

"Oh my God, Frau Hoffman!" I ran across the street, careful not to trip on any debris, and shouted up to the second floor, "Frau Hoffman! Frau Hoffman!" I waited, but there was no answer and no movement. I scanned the wreckage for something to climb up to the second window but couldn't find anything. Finally, I pulled Martha's hand and started walking quickly down the street toward the police station.

The young police officer took pity on me and carried a ladder back to Frau Hoffman's apartment. After setting the ladder close to what was the hallway between what used to be my apartment and Frau Hoffman's, he climbed up and disappeared into the hallway. After about ten minutes, he climbed down and walked over to us.

"No one is there," he said. He lit a cigarette and blew out the smoke. "Aside from cracked walls and glass everywhere, the apartment was in pretty good shape." I was at a loss for where she might have gone.

The young officer's radio crackled to life, and he was instructed to go to another address. He threw his cigarette butt down and crushed it with the toe of his boot, then walked down the street. I noticed he left the ladder, but he was already around the corner.

I turned to Martha. "Let's go see your apartment."

Martha's apartment was another thirty-minute walk to the west of mine. Part of the building had windows blown out, and the roof and front wall were damaged. We walked to the other end of the building toward her apartment home. Surprisingly, her first-floor apartment was mostly intact. There was a hole in the roof and damage around the front door, but the door itself was usable.

We walked into her apartment and were surprised to see a woman sitting on the sofa and an eight- or nine-year-old girl sitting on the floor facing her. Playing cards were spread out across the coffee table between them.

After a moment of silence, Martha opened her arms and said, "Lotte!" I stood in the doorway and watched them hug for a few minutes. The girl also joined the hug.

The women stepped back, looking at each other for a few moments, and then Martha started laughing. "Karla, this is my cousin Lotte," Martha said.

We all sat together in Martha's living room as she caught Lotte up on where she was living. At some point during the conversation, the decision was made that Martha would move home and share the apartment with Lotte and Lily. Martha said it would give us more room at Herr Hermann's farm, but really, I think she wanted to be with family. I was curious about where Lotte and Lily had been during the war but didn't want to be nosey.

On Christmas Eve, I decided to make aebleskiver, Edith's favorite. I made them in Herr Hermann's kitchen, using some of his flour and sugar allotment. The specially made pan had six wells about four centimeters in diameter for making the Danish pancake balls. I placed a spoonful of dough in each well, then added a piece of apple. After three minutes, I turned them with a fork so the other side could cook. After they'd finished cooking, I placed them on a plate and sprinkled them with sugar. I separated half to bring back to the shed with me and left the rest for Herr Hermann and his family.

Edith had disappeared into the living room to play with Herr Hermann's grandson when we first arrived.

"Edith! Come in the kitchen, please," I called to her.

Edith came running in and crashed into the back of my knees as I stood at the sink cleaning my pan. I bent down and offered her a donut from the plate. She clapped and laughed, full of excitement, then looked around the plate for the best ones. I didn't know what criteria made up the best ones, but it was fun to watch her decide. She took one in her right hand, and I stood up, taking the plate with me.

Edith held up her hand. "Mutti, come back!"

I bent over again and Edith managed to squeeze two more pancake balls into her small left hand.

CHAPTER 72

April 1946

At the beginning of April, Herr Hermann's family—which now included me, Rosie, and Anna—gathered around the kitchen table at the main house to plan the next two months. Spring was a very busy time on the farm, and Herr Hermann wanted to give out work assignments. The kitchen table set included a bench against two walls and three wooden chairs. I sat on the end on the bench with Edith beside me, tucked in the corner with her doll. Herr Hermann's children and grandchildren took up the remaining seats around the table.

The back door opened and slammed shut, and then we heard footsteps. We all looked across the table from each other in surprise.

"Hello?" A man's voice was in the hall.

Adele, Herr Hermann's oldest daughter, and Heidi, his granddaughter, stood up at the same time. "Vati!" Heidi screeched then. Apparently deciding that the adults weren't moving fast enough, she crawled under the table and jumped into her father's arms as he entered the kitchen. Anna shifted her chair so Adele could get out.

I tensed at the sight of the tall balding man in his Nazi uniform. I knew from talking to Herr Hermann that his son-in-law had been a corporal assigned to the Western Front in France.

I felt tears prick the back of my eyes as I watched the homecoming, wishing it was Bruno.

I slid out from the kitchen table and took Edith's hand. "Herr Hermann, we'll come back later to do the planning," I said.

While Herr Hermann's youngest daughter, Bertha, looked after Edith and Rolf, I continued to work in the garden every day. The garden was about seven by ten meters. I pulled out all the previous season's dead vines and leaves, then used a hoe to loosen the dirt. I planted rows of carrots, onions, radishes, and lettuce grown from pieces I'd saved and put in water to grow roots over the winter. Herr Hermann provided seeds for peas and spinach. I left enough rows to plant tomatoes, cucumbers, and peppers when the weather was warmer.

I looked across the yard, about twenty meters, and saw Adele's husband, Paul, building more beehive boxes and frames. I rinsed off my shovel and hoe, then headed across the yard to the barn to put them away and get a bucket so I could water everything. Before going to the well for water, I walked over to Paul. He had a cigarette dangling from his mouth and was squatting on the ground, assembling a frame.

"Paul, do you think you could build me some wooden boxes so I can plant some herbs?" I asked.

He squinted when he looked up at me and took the cigarette out of his mouth, holding it between his first finger and thumb. "I can do that. Can you make a drawing of what you want?"

"Yes, I'll leave it on the kitchen table for you." I walked toward the well to fill the bucket with water.

CHAPTER 73

September 1946

Rolf had turned six years old, and it was time for him to go to school; however, there were no schools in Prasdorf. Even if there had been, they might not have been open; many schools were closed because most teachers had been sent to war. Adele and I decided to create our own "school" for Rolf and Heidi. Adele agreed to teach math and science. I took history, English, and writing. I also agreed to teach a sewing class each Sunday morning to anyone who wanted to learn.

Adele gave her lessons in the morning while I worked on the farm, and I gave my lessons in the afternoon. Rosie oversaw homework. I loved every minute of teaching our small class. Soon word went out to the neighbors, who sent their children. Nearly two decades after I'd given up hope, I had finally realized my dream of teaching classes.

One morning, Anna and I were working in the garden, pulling the weeds that seemed to spring up every night. We worked in tandem, each of us kneeling in front of adjacent rows.

"Karla, it's coming up on two years since Bruno was listed as missing in action," Anna said softly. "I haven't heard from Karl at all." She sat back, brushing wisps of hair out of her face with her arm. "I was thinking maybe we should have a funeral . . . plan our future."

My anger shot up as I picked up a pile of weeds and threw them in the bucket we used for gardening. *Was she kidding me?* If Bruno were dead, I would feel it.

He's not dead.

One day in February, Anna and I spent an afternoon pruning shrubs in the front of the house. I clipped the long branches with the loppers, letting the branches fall to the frozen ground. Anna then picked up the pieces and put them in the wheelbarrow. "I received a letter from my aunt inviting Rosie and me to live with her in Flensburg," she said after we'd been working for a while.

"I didn't know you had an aunt in Flensburg," I said. We had been living together for three years, and she'd simply mentioned that she was an only child and that her parents were dead. A tendril of guilt worked its way into my conscious. *Had I been so absorbed in the war and my children's survival that I hadn't thought to ask about Anna's family?* She could have gone to her aunt's house after Bruno and Karl left. Yet she had stayed with us and had been an enormous comfort and help with Rolf and Edith.

"My father's sister. She's eighty." Anna pushed her hair behind her ear and looked up at me. "Rosie and I are going to go at the end of March. I think it's time we moved forward."

PART IV

Bruno and Karla

CHAPTER 74

February 1947

Bruno

Karl tapped my arm and smiled. "Let's go to Prasdorf."

"Frau Hoffman, thank you." I looked around her apartment. "Are you going to be okay here?" I couldn't imagine how this seventy-year-old woman found food and managed the ladder.

"Of course! Go get your family," she said as she ushered us out the door. On the bus, I tried to temper my blossoming feeling of hope and happiness for fear I would be let down. Three years was a long time, and I had no idea if they were still at the camp.

We took a two-hour bus ride from Kiel to the town of Probsteierhagen. The bus depot was very small, and there were no clerks working, so we set out on foot, eventually passing a fire station.

"Let's get directions." Karl indicated the station.

The fire captain pointed north and said it was a twenty-minute walk to the camp. He was nice enough, but his tone of voice when he said "camp" seemed to have an edge to it.

Karl and I took off at a jog, slowing to a walk once the gates to the camp were within view on the right side of the road. As we neared the camp, my palms started sweating, and my heart began to race. My feet seemed to have a mind of their own as I slowed to a stop.

"What is it?" Karl looked at me with concern.

My mind transported me back to the training camp I was sent to in Berlin after the Nazis forced me into war. A sturdy metal fence enclosed the perimeter of this camp, reminding me of similar barriers I had encountered before. Beyond the fence, rows of tents stretched across the field, evoking memories of my long days of military training. Despite the familiar and upsetting scene, a surge of determination coursed through me as I drew two deep breaths and strode purposefully toward the camp office situated just outside the gates.

"Excuse me!" I said.

The clerk looked slowly up at me but didn't move from where he was sitting, his feet propped on a desk and a book in his hands.

"My wife left me a note saying that she's here," I told him.

"You can just go look for her, then." *Was he kidding?* There were rows and rows of tents with thousands of people out there.

"Can you just see if she is registered here?" Karl asked with frustration in his voice.

The young man got up, obviously irritated with two old men needing his help. He walked over to a box with ten-by-fifteen-centimeter cards stacked neatly together and looked at us. "Name."

"Karla Arnold."

The clerk flipped through the cards. "There's no 'Karla Arnold.'" My heart dropped.

"How about Anna Arnold?" Karl asked.

"There is no one with the name 'Arnold' registered."

My anger rose. "Look, we're just making it back from the war. I walked from Siberia, for Christ's sake. Look again!" The clerk's eyes got big.

"Could they have signed out and gone somewhere else?" Karl asked.

"Most people were rotated out to farms to make room for more families. The cards of those who rotated out are in a different box."

My jaw almost cracked as I gritted my teeth.

CHAPTER 75

February 1947

Karla

A day of sun and no clouds was a rare delight in February. Rosie and I were washing clothes in Herr Hermann's large sink that was located in a utility room just off his kitchen. Washing was a thankless job, but I was grateful for Rosie's help. I leaned over the washboard, scrubbing shirts, underclothes, and Edith's bed sheet. After each item was scrubbed, I passed it to Rosie, and she rinsed the soap out. It was a little crowded for two people, but I enjoyed her company.

Rosie and Anna would be leaving soon, and I knew I would have decisions to make. The children and I couldn't live on Herr Hermann's farm forever. Although I wanted to move out of the cold garden shed as soon as I could, the decision to leave was hard. Making plans for the future felt like I was giving up on Bruno.

The laundry washed and rinsed, Rosie and I worked together to squeeze as much water out of the fabric as possible before folding everything into the laundry basket. We then carried the basket, each of us holding one end, out into the frigid air. I didn't realize the temperature had dropped and paused to think whether we should hang the clothes on the line or in the house. *The sun is shining, so perhaps a few hours on the line will get the drying process started,* I thought.

I waved at Anna, who was sitting in a chair just outside the garden-shed door, drinking water from a glass. She took the glass inside when she saw Rosie and me, then walked over to help hang the linens on the clothesline to dry in the sun.

As we started pinning up the sheets, I saw Rolf trying to put a stick in the ground while Edith watched from about ten meters away. I worked one line with my back to the main house, and Anna helped Rosie on the other side.

Adele, Paul, and Heidi had gone into town for supplies with Herr Hermann. I didn't see Bertha and her children in the yard. I assumed they were in the house or had maybe decided to take a walk.

CHAPTER 76

February 1947

Bruno

My heart raced as the farm came into view, and I started running. The main house was painted white with a small front porch. There were a door and two windows at the front of the house, and when we walked up, I saw three more windows along the side. I stepped onto the porch and knocked, but there was no answer. Impatient, I knocked again.

Finally, I heard footsteps from inside the house and the door opened. A young woman holding a baby looked at us curiously. "Yes?"

"I'm Bruno Arnold. I'm looking for my wife . . . Karla."

She opened the door wider and smiled. "She's in the back." She pointed to her right.

I jumped over the railing as Karl ran around the porch behind me.

Five meters away were two young children, a boy and a girl, playing. It looked like the boy was trying to get a stick in the ground, and the girl was laughing. The boy looked up and locked eyes with me. My heart leaped out of my throat as I approached him. I knelt down in front of the children. "Rolf . . . hi. Do you remember me?"

Rolf stood up and called, "Mutti!" He grabbed Edith's hand and tried dragging her but ended up letting go and running. I followed the direction he was running and saw her hanging sheets. My wife! I picked Edith up and put her on my shoulders as she laughed.

CHAPTER 77

February 1947

Karla

A mother knows every one of the tones of her children's cries. I heard Rolf yell at me and knew instinctively he was scared. My entire body tensed as I turned around and saw Rolf running toward me. My eyes scanned behind him, and I saw a man carrying Edith on his shoulders. My stomach did a flip, and I dropped the laundry and the clothespins as I ran.

"Bruno!"

CHAPTER 78

February 1947
Bruno

I saw Karla drop the laundry and run toward me as I put Edith gently on the ground. Rosie pulled the sheets that were hanging on the clothesline back and screamed, "Vati!" She ran toward Karl just as Karla threw herself into my arms.

I realized in that moment that I hadn't come home when I crossed the border into Germany. And I hadn't been home when I stood outside our demolished apartment.

Home happened the moment Karla wrapped her arms around me.

CHAPTER 79

April–September 1947

Karla

Anna and Karl moved to Flensburg at the end of April, just a month later than Anna had planned. Karl was optimistic about finding an electrician job, and Anna was looking forward to a new chapter in her life. Rosie found a job at a hardware store in Kiel. The owner lived above the store with his family and rented a small room to Rosie. I was excited for Rosie's newfound independence.

I read the morning paper as I walked home from the grocery store in Prasdorf early one Sunday morning in June.

Postwar Progress: Updates on Jewish Communities in Germany

Germany is undergoing a period of reconstruction and reconciliation, with a concerted focus on the status and welfare of Jewish communities across the nation. Efforts toward reintegration are notable, with various programs and initiatives aimed at helping

Jewish survivors reintegrate into society. These efforts encompass the provision of housing, employment opportunities, and social support, signaling a commitment to addressing the needs of those who suffered during the war.

Legal reforms have also taken center stage in recent months, with the overturning of discriminatory laws and policies targeting Jews. These reforms represent a significant step toward fostering equality and justice within German society and include strengthening legal protections for religious freedom and minority rights.

I thought of Eli and Ilse. *Had they made it out safely?* The front-page news article went on to describe educational initiatives aimed at combating prejudice. I folded the paper and tucked it under my arm as I entered the shed.

I placed the folded paper next to Bruno's place at the dining table and poured his coffee as he walked over, pulling up his suspenders. I leaned into him as he kissed my cheek.

I sat down across from him, sipping my hot coffee and waiting for him to read the entire article. He finally put the paper down and looked at me.

"Do you think they made it?" he asked. I knew he was referring to Eli and his family.

I smiled at him, and then I pulled my purse off the empty chair where I'd laid it when I walked in. I dug into the small zipper pocket for the piece of paper I'd hidden there five years before and pushed it across the table to Bruno. "Why don't you write to Viggo and ask?"

He unfolded the paper and looked up at me. "Where did you get this?"

"Viggo handed it to me before they left. For emergencies. The Gestapo was everywhere, and I knew they were reading people's mail, looking for dissidents. I couldn't take the chance of writing him before now."

Bruno sat up straighter, and I could tell he was getting excited. "Write to Viggo," I told him. "Find our friends."

⌇

Two months later, I walked into the garden shed with a grocery bag in each hand. Bruno had taken Rolf and Edith to the park. As I put away the groceries, I saw two envelopes lying on the floor. Someone must have slid them under the door. I wondered if I should open them or wait for Bruno.

I decided to wait, but the letters continued to call to me from the dining room table where I had left them. Finally, I heard my family at the door. I grabbed the letters and ran to the door, opening it widely. Bruno was carrying Edith, and Rolf was trailing after him with grass stains and dirt on his knees. Rolf looked so happy, I didn't have the heart to reprimand him for the grass stains. I knew my boy; he had been rolling down one of the small knolls in the park.

"What a welcome from my wife," Bruno smiled.

I held up the envelopes. "One from Viggo in America, and one from Eli and Ilse in Sweden."

Bruno gently let Edith slide down to the floor and took the envelopes from me. We sat next to each other at the table, and Bruno held the first letter out so we could read together.

Dear Bruno and Karla,

We cannot tell you how ecstatic we were to get a note from Viggo with your address on it. We have thought of you so often over the years and prayed you were well. You will always and forever be part of our family.

It's hard to believe that Jacob is eighteen years old. He wants to be a doctor and is now studying at the University of Stockholm. Daniel is sixteen and is an avid football player like my brother.

I hope Klaus and Rolf are well.

With much love,

Eli and Ilse

I watched as Bruno took a deep breath. He reached for my hand and squeezed it. The room was full of emotion. It was hard to see Klaus's name in print. So much had happened in the five years since we last saw them. But our friends were alive!

"Open the one from Viggo," I said, hoping for a distraction.

Bruno slit the second envelope open and started to read the letter but then passed it to me. It was in English, so I translated.

Dear Bruno and Karla,

It was so good to see your letter. I passed your address to Eli and Ilse. You should be comforted and proud to learn that they have been living a peaceful life in Sweden near my family.

I learned of Otto's and Therese's passing. I'm so sorry for your loss. They were courageous people, and I was honored to have met them even for the short time I knew them. I traveled all over Europe with my job and met many people, but your parents will always hold a special place in my heart.

Bruno rubbed my back as I read.

It will take some time, but Germany is doing well rebuilding. I hope by now you have found housing and are feeling the progress. If I can be of any assistance, please let me know. Below is my address.

Fondly,
Colonel Axel Viggo Granholm

I folded the letter and put it back in the envelope, amazed that Viggo was a colonel.

In September, Edith convinced Rolf he needed aebleskiver for his birthday treat, so I started saving a little bit of the ingredients each week out of our food rations. The morning of Rolf's birthday, I looked everywhere for the special pan. Bruno was sipping his coffee at the dining table.

"Bruno, where is the aebleskiver pan?" I finally asked.

He blew on the hot drink and casually said, "I sold it."

Anger coursed through me. "You what?"

He turned the page of the newspaper. "We needed money to buy food, so I sold the pan."

I saw Edith in the corner with her green eyes as round as saucers. Her face crumbled, and she threw herself on the floor and cried. She cried loudly with large tears covering her face and dripping off her chin.

I picked her up to rock her. I had held this family together while he was gone for three years, and he couldn't consult with me before making a decision like this! He wasn't even reacting to Edith's meltdown. "How could you, without asking me?" I asked angrily. "There aren't many treats we can give our children, and the aebleskivers were important. I can't make them without the pan!" I put my hand on Edith's cheek and kissed her temple.

Bruno calmly folded his paper, but the movement of his clenched jaw told me he was working to keep his temper reigned in. I had never spoken to him like that before, much less in front of the children.

"Feeding our children is top priority. I won't apologize for that."

I sat on the edge of the bed with Edith in my lap and watched Bruno walk out of the room. I felt a little guilty for having snapped at him during a time when we were both feeling our way back to each other. We loved each other immensely, but we had spent three very long years apart.

CHAPTER 80

March–July 1948
Karla

I started work as a seamstress at a small dress shop in Kiel. Around this time, a friend of Bruno's let us convert an attic room into our new apartment. The room was only about forty square meters, but it was home. There was already a full-sized bed for me and Bruno. Herr Hermann gave us one set of bunk beds for Rolf and Edith. Bruno built kitchen cabinets with scrap wood for a corner kitchen. He also found a tabletop and four mismatched chairs.

It was June, a week before what would have been Klaus's ninth birthday, when I was awakened by Bruno's scream. He had been sleeping restlessly ever since his return, but that night was a full-blown nightmare.

"Bruno," I said softly. I glanced over at the bunk beds and was grateful there was no movement.

Although the air was chilly, the sheets were wet, and I could see the sweat on Bruno's forehead from the ambient light of the moon.

I pushed at his shoulder. "Bruno."

Suddenly he sat up and looked around, confused about where he was. I sat up and rubbed his back. "You're safe."

In one motion, he turned and put his arm around me while laying us back down. Ten minutes later, I felt his body relax and his breathing level off.

⌖

The man who rented us the attic room was a customer of Bruno's from before the war. He lived on the ground floor and gave the second floor to his son and daughter-in-law, Lisl. I met Lisl the day we moved into the attic room. Lisl's son was just three months older than Rolf, and it was nice to watch the boys play with one another while we had coffee.

One week, Lisl invited us to spend Sunday afternoon with them. I had just sat down at her dining table, and she was pouring hot water from the kettle into the ground coffee in a carafe. "I didn't realize Erna was your sister, Karla."

I watched as Rolf told Edith to go play somewhere else and debated whether to step in. "How do you know Erna?"

She arranged cups and saucers on the table. "I met her before the war at a party." She poured coffee into our cups and passed me mine. "I had lunch with her last week."

I blew on the hot liquid and took a tentative sip before putting my cup back on the saucer to cool.

"The clothes for Rolf and Edith were cute," she said.

I looked sharply at her. "What clothes?"

Lisl looked at me over her cup. "A package from America had arrived when I was there. It had Bruno's name on it." She put her cup down. "I was a little surprised she'd opened it, but she said you wouldn't mind if she took a peek. I'm sorry, I . . ." Lisl let her words hang. It seemed she didn't know what else to say.

"Lisl, can I leave Rolf and Edith here for an hour?"

As I rode the bus, I racked my brain for possible reasons why the package was delivered to Erna's house but couldn't make sense of it. My anger rose with every step I took from the bus stop to the front door of her house. There was no guard, and there were still boards nailed to the windows. Most buildings had their windows blown out from bombs, but by then most had been repaired. I knocked several times before the door finally swung open. Erna appeared under the weather, with greasy hair and a pallid complexion that hinted at her unwell state.

"What do you want?" she asked.

"A package from Bruno's cousins in America was delivered here." I wasn't about to let her deny something I knew was true.

She didn't invite me in. She just held the door open enough to look at me and said, "If you're here for the clothes, I sold them."

She didn't care enough to ask how I found out. I was stunned. "You sold my children's clothes? How could you?"

She said nonchalantly, "I needed the money."

I made an obvious look around her house. "You don't need the money."

She balled her hands into fists but kept them at her sides. "The British captured my husband and took all the money! They killed him! I have nothing. I have no income, and you can see the state of this house!"

The British killed him, or he committed suicide, like the other Nazi cowards? I asked myself. I wasn't a person to get angry often, but I felt so much rage toward my sister. She had done many terrible things to me in our lifetime, and now she had stolen from my children. I was livid. "Who did you sell them to? You need to get them back."

She slammed the door in my face.

CHAPTER 81

September 1948

Bruno

Karla and I had an ongoing conversation about people knocking on our door at all hours for help fixing everything from a broken window to overhauling an engine. She was angry when people knocked on our door for help after dinner. I wanted the work to support my family.

Most nights after dinner, while Rolf did homework and Edith played, Karla sat at one side of the dining table, sewing, her machine making whirring sounds every few minutes. It would go silent as she adjusted the fabric, and then she would press the pedal, and it would come to life again.

One night, I sat across from her, fixing a boat engine. As I worked, I thought about a few of the jobs I'd done over the past month. One person paid me in trade with an old bicycle after I rebuilt the carburetor to his truck. I spent a week fixing up the bicycle, repairing the brakes and the broken chain. I found an old basket in the landfill. The bicycle made it possible to get around town and take on a few more jobs each day.

I glanced over at Edith as she put her doll on top of a wooden toy car I'd made and "drove" it around the floor. I smiled as I thought about the job I'd taken her to earlier in the day. I had put glass in several windows on a house just outside of Kiel. The woman paid me with a dozen eggs stacked up in a bowl. I had lifted Edith into the bicycle's basket, then handed her the bowl of eggs. "Now, don't drop them, Edith." I laughed at how serious my four-year-old could get. She held tight to the eggs and bragged to Karla about how well she did.

⌁

One rainy Saturday afternoon, I was sitting on the bed with my back against the headboard. Edith was sitting on my lap, and Rolf sat next to me with his elbow on my thigh, engrossed in the story I was reading to them. Karla was sitting at the table, sewing.

Karla frowned when someone knocked on the door. "We should put a sign on the door with your hours of work."

I handed the book to Rolf, slid Edith off my lap, and got up off the bed. My toolbox was sitting by the door. When I opened the door, I was surprised to see a boy of around nine or ten years old. He looked distressed as he shifted from one foot to another. "Herr Arnold, my uncle sent me. He needs you to come help."

When I glanced at Karla for her acknowledgment, she rolled her eyes. "I'll put a sign up with my working hours tomorrow, Karla. I promise." She waved me off, and I followed the boy.

The boy kept running ahead and then waiting for me to catch up. We walked across the street, about four hundred meters from my family's attic room. The rain stopped and a few glimpses of blue sky appeared between the departing clouds.

I saw the boy talking to a man who I assumed was his uncle. As I walked up, the man approached me.

"Herr Arnold, I'm Herr Vogel. I'm sorry to take you away from your family." We shook hands. "I tried to find someone at the British naval base to come, but they said the best they could do was to put up that sign." I looked over to where he pointed. A sign with red letters was tied in the middle of a rope that extended from a tree to a sign across the entrance to the alley: "Bomb! Stay away."

"I hear you're the one to call when something needs to be fixed." Herr Vogel looked at me pointedly. He then gestured beyond the sign to a mound of metal next to a building. "I was hoping you could defuse it."

I scratched the side of my face, looking around at all the buildings surrounding us. Many had been restored, and families were living in them. The one with the bomb next to it looked like construction had just started on it. I glanced across the street at the house where I knew my family was. *Could the bomb blow buildings up that far away?* I took a breath and said, "Let's evacuate all the families first." I took a step in the direction of my attic room. "I'll be back in a few minutes. I need to talk to my wife."

I ran back over to our house and climbed the stairs two at a time. My family was in the same place I'd left them. "Karla, I need you to take the children to Martha's for a bit."

She stopped sewing and looked up at me. "Why?"

"Because there's an unexploded bomb just four hundred yards from here. Families are being evacuated temporarily."

"Rolf, Edith, get your jackets. We're going to visit Tante Martha." Karla grabbed her purse from the chair, and we walked out together. Instead of turning right to go to the bus stop, I turned left.

"Where are you going?" Karla asked.

I glanced across the street, then back at Karla. "No one is coming to defuse it."

Karla's face went pale. "No, Bruno. Not you."

"There's no choice. The bomb needs to be defused, and I couldn't live with myself if I walked away and people died." I had already walked away from more than thirty men in Russia.

"Don't do this," Karla whispered with tears in her eyes.

⌁

I hated disappointing Karla. She had already gone through so much. As I got closer to the alleyway, I told myself I would just assess it. If I wasn't confident that I could defuse it, I would leave it for the bomb disposal units, however long it took them to arrive. I didn't know if that would be hours or weeks or months.

The bomb had dropped down within half a meter of a brick building, in between some bushes. A few of the bushes had been cut, and their branches were piled to one side. The bomb was at an angle about halfway in the ground, its tail end sticking up. I guessed that it weighed about five hundred kilograms and was about two or three meters long. I squatted in front of the bomb, thinking about the two-hour course on how bombs work that I'd had to take as part of my military training.

So I finally found something that the Nazis taught me useful.

CHAPTER 82

September 1948

Bruno

Herr Vogel walked up behind me as I looked through my toolbox. "How did you find this?" I asked.

"My nephew was cutting down the bushes in front of it. Do you think you can defuse it?"

"I don't know. Can you get me some supplies? I need a shovel, flashlight, string, and wire cutters." I shifted tools around in my toolbox. "Actually, I have wire cutters, so just a shovel, flashlight, and string."

I dragged the cut bushes out of the way and shook my head. *Why is a boy of nine cutting bushes?* I kneeled in front of the explosive and used my hands to uncover more of the bomb, looking for a door to access the electronics while putting my ear to the device to listen. There was no sound. Since I couldn't find a door to the electronics, I had to assume they were in the head buried in the ground. Well, that was unfortunate.

By the time Herr Vogel came back with my supplies an hour later, I had removed about fifteen centimeters of dirt, and there was still no electronics panel. I took the shovel and gently loosened up more dirt so I could scoop the dirt next to the bomb away with my hands.

Herr Vogel got down on his hands and knees behind me and pulled the loose dirt further away, giving me room to work. Still the electronics door remained elusive.

"What are you looking for?" Herr Vogel asked.

"There should be a small door or panel to access the electronics." I rubbed my chin with the back of my hand. "I'm afraid if we move any more dirt, the entire thing will shift and either detonate or make it harder to disarm it."

"What if we used some of that construction equipment to hoist it up? We can put straps under it and just pull it up gently?"

I stood up to stretch my knees and thought about his idea. "My concern is that bringing the equipment will shake it too much." I walked around, looking at the bomb from different angles. "How about if we find some wood and use it to prop the bomb up safely from the sides. Then we can dig dirt until we find the door. Once we find it, we can fill in dirt around it. Leaving the door exposed and filling in dirt will give extra stability while I figure out how to disarm it."

"I'll get someone to find wood." Herr Vogel took a step toward the street.

"Can you also send someone to get some schematics?" I took a pencil and small piece of paper out of my toolbox and walked around the bomb to the place where I had seen a sticker earlier. I spit on the sticker and rubbed the area clean. "It's a British bomb, so the naval base should have something on it." I wrote down the serial and lot numbers, then handed the paper to Herr Vogel.

"I'll get right on it," he said.

Thirty minutes later, Herr Vogel returned with three pieces of wood ranging from one to four meters in length. He also brought two pieces of rebar about two meters each. I was surprised to see a man in a British navy uniform following him with rolled-up papers. The schematics.

"This is Captain Taylor with the British navy," Herr Vogel said as he put the wood and rebar next to the bomb.

"I'm Bruno." I shook Captain Taylor's hand.

We spread the schematics out on the ground. "What's your plan?" asked the captain.

I was relieved he spoke German because there was no way I would let Karla come back to translate. I walked him through the plan, making adjustments to how I thought we should place the wood as the captain asked questions. Finally, the three of us started moving dirt, pushing the wood and rebar gently under the bomb as we worked. As we moved the dirt, I felt around the outside of the cold metal for the door.

"I found it," I said after about thirty minutes. I stood up and rubbed my hands on my hips to get the dirt off. I grabbed another board and put it just under the door. "Let's fill in as much dirt as we can, keeping this area clean."

Lying on my back to access the door, I used a screwdriver to gently unscrew the four screws securing it. Next, I used the tip of the screwdriver to gradually remove the door. The inside of the door was attached to two wires, and another two wires were inside the bomb casing attached to the cylinder fuse.

Captain Taylor stood behind me, looking at the schematics and giving me directions. "Cut the yellow wire, then wrap the string around the top of the fuse and pull it out gently." Herr Vogel passed me my wire cutters from my toolbox.

At that point, my hands started shaking, so I stopped, closed my eyes, and took several deep breaths. Once I felt calmer, I held my breath and cut the yellow wire. Once that was done, I tried to gently grip the top of the fuse, but my hands were too sweaty.

Trying a different approach, I placed a slip knot around the top of the fuse and attempted to pull it out. It wouldn't move, so, after drying my fingers on my pants, I used my hand to slowly turn it a small amount. I then pulled the string again with my right hand and guided the fuse out with my left hand. As soon as the fuse cleared its casing, I cut the remaining wires. Once it was free, the captain took the fuse gently from me. I stood so we could go over the schematics to see if there was anything else I needed to do.

Once we were satisfied the job was done, I walked to the end of the alleyway and put my hands on the side of the building to take some deep breaths.

Captain Taylor held the fuse up. "I'm taking this back to the base, and I'll get someone over in the next day or two to remove the casing."

As I watched him walk off, I pulled out a cigarette. Herr Vogel saw my hands were still shaking, so he took my lighter from me and helped light my cigarette.

CHAPTER 83

December 1948

Karla

I was walking home from taking Rolf and Edith to school when I heard the drone of a plane overhead. My heart rate went up, and I started walking faster. The people around me were carrying on with their daily activities as if nothing was wrong. *Why aren't you running?* I screamed at them in my head. The closer the plane got, the more urgent it became for me to find a place to hide. The air raid shelter. People glanced at me as I started running toward the air raid shelter, but then they went back to whatever they were doing. I screamed to them in my head, *Run!*

The plane was almost directly overhead as I ran up to the shelter. Vines snaked along the roof and curtained the front door. I reached my hand between the vines and pushed, but the door wouldn't open. I forced myself to look up from the relative safety of the shelter's doorway. The silver plane was flying away toward the south.

I leaned against the door and took deep breaths, trying to calm myself. Then the tears started—slowly at first, but within a few minutes, my body was overcome with emotion. I dropped my purse and slid down to the ground.

I don't know how long I sat in front of the shelter before I felt strong enough to get up and walk home. As I walked through the door of our attic room, I decided not to tell Bruno, since he was dealing with his own demons.

"Hello, Frau Arnold!" Bruno pulled me into the room, slid my purse off my arm, and led me across the floor in a waltz.

"What has gotten into you?" I laughed.

He pulled me toward the bed.

"Bruno, I don't have time. I have sewing and cleaning, then I have to get Rolf and Edith from school," I pointed out as I went through my daily list in my head.

"I just want to tell you my news."

I sat on the edge of the bed and waited. He kneeled in front of me, just like he did the day he proposed. "I got a job with Königliche Norddeutscher Lloyd shipping company as one of three electricians they hired," Bruno announced.

I stood up and wrapped my arms around my husband. Still reeling from my earlier panic and absorbing this great information, I needed to feel his warmth. He stepped back, keeping his hands on my hips. "It comes with money toward an apartment."

⁘

The shipping company helped us find an apartment in Kiel-Pries, a suburb of Kiel only thirteen kilometers north of our attic room. The apartment was beautiful and very similar to the one I grew up in, but larger. Two-thirds of the apartment was made up of a large combined living and dining room that was about fifty square meters long and a small kitchen that was tucked behind the dining room. The other third was a bedroom, closet, and bathroom.

The air was electric with excitement as Bruno and I looked at the apartment. The apartment I had lived in my entire life before the evacuation had had a bathroom that we shared with five other families. We had used an outhouse at Herr Hermann's farm. And now, we would have indoor plumbing that we didn't have to share with anyone else. I put my hand over my mouth and laughed.

Our own bathroom!

CHAPTER 84

March 1949

Bruno

I found four mismatched oak chairs in the landfill for our new apartment. Three chairs were missing a leg, and one was missing a back. I was able to fix them over one weekend with Rolf's help. He sanded each chair by hand and helped me stain them a dark walnut color. I did some electrical work in trade for an old table I found in the customer's basement. This was a start, and we were able to move into our new apartment a few weeks later.

I borrowed a truck from a customer, and a friend helped me carry the bunk beds Herr Hermann gave us down the stairs from the attic room. Karla packed the old wagon with linens and kitchen supplies, and we carried it down to put in the truck.

"What's that?" Karla pointed to the back of the truck.

I took a drag of my cigarette and smiled. "A gift for the lady of the house."

She walked around the truck and ran her hand along the walnut top. "A sewing machine table," she whispered. She glanced at the second piece of furniture I'd picked up from another friend, then looked at me. "And a chest of drawers so we can put things away!"

Moving into our apartment felt like turning the page of a book or like transitioning from a chapter of war to a chapter of hope. Karla and I went furniture shopping for the first time in our lives and bought a soft yellow sofa with a matching chair for the living room. We had no money, but the store let us buy the furniture on credit. The children were young enough to sleep on the sofa together so Karla and I could use the bunk beds until we could afford a proper bed.

I was handing Karla the kitchen items out of the wagon and she was putting them away when I found a small box at the bottom. I pulled off the lid and saw a stack of envelopes. "Karla, what are these?"

"Those are letters I wrote over the three years you were gone."

"Do you have a boyfriend I don't know about?" I teased. I pulled the stack out and put the box back into the wagon.

Karla laughed and walked over and took them from me. "Don't be silly. These are letters I wrote to you." She shrugged her shoulders and reached for the box. "It's not like you had an address I could send letters to."

I put my hand on her arm to stop her and gently took the stack of envelopes from her hands. "Why did you write them?" I asked.

She looked away, then back at me. "I just wrote them to feel more connected to you."

I was speechless as I cradled them to my chest. "Can I read them?" Our journey back to each other had been challenging at times, but it was in that moment that I remembered the depth of love I had for Karla. My heart soared as I thought about our future together.

CHAPTER 85

June 1949
Bruno

Edith held my hand as we walked along the waterfront. I carried a basket filled with lunch in the other hand. Karla walked ahead of us, pointing to the sailboats and telling Rolf which ones she liked. The weather was a perfect combination of warm sun and a gentle cool breeze coming from the Baltic. So many people attended Kiel Week for entertainment, food, and sailing races.

We made our way inland to a small grassy area so we could eat. I pulled out the contents of the basket, handing each item to Karla as she laid everything out in the middle of a wool blanket she'd brought. Cheese, apples, bread, and a carafe of coffee. I laid back on my elbow and watched the people around us. Before the war, I would have walked around to socialize, but the war had changed me. Now I preferred to watch people first before I engaged in any conversation. Karla's nickname for me, "the mayor," was long gone.

I saw families without husbands and men with missing limbs or in wheelchairs. I felt guilty for being relieved that I wasn't in a wheelchair and Karla didn't have to take care of me. I watched as an elderly couple held hands while walking down the boardwalk. *I hope that is Karla and me when we're that age.*

"Vati, I need to go to the toilet," Rolf said, interrupting my thoughts.

I stood up, wiping bits of grass off my hands. "Okay, I saw one down this way." I started walking in the direction we'd come from.

There was a line with two men and a boy just a little younger than Rolf in front of us. I glanced down at my son, thinking how much he was like Karla in looks and personality. He was quieter and more introspective, whereas Edith was a ball of energy.

The man in front of us stepped into the stall and closed the door. Just then, a breeze carried a smell of wood mixed with urine to me. Instantly, I was transported back to the train car packed with German prisoners on its way to Siberia.

My throat dried up; my heart started racing. After a minute I felt sweat running down my face and back. I couldn't breathe. I curled my fingers, feeling my sweaty palms. I had to get out. Other men were in line behind us, blocking the way. My vision started to narrow as if I was looking into a tunnel. I turned and started pushing people out of my way to get out.

"Vati, what's wrong?" Rolf ran after me.

I bent over with my hand on my knees, taking deep breaths. "Nothing, Rolf. Go to the toilet. I'll wait for you."

I was still in the throes of my panic when Rolf returned. He put his hand in mine and squeezed gently. It took a few minutes, but his small gesture was enough to ground me back to the present. I held on to his hand as we walked slowly back to Karla.

"What happened?" Karla looked sharply at me.

I shook my head, not ready to talk about it.

CHAPTER 86

December 1949

Karla

Each month, life continued to get easier. Roads were repaired, making it easier for supplies to enter the city. The new currency was distributed, and more people paid us in cash for any odd jobs. The inflation rate dropped to something more manageable. Bruno worked during the week at the shipping company and took odd jobs on the weekends or evenings. I continued working at home, sewing for the dress shop. We were slowly putting our lives back together.

One Sunday afternoon, Martha came to see the apartment and have coffee while Bruno took Rolf and Edith to a small Christmas market in the old town at the center of Kiel.

I poured coffee into two cups as Martha put a pastry box in the middle of the table, then sat across from me.

"I have news!" she announced.

I took a tentative sip of the hot coffee and felt instantly nauseated. I put the cup on its saucer and took a deep breath. "Tell me," I said.

"Well, Charles and I are getting married!" she said with excitement. Charles was a captain in the British navy stationed in Kiel. They had met in 1946 when Martha found a job as a clerk in the same building Charles worked in. "Also, you're going to be an aunt."

It took me a minute to absorb the news. Then I reached over and squeezed her hands. "That's wonderful."

Martha shifted in her chair. "I know you are very busy but . . ." Her words drifted off. I nodded, encouraging her to ask. "Will you make my wedding dress?" she asked.

"I would love to!"

I opened the pastry box, then immediately closed it, feeling a wave of nausea.

"Your face just turned pale. What's wrong?"

"I don't know. Suddenly coffee and the apple smell from the pastries are making me ill."

Martha's face got serious. "Do you have any other symptoms?"

I waved my hand, dismissing her concern. "I probably just need a nap."

"Are you pregnant?" Martha blurted out.

I thought back to the last time I had my period. I had gone without my menstrual cycle during the war several times, probably because of lack of nutrition or long hours of working or a combination of the two. This time, though, was different, and when Martha brought it up, I knew in my heart I was pregnant.

By New Year's Eve, I was certain. In addition to feeling nausea every time I smelled coffee, my breasts were larger and tender. One afternoon, Edith invited two friends over to celebrate her birthday. I made aebleskiver with the new pan Bruno bought and bee sting cake for the girls. While they played in the living room, Bruno and I went for a walk and enjoyed the newly fallen snow from the previous night.

"Bruno, I have a present for you."

He held my hand as we walked across the street toward the park. "It's not my birthday."

"I'm pregnant."

Bruno stopped walking and stared at me. I started to get nervous. Maybe this wasn't the present he wanted.

His face lit up like a sunrise. "Karla, this is the best present you could give me." He hugged me fiercely.

We told Rolf and Edith the next day. Rolf was indifferent. Edith was excited until she found out there was a possibility she would have to share her bed if a sister was born. Eventually, both children became excited about the prospect of a little brother or sister.

Life continued as we prepared for another child. After working all day at the shipyard, Bruno spent evenings repairing small engines for motorboats. The days were long, but we had a roof over our heads and food to eat. Mostly, we immersed ourselves in a world of peace that we had not had since before the war that ended in 1918.

CHAPTER 87

May 1950
Karla

On Friday evening, Bruno entered the apartment, took off his rain jacket, and shook the water all over the floor. Things like that used to bother me before the war, but now I didn't care. The wet floors would dry on their own. It had been pouring all day.

I sat in front of my sewing machine, making a baby blanket for Martha out of alternating squares of yellow and green material that I'd found on sale at the fabric store. Leek soup was simmering on the stove and was nearly ready to eat. Rolf was doing schoolwork at the dining table. I touched my huge belly as I felt a kick from the life growing inside me.

"Mutti." Edith looked up from the marbles she had spread out in front of her on the floor. "Is it bad for me to be friends with Erika?"

I turned to look at my six-year-old daughter. "Why would you ask that?"

"The kids in school tease me. They say that she is a gypsy, and she's dirty for living in the camp," she answered solemnly.

"Come over here." I shifted around in my chair and pulled Edith to stand between my knees. I pushed her braids behind her shoulders. "If you like playing with her, you go right ahead and ignore those people with closed minds. We judge people for what is in their hearts, not how much money they have or where they live."

"Are any adults saying things to you, Edith?" Bruno asked as he dried his hands on a towel.

Edith nodded, and my anger surged as I looked over her head at Bruno.

Bruno tossed the towel on the dining table. "Edith, it's Saturday tomorrow. How about if we walk to the camp together and visit your friend?"

⌁

On Monday night at dinner, Bruno asked, "Edith, what did you learn at school today?"

Always eager to share, she replied proudly, "We are the Federal Republic of Germany led by Herr Adenauer."

Rolf chimed in, "That's because Germany started the war, and we now have a new government."

Edith looked at him with a mix of confusion and anger. "That's not true! The Polish started the war."

Bruno put his fork down. "Where did you hear this, Edith?"

"My teacher told me."

Rolf looked at Bruno and confirmed this. "That's what they're teaching us in school, Vati, but I know it was the Germans. The old German government forced you to fight." He paused and looked at Bruno seriously, then said, "Did you kill people, Vati?"

I saw Bruno turn pale and take his time wiping his mouth with his napkin while he tried to think of a suitable answer. I could tell he was struggling with the memories of leaving those men in the prison camp. I stood up and said, "Let's save this discussion for later, shall we?"

Bruno ignored Rolf's question. The answer was too complicated to understand. Instead, he said, "Edith, Rolf is right. The Germans started the war."

"No, Vati! It's not true. My teacher told us it was Poland."

I stepped in and said, "Edith, maybe you misunderstood. The Germans invaded Poland, and that was what started the war."

Edith shook her head and remained silent as she sat back and put her heels on the edge of her seat, then wrapped her arms around her knees.

CHAPTER 88

May 1950

Bruno

The next morning, I walked the children to school and stopped in to talk to Edith's teacher.

"Herr Becker," I said as I shook his hand, "may I speak to you in private? It will only take a moment."

The man was shorter than me and walked with crutches because the lower part of his left leg was missing. He looked concerned but said, "Yes, let's walk outside." I glanced at Edith, who was standing next to a friend and watching my every move.

The classroom was just inside the back door to the school. I held the doors open so that the teacher didn't have to struggle to get through. I briefly saw children running out the front door and turning left. *Was that my daughter among them?*

Herr Becker and I were standing just outside the back door when I saw Edith and her friend crawling behind a bush next to the brick building. Herr Becker's back was to them. I wondered if I should tell the girls to go back into the building. A glance at Edith's curious eyes helped me decide. *Nope, she should listen to how respectful adults solve problems.* Hopefully Herr Becker was going to be amenable.

"Herr Becker, Edith informed us last night that you told the children Poland started the war. I thought maybe she was confused since the war started when Germany invaded Poland."

"Yes, I suppose I did tell the children the war started with Poland."

I tried to keep my anger in check and crossed my arms over my chest. "Herr Becker, Germany needs to take responsibility for the war. The people of Germany voted for the Nazis, and the Nazis, along with Hitler, destroyed our country and many others." Herr Becker looked down at the ground. He knew I was correct. For Edith's benefit, I continued. "Hitler used his power to murder people, which resulted in seventy-five million people dying and millions of additional people living with wounds. You cannot deny the truth."

"At this age, it is better for children to have confidence in their country."

"No, everyone should have the truth so they can make better choices," I said with a stern voice.

"You don't know anything about—"

It had been ingrained in me from an early age how disrespectful it was to interrupt someone, but my anger was building. "Herr Becker! I beg your pardon. First, I am a father and an uncle. I know exactly what is right in terms of raising children, and it is not to lie to them! It is also appropriate to give them accurate information, so they make better decisions . . . and I know exactly what it is like to fight in a war!"

I glanced at Edith; her eyes were as big as saucers. She had never heard me raise my voice in anger; at least I didn't think she remembered ever hearing that. I continued, "I would think that with your experience in the war, you would prefer truth for our future generation."

Herr Becker was silent for a few moments before responding. "Perhaps you are right, Herr Arnold. I was trying to think of the children and the chaos around them."

"Tell them the truth. Today. This morning." I turned to Edith and her friend and said, "Let's all go into the classroom."

I held the door, and Herr Becker turned to go into the building. He paused. Looking at Edith and her friend, he opened his mouth. I thought it was good that the girls heard our conversation. The children learned that adults could make mistakes and, more importantly, admit them. I cut Herr Becker off from speaking. "After you."

I stayed in the classroom as Herr Becker clarified his lesson about who started the war. The children raised their hands to ask questions. "Herr Becker, why did the Germans start the war?"

Herr Becker sat down in his chair behind his walnut desk and looked at me, so I stepped forward and answered. "I think most Germans would have preferred no war. Germans were scared, frustrated, and sad about the first war. They voted for people who used their fear as a way to gain power." I walked to the front of the classroom. "I think it's important for everyone to know this so they can do more research and make better choices about who is voted into power."

Another student asked, "Were you a soldier?"

I nodded. "I was. I was forced to be a soldier in order to keep my family safe."

There was a knock on the door, and I saw my neighbor walk in, out of breath. "Herr Arnold, your wife sent me. You're needed at home."

CHAPTER 89

May 1950

Bruno

As soon as I returned home, I stopped at Frau Schwimmer's apartment on the first floor and used her phone to call Frau Kraus, the midwife. After many discussions and tears, I had finally agreed to Karla giving birth at home. It was one thing for Edith to be born at home during the war, but the war was over. It seemed Karla couldn't go near a hospital without suffering an attack of panic and anxiety.

I had the boiling water, towels, and sheets ready to go as Frau Kraus walked in. She glanced around and smiled. "I see this isn't your first time."

I showed her to the bedroom where Karla was lying on her side. Another contraction had just started. I ignored the look on Frau Kraus's face as I climbed into bed next to Karla and rubbed her back.

"Do you want to wait out in the living room while I check her?" Frau Kraus asked.

Karla and I both answered at the same time. "No!"

"Bruno stays," Karla said with a firm voice.

I shifted to sit with my back to the headboard and settled myself around Karla. Then I looked pointedly at Frau Kraus.

Two hours later, our beautiful baby girl was born: Brunhilde Gertrude Martha Arnold.

CHAPTER 90

October 1959

Frankfurt, Germany

The sun was setting, casting an orange glow through the windows. Karla and Bruno sat next to each other, holding hands and smiling.

Fräulein Neumann adjusted her glasses and flipped through her notebook until she found the page she was looking for. "Do you still write to Eli and Ilse?"

"We do. They opened a grocery store in Smedjebacken, a town just two hours west of Stockholm. Jacob graduated medical school and lives in Stockholm with his wife and three children. Daniel became a pilot for the Swedish Air Force," Karla explained.

"How does it feel to know you saved not just four people's lives but seven if you include Jacob's children?" Fräulein Neumann asked.

"There are no words to describe how grateful we are that they are safe," said Bruno.

Fräulein Neumann shifted in her chair, then closed her notebook and looked at him directly. "Did the Nazis murder your parents?"

Bruno sat back and considered the question for a moment. "It's a mystery but . . . there is no disputing the timing of our friends' rescue and my parents' deaths."

"Tell me about your children," Dr. Schmidt said to Bruno and Karla.

Karla smiled with pride. "Rolf is nineteen years old and about to finish the classroom portion of becoming an electrician. Edith is sixteen and goes to a Danish school in Flensburg. Her Danish and English are very good. Pit—that's what we call our youngest daughter—is nine and loves gymnastics."

"One last question, Herr Arnold." Dr. Schmidt clicked his pen a couple of times. "You lived through two world wars, were a prisoner of war, and walked home practically all the way from Siberia." Dr. Schmidt paused and flipped to a blank page in his notebook. "If there is one lesson you've learned from all this that you could teach the world, what would it be?"

Bruno rubbed his chin, as if thinking about how to best articulate a straightforward answer to a complex issue. "If people have the privilege of living in a democratic country, they should understand their power to vote comes with great responsibility." Bruno glanced at Karla. "Centuries of history have taught us about extremists who gradually erode civil liberties. I would like people to think beyond any rhetoric and propaganda to see what is in the candidate's heart before they cast their vote."

+~+

Dr. Schmidt and his colleagues watched out the window as Bruno and Karla made their way down the sidewalk from the building. They were holding hands.

Dr. Schmidt's eyes lingered on the couple. "An amazing love story they have."

"I hope my future husband and I are holding hands at that age," said Fräulein Neumann.

Dr. Schmidt laughed and thought to himself, *Fifty is old?*

As Dr. Schmidt gathered his notebook and tape recorder, he took one more glance out the window to see Bruno put his arm around Karla's shoulder and pull her closer as they rounded the corner and walked out of sight.

REFERENCES

"Adolf Hitler Collection of Speeches 1922–1945." (n.d.).
   [PDF file]. https://ia801903.us.archive.org/17/items
   /AdolfHitlerCollectionOfSpeeches19221945/Adolf%20
   Hitler%20-%20Collection%20of%20Speeches%201922-1945.pdf

(August 17, 1934). "Adolf Hitler—Speech in Hamburg at the Blohm
   and Voss Shipyard." https://der-fuehrer.org/reden/english
   /34-08-17.htm

Arnold, B. (n.d.). Brunhilde Arnold [Personal interview with the
   author].

Arnold, E. (n.d.). Edith Arnold [Personal interview with the author].

Arnold, R. (n.d.). Rolf Arnold [Personal interview with the author].

Birkbeck, University of London. (n.d.). "Concentration Camps
   Inspector: Document 021." http://www.camps.bbk.ac.uk
   /documents/021-camp-inspector-eicke.html

Cultural Atlas. (n.d.). "Judaism—Rituals and Practices."
   https://culturalatlas.sbs.com.au/religions/judaism
   /resources/judaism-rituals-and-practices

Dinner, L. (April 16, 2024). Rabbi Lucy Dinner [Personal interview
   with the author].

Encyclopedia Britannica. (n.d.). "Battle of Jutland." https://www
   .britannica.com/event/Battle-of-Jutland

Encyclopedia Britannica. (n.d.). "Gestapo." https://www.britannica
   .com/topic/Gestapo

Encyclopedia Britannica. (n.d.). "Kiel." https://www.britannica.com
   /place/Kiel

Fordham, O. (n.d.). Olga Fordham [Personal interview with the
   author].

History.com. (n.d.). "How Germany Is Still Paying World War
     I Debt." https://www.history.com/news/germany-world
     -war-i-debt-treaty-versailles

History.com. (n.d.). "World War I." https://www.history.com/topics
     /world-war-i

Imperial War Museums. (n.d.). "What You Need to Know About the
     British Naval Blockade of the First World War." https://www.iwm
     .org.uk/history/what-you-need-to-know-about-the-british-naval
     -blockade-of-the-first-world-war

Library of Congress. (2022). "Photographs Show World War I,
     German Military." https://www.loc.gov/item/2021667903/

The Holocaust Explained. (n.d.). "The Early Years of the Nazi Party."
     https://www.theholocaustexplained.org/the-nazi-rise-to-power
     /the-early-years-of-the-nazi-party/

The National WWII Museum. (n.d.). "How Did Adolf Hitler
     Happen?" https://www.nationalww2museum.org/war/articles
     /how-did-adolf-hitler-happen

United States Holocaust Memorial Museum. (n.d.). "Ministry of
     Propaganda and Public Enlightenment." https://encyclopedia
     .ushmm.org/content/en/article/ministry-of-propaganda
     -and-public-enlightenment

United States Holocaust Memorial Museum. (n.d.). "State of
     Deception: The Power of Nazi Propaganda." https://exhibitions
     .ushmm.org/propaganda/home/state-of-deception-the
     -power-of-nazi-propaganda

United States Holocaust Memorial Museum. (n.d.). "The Nazi Party."
     https://encyclopedia.ushmm.org/content/en/article/the-nazi
     -party-1

United States Holocaust Memorial Museum. (n.d.). "The Nuremberg
     Race Laws." https://encyclopedia.ushmm.org/content/en/article
     /the-nuremberg-race-laws

United States Holocaust Memorial Museum. (n.d.). "The Reichstag
     Fire." https://encyclopedia.ushmm.org/content/en/article
     /the-reichstag-fire

Wikipedia. (n.d.). "Otto-Heinrich Drechsler." https://en.wikipedia.org
     /wiki/Otto-Heinrich_Drechsler#:~:text=Otto%2DHeinrich%20

Drechsler%20(1%20April,the%20extermination%20of%20
Latvian%20Jews
Yad Vashem. (n.d.). "Prewar Hanukkah Menorah from Kiel,
Germany." https://www.yadvashem.org/artifacts/museum
/prewar-hanukkah-menorah-kiel.html

ABOUT THE AUTHOR

Monica Granlove is a storyteller and social commentator dedicated to motivating future leaders. Monica engages audiences in thought-provoking discussions, emphasizing the importance of applying historical perspectives to today's world. She believes that by exploring the past, we gain a deeper understanding of our shared humanity and can make informed decisions for the future, especially when it comes to voting for political leaders.

Based on the true story of her own grandparents, Monica wrote *The Electrician and the Seamstress*, her debut novel. When she's not writing, Monica is traveling with her husband, Axel, and their spoiled dog, Abby, or spending time with her three adult daughters. She lives in Raleigh, North Carolina.

www.ingramcontent.com/pod-product-compliance
Lightning Source LLC
Chambersburg PA
CBHW022004310726
48972CB00006B/1514